LOVE ME LIKE YOU DO

ERIKA KELLY

LOVE ME LIKE YOU DO

Erika Kelly

ISBN: 978-1-955462-15-0

Copyright 2022 EK Publishing, LLC

Cover image by JoEllen Moths
Cover design and Formatting by Serendipity Formatting
Editing by Sharon Pochron
Editing by Olivia Kalb Editing
Proofreading by Emily A. Lawrence

Titles by Erika Kelly

Have you read the Rock Star Romance series? Come meet the sexy rockers of Blue Fire:

Sign up for my newsletter to read the EXCLUSIVE novella for my readers only! You'll get two chapters a month of this super sexy, fun romance! #rockstarromance #teenidolturnedboyfriend Also, get PLANES, TRAINS, AND HEAD OVER HEELS for FREE! I hope you'll come hang out with me on Facebook, TikTok, Twitter, Instagram, Goodreads, and Pinterest or in my private reader group.

This book is dedicated to my publishing team. Each book has its own process, and with this one, I drew you all into the whirlwind!

Acknowledgments

- To Superman, all my love, always.
- Everyone should have a friend like Sharon Pochron. I don't know what I'd do without her.
- The world needs more people like Erica Alexander. She's one of the rare people I can totally count on.
- Thank you to Melissa Panio-Peterson for being the other half of my brain.
- A huge shout-out to Christian Sarlo of the Penn State University hockey team. He gave me outstanding help, and I couldn't have written this book without him. I'm forever grateful for his time and the care he took in answering my questions. Any mistakes are mine.
- Thank you to Kyle Gipe, Managing Editor of The Hockey Writers. He was so generous with his time and knowledge and gave me a much better understanding of the game.
- To Emily, thank you for taking me on at the last minute and for making my book better!
- Thank you, Olivia, for seeing the things I couldn't. You filled all the holes.

- And thank you to the readers, bloggers, reviewers, and all my author friends who make this job so richly rewarding and worthwhile.

Chapter One

COLE MONTGOMERY WAS FUCKED.

Over his eight years in the NHL, he'd been slammed against the boards so hard his helmet had flown off, whacked on the head with a hockey stick, and tripped while skating twenty-three miles per hour...

And now, he was sitting on the examination table, waiting for a diagnosis...after cracking his head on the floor of a *roller skating rink*.

Coach stormed into the room. "You had better be okay."

Leaning back on the table, Cole gave him an easy smile and crossed his ankles. Pain exploded in his knee. "I'm fine."

They both looked at the team doctor for confirmation of the lie. "He's got a concussion."

"How did you *do* this?" Coach bristled with anger. "What the hell were you thinking?"

Like he didn't feel shitty enough? The last thing he wanted was to miss a game. They'd won the Cup last season. He fully planned on winning it again this year. "I threw a holiday party for my guys like I always do."

"At a *roller rink*?"

"I wanted to include their families." Hockey took them away from their wives and kids enough, so he figured this year, he'd go all-out with a fun event. "I wasn't even skating. You know I wouldn't do anything to put myself at risk."

"And yet, here we are."

"As I understand it," Dr. Hansen said. "The guys were messing around, racing each other, and they were about to crash into Peck's daughter. Cole grabbed her and saved her from serious injury."

"Yeah, well, Mr. Fucking Hero, the captain of this damn team, now has a concussion." Coach got right up in his face. "Why do you do this shit? Why do you always have to take things too far? You want to give the guys presents? You hand them out in the locker room. Take them out for a fucking drink. But no, you always have to turn it into some over-the-top event." He spun around, cocking his arm back like he might hit the wall. Instead, he punched the air. "How long is he off the ice?"

"Four games."

Coach's eyes bugged out, and his features flamed. "*Four?*" The heel of his palm smacked the padded exam table. With his jaw clenched tightly as if biting down on a rash of words he might regret, he turned and stormed out the door.

In his absence, the room pulsed with tension. Cole couldn't believe it. He rarely got injured. This was only his second concussion over a lifetime of playing hockey, BASE jumping, rappelling, glacier snowboarding... Name an extreme sport, and he'd done it. But to have it happen like this—not even halfway through the season?

I can't afford to miss any games.

"Well, that went well." He slid off the table, landing on the knee he'd twisted. Fire blazed up his thigh, but he quickly schooled his features.

Doc watched him with a guarded look. "Is there any other pain you need to tell me about?"

He shook his head. Not a chance would he mention it. They had six more games until they got a break for Christmas Eve and Day. He'd miss four of them, giving him time to ice and rest his knee.

When he reached the door, Doc called, "You need any painkillers?"

"Nope. It's all good."

Liar.

Fuck.

Cole sat on his leather couch, leg propped, ice on his knee.

"You okay, slugger?" Birdie, his twenty-two-year-old assistant, came into the room with a protein shake.

"You know I play hockey, right?"

Around him, she referred to every sport other than the one he played, always pretending she didn't know the first thing about hockey when in fact he'd met her at a coaching clinic at Boston University. Her long-term boyfriend had just dumped her through a text, and she'd come to the rink to hurl his belongings onto the ice.

She'd worked for Cole ever since. Now, though, she was about to graduate with a master's degree in education and would be leaving him to teach smelly middle school kids. "Maybe one day, I'll catch a game."

"You know, some people are impressed with me."

"And yet you hired *me* to be in your face every single day. Huh. Wonder what that means?" She set down his drink and pulled a letter out of her back pocket. "This is the fourth one you've gotten. Now that you have some free time, maybe you can deal with it."

He glanced at the envelope from a law firm in Calamity, Wyoming. This past summer, his old hockey coach had passed away, bequeathing him and his three high school friends a hockey team, but the estate was handled by a different practice. So what could it be? He and his dad owned homes there, but neither was involved in litigation.

Tearing it open, he scanned the letter.

"What's it say?" Birdie asked.

"They need me to call them." He tossed it aside. "Can you please hand me my phone?"

"Wait, is this for real? You're actually going to do something that isn't hockey related?" She grabbed it from the kitchen counter and handed it over.

As he dialed, he considered the possibilities. His land backed up to Grand Teton National Park, so he didn't have neighbors who'd sue him over property lines, and he wasn't home enough for anyone to file a noise dispute. He really had no clue.

"Whitten Rose and Vasquez Attorneys," the receptionist answered. "How may I direct your call?"

"Hey, this is Cole Montgomery. I got a letter from"— he read the signature line—"Ashley Stephenson, asking me to call."

"One moment, please."

"All right, I'm out of here." His assistant grabbed her backpack. "Need anything before I leave?"

"Nah. I'm good. Hey, how're you getting there?" In order to graduate, she needed to complete her requisite student teaching hours. But with her car in the shop, it would be difficult to interview at the schools.

She looked at him like he was an airhead. "Uh, public transportation? This is Boston."

"Take my car." He gave a chin nod to the bowl where he kept his keys and spare change.

"Are you out of your mind?"

He patted the ice pack. "I'm not going anywhere for a few days."

"How are you even offering me something like that when I totaled your car the first time you loaned it to me?"

"You were nineteen and upset over your ex."

She shook her head. "I'm a terrible driver, and that's why my car's in the shop."

"Hello?" A woman came on the line.

He held up his finger to his assistant. "This is Cole Montgomery. I got a—"

"Yes, Cole. Thank you for getting back to me."

His assistant waved to him before heading out the door.

"Sure. What can I help you with?" A lawyer only reached out for a good reason. If it wasn't about the Renegades hockey team, then what else could it be? "Is something wrong?"

"I'm sorry to inform you that Darren Leeson passed away."

He jerked upright so quickly he knocked the ice pack off his knee. "*Darren?*" Immediately, an image dropped into his mind. A red-haired, freckle-faced skater kid with an easy laugh and lazy eyes. Cole's closest friends were on his hockey team, but since they'd always had family obligations, girlfriends, and jobs, he'd wound up spending a lot of time with Darren, another loner. "What happened?"

"He and his wife were on their way back from Las Vegas. An eighteen-wheeler spun out on black ice on I-80 in Echo Canyon and…" She sighed. "He and Lindsay didn't make it."

"Jesus." He squeezed his eyes shut, and there it was again, an image of that dopey grin.

He just couldn't believe he was gone.

The summer after high school, Cole had fucked things up with his hockey friends, so instead of playing in the States, he'd moved to Canada. It had been a terrible time. Riddled with guilt, he'd lost touch with everyone except Darren.

Easy-going Darren, who'd accepted Cole just as he was.

"I'm sorry for your loss," the attorney said.

"I can't believe it."

When had they started to drift apart? Because even after he'd moved to Boson, he and Darren had kept in touch. Somewhere along the way, between his career and Darren's marriage and kids… It must've been a good four years since they'd last talked.

But he pulled himself together because the lawyer wasn't calling to announce their passing. "Is there anything I can do to help?" Last he'd heard, Darren worked construction, and Lindsay worked part-time for a florist.

"You—"

Actually, he knew exactly what he could do. "I can set up a trust fund for the daughter."

"Oh, that's… Well, actually, there are two girls."

"That's fine. I can set one up for both." There was something in her tone, though. Something that made his senses perk up. "But that's not why you reached out. Are you letting me know about the funeral?" If there wasn't money for that… "I can cover the costs."

"Mr. Montgomery, this is all very generous of you, but that's not why I'm calling."

"Okay." A weird sensation crawled up his spine and twisted around his chest. In hockey, intuition won games. He'd honed his well over many years and countless games.

His sixth sense was going haywire.

"You're named as the guardian."

One good squeeze yanked the air out of his lungs. He scrambled to make sense of what the woman had just said. "You mean godfather." He'd gone to the christening, and his assistant sent presents every year on the girl's birthday.

"No, I mean, Darren listed you as the man he'd like to raise his daughters."

"Me?" He flung back against the couch hard enough to rattle his bruised brain. *Wait.* "When did he have a second kid?"

"The oldest is six, and the littlest one's three."

Two little girls—their whole lives ahead of them. *Damn, that sucks.* Still, he'd be the worst person in the world to take care of them. *Fuck.* His heart thundered, and perspiration broke out over his lip. "That's not…no, I can't do that."

"That's fine. You certainly don't have to. It's just a request."

"He never told me about it. This has to be a mistake. You must be looking at an old will or something. We haven't talked in four years."

"He and Lindsay updated their will when their last child was born three years ago."

"Okay, but there must be someone else. A cousin, an aunt...*someone.*"

"Mr. Montgomery, it's okay. I'm only informing you of his request. You're in no way obligated to become their guardian."

"That's good." He let out an awkward laugh. "Trust me, no one wants me responsible for their kids." He got a flash of Booker's landing that horrible night ten years ago, the way his legs had crumpled. Thanks to Cole, his friend had lost his shot at playing hockey.

He could've died.

But no good came of remembering the terrible decisions he'd made in his past. "All right, well, as I said, I'll talk to my lawyers and get trust funds established for both of them."

"That's fine. Thank you for your time."

His pulse rocketed, and he panicked at the thought of disconnecting. Of not knowing what would happen to those girls. "Hey, is there a funeral?" Better to ask that instead of learning about a fate he could do nothing about.

"Not that I'm aware of."

"What do you mean?"

"As I mentioned, there's no known family. Lindsay's father passed away five years ago, and her mother lives in a senior care facility. Darren has no one that we're aware of."

He shifted uncomfortably, afraid to voice the words taking form in his mind. But he had to do it. "So, where are the girls now?"

"In a temporary foster home."

"And where will they..." He swallowed. "Wind up?"

"They'll go into the system."

Fuck. Fuck, fuck, fuck. Darren had terrible stories of foster care. Horrifying. "They'll be together, though, right? Sisters go together?"

"I really can't say what will happen. It's always harder to place siblings."

"But you'll try, right? You'll try to keep them together?"

"It's not up to this law firm. I'm just the administrator of the will. Without guardians, they'll be handed over to Wyoming's Department of Child Services."

No. Panic mixed with dread, creating a volatile brew. Darren would hate that. "I wish I could help, but I live in Boston." He gripped the back of his neck. "I play eighty-two games a year. How would it even work?"

He was used to battling two-hundred-pound walls of muscle and blocking one-hundred-mile-per-hour shots. He'd done extreme sports his entire life. He knew how to keep a sharp focus and clear mind. If he didn't, he'd be dead. But at that moment, his mind was crashing.

Caught between two absolutes, Cole closed his eyes, sealing himself inside the throbbing pain in his head. How could he let Darren's kids go into the system?

But at the same time...

He didn't know much outside of hockey, but he did know one thing for sure.

He was the worst thing for those girls. "I'm sorry. I can't do it."

Chapter Two

"ARE YOU KIDDING ME?" HAILEY CASSELTON STOMPED her boots in the freezing cold foyer of her Brooklyn apartment building. With her wool glove caught between her teeth, she jiggled the lock of her mailbox, but her fingers were too stiff to turn the key. Setting her messenger bag down, she cupped her hand and blew, warming it. Finally, she regained some flexibility and got it open, pulled the envelopes and catalogs out, and then headed up to her fifth-floor walk-up.

The scent of grilled meat wafted out of Mr. Nozu's apartment, the kids were shouting and running wild in the Posners' place, and Lynn's rebellious cat had gotten out again. He sat facing the door, waiting to be let in.

Hailey gently twisted the knob, and the kitty rushed in. She closed it and continued up one more flight. Letting herself into her tiny studio, she could've sworn she got a whiff of her mom's patchouli scent. *Is she here?* With Christmas less than two weeks away, it would make sense. They always spent the holidays together.

Yep. She spotted her tattered suitcase in the corner.

As she dropped the mail on the counter, she noticed an official-looking envelope from a law firm. *Huh, that's weird. Am I in trouble?* She noted the Calamity, Wyoming return address, a town she'd lived in for most of her senior year in high school.

She could never think about that place without remembering the fuckwad who'd ruined her experience. Cocky, privileged, larger-than-life Cole Montgomery. Just because his dad was the star of *Clan Wars*, one of the longest-running movie franchises in history, he thought he could impress everyone with his private jets and limos.

Okay, you're rich. Cool.

So what?

He could never just do normal things—like have a basic conversation.

What a douche.

Before she opened the letter, she headed to the closet to hang her parka…and found the door gaping open. Her entire collection was gone.

Shock froze her in place. Had her mom taken it? *I mean, yes. Obviously.*

But why?

It had taken her eighteen months to design and sew them. But before she panicked—*let's not assume the worst*—she called her mom. It went straight to voicemail. She shot off a text.

Hailey: Did you take my robes?

She waited, but the message went unread.

Oh, my God. This isn't happening.

To reach her goal of owning a fashion line, Hailey had two jobs. She could barely make ends meet with her salary as a designer for Abbott's of London, so she worked weekends in a high-end designer's boutique in SoHo. Not only did she need the money, but she got to learn the retail end of the business.

As soon as she saved up two—well, maybe three—years of living expenses, she'd launch her line. In the meantime, she'd spent every free moment since graduating from the Fashion Institute sketching and sewing all kinds of sexy lingerie, giving herself time to find her own voice. She'd wanted to find something that distinguished her from all the others in her field.

And then, about two years ago, one of her favorite fabric shops began stocking materials made from sustainable products. She'd fallen wildly in love with one made from bamboo and modal because it felt like wearing liquid silk. She'd known immediately what textiles and colors would work with it. The result was feminine robes and sleep sets that looked luxurious, bohemian, and sexy all at once.

Just as she went to check her phone again, she found a note taped to the wall.

Surprise, baby! I'm here. And I've got the most amazing news for you! Come to this address and find out what it is!

Dammit, Mom. What have you done now?
Stuffing the attorney's letter into the pocket of her parka, she headed out the door.

Standing on the sidewalk, Hailey took in the unlighted façade.
What the hell's going on?

Hailey: I'm outside a place called Strike a Pose. It looks closed.

This is ridiculous. All she wanted was to eat dinner, take a hot bath, and work on her robes while watching a holiday baking competition on television. God, it was cold out here.

Hailey: I think I'm at the wrong place. I'm going home.

Mom: No, no. This is it. Don't go anywhere. I'll be right out!

Oh, now she responds.

Hailey: Do you have my robes????

Normally, she loved when her mom visited. They were both fashion designers, so they talked shop, took long walks around the city and discovered new restaurants and interesting boutiques, and had a fun but quiet holiday. They knew each other so well that it was always easy.

But there'd always been a mutual respect for each other's work. Her mom knew better than to touch her robes. *Imagine if I took one of her costumes?* She'd pitch a fit. *And rightfully so.*

Just then, the door burst open, and her mom emerged, eyes bright with happiness, arms outstretched. She pulled Hailey into a hug right there on the busy, bustling streets of Manhattan's Lower East Side. "It's so good to see you." Holding her close, her mom rocked her from side to side.

She couldn't help but sink into her embrace. As frustrated as she got with her mom's unorthodox approach to life, she still loved her, and it had been far too long since they'd seen each other.

But right now, she needed answers. Hailey pulled back. "What's going on? Why are we here?"

"I'll show you. Come in. Let me introduce you to my new friends." Taking her hand, her mom slipped into the building. It smelled of new carpet and fresh paint.

In the dim lighting, Hailey could see a stage, a bar, and loads of café tables. "This is a club?"

"Yes. Burlesque, and it's opening in January." She pulled Hailey close, her smile stretched wide. "And they've hired me to make the costumes. It's a full-time job."

Well, that's a first.

"Naomi," someone shouted. "Introduce us."

"You're going to flip out when you see my surprise." Her mom led her to a table surrounded by gorgeous, vibrant women. "Everyone, meet my daughter, Hailey. Hailey, this is the cast, the owners, the bartenders, and the servers of Strike a Pose."

Someone got up to hug her, and others called out from their seats, but everyone seemed welcoming and lovely. But —for the love of God—they were all wearing her robes.

She went boiling hot. Her mom had *given them away?* What was she thinking? But the women were introducing themselves, so Hailey gave them the courtesy of her attention. "So nice to meet you."

"Your mom is the *bomb*," one of them said. "I never thought about who designed a rock star's costumes, but to find out your mom did Kaley McCutcheson's last tour? I'm dying."

"And Alexis de la Cruz." The woman fanned herself. "I can't believe she came up with crazy-ass looks like that."

Her mom had been working since high school. She'd started out in her drama program in New York City, and since there were a lot of celebrities' kids there, she'd gotten her first job right here in the city making costumes for Shakespeare on Lex when she was nineteen.

She tried to hide it, but Hailey was livid. So, when her mom brought a chair to the table for her, she said, "No," a little too harshly.

Hurt wrenched her mom's features.

"I need to talk to you in private."

"Sure." She ushered Hailey to the bar. "What's wrong?"

Hailey kept her back to the table, so they wouldn't see her expression. It wasn't their fault. "You gave them my robes."

"Oh, honey. They're stunning. You've really hit on something here. The girls are obsessed with them—"

"*Mom.* That's my inventory. I'm building it up for when I finally launch my own line."

"I know that. But seriously, what're you waiting for? You've always been so cautious, and where has it gotten you? You're wasting your talent on that boring nightgown company."

Because I don't want to be like you. I don't want to go from gig to gig, one friend's couch to another. I don't want to jokingly ask someone to buy me dinner because I have no money for food.

I never want to eat tuna out of a can again as long as I live.

But she didn't say that. Instead, she said, "It's my career, and I'm going to run it the way I want. I have a great job, and I'm very lucky to work for a company like

Abbott's. But most importantly, I'm saving money until I can afford to go out on my own."

"You're twenty-eight years old. Instead of that second job, you should be selling your designs on your own website."

"Please don't tell me what to do." *You're not exactly a model for entrepreneurism.* "I have a plan."

"Okay, but in some ways, don't you think your *plan* is a cover for your fear of failure? Honey, you can do your job in your sleep, and I know designing flannel nightgowns doesn't feed your creative fire. At some point, you've got to just jump in. Come here." She led her back to the table. "Guys, tell her how much you love the robes."

"Oh, my God. This is insane." A brunette stood up, swayed her hips, and lifted her arms to show off the bell sleeves. "I've never worn anything like it."

"I'm never wearing anything else again," another woman said. "It's better than being naked."

Her mom shot her a delighted look. *See?*

"Oh, thank you." Hailey gave the women a genuine smile. "I really appreciate it." And she did. It was the first bit of feedback she'd gotten.

"Give us your business card," a tall redhead said. "We'll hand them out to everyone. I promise you're going to make a killing on these. You won't be able to keep them in stock."

And that's the problem in a nutshell. "Thank you so much. You've made my day." Fed up, she had to get out of there. "Well, I need to get going, but it was nice to meet all of you." She headed toward the glowing red exit sign, her mom hot on her heels.

"Hailey, hang on."

She couldn't even look at her. She pushed the lever and stepped outside.

"Wait." Her mom seemed out of breath. "Why are you so angry?"

"Because I don't have a business yet. I make these robes in my spare time."

"Not for long. Once the word spreads, your sales are going to explode. We'll sell them here in the gift shop. Well, we don't have one yet, but we can start one."

"How on earth am I going to keep up with that kind of demand? It's just me."

"You'll hire people. We'll get you a warehouse in Brooklyn."

"With what money?"

"With your savings."

"That savings is meant to float me when times get tight." Briefly, she squeezed her eyes shut. This conversation was way too familiar. "Let's stop talking about it. It's not something we're ever going to agree on."

Her mom's forehead creased with concern. "You're seriously upset."

"Yes. You had no right to give away my robes. Do you know how much that material cost? How many hours I spent designing and sewing them? I had a plan, and you've just reduced my inventory to zero."

"Oh, honey. I'm so sorry. I thought you were just scared about putting yourself out there. I thought I was helping you take that first step. You're so talented, and you're not doing anything with it."

"But I am doing something with it. I'm building up inventory so that when I have enough money, I can safely take the risk of opening my own business."

Her mom just stared at her. She truly didn't understand.

"I'm not like you. I can't just hope another gig will show up when I need it. I need an income, groceries…a roof over my head that *I'm* paying for."

"I'm so sorry. How can I fix this? Do you want me to take the robes back?"

"No, Mom. They're wearing them." *Naked. Sitting down. I can't sell them now.*

"I can ask them to pay. I'm sure they will."

"No, it's too late for that. What's done is done." The brutal wind hit her cheeks and bare hands. She jammed them into her pockets to grab her gloves. When she pulled them out, the letter from the law firm hit the ground.

"What's that?" her mom asked.

"No idea. It came in the mail today. I can't imagine what business anyone from Calamity would have with me." She never stepped out of bounds, so she shouldn't be on anyone's radar. "I'll open it when I get home." She'd been seventeen when she'd lived there, and she'd only gone back to visit Lindsay a couple of times.

A zing of dread shot through her when she realized her friend was her only connection to that town. Tearing it open, she unfolded the letter.

"What does it say?" Her mom moved closer, her patchouli scent swirling in the air.

Shock pierced her heart. "Lindsay Leeson died."

"Oh, no. How can that be?"

Memories slammed her. So vivid they hurt. Lindsay, with her blue hair and side-cheek piercings placed right in the center of her dimples, laughing so hard she fell to the ground, rolled onto her back, and kicked her legs like she was cycling.

Secrets whispered under the covers at sleepovers, long hikes with the guys to a glacier lake, and countless late-night conversations over pints of Bliss ice cream.

The summer between junior and senior year, her mom had moved them to Calamity to design costumes for a country music star in residency at the outdoor theater. That's where Hailey had met Lindsay. They'd become fast friends, and when it was time for her mom to move on to the next gig in Florida, Hailey had begged to let her live with Lindsay for senior year.

It was her last shot to have a normal school experience.

And she'd wanted it so badly…homecoming, football games, prom… She'd have done just about anything to convince her mom to let her go.

That year would've been everything she'd ever wanted had it not been for Cole Montgomery, the asshole hockey player. Thanks to him, her time had been cut short, and she'd missed prom. *Whatever*. She'd made a best friend, and it had been a great experience.

But she'd gone off to school in New York, and Lindsay had stayed in town to build a life with her boyfriend.

Husband.

The father of her children.

And now they were both dead.

Her mom brushed the hair off her shoulder. "What're you feeling right now?"

Good question. She was a mess of emotions. Sorrow, certainly, but also… "Regret. I fell out of touch with her." Her life had become all about work, about saving money so she could live her dream of being a fashion designer.

She had two jobs, and Lindsay had two kids.

"Isn't that just life?" her mom asked. "People drift apart. And you two were on such different paths."

"That doesn't make me feel better." Regret nearly suffocated her. "She had two children. I was—am—the godmother—of the first one, but I never took it seriously. I sent presents on her daughter's birthday, but I wasn't there for her. I haven't been there for Lindsay in three years." *And now she's gone.*

"Why's the law firm writing you?"

"I don't know. It just says they have a 'matter they need to discuss with me.'"

"Well, go on and call."

"I'll do it when I get home." Not here, where she was freezing her butt off as traffic piled up, horns honked, and pedestrians raced by.

"There's a two-hour time difference, though. If you wait any longer, you'll have to call tomorrow. Are you going to be able to sleep tonight wondering what this is about?"

"No." Numbly, Hailey started to dial the number on the letterhead, but her mom tapped the paper.

"Look, she says to call her direct line."

"Right. Thanks. I'm totally freaking out." Hailey started over.

Her mom wrapped her arms around her, a bulwark against the bitter cold. "Whatever it is, we got this."

As the line rang, Hailey's heart fluttered in her throat.

"Ashley Stephenson." The woman sounded professional and rushed.

"Hello, Ashley? This is Hailey Casselton. I just got a letter from your law firm telling me Lindsay Leeson…" A sting of awareness sped through her. "Passed away." A gust of icy wind had her lowering her head.

"Yes, and I'm so very sorry to deliver that news to you.

But I'm glad you called. We've had a hard time getting a hold of you."

"I've moved a lot. Can you explain what's going on? As you can imagine, this comes as quite a surprise."

"Yes, of course. As I understand it, Lindsay and Darren had gone to Las Vegas for their anniversary and on the way back, an eighteen-wheeler spun out on black ice and, unfortunately, collided with them."

Hailey sucked in a breath of frosty air. It punched the back of her throat, the burn so painful it brought tears to her eyes. "I can't believe it. I can't believe they're gone. How are the girls?" She tried to think of what family either of them had…but other than Lindsay's parents, she couldn't recall anyone. "Where are they right now?"

"They're with the same neighbors Lindsay and Darren left them with when they went away. Which is actually why I'm reaching out to you. Lindsay and Darren named you a co-guardian."

Her mom's arms fell off her shoulders, her hands clapping over her mouth. She looked as shocked as Hailey felt.

"Me?" She was in no way equipped to take care of two little girls. "I don't understand. I know I'm Paisley's godmother, but you said guardian, and I'm just trying to understand. Am I supposed to raise Lindsay's daughters?" She took in the filthy street, the taxis jockeying to outmaneuver each other. "I live in New York City."

"The parents have requested a sale of the home to provide for the girls, so there's some money if you need a larger place. And they did have some life insurance."

"I don't know what to say." Her mind raced ahead to school, homework, family meals, and dance classes…a lifestyle she'd only ever seen in movies. "You said co-guardian. So, there's someone else involved?" Hopefully, someone more, appropriate.

"Yes, but he's opted not to do it."

What should have scared her—being solely responsible for two children—somehow made the decision that much more compelling. "If I don't claim them—" Wait, that didn't sound right. They weren't pieces of luggage. "If I don't step in, then what?"

"They go into the foster care system."

No. That would be Darren and Lindsay's worst nightmare for their babies. "But at least they'd stay together, right?"

"That I can't answer. I can only tell you that statistically around seventy percent of siblings are separated."

"You're killing me here." She looked at her mom and mouthed *What do I do?* But she didn't wait for an answer. Because she knew.

These are Lindsay's daughters.

"I'll be on the next flight."

Chapter Three

THIS CAN'T BE LINDSAY'S NEIGHBOR. **AFTER SEVERAL** miles of driving up a mountain road, Hailey reached a fancy gate. She checked her phone for the code, rolled down her window, and punched it in. Icy air rushed into the heated car.

Holy moly, the mountains were a whole other level of cold. She'd forgotten about that.

Once it opened, she drove through. The driveway rounded a bend before exposing a huge stone, wood, and glass home. One so stunning that it could easily be featured in *Architectural Digest*.

Unless her friends had won the lottery, this couldn't be right. She cut the engine and grabbed her phone.

Hailey: I'm at 41802 Skyline Drive. Is this the right address?

When she'd come here for the christening three years ago, the Leesons had lived in a neighborhood behind a strip mall that consisted of one-story homes and small, neat lots. Nothing like this. Also, she didn't see the social worker's car. He'd said to look for a white Ford F-150. No way would he want her to pick up the girls by herself.

They don't even know me.

Chase: Yes, sorry. I had other appointments today, so I couldn't wait any longer.

Crap. After all her travel issues—a delayed flight, snowy roads on her two-and-a-half-hour drive from Idaho Falls to Calamity—she couldn't blame the man. Fortunately, she'd talked to him over the phone, plus she'd done a lot of reading on the plane, to get a handle on how to help these little girls process the loss of their parents.

God, this is going to be hard.

Hailey: So sorry about that.

Chase: Not your fault. But there's been a change of plans. The co-guardian picked the kids up. He can only stay in town a few days, but he's going to let you use his home for as long as you need it. I've already done the home inspection, and we've begun your background check, so everything's looking good. I'm here if you have any questions.

Wait, seriously? He's just going to let me have these two little girls? He hasn't even met me.

How is this okay?

But she kept her thoughts to herself. She didn't want to say anything that would cast doubt on her. Not for anything would she let them become wards of the state.

Hailey: Okay, thank you.

Well, here we go. She got out, grabbed her suitcase, and turned to take in the view. *Holy wowza.* The lowering sunlight reflected off the plate glass windows of the massive house that was tucked into the Teton Mountain Range. Several feet of snow covered what she imagined would be bright green, neatly mowed grass in the summer.

She'd lived in a lot of places in her life but never anywhere like this. Since the co-guardian had opted out, she hadn't asked for any details, but now she was curious. Maybe it was the owner of the construction company where Darren worked?

Her immediate thought would've been Cole since the guys had been best friends. But he hadn't been at Everly's christening, and when she'd asked about it, Lindsay had said they'd fallen out of touch. So, thank goodness for that.

Lifting her wool scarf to cover her mouth and nose, she headed up the stone walkway. After ringing the doorbell, she tipped her head back and took in the gray sky. She might never see her friend again, but she would always feel her in her heart.

I'm here, Lindsay. And I swear I'll do whatever I can to make sure your babies wind up in a safe and loving home.

When no one answered, she turned the knob and let herself in. The eerily quiet house was a showcase with soaring ceilings, floor-to-ceiling windows, and a hearth meant for a fancy resort. The whole place was spotless and looked like it could be featured in a magazine shoot.

The only things that didn't fit were the two black garbage bags. Hailey had a sickening feeling about what she'd find inside them. Kneeling, she opened one to find sneakers so tiny her hand wouldn't fit inside, a flannel nightgown similar to what she designed for Abbott's of London, a blanket that smelled of laundry detergent, and a stuffed animal.

Sorrow crashed over her as she held the well-loved bear against her chest. Discolored from endless hugs and a torn arm, it surely held every memory of the life the girls had just lost.

She couldn't bear to think of how terrified they were. She'd lived through plenty of scary times herself. Packing her bag every few months, climbing into her mom's car, and driving to an *exciting new city where you'll make so many friends!* and running out of food and wondering when she'd be able to fill her belly.

But on every step of her journey, she'd at least had her mom. The one consistent person. These girls had lost both of their parents, their home, and their sense of safety in the world.

I don't know how to make things right for them, but I'm not going to leave them until I do.

Gently placing the bear back into the bag, she got up. "Hello?" The place was so big, she couldn't decide which direction to take. She was ready to text the social worker again when she heard a scrape that sounded like a chair on a tile floor. She headed in that direction.

As she made her way across the sprawling, airy living room and through the dining room, the kitchen appeared like something she'd seen on one of her cooking shows. Shiny, expansive, and not a glass or mug out of place. Despite its size, though, the low wooden beams and glass-fronted cabinets filled with colorful plates gave the room a surprisingly cozy appeal.

At a large rustic table sat two little girls, their legs

swinging, and a huge, broad-shouldered, dark-haired man. *Oh.* Was that—

"*Cole?*"

He didn't move—not the tiniest flinch of a muscle—and yet his eyes sharpened. Sitting sideways, long legs out in front of him, ankles crossed, he said, "Hey," before taking a big bite of a sandwich.

"*You're* the co-guardian?"

"Sure am. Who'd you think it would be?" He hadn't changed a bit. Still the most physically perfect man she'd ever seen, he had large, rounded biceps, powerful thighs, and big, strong hands. Underneath that casual slouch, though, hovering just below his air of good-time party boy, she caught a watchfulness, an intensity.

No matter how easygoing he liked to present himself, this man was aware of everything going on around him.

"I…had no idea." Why in the world would they leave their children with *Cole Montgomery?*

He broke into a grin. "It doesn't compute, right? Me, of all people?"

And that's why everyone loves him. Because he was gorgeous, rich, a superstar hockey player and yet, he was totally and completely earnest. His humility was so disarming that she immediately relaxed.

He sat up, sliding his bare feet under the chair. "I don't know what they were thinking, but I guess they needed to make sure the girls were set financially."

She took a moment to read his features. With a comment like that, anyone would think he was bragging about his obscene wealth, but she could see he actually believed his only value came from his bank account. "Oh, I don't know about that. Darren thought the world of you."

It was the only reason she'd agreed to go on that damn date with him. Her friends had convinced her Cole was a great guy.

She turned her attention to the two girls quietly eating their sandwiches. *They must be terrified. New house, strange man.* She pulled out a chair and joined them, smiling when she saw the peanut butter and jelly smeared around their mouths.

"Hi. I'm Hailey."

Tense with awareness, they continued munching.

"Now, you must be Paisley." She leaned closer to the older one. "I know because I'm your godmother. You probably don't remember me since the last time I saw you was when your sister was born." She turned to Everly, the three-year-old. "I was at your christening."

Paisley gazed up at Cole. "May I have milk, please?"

Lovely manners.

Damn, Lindsay. You done good.

"You got it." Rising out of his chair, he strode to the refrigerator.

The six-year-old watched him in awe. *Well, let's be honest.* All three of them did. Cole had an athletic grace and a commanding physicality that made it impossible to look away. Because while the rest of the world went through puberty and a gawky phase—weight gain, acne— Cole had bypassed all of it.

He came back with a glass for each girl and sat back down.

"Do you have a dog?" Paisley's legs kicked rhythmically under the table, while her sister was entirely focused on eating.

"I don't." Cole drank from his water bottle, his Adam's

apple bobbing, the tendons in his neck flexing. "But I always wanted one."

Paisley tipped her head. "Then why don't you have one?" She sounded like it was the most obvious thing in the world.

You want something, you get it.

That was exactly her mom's thinking. *You want to be a designer? Be one!*

"Because I'm not home enough. But when I was a kid, it was because my nannies didn't want 'one more thing to take care of.'"

"What's a nanny?"

"A babysitter." He spoke to her like an equal.

That's nice.

"Were they mean to you?" Paisley asked.

Looking at his water bottle, he cracked a grin. "One of them was. But not the last one. She was cool."

Paisley took a slug of milk, then licked her lips. "I don't like horses. I got hit by one when I was little, but I like dogs. And kitty cats. And I like swimming. Do you have a pool?"

While Hailey had a hard time following the conversation, Cole rolled with it. "I do. But it's covered in snow right now." He perked up. "Actually, I've got an indoor lap pool if you want to swim in that. It's not very deep, but it could be fun."

"An inside pool? I want to go. I want to go now." She swished her bottom until her butt hit the edge of the chair, and then she dropped to the floor. "Come on, Evvie. Let's get our swimsuits."

"I not finished." The littlest one took another bite.

"Take it with you," Paisley said.

Evvie seemed to find that a reasonable option because

29

she grabbed the last quarter of her sandwich and followed her out of the kitchen.

Without the kids, an awkward silence settled between her and Cole.

She hadn't seen him since high school, where he was a total smoke show, hugely popular, a hotshot athlete—in other words, totally intimidating—but also such a tool. He'd ruined her senior year.

But her petty issues from a decade ago had no place in today's situation. "I'm surprised to see you. The attorney told me there was a co-guardian, but that he wasn't going to be involved."

"I wasn't." Cole got up, stacked their plates, and brought them to the sink. "But I've got a concussion, so I'm out for the next four games. Figured I'd come out here and see what's up."

See, there it was again. That cavalier attitude. But she knew how close he and Darren had been. Even more, this man was in the middle of his hockey season—he needed to be with his team—but he'd chosen to come and pick up the girls.

"Bullshit." She came up beside him and got walloped with his expensive and masculine scent. *Whoa. The pheromones radiating off him…that's powerful stuff.* "These are Darren's kids. You couldn't *not* be involved."

He gazed out the window at the snow-covered mountain range. "No. I couldn't." Steam rose out of the sink, and he fiddled with the faucet to get the right temperature.

"I can't believe they're gone." If they had any other history, she'd have hugged him. They might not have much in common, but they did share Lindsay and Darren.

"I know."

"Mostly, I'm so angry."

He cut her a surprised look.

"At myself. I haven't talked to Lindsay in *three* years. I came out here for the christening, and then…I don't know what happened. I took a second job, she got busy with two kids, and somehow, we drifted apart. I hate that I let that happen."

"I get it." He rinsed the plates and stacked them in the dishwasher. "I lost touch with Darren, and I don't remember when." He braced both hands on the rim of the sink and lowered his head. "Why didn't I fly him out for a game? I should've sent his family to Disneyland. At some point, I should've checked in with him."

"I noticed you weren't at Everly's christening."

"I was thinking about that on the flight out here. I got an invitation, but I don't remember if I RSVP'd or just blew it off. I hope like hell I didn't give it to my assistant to handle." He went back to rinsing a glass. "I'll have to ask her. Darren… He was the best."

"He really was. And the way they loved each other? Even after two kids and financial stress and everything they'd gone through, they were still so wildly in love. Total soul mates."

"You believe in that stuff?"

"How could you know them and not believe it?"

"Because they were both lonely. And they both needed family."

"So? Lots of people are lonely, but that isn't what makes a long-lasting bond."

"That's fair. So, what makes that kind of bond?"

"I think it's a soul-deep connection. I think it happens on a subconscious level. It's a bond that can't be broken."

"Plenty of people break it."

"Then, they're not soul mates."

He cracked a grin. "I like this romantic side of you."

"What does that mean?"

"You only ever showed me your badass bitch side."

"Excuse me?" *What did he just say?* "Did you just call me a bitch?"

"No. I said you gave me attitude. Badass bitch attitude." He turned off the faucet. "You didn't take shit from anyone, and I admired that. Everyone else went along with things because they wanted to be liked and accepted, but you stood your ground. You knew who you were and didn't compromise it." He reached for a dish towel. "You going to get changed?"

"I didn't bring a swimsuit. It's December in Calamity, and I didn't plan on staying longer than a few weeks. Besides, in a million years, I would have never expected to be staying someplace with an indoor pool."

"You underestimated me."

She smiled. "I didn't know it was you."

In her frilly bikini, Evvie marched back into the kitchen, her plastic sandals slapping on the floor. She wore goggles and a blue plastic backpack. "I weady."

Paisley followed, wearing a red one-piece and flip-flops. "We're ready. Can we go now?"

"Sure. Let me get changed." Cole tossed the dishrag onto the counter. "And I've got to grab some towels."

"Come on." Everly lifted her arms as if the big hockey player had always been in her life. "Go wif you."

And look at that. He hitched her on his hip like it was the most natural thing in the world. "You're going to have to help me pick out the towels. Any color you want. We have blue, green, red—"

"Wed." The little girl punched the air, and the two left

the kitchen, chatting quietly like two old friends out for coffee.

Which left Hailey alone in the kitchen with Paisley. *Well, shoot.* She wasn't sure what to say. Did she bring up her loss? It felt important to ask how she felt, to see if she needed to talk about her parents, but everything she'd read said to let the girls bring it up on their own, and that when they did, she should answer the questions directly but specifically—not to go off on any tangents or deliver information they weren't ready to hear.

Apparently, those conversations came most often in quiet moments while they were doing other things. So, while they waited for the other two, Hailey got her sketchbook out of her tote along with a case of markers. Taking a seat at the table, she pulled off the cap and started filling in a design she'd started on the plane.

The girl sat beside her, watching. "That's pretty." And then, "Are you a mommy?"

"No, sweetie. I'm not."

"Why not?"

"I guess I haven't met the man I want to have babies with." She'd always gotten that funny feeling in the pit of her stomach from books and movies when the hot boyfriend entered the scene. When the powerful man fell madly in love with a regular woman like her. The images on social media of couples holding hands, giving piggyback rides, laughing hysterically over a shared joke, and snuggling under covers, made her yearn for it.

She met plenty of people at school, in bars, and at work, and she'd done her fair share of dating, but she'd never connected with anybody that way. And she'd rather be alone than spend time with someone who didn't excite her.

33

"Do you want to be a mommy?"

"I do." The sharp wrench in her heart told her just how much she did. *Well, let's be honest.* She wanted everything she didn't have as a child.

She didn't need a therapist to explain her difficulty making friends. It stemmed from moving so often growing up. When she saw a group of people talking in yoga class, she quickly left the studio. Afraid of rejection, afraid of breaking into a clique… A lifetime of being the new kid still impacted her.

It wasn't all that long ago that she'd accepted her fate. She would be a single woman in this life.

And that was okay. She'd made peace with it.

Paisley got up on her knees to look more closely at her drawing. "What're you making?"

"A robe. Do you like it?"

"What's a robe?"

"Sometimes, when you wake up in the morning and it's cold, you put a robe on over your pajamas. Or maybe it's a lazy Sunday, and you want to lounge around the house drinking tea and watching movies. You don't want to get dressed, but you don't want to be in your pajamas, so you throw on a robe."

"I don't have a robe." She was quiet for a moment. "My mommy doesn't have a robe."

An alarm rang in her body. Here was an opportunity to talk about her parents. "Oh, yeah? What did your mommy wear around the house?"

Paisley shrugged. "I don't know."

"I never used to wear robes, either. But then I started making them, and now I wear them all the time. They're pretty, and they're comfy."

"How do you make them?"

"With fabric and a needle and thread."

"Can you make me one?"

"I'd love to."

"Yay. Thank you. Can you make one for Evvie, too?"

Ah, Evvie. Good to know her nickname. "You bet I can. Matching or different?"

Paisley gave it some thought. "Different."

"You got it. So, first, you've got to tell me your favorite colors."

The little girl sorted through the markers and pulled a blue and an orange. "I like yellow, too. And green. Green is like grass."

"So, you like colors you find in nature Blue like a lake and yellow like the sun."

"Yes, but do I have to choose just one?"

"Nope. My robes have lots of colors. Here, let me show you." She pulled her phone out of the zippered pouch in her tote and opened her photo file, scrolling until she found the robe that hit all Paisley's favorite colors. "See how it's got blue, yellow, orange, and a little green? I could make that for you."

"That's pretty." She scrunched her nose in disapproval. "Do you have purple? That's my favorite color."

"Yes, I do. Hang on." She scrolled some more. "This one?" She'd used muted jewel tones, making the robes look like a favorite T-shirt that had gone through the wash a hundred times.

"Yes." Paisley gave her a big smile. "I like that one."

I'd give it to you, but I'd have to yank it off my mom's new friend. "And what about Evvie? What colors does she like?"

"Evvy likes red."

"Should I put other colors in it?"

"No. Just red. I'll make hers." Paisley reached for the red pen and began drawing.

In the quiet kitchen with nothing but the scritch of markers and Cole's footsteps on the floor above, Hailey calmed down for the first time since she'd read the attorney's letter. After the rush and drag of travel, the research on grief, and the anxiety of the unknown, she finally let out a breath.

But it didn't last long. *Nope.* In the quiet, all the questions broke loose and chased each other around her mind.

How long do I need to stay here?

Is someone currently looking for extended family who can take the girls? I mean, if social services hasn't found anyone, who can? And how long would it take?

What about her job? Fear pinched the back of her neck. Abbott's of London was a family-owned company, so she hoped they'd understand why she needed to be in Wyoming right now. As it was, she worked remotely three days a week. If she got everything done, it shouldn't be that big a deal.

God, she couldn't lose her job over this. *I mean, I will. I won't abandon the girls, but…* There were just so many unanswered questions.

Those big blue eyes watched her carefully. "Are you scared?"

Yikes. She had to be careful. Paisley might be six, but she picked up on adult emotions. On the other hand, here was an opportunity to get the girl talking. "It's always a little scary to be in a new place with people you don't know very well, right?"

Paisley shrugged. "Are you going to live here with us?"

Oh, boy. Go for the hard-hitting question right off the bat, why don't you? "For now, yes."

Paisley's features tightened. "Are we going to have Christmas here with you?"

She couldn't even commit to something that was twelve days away. "I would like that very much." What if they found a home for the girls tomorrow? A week from now? She wouldn't make promises she couldn't keep.

"What about Cole?"

She couldn't speak for him. "Tell you what. While you guys are swimming, Cole and I will come up with a plan. Does that sound good?"

"I guess."

"But while we're waiting, let's make some pretty pictures because this house might have nice furniture and fancy chandeliers, but it's definitely missing the fun stuff like drawings and seashells and cute magnets."

A secret smile curved Paisley's mouth, and she went back to work.

Ever since the conversation with the attorney, she'd been in a race to get here and assess the situation. But now, she knew her purpose, and it energized her, sweeping away her doubts and fears.

No matter the personal cost, I'll get these girls settled in the right situation as soon as possible.

Could she count on Cole? She honestly had no idea.

Chapter Four

In the warm humidity of the lap pool room, Hailey stood at the window overlooking a snowy forest. It was literally a winter wonderland, and given the circumstance, she couldn't think of a better place for the kids to spend Christmas. Behind her, they splashed and giggled, and for one precious moment, all seemed right in their world.

For them, this was a vacation, a weekend away.

But she knew on a deeper level, they had to miss their mom and dad. They had to sense something was wrong. They had to be scared.

Water ran through her toes, and she turned to find that a red plastic cup had tipped over. They didn't have real toys, but the girls seemed content to play with cups and corks. It might be relatively shallow, but until they bought floaties, they'd confined the girls to the stairs.

They're just babies, just starting out, and now their lives are shattered.

She felt so helpless. She and Cole needed to come up with a plan to make things right for them. Joining him at a café table, she said, "Hey, so, Paisley asked me about Christmas." She sat down. "We need to figure things out."

His big frame slouched low in the padded chair. "Well, we're doing Christmas with them." He watched the girls like they were the most adorable things he'd ever seen. "That's for sure."

"*I* am." Her stomach squeezed. "You'll be gone by Thursday." *And then I'm in this alone.*

His senses sharpened in a way that made her think he was worried about her. "I can come back. We get two days off for the holiday, so I can be here for Christmas Eve and Day."

"You can?"

"Absolutely."

"Oh, thank God." She stuttered out a laugh. "I'm not ready to do this alone."

He grew even more intense. "You won't, Hailey. I may not be here physically, but I'm still here for you. I can give you this house. And I can hire nannies. A chef. Whatever you need."

There it is. "And there's the Cole I've always known. Always throwing money at the situation."

"What does that mean?"

She shook her head. "Why take a car to the dance when you can rent a limo? Who needs to hang out at the river when Cole can fly you to the ocean?"

He hardened. "We're not talking about a party here. We're talking about two little girls who lost their parents."

"I know that. And you just told me what you're willing to do—throw money at them. Which leaves the hard part to me." She leaned closer so the girls wouldn't hear. "It's not about making them a sandwich or getting them to school on time. It's about what happens when they start acting out because they miss their mom and dad. Cole, these kids are going to need therapy. They're going to need comfort and love. They'll need advice and...and discipline. Finding someone to cook our meals is the least important thing here."

"I don't know what you want from me. I can't just"—he snapped his fingers—"find them a family. *I* sure as hell can't be their parent. And I'm not saying you should do it. I'm not assuming you're going to adopt them. But there are some things I can provide to make sure their physical needs are met." He tapped his knuckles on the glass table. "Believe me, that's every bit as important as the emotional stuff."

The conversation was pointless. He'd made himself clear. He had nothing to offer but his credit card. Besides, she'd known from the start she was in this alone. "Look, I've only talked briefly to the attorney and Chase, so I don't know much about the situation. Is *anyone* looking for family? Are we really all they have?" *That can't be right.*

She hadn't given it much thought back then, but in high school, Lindsay's parents were in their late fifties, and they'd come from Hungary. They'd shared some of their stories, and as far as she'd understood, they hadn't kept in contact with their families. And Darren had been in foster care. On his Emancipation Day, he'd married Lindsay at the courthouse.

Reality knocked her on her ass. Up until this moment, she'd assumed she'd take care of the girls *until* they found their permanent home. But what if there wasn't one?

Oh, come on. There were plenty of people who would love to take in these girls. "Maybe they have close friends who wouldn't mind adding two little girls to their family."

"They chose *us*, Hailey. People they hadn't talked to in

years. That should tell you everything you need to know about who else might be waiting in the wings."

"But I can't...I can't raise two children in my studio apartment in Manhattan. I'm a fashion designer—I hardly make any money."

He gave her a patient look.

"Right." *I just made his point for him.* She was an emotional mess, and he was being practical. They needed food, clothing, shelter...*God.* They needed so much more than she could ever afford. "You're absolutely right. I'm sorry for jumping on you."

"I've had a little more time to wrap my head around this situation."

"So, then...I mean, let's be honest here. The only thing standing between them and foster care is me, right? If I don't take the girls, they'll become wards of the state."

He reached out as if he wanted to grab her hands but stopped himself before touching her. "Hang on. You're trying to solve all the problems at once, and that's not possible in this situation. If I went into a game worrying about all three periods, I'd flame out within five minutes. I have to break it down and handle it one step at a time. First, I think about the puck hitting the ice and where I'm going to shoot it. Then, I see who's got control of it and come up with the next strategy."

"This isn't hockey. These are Lindsay's *daughters.*"

"And you got here this afternoon. So, we're not even close to making big decisions yet. Let's take it one step at a time. Step one is Christmas."

Tension eased in her neck and shoulders. "Okay." She liked his approach. "That's good. I can handle that." A tree, some stockings, a few presents. A nice meal. "What's step two?"

"I'll hire a private investigator to look for extended family."

"Okay, I'm doing a one-eighty here. I *totally* appreciate your money."

When they both smiled, something happened… shifted. For one moment, she could believe they were in this together.

This big, muscular jock with his shocking blue eyes and dark hair acted like he didn't have a care in the world, like he was all about hockey and living this decadent lifestyle of parties and yachts, supermodels, and pop stars. He looked like a man who could give one hot, commanding look to a woman in a bar and have her follow him out the door and right into his Maserati.

But she was starting to see a whole other side of him. A man who was good in crises.

"I promise I won't walk away until they're in a good home," he said.

A man who cared.

She believed him. "And if we don't?"

He chuckled. "You're doing it again. Can we get through steps one and two before we tackle that one?"

She blew out a breath. "I'm a planner. What can I say?"

"Unfortunately, this is one situation you can't map out. I'll get an investigator on it right away, but I don't think we should tell Chase we're not sure about taking the girls. He made it clear the courts don't look for family. Which means if we're just here for the holidays—"

She held up a hand. She didn't want to hear the rest of that sentence. Lindsay's girls would not go into the system. "I agree. I won't say anything."

"You realize that means he'll go ahead with the adoption proceedings, right?"

Even if she wasn't confident they'd find a home, she still knew she couldn't put them in foster care. "Yes."

"Okay." He sat back in his chair. "Now, as far as that emotional stuff, my dad gave me the number of a therapist friend of his. I've been talking to her, and she's given me tips. She says to only answer the questions the girls ask."

"Yeah, that's what I read."

"And she also said to keep them on their usual schedule. Chase found a calendar on the wall in Lindsay's kitchen, so I've got that. He's already talked to the school and arranged for the bus to pick Paisley up outside the gate tomorrow morning at six-fifty."

"When are they out for the Christmas break?"

"Not till the twenty-third."

"Okay. So far, that sounds good." Her chest tightened, and she dragged her clammy hands on her jeans.

This time, he did reach for her. "Hey, talk to me."

And that big, strong grip kept her from going under. "I'm scared."

"I know. I get that. But try not to let your mind race ahead, okay? We can only deal with what's on our plate right now." With his free hand, he pulled out his phone and tapped the screen.

"What're you doing?"

"I'm getting the ball rolling." He waited a moment before speaking. "Hey, this is Cole Montgomery. I've got a project I'd like your help with as soon as possible." He left his number and then disconnected.

"Was that the private investigator?" When he nodded, she squeezed his hand. "I like a man who makes things happen."

His chair scraped on the limestone floor as he dragged it so close their knees touched. "Here's the thing. We *are* in this together, but when I go back to Boston, I'll get hyper-focused, so I'm telling you now, if I forget to check in occasionally, all I need is one reminder—one text that says, Hey, asshole, where are you? And I'll get back on track."

"You know I'll do that."

"I do. And that's why I liked you so much. Now, what else is on your mind?"

That's why I liked you so much.

The world quieted to nothing but the gentle lapping of water as she considered the words he'd tossed out so carelessly. She'd known, of course. He'd asked her out for months before she'd finally agreed to a date. But she'd always figured he'd pursued her because she was the only one who didn't fawn all over him.

Had she been wrong? She'd never know because they weren't going there. She had way bigger concerns. "My job."

"Do they know yet?"

She shook her head. "I don't want to ask for time off until I know what we're doing."

"Sounds fair. Are you worried they'll fire you?"

"I honestly don't know. They're family-owned, so I think they'll understand what I'm doing—up to a point. As long as I get my work done, and as long as there's an end date."

"Hence, the nanny."

"We can't hire a nanny. That's a full-time job."

"Fine. I'll get a babysitter."

"You've got an answer for everything." She let out a breath. "And I'm really, incredibly grateful for that. Well."

She got up. "We better get these girls some dinner." Reaching for the towels, she was surprised when he snatched the top one out of her hands.

"Divide and conquer." That voice—so deep and rugged—connected with something deep in her core.

It felt dangerous to revise her opinion of him after what he'd done to her in high school, but she couldn't judge him for anything other than how he was handling this situation. "I like that." As they each lifted a child out of the pool and wrapped them in towels, she asked, "By the way, where am I sleeping?"

"The lower level's got a gym, a theater, a wine cellar, and a couple of bedrooms. There's a nanny suite off the kitchen. The third floor's pretty cool because it's got an observatory. You live in the city, so you'll appreciate the night sky out here."

"Yes, fancy boy, you've got a great big house. Can you just point me to a bedroom?" With the girls bundled up, they headed out of the room.

"My point was not how cool my house is—though it is pretty sick." His voice grew more intimate—like something his lover might hear under the covers at night —in the narrow walls of the staircase. "But to say you've got your pick of rooms. In case you're uncomfortable being on the same floor as the girls and me."

When they reached the kitchen, she turned to the little ones. "Do you want to grab pajamas out of your bags, and I'll get a bath started?" Once they left, she said, "I'll take the room next to them. Just in case they wake up with a nightmare or need a glass of water or something."

He flinched as if nearly walking into a sliding glass door. "Shit."

"What?"

"*Nightmares?* I didn't think about that." His concern gave way to a thoughtful expression. "Well, it didn't happen last night."

"Would you have heard them if it did?"

His cheeks colored. "Probably." He brushed past her. "Better get to the girls before they put on their dog and cat costumes."

"Wait. What does that mean?"

"Chase told them to pack a few things, and they chose costumes, tutus, and swimsuits."

"No, I meant about the nightmares." She followed him across the living room. "Where did you sleep last night?"

"Close enough that I would've heard."

She caught up with him, grabbing his shoulder. "Why are you being so weird? Just tell me."

"Why?" For the first time, he looked rattled. "They slept through the night. That's all that matters."

"Then, why are you blushing? Either you stayed up all night watching them—"

"Why would I *watch* them? That's creepy."

"Fine, so where did you sleep?"

"Nearby."

"In the bedroom across the hall?"

"Outside their room, okay? I have a very nice sleeping bag, and for your information, I slept like a log." He found the girls in the living room, lifted them up, and headed for the stairs.

Floored, Hailey stood there and watched him take off. He wore jeans like every other mountain man in Calamity, and the flannel shirt and his overlong, dark hair that curled at the back of his neck completed the look. But few had an ass as tight and round, shoulders as broad and muscular, and she guaranteed nobody smelled as good as he did.

The scent of him lingered in the air. Clean clothes, expensive shampoo, and rugged, outdoorsy man.

He was the son of an A-list actor. He'd traveled the world, had more money than he could spend in ten lifetimes, and was the hottest player in the NHL. He lived recklessly, wildly—like only someone who'd never known a minute of insecurity could.

And yet he'd slept on the floor outside the bedroom of two orphaned little girls.

As he carried them upstairs for their bath, he'd never been sexier.

But before she became yet another star in his orbit, she had to remind herself he was a man who lived at a whole other level. She didn't want to live at another level. She preferred the simple things. She appreciated all the things he took for granted.

She wanted normal.

But Cole didn't do normal. If someone said they were having a party, he turned it into a screening of his dad's latest movie or a catered pool party. Something small, real, and intimate was never good enough.

All of that was true, but tonight, she'd gotten a glimpse of another side of him. A deeply caring man with a sense of responsibility and innate leadership skills.

A man who'd slept outside the bedroom of two little girls.

And, oddly, that seemed the most dangerous side of all.

Normally, when Cole visited Calamity, his housekeeper stocked the kitchen. He tended to travel with a group of friends who wanted to take advantage of everything the area had to offer like rappelling, white water rafting, and hardcore snowboarding, and she knew exactly what to buy. But since he never came home during hockey season, and she spent winters in Arizona, this time, he was on his own.

Which meant he had nothing to feed four empty bellies.

When he'd picked up the girls yesterday, he'd gotten the car seats, so he supposed they could go out to dinner. But where did you take kids? What did they eat? Maybe they could just grab burgers at Wild Billy's. *No, that's a bar.* He could just see Hailey's expression when they walked into a place with a mechanical bull and line dancing.

And fast food's out of the question, right?

He was totally out of his element here. He'd have to ask her.

Hailey Casselton. Of all the people to be stuck in this house with... Man, he'd had a thing for her. With her long, wavy hair, lips that drew a man's attention, and funky clothes she'd designed herself, she'd looked so different from the other girls who wore cowboy boots and jeans, rode horses and snowboarded. For all its billionaires and celebrities, at its heart, Calamity was a mountain town. Kids trained for barrel racing and bronco riding, worked the ski lifts in the winter, and a fun night out was a bonfire and kegger at Horseshoe Bend on the river.

Hailey was different. She had a sophistication that came from growing up in a big city. He hadn't known how to behave around her, so he'd made the mistake of treating her like everyone else in a social situation—with banter and superficial conversations. His buddies joked, teased, and lobbed one-liners at each other, but she didn't find him funny or charming, and she sure as hell didn't want to spend time with him.

Hailey was real. She was smart, driven, creative—a whole mix of qualities that made him want her in ways he'd never felt before. Still, to this day, no one stirred him up the way she did.

She was special, and he knew without a doubt Lindsay had been right to name her guardian. Why the hell they'd chosen him, he had no clue. It had to be money. Hailey would raise them, and he'd provide for them.

Following voices, he found her in the bathroom. The girls played with cups and corks in the tub while Hailey sat on the toilet lid, typing on her phone.

She glanced up, relief easing the tightness across her forehead. "I talked to my boss. He's okay with me working remotely here until January third."

He breathed in the scent of lavender bubble bath. "That's good."

When she broke into a grin, his heart nearly exploded. She looked so pretty, her light brown hair a cascade of loose curls, those hazel eyes trained on him with so much excitement, like they were in this thing together.

And they were. But thank fuck he'd be helping from Boston because there wasn't a chance he could live under the same roof with this woman and not want to touch her, talk to her, be near her. Water splashed onto her blouse, making the silky material cling to her plump, round breasts, and the low hum of arousal kicked in.

"Maybe we'll get lucky, and the PI will find a family for them by then," she said. "But whatever happens, I'm not going to worry about it till January. I'm going to take your advice and go one step at a time."

She wasn't businesslike anymore. She wasn't anxious. And the relaxed version of Hailey dazzled him to the point that he couldn't form a coherent thought.

Fortunately, Evvie handed Hailey a plastic cup, so she turned her attention to the little girl and didn't have to witness a grown man standing there tongue-tied. Setting her phone down, she pretended to drink from it. "Mm. This is good. What is it?"

"It hot." The three-year-old's eyes were lit with mischief.

"Hot soup?"

Evvie nodded, her grin widening.

"Hm." Hailey sipped again. "Ooh, it is. It's hot. So hot." She made faces and waved a hand near her mouth. "Oh, no. It's boiling hot."

The girls laughed, and Paisley dipped a cup into the bath water and handed it over.

"Maybe this one's better." Hailey pretended to take a sip. "Ow. It's burning hot." Her eyes went wide as she tossed the cup, water arcing across the tub and hitting the wall. The girls cracked up, and he couldn't help but laugh with them. They continued filling cups and handing them over for several minutes, and not for a second did Hailey lose interest.

Yeah, she's exactly the right choice for these girls.

When the girls moved on to another game, Hailey reached for a white towel and dried off her face and hands.

He leaned against the counter. "You're good with them."

"Oh, well. This part's not hard."

He'd never met her mom, but she'd obviously done a great job. "You must've had a good role model."

When her gaze cut away, he knew he'd touched on a sensitive subject. Back in high school, she'd lived with Lindsay for most of senior year. She'd said it was because her mom moved around a lot for work, but maybe there was more to the story.

He'd never really questioned it back then. Given how he'd grown up, what did he know about families? He'd only ever known a dad who filmed two hundred days a year thanks to a massively successful movie franchise. And when his dad was home, he always had friends and business partners visiting.

Cole had bonded with a lot of people who hadn't stayed in his life all that long. "You're an only child like me, right?"

"Yep. My mom's great."

And yet he heard the hesitancy in her tone. "But?"

"No, nothing bad. We're just different. And I guess when you said role model, it threw me. I don't see her like that." She busied herself by draping the damp towel over the rack.

He hoped for more but didn't want to push. "I know you moved around a lot."

She came closer to him. Weirdest thing, but it was like the cells in his body heated up and started moving like bumper cars at a county fair. Crazy because no other woman had the power to excite him like this.

"We did. All the time. And it wasn't like she'd wait until the start of a school year. If she got a gig, we packed up and left. Don't get me wrong, if you met her, you'd love her. She's warm and fun...I mean, everyone loves her. It's just..." She stood so close their arms brushed. "My mom works hard, and she loves what she does, but in between gigs, it doesn't occur to her to get a job. She trusts that the universe and her reputation will provide for her. And they usually do. The phone always rings, and she gets another gig."

"But you need stability."

"Oh, yeah. In a way my mom can't possibly understand. She keeps in contact with everyone, so when she needs a place to crash, she just starts texting. I don't think anyone's ever turned her down. And it doesn't bother her a bit when they eventually tell her it's time for her to move on."

"Sounds like you hated that part."

"It was mortifying." Briefly, her eyelids fluttered closed. "I remember when I was twelve, she met this music executive who had a fancy house in the Hamptons. He only came out on the weekends, so he didn't mind letting us use the downstairs suite during the week. It had its own entrance, so we didn't need to go into the main part of the house." She did it again, closing her eyes briefly as if blocking out a terrible sight. "We hadn't eaten all day, and I was starving. I remember creeping up the stairs and peering around the dark house, listening to make sure no one was home. It was dead silent, so I went into his refrigerator and scarfed down anything I could find. And there wasn't much, believe me. An expired yogurt, a jar of pickles, and some sliced cheese with hard edges. And then, I was scooping out ice cream—like being so careful to carve it out in the exact same pattern so that no one could tell I'd taken a few bites—when I heard this deep voice go, What're you doing? I nearly jumped out of my skin."

What the fuck was wrong with her mother? *She* might

not mind going without food or a roof over her head, but she had a *daughter*. How could she not feed her little girl?

"I wanted to die."

"Was the guy a dick about it?"

"You can't blame him. He'd made it clear to my mom that she could stay a few nights, but she couldn't come into the main house. I was old enough to know not to go up there and root through his belongings. He pulled the ice cream container out of my hand and asked me to get back downstairs. The thing is, if he'd caught me eating a can of tuna, he wouldn't have minded. He'd have understood I was hungry. But he thought I was just a kid wandering through his house and randomly eating ice cream. You know? I'm sure he checked his jewelry box to make sure I didn't steal a watch."

He nodded like he understood, but he didn't. Because the man knew Hailey's mom. He knew if she needed to couch surf, she probably didn't have money for other things. Like food. He should've let Hailey have the ice cream and asked if she needed anything else. Like toothpaste or a fucking sandwich. He should've given her a few gift cards.

"So, no, I don't see my mom as a role model. That doesn't make her a bad person. It's just that I need stability and a reliable income."

"I get it." *This.* This was the conversation he'd always wanted to have with her in high school. Maybe he hadn't been mature enough. He'd hoped they'd talk on their date, but he'd been so damn nervous.

"She never treated me like a child. I was her friend, her partner in crime. Instead of mowing lawns or babysitting, I made money by helping my mom's clients. So, I'm a boss at pet sitting and watering plants and taking in the mail, but I don't know the first thing about children."

"These two make it seem pretty easy."

"They do." After a quick glance at the girls, she lowered her voice. "But right now, they're on vacation. We're just another stop along the way of where they wind up. How many passes before they stop opening their hearts and trusting?"

It was like missing a step, that shock of sensation ricocheting through his body. Because it had happened to him. With each babysitter, nanny...even his dad's girlfriends who tried to be a mother to him. He couldn't say when it had happened, but he'd lost interest in getting to know anyone. He'd stopped trying.

"I hate this so much." Her eyes glistened, and her bottom lip wobbled. "They're such good, sweet kids. They deserve the best life. And I just don't think we're the right ones to give it to them."

You sure the hell are. But he had no answers, and he couldn't bear to see her upset. "It's too soon to know anything right now. All we can do is try to find them the right home. And once they're there, we can stay in their lives. We *are* the godparents. We'll always look out for them."

"You're right." She touched his arm—just a simple brush of skin—but it was like making eye contact with a rock star—a pinch to his nervous system. "Thank you. You're good at calming me down."

"Well, I'm in a lot of high-pressure situations. If I lose my shit, I don't score goals. But I'll talk to the PI tomorrow, and in the meantime, we'll give them the best damn Christmas they've ever had."

Gratitude welled in her eyes. "I'm so glad you're in this with me."

He let out an awkward laugh. "Never thought I'd hear you say something like that."

"Well, you've changed a lot since high school." The way she gazed up at him…was that…admiration?

It fucking was. Somehow, it knocked down the gate, letting all the longing and yearning his teenage heart had felt for her flood in. Countless times, he'd dreamed of her hands on his body and kissing that sexy-as-fuck mouth. He'd wanted to see those hazel eyes filled with love and lust.

But he'd never understood until this moment that what he'd really wanted was her respect. He'd wanted her to like him.

As much as it meant to him, though, he knew it didn't count. She just didn't want to be alone in this impossible situation. He had to remember that and not get carried away. He took a step back. "Hey, so, I came up here to ask about dinner. Should I order in? Take them out?"

He'd startled her with the abrupt change in conversation. She looked confused…almost hurt. "Uh, well, they've just had a bath. Probably better if we order in."

He watched the kids take turns pouring water over each other's heads, their blond hair glassy, flattened against their backs. "What should I get?"

"I don't really know. I haven't been in Calamity in ten years, and when I was, I didn't eat out all that often."

"I meant what do kids like? Burgers?"

"Ask them." She sat back down on the toilet lid. "Or just get whatever you ate when you were their age." She picked up her phone. "While you're doing that, I'll order groceries." She turned her attention to the girls. "Hey, cuties. I'm going to get some stuff for breakfast. What do you like?"

Evvie looked up, eyes bright, cheeks rosy. "Faffles."

"Waffles, cool. I like them, too. What else?" When neither answered, Hailey asked, "Do you like juice, milk, or water?"

"Milk, please," Paisley said. "Mommy wants our bones to be big and strong."

"Smart lady. How about eggs?"

As they created a list, Cole kicked himself for shutting her down. He'd had a genuine moment with her, one where she didn't hate him, and then he'd ruined it.

Why couldn't he relax around her?

Chapter Five

As Cole headed downstairs, pain flared in his knee, so he sat in a club chair. He had to be better about staying off it. Yeah, he was here to get the kids set up, but he also had to use the time to heal.

Scrolling the food delivery app, he had no idea what to choose. *She said get them whatever you ate as a kid. Fine.* He clicked on Harley and Lu's Emporium, a gourmet market that sold prepared foods, and ordered enough to last a month. Which was good. The more he gave them now, the less guilt he'd feel when he left.

His phone had been blowing up for hours, so he took some time to check in with his teammates. They had an important game tomorrow, so mostly, it was the guys begging him to get back on the ice.

Half his brain was focused on responding to his teammates, his coach, and his trainer, and the other half was listening to the squeals and chatter coming from upstairs, wishing he hadn't cut Hailey off. She probably thought he didn't give a shit, that all he wanted was to get out of there.

Couldn't be further from the truth.

Finally caught up, he was left with only a couple of unanswered messages.

First was Jaime Dupree, one of his oldest hockey friends.

Jaime: You okay?

Jaime: Saw you weren't on the ice. Heard you've got a concussion?

Even though his closest friends had broken the barrier of silence this past summer when their former coach passed away, he still felt sick to his stomach when he saw Jaime's name. He'd failed them all so badly.

He wasn't going to ignore him, so he tapped out a response.

Cole: Yeah, I'm good.

Jaime: Sorry that six-year-old took you out. Need a juice box? Some animal crackers?

Cole chuckled.

Cole: I was saving her. It was a heroic act, asshole.

Cole: Who the fuck told you anyhow?

Jaime: Don't know if you heard, but I own a team now. Basically, I'm the shit. I've got eyes and ears everywhere. But yeah, it was your agent. You really should fire him. He gave up the details way too easily.

Cole: He has his good points.

Grinning, he sent him a GIF of money raining.

The obvious thing was to mention that he was in town, but did he really want to see him? He liked living on the East Coast. Being far away. Keeping too busy to revisit the past.

He moved on to the next message. It was from Declan, another friend in their foursome. Now that Declan had agreed to coach the Renegades, half of them were fully reunited. He got a twist of longing to be part of that.

Declan: I shipped you some Band-Aids for your boo-boo. I know you like the ones with dinosaurs.

Okay, fuck it. He'd just start a group text.

Cole: Listen, fuckwads, I'm out for four games, so can we not make fun of my concussion?

Jaime: Nah.

Declan: Nope.

A powerful wave of nostalgia hit him so hard his chest ached. These guys, they'd been his family. He remembered making rafts out of branches and trying to float down the river (crashing within minutes, of course), racing each other on dirt bikes (that time Booker tried to overtake Jaime on the narrow edge of a mountain path and careened off it), flying them all out to New York City for his dad's première (where Jaime tried to hook up with a supermodel—though, they still didn't know whether he'd actually slept with her).

These guys were his brothers. Yeah, he'd fucked it all up, and Booker would never forgive him, but at least he could get these two back.

Cole: I'm in Calamity right now because I got some bad and weird news.

Jaime: Bad first.

Cole: Darren and Lindsay Leeson died.

Declan: No fucking way. Died?

Cole: Yeah. Ten days ago.

Declan: Jesus. That sucks. Don't they have kids?

Cole: And that brings us to the weird news. Darren named me as guardian.

Jaime: Why's that weird? You were his closest friend.

These guys knew why better than anyone.
I'm a menace.

Cole: I'm the last person anyone wants raising their kids.

Jaime: That's bullshit. You're generous, smart. You're a good man.

Declan: And rich.

Cole laughed.

Cole: Okay, quit soaping my ass. I'm not donating to your new training facility.

Jaime: Did you forget it's Kurt's team? Trust me, we're well-funded. Since you've got nothing better to do, come to the rink tomorrow. We've got practice at eleven.

Paisley would be at school, so Hailey wouldn't need him around. Yeah, he could do that.

Cole: See you then.

He set the phone down, letting it sink in that they didn't hold a grudge. That this banishment was self-imposed and reconnecting with them meant this town could feel like home again. He'd like that.

By the time he got the notice from the delivery driver, the girls were coming down the stairs in their flannel nightgowns, looking fresh-faced, their cheeks flushed pink as cotton candy. Hailey started toward him. "So, what're we doing for dinner?"

But he'd made such a mess of his conversation with her that his brain scrambled as soon as he saw her. He blurted, "Food's here. Be right back," and turned his back on her, heading for the door.

What the hell is wrong with you?
Get a hold of yourself.

"Good timing," she called. "They just dropped the groceries outside the gate."

"On it." He threw on his leather coat and escaped into the freezing cold night. What he had to realize was that one, he wasn't eighteen anymore. He was a grown-ass man who didn't need to get flustered around anyone. And two, he wasn't pursuing her. The only reason they were under the same roof was because of the girls. *That's it.*

There's not going to be some big romance.

His breath came out in white puffs, and his knee hurt as if he'd jammed a spike through the patella. As he rounded the bend in the long driveway, headlights blinded him, and he shielded his eyes.

They flicked off, and a young man jumped out of the idling truck. "Sorry, man."

He hit the button to open the gate, and while the guy unloaded stuffed tote bags from the cab, Cole collected the box with the groceries.

The driver handed them over, gaping in that very familiar way. "Are you...holy shit. Cole Montgomery?" The man spun around, bending over and clenching his fists on his knees. "You're fucking *Cole Montgomery*. I can't believe it. I grew up here and never once ran into you. This is insane."

"Good to meet you, man."

"What're you doing here? You've got a game tomorrow."

His concussion had already hit the news, but he should be sitting on the bench with his team. "I've got some family business to take care of. I'll be back by Thursday."

"You're playing, right? Because we can't afford to lose you. Not when we're up against the Chargers."

Conversations like these could go on for a while, so he had to cut it short. The girls were hungry. "Absolutely. Listen, thanks for bringing food to my crew. You have a great Christmas." He gave him a tip and a chin nod and headed back up the long driveway.

The wind cut through his jacket, and his knee throbbed. *No more screwing around.* He had the next three days to heal, so he had to take it easy. He'd hang out on the couch while the kids played or whatever. He just had to keep the weight off.

Hearing little girl chatter and Hailey's sexy voice as he entered the house was jarring. Usually, he had his friends with him, which meant there was always laughter, booze, and music. It was a raucous energy.

But with kids and Hailey, it had a whole different vibe, and he liked it. Throughout his childhood, he'd been obsessed with watching other families. At restaurants, parks, school events—and especially when he'd hung out at someone's house—he keyed in on the dynamics. More than anything, he liked when the Duprees invited him over the holidays.

Jaime's dad cooked the meals, and his mom sat in her Barcalounger holding court with her extended family. Kids ran amuck, adults sipped cocktails, and the house smelled of pine, cinnamon, and roasting meat. Cole smiled at the good memories.

It struck him that he'd be hosting Christmas here. Which meant it was up to him to create the magic for the girls. He was surprised at how much he liked that idea, giving Darren's kids the kind of holiday he'd missed out on.

Yeah. He liked it a fuck of a lot.

He came into the kitchen with his bags held high. "Who's hungry?"

"Me, me, me." Evvie danced with excitement.

He set them on the counter and started pulling out food. "Let's get some plates and forks." As he went to the cabinet, Hailey started unpacking the groceries.

"Why did you get balloons?" Paisley waved the bag toward her sister. "Look it. She got balloons."

Hailey's grin blinded him like a paparazzi's flash. "They're for tomorrow. We're going to play some games with them."

"But I have school tomorrow." Paisley looked devastated.

"Don't worry. We'll wait until you get home."

"Evvie play?" the three-year-old asked.

"Absolutely. We all will." The light from the refrigerator made Hailey's hazel eyes sparkle and accentuated the different shades of blond in her wavy hair.

She was so damn pretty. But as long as he kept seeing her like that, he'd keep being awkward. *So, snap out of it.* "Okay, let's eat." The girls ran to the table, chairs scraped on the hardwood floor, and he held up a container. "Who wants chateaubriand?" He lifted another one. "We've got paella in case you prefer fish. There's chicken pot pie—that was my favorite when I was a kid. And in case you're not meat eaters, I got pesto pasta with fresh mozzarella." He reached for a serving spoon. "Who wants what?" Three pairs of eyes stared at him.

Evvie turned her nose away. "I not eat dat."

"You don't eat what? I got a little of everything." He looked at Paisley. "What about you? You want noodles?"

She peered into the bowl. "Why are they green?"

"Because of the sauce." He shot Hailey a look. "What kid doesn't like noodles?"

But she was too busy laughing to answer.

"What? You said to get what I liked when I was a kid."

"Yes, like chicken fingers or fish sticks. Not chat—" She laughed so hard she couldn't finish the word. "Chateau—" Another burst of laughter had her doubling over.

"Chateaubriand? It's steak."

After Hailey caught her breath, she said, "Pretty sure kids eat chicken fingers and mac and cheese."

"I want shicken fingers," Evvie said.

"Well, that's not what I had when I was a kid." He ate whatever Chef served him. "I ate Chateaubriand." What was wrong with that? Everyone liked steak. "It's the tenderloin. It melts in your mouth like butter." He dropped a slice onto Paisley's plate. "Here, try it."

She shook her head, slapping her hand over her mouth.

"You're not going to eat *steak*?"

She shook her head.

"Well, what do you want?"

"Chicken fingers."

"I don't have any. But I do have chicken pot pie. You can't not like that." With a serving spoon, he dumped some onto a plate. "Here, try it." The steam wafted out, so he blew on it.

Both girls screwed up their faces and shook their heads.

"It looks like doggie throw-up," Paisley said.

It kind of did. He took a bite, just to be sure. *Delicious.* "You're seriously not going to even try chicken pot pie? Fine. Noodles, it is." He served two helpings and pushed it in front of each girl.

Paisley stared as if he'd just spa,t on a plate. "It's green."

"We've already gone over that. That's pesto. Everyone loves pesto."

"It's green."

"Trees are green. Grass is green. Green is good. Try one bite, and you'll never want to eat anything else again." His sales pitch was met with twin stubborn, tight-lipped scowls. "Oh, it's like that, huh? Well, if you don't like this, you're definitely not going to like the paella."

Paisley pointed to a mussel. "What *is* that?" She made gagging motions, her tongue sticking out.

"Yeah, okay, I can see you wouldn't want to suck down a bivalve mollusk that maybe looks like a woman's special garden. How about we skip the fish, and you just eat the rice?" He shot Hailey an impatient look. "Some help here?"

But she was of no use because she couldn't catch her breath. She was wheezing with laughter. With a hand on her belly, she sucked in a deep breath. "Oh, my God. Special garden? You're hilarious." Then, she waved him off and opened the refrigerator. "I'm making mac and cheese."

"Yay," Paisley said.

Evvie clapped. "Mascaroni and sheeze."

"This..." He pointed a finger at the pesto. "Is a hell of a lot better than that boxed stuff."

"How do you know?" Hailey asked. "Have you ever had it?"

Ignoring her, he used his boot to kick out a chair and sit down. He figured if he ate with relish, they'd want to try it. So, he served himself a little of everything, sawed off a piece of steak, and chewed. He sighed at the warm, rich goodness of the meat. "Unreal." But the girls just stared at him. "What?"

"You're going to eat all that?" Paisley asked.

"Well, sure. I have to eat a lot of calories every day."

"What's a calorie?" Paisley asked.

Okay, this was something he could talk about. "It's a unit of energy. And our body—our brains and muscles and cells—need nutrients, which the calories provide. A car needs gas, right? Our bodies need good food."

"Faffles good food." Evvie spoke with absolute sincerity.

"Whole wheat ones, maybe." *Wait.* He was being a dick. She was three and didn't need a lecture on white versus wheat flour. *Stay on topic.* "Yeah, so, I play hockey, and I burn about two thousand calories in a game. I've got to replenish that with good food. Like fish and fresh vegetables and meat. Like good carbs." The girls seemed enthralled, so that was a good thing. "Multigrain bread, rice, vegetables...you get me?"

Paisley pointed to his forearm. "You got lots of hair."

"I...what?" What did hair have to do with calories?

She rubbed her hand on his arm. "You're like a bear."

"I don't have *that* much." He wasn't unusually hairy. "I have a normal amount for a guy."

Paisley got up on her knees and leaned across the table to tug on a few strands. "You look like Wild Man Jack." She giggled, which set Evvie off, and soon the two were squealing and stomping around the kitchen like some weird mountain beast.

"Who's Wild Man Jack?" he asked.

"He's that man in the stories Mommy reads to us. We

love Wild Man Jack." Paisley continued to roar like a grouchy old hermit.

Is that me? Am I the grouch? Dropping his fork, he pushed his chair back and joined Hailey at the stove. "Is this because I talked about whole wheat waffles?"

She burst out laughing. "Oh, my God."

"Am I the mean old man in the house who hoses kids off his lawn? Is that how they see me?"

"No, Cole. It's just the hair."

"But I'm not hairy."

Chuckling, she ignited a flame under the pot of water.

He loved seeing her relaxed and smiling. "What?" He rubbed his arm to make a point. "I'm not."

"You remember Darren, right?"

"Of course." His friend had a head of coarse, wiry, red hair, so he'd kept it buzzed.

"Remember when we'd go to the lake? And he'd be shirtless?"

He went back there…back a whole decade to when he hadn't fucked up someone's life, to when he had a bunch of different friend groups—his hockey buddies, the kids of actors his dad had worked with over the years, and the foursome of him, Darren, Lindsay, and Hailey.

To when he'd had a hardcore crush on a girl who didn't look or act like anyone he'd ever known.

He remembered taking the four of them out on his dad's boat, stopping in a cove, and spending the day on a private beach. Mostly, he remembered wanting to get Hailey's attention. Wanting it so badly he acted like a fool.

And that's when he remembered Darren's pale body. He grinned. "He had no hair. Like a hairless cat."

"Exactly. So, compared to their dad, you're Wild Man Jack."

She was right, so he turned around, held out his arms, and roared. "I'm Wild Man Jack, and I eat little girls with empty bellies."

They squealed and ran away from him, darting back and forth as he pretended to grab at them. He rarely spent time around kids. Sometimes, when his teammates got together, he'd meet their families and see the kids running around. But he kept his distance. Just wasn't his thing.

But seeing the sheer delight in the eyes of Darren's girls? It filled him with satisfaction. Like maybe they'd be all right. And it fueled him to make *sure* they'd land right where they should. Eventually, they each grabbed one of Hailey's legs, hiding behind her, and he stopped messing with them.

While she served neon orange mac and cheese and buttered green beans, Cole closed all the Harley and Lu containers and stuck them in the fridge. As the three of them sat at the table, chatting and eating, he brought his plate to the counter, leaned his back against it, and ate the rest of his dinner. Between bites, he shot off a few texts to his teammates, who were anxious about tomorrow's game without him.

Cole: We got this. We're on fire.

Hailey's laughter drew his attention to the table. He liked looking at her. There was intelligence in her eyes, mischief in her smile, and an innate sexiness in how she moved her body. He could tell she was a sexual woman.

But it was more than that, of course. It was her ballsy nature. Her confidence. She'd never been shy. In fact, from the moment she'd arrived on campus, she'd strutted down the halls like she'd grown up in Calamity. She'd even started a fashion design club. That was another thing he liked about her. She'd always known what she wanted, and she'd gone after it.

His phone vibrated, and he saw a text from his dad.

Aging Movie Star: How's it going with the kids? You never called back.

Cole: Sorry. It's been mayhem, but the girls seem okay. Thankfully, the co-guardian's here and handling it way better than I ever could.

He glanced at her again. Her green bean was talking to Paisley's, and Evvie was cracking up.

Cole: You'll never believe who it is.

Aging Movie Star: Hit me

Cole: Hailey Casselton

Aging Movie Star: Get out of town. You serious? Does she still hate you?

Cole grinned. He loved his dad.

Cole: You're supposed to be my greatest supporter, the shoulder I cry on, my warrior against a harsh cruel world.

Aging Movie Star: Sure, but aren't we talking about the same woman who moved out of town about five minutes after you took her on a date? I have resources

but getting that woman to like you is beyond even my means.

He sent a few crying and wincing emojis, but for all the hijinks Cole had pulled over the years, he'd given his dad a permanent pass on giving him shit.

Cole: We're actually getting along okay. Looks like the old Montgomery charm might be working.

Aging Movie Star: Now, I'm really worried. Sounds like that concussion's really bruised your brain. Look, the charm didn't work ten years ago, and now that she's got some life under her belt, it's gonna be even less effective.

Cole: Thanks, Dad!

Aging Movie Star: Anytime, Son! Hey, listen. We should wrap in the next week or so, which means I'll be home for Christmas. I'll fly straight to Boston and catch a few games.

His dad had always made a big deal out of holidays and birthdays, taking him on wild adventures. Cole had truly seen the world.

But he'd never—not once—had a traditional Christmas.

Cole: Sounds good. But come to Calamity.
Hailey and I are going to go all-out for the girls.

Aging Movie Star: Sounds good. I'll do that. And let me know how I can help. You talk to Deborah yet?

His dad had sent him the number of a therapist he'd dated years ago. The woman had been invaluable.

Cole: Yep. She's retired but said she's here for me when I need her. She's good.

Aging Movie Star: Glad to hear it. My manager will send presents, but longer term, he can buy a house for them, hire a couple of nannies.

Cole: For now, they're going to stay here. Hopefully, the PI will come through for us with a good family.

Aging Movie Star: And if not?

Cole: One step at a time...

Aging Movie Star: Got it. Okay, they're calling my name. 'Night.

With Christmas ten days away, he had to get going. Starting tomorrow, he'd have a fire in the hearth, decorations everywhere, a tree lit up... He'd look up how to make sugar cookies and shit like popcorn garlands.

Just thinking about it yanked his heart into a painful knot. He'd always known he led a privileged life—the chef, the drivers, nannies, jets, yachts. He knew he wasn't like other kids. But where Jaime had envied Cole's freedom and money, Cole had longed for the classic father who grounded him for not doing his chores and the mother who helped him with his science projects.

Shipping this late might be an issue, so he'd better start ordering presents. With no clue what kids their age would like, he typed the question in the search bar. *Toys for Six-Year-Olds.* He'd just get one of everything recommended.

Right when he'd put ten things in his cart, Hailey came up to the counter armed with plates. "You missed out on a delicious dinner." She stuck out her neon orange tongue to let him know she was kidding. "At least their bellies are full. What're you doing?"

He turned the screen toward her.

It took her a moment to figure it out. "You're buying presents?"

"Yeah, I figured we should start ordering now, so things get here in time."

"But we don't even know what they like. Or what they already own." She shut off the faucet. "Speaking of which, I saw their garbage bags."

"Yeah, that was awful. I went to pick them up, and the neighbors handed them to me. They said something about grabbing what they could."

"Do you think we can go to their house? There must be important documents, baby books—"

"Chase got all that, but yeah, I'll ask him if we can get in there."

"Good, because even if they don't know it now, they might want their mom's favorite necklace or their dad's baseball hat. You know?"

"Makes sense." He brought up his chat with the social worker. "How about tomorrow morning?"

"Paisley will be in school."

"You want to go *with* the girls?" He could only imagine their expectations about going home—and finding it empty. The impact might be devastating.

"We should probably ask Chase about it. I mean, I know they're young, but this is their only chance to get things that might be meaningful to them."

He figured Deborah would be the better resource. "My dad hooked me up with a therapist. I'll ask her." He shot off a message asking her if she had time to talk, and then set his phone down. "I'm not good at waiting. I want to fix all their problems before I leave on Thursday. Well, I play on Thursday, so I'll actually leave on Wednesday."

Hailey wasn't one to hide her emotions, and her irritation bristled like static electricity. "We can't fix anything in three days."

"No, we can't. But I'm doing everything I can." He held up his phone. "Like buying them presents so they have a good Christmas."

"Look at us. We're the perfect team for these girls. You've got their physical world covered, and I'm all over the emotional."

"That's not fair. I care about their feelings, but they're six and three. They can't even begin to understand what's happened to them. I don't know what you want me to do."

"Well, for starters, instead of standing over here buying things, you could be sitting with them." She pointed to the kitchen table. "And from my perspective, they need us more than all the toys in the world."

"They can't *have* us, Hailey. We can give them a great Christmas, but we can't let them get *attached*." He lowered his voice. "They just left their neighbor's house. Now, they're with us. Pretty soon, they'll move on to someone else. The best thing we can do is keep them alive and happy."

"Maybe you can do that, but I can't." She stepped closer, her back to the girls. "Given what's happened to them, how can we not comfort them? Honestly, it hurts my heart to think of them eating alone at the table with you standing over here looking at your phone. I don't mean to be harsh but come on. We have to give them more than a pillow and mac and cheese. We have to make them feel safe. Loved. They need to know they're not alone. That we've got them."

While everything she said rang true, he was coming at it from a personal perspective. He knew what it felt like to get attached, to have expectations, and to have that person move on as though he'd never existed. *There comes a point where a kid just shuts down.*

She glanced at the girls over her shoulder, an impassioned look in her eyes. "I don't know what will happen tomorrow, let alone next week, but I do know we're the only ones here right now. They're lost and alone, and I have to make sure they feel loved and safe. I *have* to."

"I hear you." And maybe the difference was that no nanny had ever been as invested in his welfare as Hailey was in these girls. "I'll be better." He watched the girls for a moment, Evvie chomping away, and Paisley slugging back her milk. "I know you think I just want to throw money at the situation, but I do care about them." Well, he should clarify. "I care about Darren's kids. And since I'm going back to Boston soon, my focus is on providing for them."

"No, I get that. And it's equally important." She

grinned. "I guess it turns out us being opposites is a good thing."

"I don't know why you'd say we're opposites. You don't really know me."

"Sure I do. Because of Lindsay and Darren, we spent a lot of time together that year. And now, everything I see of you in the media confirms it."

"Confirms what, exactly? Are you saying you know me because of how I'm portrayed on social media? Come on, Hailey. You know better than that."

"No, that's not—" Now, it was her turn to be flustered. "Look, we're getting totally off the point. We're talking about the girls, and what we need to do for them."

"Oh, hell no. I want to hear it. Go on and say what you think of me. We're stuck in this house together. Might as well put our cards on the table."

Chapter Six

She let out an exasperated huff of breath. "You're obviously smart, and you've got a lot going for you."

"A lot going for me, huh? Well, damn, Hailey. Don't make me blush." Did she really think so little of him that she couldn't come up with a single compliment?

She flicked a hand dismissively. "You know you're good-looking and have a great body. You're charming and fun. Blah blah blah."

"Oh, no. See, that's not how conversation works. 'Blah blah blah' isn't an actual sentence, and it's not descriptive. Come on. You took AP English. Do better."

Smiling, she shook her head. "Does your ego never get its fill? Cole, everyone likes you. How much more reinforcement do you need? Okay, let's see. You were homecoming king, voted most popular and most likely to succeed…you're the top scorer in the country. You've dated the world's hottest models, actresses, and singers—"

"So, that sums up everything there is to know about me, huh?" It shouldn't come as a surprise. Hadn't he always figured she'd seen him that way? "The only things I've got going for me are looks, money, and athleticism." None of the things that mattered to a woman like Hailey Casselton. She would only care about a man's character. And she'd never cared for his.

But what have you shown her? Have you had an actual conversation with her?

Or did you just act like a fool to get her attention?

With concern in her eyes, she touched his arm. "Hey, we're just joking around, right?"

"Sure." None of this should come as a surprise, so he swung around to drop his plate in the sink.

Chairs scraped back, and little feet hit the floor. "We want a snuggle movie night," Paisley said.

"Let's do it." He was glad for the distraction. It sucked, her opinion of him, but he was mostly pissed at himself for not being authentic around her. Then again, as she'd pointed out a decade ago, who was he real with?

He'd thought about it a lot over the years.

With his teammates, he was a cheerleader, always rallying their spirits to win games.

He was an easy-going son, so his dad would want to spend time with him.

And around his friends…he was fun. He brought the good times and delivered experiences they couldn't afford on their own… so they'd want to spend time with him.

Well, that's fucked up. He'd even worked hard to get his *nannies* to like him.

He'd never been himself around anyone because he'd been working too hard to keep them around. He looked at the girls, jumping around with excitement.

I don't want that for them.

Which meant Hailey was right. They needed more

from him than a place to crash for a few nights and a college fund. "Come on, you little monsters. But I get to pick the movie."

"No," Paisley cried. "We get to pick it."

"No way." He headed for the stairs. "You'll pick something with balloons in it."

"No, I won't." Giggling, Paisley followed behind.

"Okay, but it'll for sure have puppy dogs and peanut butter." He opened the door and headed down the stairs.

"It will not." Paisley practically shrieked, and he loved the happiness in her tone.

"Hey, do you have popcorn?" Hailey called.

"Yep. It's in the theater." He only noticed how far ahead he'd gotten when he was halfway down the stairs. He stopped and waited for them to catch up, and the sight of those bare baby feet and little pudgy calves nearly undid him. Evvie pressed her hand to the wall, dipping her toe until her foot hit the next stair. It might've been the cutest thing he'd ever seen.

But really, it was the innocence, the helplessness, that got to him. An intense sense of protectiveness surged through him, and he scooped her up. "I got you."

Just as he started to turn back around, he caught Paisley's gaze, caught the longing, the stark loneliness, so he picked her up, too, and held her tightly against him. "I see you, little one. And I got you."

She cracked a tiny smile, and an unfamiliar emotion swept over him, loosening his joints and softening his bones.

One girl on each hip, he made his way to the theater and set them down in recliners. But he couldn't get her expression out of his mind because this was what Hailey meant about having to be there for them. They were scared and lost and needed an anchor now. Not later, when the PI found the right family.

Yeah, he got it.

He picked up the remote and turned on the big-screen television. "Okay, so, what're we watching?"

They started shouting out titles completely unfamiliar to him.

"Hang on. Let's do this." When he found a popular cable network, he clicked on children's programming and then sat on the arm of Paisley's chair and started scrolling. "Tell me when you see something you like." These leather recliners were built for giant, muscled men—not these two little lima beans.

Damn, they're cute.

Paisley pointed to the screen. "That one."

"You got it." Thinking of Hailey, he glanced at the stairs, but she wasn't on her way down. As the kids settled in, he fired up the popcorn machine, and a few minutes later, the scent filled the large room that was illuminated only by the screen and the line of cinema lights on the floor. With a red and white striped box, he scooped out some buttered popcorn and gave it to the girls to share.

As he settled into his own recliner, everything hit at once. Missing four games. *That sucks.* Being back in Calamity with Hailey, of all people. That was good because he'd always had a thing for her. But also bad because no one disliked him as much as she did.

And the girls. The situation was becoming clearer by the minute, the massive responsibility Darren had laid in his hands. And the devastating loss of two great parents. His friends.

A wave of exhaustion hit, making it impossible to hold onto all those heavy thoughts.

He'd close his eyes just for a minute.

The earth rumbled, and Cole jerked awake. Disoriented, he blinked against the source of bright light in an otherwise dark room. His ass was numb, his left hand had fallen asleep…and was he sweating?

Where am I?

Coming fully awake, he placed himself in his home theater, loud noise coming from the speakers, and an animated movie on the screen. And the reason for sweating? He had little furnaces nestled under each arm.

Evvie had her knees drawn up, so all he could see looking down were her tiny little toes—each one no bigger than a corn kernel. And Paisley had one hand on his thigh, her fingers delicate as little twigs.

He felt eyes on him, and he turned to see Hailey watching from two chairs away. Biting her lip to keep from laughing, she got up and moved to the empty seat next to him. She leaned so close her silky hair brushed his cheek. "See that? Even kids like you."

"This room gets pretty cold, and I run hot. They like me for my body heat."

"Yeah, that's what it is." She shook her head. "I remember when I was living with Lindsay." She kept her voice low so the kids wouldn't hear. If he looked at her, they'd be close enough to kiss. "Her parents had a very old-school relationship, and her mom once said that she did all the nurturing stuff. She made Lindsay's favorite foods, took her to the mall for back-to-school shopping, and gave her advice about boys and life. But whenever her husband came home, he was the hero. Lindsay wanted *his* attention, *his* praise. There's something powerful about a father."

The intimacy of her voice, her breath on his cheek, coaxed chill bumps on his arms, and that's what made him do it. He turned. Not all the way—because he didn't want her to see how much he wanted to kiss her—but enough to see the shine on her lips from the buttery popcorn, the gentle curl in the hair framing her lovely face. "Did you ever know yours?"

"No. Which is funny because my mom's a keeper. She's still friends with people from childhood even though she's never lived anywhere longer than a couple of years."

"What's the story there? Did you *want* to meet him?"

"It wasn't the kind of situation where I could."

"Bad guy?"

"I don't talk about it much because it sounds awful, but my mom's not sure who he is."

"She told you that?"

"Sure. My mom doesn't believe in secrets or shame. She's a firm believer that every morning is a fresh start, and there's no point in holding onto the mistakes we made. We learn from them and move on."

"So, your father was a mistake?"

"It's complicated. My mom's a costume designer—"

"I know. It's what brought her to Calamity. She made the outfits for Shayla McFadden at the festival the summer before senior year."

"How do you remember that?"

He shifted a little, rearranging the girls, so he could fully face her. The moment their gazes locked, his heart jolted. With his attention fixed on her mouth, he said, "Because I liked you. And I listened."

"You listen to a lot of people. You go through life with

an entourage. I can't even imagine how many people tell you their life stories."

Irritation pricked the back of his neck at the easy dismissal. "I hate when people say that. My friends are not an entourage."

He must've said it with more force than he realized, because she reared back.

And yet, as much as it pissed him off that she'd see him like that, what other side of him had he ever shown her? "I make friends easily, and I keep them. And if I can help someone, I do." That's why most of the people who worked for him were people he'd met along the way. Like his assistant.

"I'm sorry. I didn't mean it the way it sounded."

"Yeah, you did. I get it. You think I'm superficial. My point is that I liked *you*, and I paid attention to what *you* said." *And how you looked and smelled, and the way you shook your head to get the hair off your shoulders.* "I was greedy to know everything I could."

"Oh." Even in the dark, he could see her features flush and her eyes go wide with surprise. "I just figured, you know, because I was the only one who didn't fawn all over you…"

"That didn't make me want you more. All it did was hurt my feelings."

He'd shocked her. He could see that. But he didn't care. Her opinion of him sucked, but it was wrong, and he was tired of hearing it.

Right away, though, shock gave way to a softening, a sweetness. The tension around her eyes eased. "Cole."

And that calmed him enough to tell the truth. "I was nervous around you. I *am* nervous around you. Because I know you don't like me, and I don't know how to change that."

She reached for his shoulder. "You're already changing it. In just this short time, watching you with the kids, talking to you. And I've been kicking myself all day for not giving you a chance back then." She ran a fingertip along the edge of the popcorn tub. "It's just I moved so many times that I just stopped trying. And here you were this popular jock, the best-looking guy in school—and I was determined to push you away. To be honest…" She let out a shaky breath. "You intimidated me. I've always felt like an outsider, and you're the sun in every room. People flock to you. I used to think it was because of your money, your dad, all the upgrades—you know, the limos, the screenings, the flights—but it just isn't true. I see it now. It's your strength that draws people to you. Your confidence. It's how you take charge of a situation where everyone else is floundering. I think I wanted to see you as a show-off so that I didn't fall for you." She paused, watching her finger make a slow tour of the tub. "Because I knew I could never keep a guy like you."

"You could've kept me."

He'd done it again. Shocked the hell out of her. She searched his expression. "God, Cole. Why weren't you this honest back then?"

"Because you were the first person I ever really liked. And if I was obnoxious around you, it was because you didn't want the Cole Show, the guy who entertained everybody. You wanted the real me. But what if I'd shown you, and you didn't like it? I think that would've destroyed me." He'd given her too much. He felt too exposed. So, he pulled back and changed the subject. "Yeah, so, anyhow. You were telling me about your mom."

Her jaw snapped shut. He'd shifted gears too abruptly again. *Dammit.* He had to stop doing that.

"Right. Uh… So, where was I? So, she was touring with Don't Ask, doing the costumes for the band and the dancers, and she wound up pregnant. She said it was a wild year, with lots of partying, and she doesn't know who got her pregnant."

"See, there you go. You say we're opposites, but that's something important we have in common. Neither of us knows one of our parents, but we're close with the other."

"You don't know your mom?"

He shook his head. "But we got lucky to have one good parent."

"Yeah, I mean, in a lot of ways, my mom and I are close, but…" She had a thoughtful expression, and he could tell she was wavering…unsure if she wanted to open up to him.

And he wanted it more than just about anything. "But?"

He saw the moment she decided to trust him. The tension in her shoulders, around her mouth and eyes… everything in her relaxed, went easy. "I guess I have a lot of resentment. She bases her business on word of mouth. So, we moved from one job to another, and while I've been to some very cool places—she's done summer theater on Martha's Vineyard and a cabaret show in Miami—we never had a home base. Without a reliable income, we often went without the basics, the stuff everyone takes for granted. Like electricity and Wi-Fi. And, as you've already heard, food. And I can't tell you how badly I wanted to sleep in the same bed, have milk in the fridge…how much I wanted her to get her shit together and take care of us."

"I'm sorry. That sounds awful."

"It was." As she watched the screen, the light danced across her features. "And what made it worse was her relentlessly happy attitude about it. Like being homeless or foraging for food was some kind of adventure. Every time she'd move me in the middle of the school year, she'd be all smiley and like, I can't wait for you to make some new friends. You're going to love it there. She had no idea how brutal it was to be the new kid over and over."

"Now I understand why you wanted to live with Lindsay."

"Well, it was more than that. I got this idea in my head that it was my last shot at a normal experience. I wanted to go to homecoming and prom. I wanted to date the quarterback and get a promposal."

"You liked Brock Dirtbag?" She hadn't liked Cole, but she was into a tool like that asshole football player?

"Who? Brock Durnbaum? Oh, no. Not literally him. No, I just meant the movie version of high school."

"And then I went and blew it."

"Yeah. You did."

"I'm sorry."

"I know. I got your text messages."

"Before you blocked me."

"At the time, I blamed you, but you know what? Lindsay's parents didn't have to send me away. They could've taken into account that I was a good student, a responsible person. I mean, I lived so quietly in their house. I didn't leave a trace of myself because I didn't want to be a bother. So, when they kicked me out...well, it just wasn't fair. I'd been so good, and I'd only made one mistake."

"You didn't make the mistake. I did."

"Didn't matter to them."

"Well, I'm sorry for my part in it. I hope you can forgive me."

She studied him for a moment, a slow smile breaking across her features. "Yeah, Cole. I forgive you."

Like a puck-drop at the start of a game, energy raced through him. If he didn't have the girls on either side of him, he'd haul her onto his lap and let her know with his mouth how much that meant to him. "Okay. Time for bed." He started to get up, but the girls clung to him like monkeys.

"Not yet," Paisley said.

Evvie gazed up at him with her puppy dog eyes and held up a finger. "One more. Pease?"

He looked at Hailey for help, but she just laughed. "Fine. One more episode, and that's it."

He'd gotten carried away, as he always did around her, so he was glad for the interruption. What was the point? After Christmas, he'd be gone until June.

He'd never have the kind of relationship he wanted with her.

Tell that to my heart.

Because the gate that had been locked for ten years had suddenly swung open.

Most mornings, Cole woke up raring to go. He liked his life. Whether it was hockey or a vacation or plans with friends, he always had something to look forward to. But this morning, pain pinned him to the mattress. The extra weight of carrying the girls up and down the stairs last night had done some damage. It felt like a gremlin was repeatedly stabbing his knee with a burning hot pitchfork.

But he had to get Paisley off to school, so he got

dressed and brushed his teeth, then headed down the hallway to the girls' bedroom. He found her in a deep sleep. "It's time to get up." When she didn't rouse, he patted her shoulder. "Pais? Got to get moving. You've got school today." Still nothing. *Huh. That's weird.* He gave her a shake. *Out cold.*

With his hands on his hips, he stood at the side of her bed. Had they kept her up too late?

Hailey came into the room. "Morning." She stopped when she saw Paisley still sleeping. "What's going on?"

"She's not budging." He sat on the edge of the mattress and put his hand on the girl's back. "Paisley, let's go. You've got school today. Come on."

Hailey stared at the sleeping child. "What do we do?"

"Let her skip it. Who cares? It's kindergarten."

"No, Chase said to stick to the schedule."

"Chase isn't here."

Evvie turned onto her belly and dropped out of her bed. With a sleepy expression, she padded over and raised her arms for him to pick her up. He lifted her onto his lap. She was light as a hockey stick and smelled like baby shampoo and laundry detergent.

How did they trust him so easily? It was…sweet. And weird. "Your sister's not a morning person, huh?" Mostly weird.

"Pay-wee sweepy."

"I see that. How do we get her up?"

The little girl launched herself onto the mattress, curled up next to her sister, and stroked her hair. "Time to get up, sweepy-head."

These two. Damn, they're close. He remembered something Chase had told him. "Something like sixty-five percent of siblings gets separated in foster care." He whispered it so the girls wouldn't hear.

"I know. I heard that, too." Underneath the fear in Hailey's eyes, he saw determination. "We won't let that happen."

"No. The PI's bound to find someone."

"Not just *someone*. It has to be a good, loving home. People who treat them like their own flesh and blood."

If Darren and Lindsay had family or friends like that, he and Hailey wouldn't be here. But there was no point in saying it again. They'd just have to wait and see what the PI came up with.

Evvie stroked her sister's hair. "Wise and shine, Pay-wee."

Jesus. The cuteness was killing him.

Hailey's hand went to her heart. "They did a really good job with these girls."

Finally, Paisley stirred and swiped the hair out of her eyes.

"Oh, wise and shine, and sing out your gory gory, wise and shine—"

"And sing out your glory glory." Hailey joined in. "Rise and shine and—" She clapped her hands. "Sing out your glory glory."

Paisley rolled onto her back, narrowing her eyes at the two singers. But when Evvie peered solemnly at her and said, "Gots to get going, Pay-wee," the older sister threw back the covers, stretched, and yawned.

"Okay, girls, what're we having for breakfast?" Hailey asked.

"Faffles." Evvie answered for both.

"I'll get 'em in the toaster." He started to go, but Paisley lifted her arms in his direction. It jarred him, the way they felt so comfortable with him. Why weren't they looking at Hailey for comfort and safety?

You're backing the wrong horse, girls.

Hailey grinned like it was adorable. "I got it." She started out of the room.

"Well, wait," he said. "What do I do with her?"

"You act like there were secret rituals in the Leeson family. Just do the same stuff you did before school. Take her to the bathroom, wash her face, brush her teeth and hair, and get her dressed."

Right. Sure. He thought back to his childhood, how he'd awakened to the smell of bacon or pancakes. He'd gotten himself up and dressed, brushed his teeth. His nanny had breakfast waiting and lunch packed. She'd never walked him to the bus, and he'd hated that. So, he'd definitely go with Paisley.

When he picked her up, she collapsed against him. Literally draped herself over him, her cheek resting on his shoulder. One hand absentmindedly patted his biceps. *Christ. This kid. So trusting.* Even though he should get moving, he held her for a minute. Kind of rocked a little, though he didn't know why. She wasn't a baby. And then…

She sighed in utter contentment.

What choice did he have but to hold her and give her what she seemed to need? This was Darren's little girl, and he wouldn't let his friend down. Only when she finally lifted her head did he carry her into the bathroom and set her on her feet. "I'll wait out here while you do your business."

But she stood there, swaying slightly, her gaze unfocused. This girl was genuinely out of it. So, he lifted her nightgown and set her on the toilet. While she did her business, he brushed her tangled hair. Immediately, he could see he'd made a terrible mistake. Her springy blonde curls turned into clouds of frizz.

Oops. Shit.

Well, thank goodness she's only six.

She probably wouldn't notice. "Let me grab your clothes." He rummaged through her black trash bag until he found underpants, jeans, a long-sleeved shirt, socks, and a hoodie. Then, he went back to the bathroom to find her staring at herself, tears glistening on her cheeks.

"What's wrong?" But of course, he already knew.

"I can't go to school like this."

"I'm sorry. I messed up." He didn't know what to do about it.

"You only brush my hair after I wash it." She sounded betrayed.

He crouched beside her. "Hey, I'm really sorry. I didn't know that. But I do now, so it won't happen again." He caught a teardrop on the tip of his finger. "Tell me how I can make it right?"

"Breakfast, you guys," Hailey called from downstairs.

"Coming," he shouted back. Checking his watch, he saw the bus would arrive in fifteen minutes. She needed to eat, then brush her teeth. "Tell me how to fix it."

Her bottom lip trembled, and he felt like shit.

"How about a ponytail?"

She jiggled and bounced in obvious frustration.

"Let's go, guys," Hailey called. "You can't go to school on an empty stomach."

A ponytail would have to do. He rummaged through the accessories on the counter and found an elastic. Then, with two hands, he gathered her hair and tried to wrestle it into submission.

"Ow. Stop." Paisley clutched the side of her head. Looking into the mirror, she cried harder. "I hate it."

It was pretty awful, puffed out on one side, lopsided. *Fuck*. He couldn't let her go to school like this. "I'll bet Hailey can fix it."

But by the time they came downstairs, Hailey was shoving a waffle into Paisley's hand and hanging a backpack off her shoulders. "Your lunchbox is in there, sweetie."

On the long, cold walk down the driveway, Paisley didn't say a word, but he could tell she was fighting back tears. He couldn't put her on the bus while she was this miserable.

Once outside the gate, he dropped to his good knee and looked her in the eyes, smoothing the section that puffed out of the elastic. "Little one, there's nothing more I want in the world right now than to make you happy. But it's my first day doing this, and I don't have it down yet. All I can do is promise to do better."

He also couldn't help wondering how much of these tears had to do with waking up in a strange home and being herded by strangers. But the bus was rumbling toward them, and he only had a few seconds to pull her together. "Can I make it up to you after school? What about a hot chocolate with a mountain of whipped cream on top? Does that sound good?"

She nodded, glancing back to the house she couldn't see behind the gate and up the winding driveway. "Who's going to take care of Evvie while I'm at school?"

"She'll hang out with me and Hailey today. Is that okay?" She nodded, and he thumbed away the tears. "You're pretty cool, you know that? I like how you take care of your sister." He watched her climb the steps and waited until the bus disappeared at a curve in the road.

Cole had faced a lot of challenges in his life. But this one? This was the toughest.

Right then, a text came in. He pulled out his phone.

Jaime: Yo, Phenom. Change of plans. Got to head to LA later this morning. Why don't you come by for breakfast?

He rarely got to be in the same town as these guys, so he wanted to take this chance to hang out with them while he was here.

Cole: Sure. What time?

Jaime: Now. Meet us at the rink.

They'd taken their first step in repairing things over the summer.

Now, he needed to see if it was possible to get their friendship back on track.

Chapter Seven

Cole sat with his two oldest friends, watching the Renegades hockey team skate. He welcomed the chill in the air and the smell of fresh ice. It brought him back to his real life—hockey—and away from the complicated emotions going on inside his house.

"Is there anything we can do to help?" Jaime asked.

"I talked to a PI on my way over and gave him all the information I have. He's going to see if he can find some family we don't know about."

"There's probably a reason you don't know about them," Declan said. "You might want to be careful there."

"I agree. We'll vet anyone he finds and meet them personally. In the meantime, I need to find a temporary babysitter so Hailey can work."

"Let me ask Phinny," Declan said. "She joined a women-in-business group to get help with her store. I'm sure someone'll have a lead for you."

"Cool. Thanks. I didn't have a starting point with that one."

"You know, there's one solution that solves

everything." Jaime broke into a slow grin. "You could move back home. Play for us." He clapped him on the shoulder. "It's what Kurt wanted."

"Yep. I know." Out of high school, he'd been drafted to the Renegades, but after what he'd done to Booker, his guilt had sent him running to Canada, where he'd played in the junior league. It hadn't seemed fair that he'd get to play professionally while his friend suffered in physical therapy.

Boston's GM had pulled him out of a downward spiral. He'd shown up at the rink, taken him out for lunch, and talked to him about his potential and how to overcome the destructive chatter in his head. From the moment Cole signed with the Brawlers, he'd worked his ass off to live up to the potential they'd seen in him.

He'd come a long way—and now, he'd won two Cups and would bring home a third this season. "But you know I can't do that." His teammates relied on him. He was their captain. "Besides, you couldn't afford me."

"You're right about that." Focused on the ice, Declan tracked his left forward. "Not when Kurt gave massive contracts to Olinsky, Traeger, and Herr. But once those contracts are up, we'll be going in a different direction."

"We're building the dream team." Jaime grinned.

"Man, Kurt would be so damn happy to see you two working together." He'd found them when they were kids tearing up his land and turning it into a dirt bike course. Instead of punishing them, he'd asked their parents if he could teach them hockey. The guys had been so good, Kurt wound up starting an elite training center and then buying a professional team. All for them.

"He wants us all together," Jaime said.

But Cole didn't miss the way Declan dropped his gaze

to his hands. Out of all of them, he'd been the closest to their former coach. He'd taken the loss hard. "Must be tough living in that house without him."

"Nah. Not with Phinny there." Declan grinned in a way Cole had never seen before. "Life's pretty good with her around." It was the bone-deep satisfaction of a man in love and living his best life.

That kind of love… It wasn't something Cole could relate to. Sure, he had an indestructible bond with his dad. His last nanny thought fondly of him. His teammates respected him. Women seemed to like him.

But he couldn't relate to the kind of love Declan and Phinny had, the kind that made a man secure in the knowledge that he was safe and didn't have to turn himself inside out to earn it.

And the one woman he could possibly love like that, he couldn't have. Even though Hailey had changed her view of him, the only thing that tied them together were those girls. They took precedence.

But he was okay with being alone.

Well, he'd been more okay before he'd found Hailey again.

"Speaking of the dream team." Jaime had a gleam in his eyes. "You'll never guess who reached out to us." He waited a beat before dropping the name. "Ross LaRoux."

"No shit?" Ross was one of the best goalies in the league.

"Right? We're in talks with him."

"How'd that happen?" And then it clicked. "Wait, isn't Booker his agent?" A spark of excitement got his blood pumping. Most good teams had a couple of superstars on pricey contracts, a core of good and appropriately paid players, a few players on rookie contracts, and a few underpaid vets who wanted to chase the Cup.

Ross, on the other side of his career, wanted it. And the fact that Booker would bring him to the Renegades could only mean one thing.

The missing piece of their four-link chain wanted to reconnect.

Could that mean he possibly forgave Cole?

"Seems like he's invested in Kurt's team, after all," Jaime said.

"Have you talked to him since the funeral?" Declan asked.

"Me? No. Why would I?"

"Because you two need to have a conversation," Declan said.

"We tried, remember? He ran off." The four of them had met for a barbecue at Jaime's ranch, but the second they'd brought up that horrible night, Booker had excused himself to hit the head, and he'd never come back.

"Which is the point." Declan rubbed his jaw. "Until we talk about that night, we're never going to get past what happened. It's this heavy cloud hanging over all of us. And I just think him bringing a player like Ross to a team that's never won a Cup?" He shrugged. "He might be ready now."

"He's reached out to you guys. Not me. And I can't blame him. I wouldn't want to talk to the man who killed my shot at the big show."

"I don't get why you carry all the blame," Declan said. "What was so different about that night? I can't think of a single time we got together when it didn't turn into night skiing or BASE jumping or some fucked-up shit like that."

"Except that night, everyone was already in bed." He

should've been excited to join the Renegades the next day. Instead, he'd been anxious, and Jaime's text had been a relief. "We were all packed and ready to go. If I hadn't stolen my dad's plane, it never would've happened."

"Not true. Jaime's the one who got bad news and asked if we could come over. He's the one who got us all out of bed. So, is it his fault?"

Jaime sat still as a statue.

"Not at all." It was perfectly clear to Cole. "If we'd just hung out at his place and had a bonfire like Jaime asked, Booker would be playing hockey right now. I'm the one who brought us to my dad's cabin."

"Right, but what I'm saying is we never did that. We never just sat around a bonfire and shot the shit." Declan looked a, Jaime for confirmation.

"It's true. That's not who we were." Jaime's relief was palpable. "Within five minutes of hanging out, someone would suggest we go dirt biking or rappelling or... Fuck, man, anything. That's who we were." His tone grew stronger with each word out of his mouth. Clearly, he'd been carrying just as much guilt as Cole had.

"Yeah, so call Booker," Declan said. "Talk to him. Even if he *does* blame you, give him the chance to get it off his chest. Have the conversation, and then let it go. It's done. We've all moved on."

"And then," Jaime said, "when you get tired of the big city and you're ready to come home, you can help us build the team."

That wouldn't happen for a long time. He owed it to the city and his teammates. "All right, I'd better get back."

As they got up, Jaime chuckled. "So, you and Hailey Casselton. How's that working out?"

"Better than I expected." And worse. Because he

wanted her even more than he had back then. "She's actually civil to me."

"Still got a thing for her?" Jaime asked.

"Hey." A young, fit man jogged over, giving Cole a chin nod. "How's it going?" He reached out his hand. "I'm Mark."

"Cole Montgomery."

"He's our team doc," Jaime said.

"Listen, I'm going to take Lukas to get an MRI. His shoulder's still giving him trouble, and I want to see if there's a tear."

"Okay," Declan said. "Let me know what you hear."

He nodded, then gave Cole a chin nod. "Nice to meet you." He gestured to Cole's knee. "You taking care of that?"

Fear squeezed the base of his spine. "Of what?"

"Your knee. I saw you walk in and the way you got up just now. It's giving you trouble."

"I twisted it."

"Yeah? When the little girl knocked you on your ass and gave you a concussion?" Jaime teased.

"No, it happened when I heroically saved a small child from being crushed under the weight of two big, bad hockey players." Cole turned back to the doctor. "It's fine, though. Just needs rest."

Mark held his gaze a little too long for the situation. "Okay, then. Well, I'm off."

"Hang on," Jaime said. "If Doc's noticing it, there's got to be something going on."

"The way you're walking, and the pain I see on your face, I'm going to guess you tore your meniscus," Mark said. "And if you continue to play on it, you might miss more than a couple of games this season."

"It's that bad?" Declan checked him out, as though assessing his pain level.

He wasn't going to lie. "Yeah, it hurts when I go up and down the stairs. With everything that's happening with the girls, I haven't had a chance to rest it."

"It is getting stiff?" Mark asked. "Swollen?"

Cole gave a curt nod.

"I'd check your ACL, make sure it didn't tear, too. But also, if the torn part breaks off, it can get lodged in the joint, and then you'll have much bigger problems. But you know all this. Look, I'm headed to the hospital right now, and I can get you an MRI."

He knew the doctor was right, but fuck. If they found something wrong…

Come on. Something is wrong.

"Better to be out six weeks right now than face the kind of setback that comes with a more invasive surgery," Mark said. "Let's see what's going on. Could be nothing. We'll come up with a game plan after we get a look at it."

"Do it." Jaime nudged him. "We can get you into the hospital's imaging center right now."

"The sooner we get the results back, the sooner we start treatment." Then, more gently, Mark said, "And the sooner you get back on the ice. What do you say?"

His coach would be pissed, and his teammates would lose their shit, but he couldn't deny the worsening pain in his knee. "Yeah, okay. Let me just check with my trainer."

When Cole got home, he found multiple trucks in the driveway. The team he'd hired had nearly finished the job, and it looked fantastic. They'd positioned Santa and his sleigh on the front slope of the roof right where the girls could see it. Strings of white lights dripped off the eaves like icicles and wound through the surrounding trees, and giant presents with big bows looked like they'd toppled out of the sleigh and landed in the snow.

He couldn't wait to show the girls what it looked like all lit up at night.

Waving to some of the crew, he let himself in. The scent of pine hit him first, and then the warmth from the fire in the hearth. He couldn't help smiling when he heard the Christmas carols piped in through the speakers.

Now, this is the magic.

Happy chatter drew his attention to the coffee table where the girls worked on an art project.

The strangest sensation hit. It was almost like déjà vu, though he'd never lived this moment before. But it was everything he'd ever wanted as a boy.

He'd bought this house because it came stocked with every luxury imaginable, perfect for entertaining whatever group of friends he brought with him. In this moment, though, for the first time, it felt like a home. Warmth rushed through him, and his heart swelled painfully.

Until he noticed Hailey glowering at him.

Oh, shit. What'd I do?

Thanks to the MRI, he'd gotten back later than he'd expected, but they still had plenty of time to take the girls to their house. "Hey, guys."

Two little heads popped up. "Cole." Excited, Paisley ran over to him. "Look what I made." She held up a piece of white paper with holes cut out all over it. "It's a snowflake." She turned to Hailey. "Can we put them on the tree now? Please? I want to show Cole how it looks."

Damn, he was glad he'd hired a company to create a holiday wonderland for these girls. He'd ordered a fourteen-foot Douglas Fir, and they'd stuffed it with glittering ornaments and garlands. They'd have to remove some of it to make room for the homemade ones.

"Sure." Hailey brought a stack of paper cut-outs to the tree and then taught the girls how to hang them by the red ribbons she'd strung through the holes.

Except…they didn't go to his magnificent tree. "What the hell is that?" They went to an anemic thing with more brown pine needles than green.

"Cole." Hailey's admonishment had his jaw snapping shut.

Evvie patted his thigh. "Issa Kwismas twee."

"If you're Charlie Brown." It was the saddest thing he'd ever seen.

"Who's Charlie Brown?" Paisley asked.

"Come on, girls. Put them on." Hailey tied ribbons on the drooping branches.

They could only be interested in this sad sack tree because the team he'd hired hadn't turned on the lights yet. "Hang on." Crawling underneath, he found a quilted bright red and green skirt. *Nice.* This was everything he'd ever wanted as a kid. The girls were going to flip out.

After plugging it in, he crawled back out and gestured to the picture-perfect tree with a flourish. "Now, that's a Christmas tree."

All three turned as one, the girls' eyes widening, their jaws dropping. "That's so pretty," Paisley said. But then, not a moment later, she grabbed her sister's hand. "Come on, Evvie. Let's make some more." And with that, she skipped back to the table.

That's it?
What just happened?

"Can I talk to you a sec?" Hailey asked, all clipped and terse.

"Of course."

"Girls, finish up the snowflakes, and then we'll do the popsicle stick ornaments next, okay?"

"Yay," Paisley said.

Evvie dropped her crayon. "I do pock-sticle now."

"Not yet, sweetie. I have to get it all set up." Hailey made her way over to him, the set of her jaw and frosty eyes letting him know she was pissed. "Where have you been?" she whispered harshly.

"I went to the rink to see my friends—"

"You hung out with friends all day?" She sounded almost hysterical.

"What? No. I was only with them for an hour. We had a breakfast sandwich. Why are you so pissed? I'd planned on being home in time to meet Paisley, but I ran a little late." He never wanted her to be that kid who watched her friends get off the bus, swooped into the arms of a parent or nanny, and then feel the emptiness of finding no one at her stop.

"If you were only with them for an hour, what did you do for the other *three hours*? And what in the world made you think it was okay to be gone half the day? Did it occur to you that I might have something to do? Who did you think would watch Evvie?"

"Ah, shit. I've got the car seats in my car. I stranded you."

"Yes, you did, but that's not the point. We're supposed to be in this together. I have work to do. I have a *job*."

Remorse twisted in his belly. "You're right. I wasn't thinking."

"Well, you have to think. I know you're only here one

more day, but yesterday was a travel day, and today, you bailed on me, so that means I've taken two days off." She blew out a breath. "I can't lose my job, Cole. I have bills to pay and no safety net."

"I'm sorry. I fucked up."

"And you have to stop swearing."

"Dammit, I know." What did she want from him? "I'm around hockey players all day."

"Well, now you're around a three and six-year-old."

"I'll do better. I promise." He pointed to her tree. "Where did you find that?"

She gestured toward the giant bay window. "In your yard."

He'd totally fucked up. He'd taken Evvie's car seat, so she couldn't go to a tree lot in town and buy a decent tree. "You carried that in by yourself? How did you get it to stand up?"

"I had to use some two-by-fours I found in your shed."

"I'm sorry. I hate that you did that by yourself."

"I live alone, Cole. I do everything by myself."

That would change starting right now. He'd only ever been a single guy. He wasn't used to checking in with anybody.

Intent on their art project, the girls sat with their backs to the massive, sparkling tree. "Don't they like it?"

"I mean, it's fun to look at. It's like the tree in Rockefeller Center. You walk by and admire it, but they didn't have a part in creating it. I can only tell you that the best part of Christmas for me was the time I spent with my mom. Making our own decorations and putting them on the tree together. Every year, we'd make our own hot cocoa and walk along the streets, looking at all the pretty storefront windows. That's what I look forward to about the holidays."

He glanced at the table but didn't see the cocoa. He'd fix that. "I should've told you my plans. I promise it won't happen again. Will it help if I handle dinner and bath time? Can you get your work done tonight?"

"Yes." Relief loosened the tension around her eyes. "That'd be great."

"Okay, so let's take them to their house right now and then, after, we can stop at the store and get whatever supplies you need to make decorations. Also, I do have other cars, so we can go ahead and return your rental. That's one less expense you'll have to worry about. Then, tonight, when they're in bed, we'll come up with a plan to make sure you can get your work done."

All that angry energy drained away, leaving her looking nothing but confused. "Thank you."

"What's wrong? Talk to me. Whatever you need, I'll fix it."

"Well, that's the thing. You just did. I spent the entire day building up anger toward you, and then you just... apologized. Like...you owned everything you did. I can't be angry anymore."

"And that's a bad thing?"

"No, it's really sexy."

Whoa. "Did you just say I'm sexy?"

"I did." It seemed to take her by surprise.

"Because I apologized?"

"I mean, yeah. For me, it's not about your looks or your bank account, or the fact that you're a famous athlete. It's because you jumped right in with these girls. You care about them, and you show it. The whole reason I didn't want to go out with you in high school was because you never got real with me. And now? You're real. And I…" She lifted both arms and let them drop. "I *like* you."

He'd never expected to see that heat in her eyes when she looked at him, hear the hitch in her breath. The low hum of desire running through him every time she was near kicked into full-blown arousal. And if the girls weren't right over there, he'd pull her close, cup those rosy cheeks, and kiss the ever-loving hell out of her.

To win this woman's respect, to know she was *attracted* to him? It was fucking everything.

But with a slow shake of her head, she looked away. "We should go." Almost as soon as it began, the moment ended. "Come on, girls. Let's get our jackets."

She got busy as though she hadn't just rocked his world. But she had. His heart thundered, and his body vibrated with a mix of lust and excitement. He stood there, unable to get his legs to move, wanting more from her.

But there was no more. There never would be.

Because he was leaving the day after tomorrow. He might be back for Christmas, but those two days would be filled with activities centered around the girls. And then he'd be gone for the rest of the season.

That was, if the MRI came back in his favor.

The shiver of fear got him moving. No point in worrying about it until he got the results. He headed to the coffee table where the littlest one was hunched over, drawing with a red crayon. "Come on, Evvie. We're going to your house."

"I *working*." Her irritation made him smile.

Already in her coat and boots, Paisley sidled up to him. "Are Mommy and Daddy there?"

Shit. That wiped the grin off his face. He'd been

wondering how much they understood. Now, he knew. *This is so damn hard.* But he gave himself an internal shake because he had to get it right. Between Deborah's advice and the research he'd been doing, he'd prepared for this moment. "No, sweetie. They're not."

She bravely held his gaze as her bottom lip wobbled. "Where are they?"

Fuck. It didn't matter that Chase had broken the news to her or that the neighbors had reinforced it. She'd probably keep asking as she both tried to process it and hoped for a different outcome.

He dropped to a crouch, doing his best to ignore the blinding pain in his knee. These would be the toughest words he'd ever have to say. But Deborah had told him to be honest. To always be direct and only answer the question asked. "Your mom and dad died in a car accident, and they can't come back."

She stood there, scared, lost, and confused.

The vulnerability of this child ripped his heart out. "I don't know about a lot of things, Pais, but I do know they love you with all their hearts, and while they might be in heaven, their spirits are with you and Evvie. And they always will be. Even if you can't see them, you can feel them in here." He pressed his hand to her chest. "But we're going to your house right now, and you can take anything you want with you, so you never forget them. Does that sound good?"

"Are we going to live with you now? You and Hailey?"

He understood the importance of that question more than this child could ever realize. His biological mom died when he was two, and his dad filmed more than half the year. Cole's number one concern had always been: *who's taking care of me?* He'd had a series of nannies until Miss Mary had come to stay.

But while he might've understood, he couldn't give her the answer she needed. He simply didn't have it. "You and Evvie will stay here, and we'll all spend the holiday together. But I have to go back to Boston to play hockey —that's my job. I'm a hockey player. So, I can be here until my next game on Thursday. Then, I'll come back for Christmas." And right then, he knew what he had to do. "After that, I'll be back here every chance I get." *Until we find you a home.* "Okay?"

That seemed to ease her mind. She nodded.

"I'm sorry, Paisley. I'm so damn sorry for your loss, but I'm going to do everything in my power to make sure you and Evvie are okay."

"You promise?"

He grew uncomfortable. He'd had a bad nanny, and his dad hadn't known about it until he'd installed cameras throughout the house. So, he knew better than anyone that once Paisley was out of his sight, he had no control over how people treated her.

But this girl looked at him with those earnest brown eyes, and there wasn't a chance in hell he could let her down.

"I promise."

Chapter Eight

THE LAST TIME HAILEY HAD VISITED, THE LEESONS had lived in an apartment. She hadn't even known they'd bought a house.

As they pulled into the driveway, she was hit with a wallop of true, deep remorse.

Lindsay's gone. There was no turning back the clock to respond to the last text, email, or voice message she'd blown off.

She'd let her career take precedence over the things in life that really mattered—relationships. Other than her mom, who did she have in her life? She worked remotely three days a week, so she didn't have many office friends. And she spent weekends in a boutique and every second of her free time designing lingerie.

Meanwhile, Lindsay was having babies and moving into a new home... Big life changes Hailey had known nothing about.

"Come on, Evvie." *Ach. That sweet little girl voice.* Paisley released her own booster seat buckle and went to free her sister's.

Shaking off the weight of regret, Hailey let them out of the car. Instead of heading for the house, though, the girls took off toward some bushes on the edge of the snow-covered yard.

"So, what did the therapist say?" They'd been around the girls, so they hadn't had a chance to talk since he'd made the call.

"She thinks we should give them space. If we're too involved, we'll distract them from the experience of being home."

"Huh. My impulse is just the opposite. I want to stay with them. Protect them."

"She said at this age, they're still expecting their parents to come back. So, the best thing we can do is just let them *be home*."

"No, it makes sense." With her heart hurting, she watched the girls. "They're so young. I don't know how they can understand this."

"They can't. That's why we keep checking in with them. And we explain things in stages, as their intellects grow."

But we won't be there for that. That'll fall into the hands of the forever family.

Why does that feel so wrong?

"You okay?" Cole asked in that deep, caring voice.

She wanted to fall against his chest and have those big arms wrap around her. Instead, she tightened her scarf and lowered her chin to warm her face. "I'm just so damn sad."

"Yeah."

"I moved all the time as a kid. I didn't take a single friend with me...until I met Lindsay."

"You met her at the music festival?"

"Yep. She sat down next to me and looked at my

sketches, and from that moment on, we were best friends." She watched the girls stand on their toes, reaching into the bushes. "What on earth are they doing?"

"Seeing if the fairies left any magic boxes for them. Apparently, Darren used to hide them. He said they were from fairies, but Paisley suspected it was him because she peeked into a bag he brought home from the store once and found the same candies in one of the boxes."

"Smart girl. Is that what you guys were talking about while I was getting Evvie ready?" He had such an ease with them. While she was all business—bath time, dinner, schedule, schedule, schedule—he was just in the moment.

The girls had instantly taken to him. Trusted him.

That's his charm, though, right? Cole Montgomery didn't know a stranger. It was disarming. *Makes you believe he's totally into you.*

She should probably keep that in mind before she jumped into the deep end of all these feelings.

Though, let's be honest. She was crushing on him hard.

"Mostly, we talked about why we're coming here. I asked her to think about the things she wanted to keep with her forever, so she'd remember to get them."

"You did?" How thoughtful was that?

"Well, Deborah suggested we talk about memories as much as we can. That's how they hold onto them."

The girls ran to a hedge that bordered the neighbor's driveway, their noses red, their expressions earnest and intent. "Magic boxes. What a great idea." Her ears ached from the cold, so she fluffed the scarf to cover them. "That's not something I'd ever think to do." Which was pretty depressing, frankly. "I'd be the mom with to-do lists. 'Make haircut appointments, buy gym shoes, don't forget supplies for the science project...' I'd be rushing them from one activity to another."

"Hey." Tilting her chin, he gazed into her eyes. The bright blue was a shock against his dark hair and the gray sky. "You've been thrown into a situation no one could be prepared for. You haven't had the luxury of time and experience, so you have no idea what kind of mom you'll be."

Maybe he noticed her pulse fluttering wildly in her throat, or maybe he could see the yearning in her eyes, but he cupped her cheeks with both gloved hands as if he might kiss her. *Holy hell.* His blue eyes burned, and his tongue swept along his plump bottom lip.

Touch mine.

Just the thought of his mouth on hers sent an electric current through her body.

"I think you'll be an amazing mom."

"You do?" She liked his hands on her. While the world reeled, and she tried to get her bearings, he pinned her in place.

"I know you, Hailey. I know how much you care. And Darren only came up with that idea because he loved his girls. Believe me, he never offered to make *me* a magic box." He grinned.

And it was like the first ray of sunshine breaking over a mountain peak. It cracked something in her, released a flood of heat, happiness...and potent desire. *Oh, this man.* Had anyone ever looked at her the way he did? She knew they hadn't. If she could trust anything about him, it was his feelings for her. They'd never wavered.

But really, what good could come from all this longing? She was here for one reason, and that was to get the girls settled with a family.

There's not going to be some grand romance with Cole Montgomery.

She took a step back, surprised at the rush of cold air when he lowered his arms. "Let's check on them."

But he didn't let her get away that easily. "They're doing exactly what we brought them here to do. They're happy. I promise, if they need us, we'll know." He looked deeply into her eyes. "You all right?"

Oh, she really liked that about him. After a lifetime of pushing people away, she liked a man who didn't give up on her.

But before she could answer, Paisley pulled a freezer bag out of the bushes. "I found one."

"Yay," Hailey said. "Can I see?"

"Wait." Paisley ran to the mailbox, her sister hurrying to keep up. "I have one more place to look."

Watching them, a fierce sense of purpose took hold. "You know, I look at these girls—Lindsay's babies, her daughters, the most important people in the world to her —and the fact that she chose *me* to raise them... I mean, it's...it's an *honor.*" Only now that she'd had some time to get her bearings was it starting to sink in. The importance of this...well, *gift.* "I don't know that I'm the right person to do it, but I do know without a doubt, if she had anyone else, the girls would be with them right now." She was getting all worked up. "I want to do the right thing. It's just—"

"Hey." He pulled her closer. "Remember, we're going to take this one step at a time. Right now, our only focus is giving them a knock-out Christmas."

"Right. One day at a time."

The girls ran up to them. "We only found this one." Paisley held it up. "Can we open it now, please?"

She didn't see why not. "Sure. Let's do it inside, though. It's freezing out there."

"No, I want to open it now. Please?"

Neither girl seemed bothered by the bitter cold, so Hailey pulled the black lacquer box out of the freezer bag and handed it to her. Paisley opened it to find two candy canes, some icicle ornaments, and two little snow globes.

The six-year-old shook hers. She watched in awe as the glittery snow fell over the cabin in the woods. "It's so pretty." Handing the other one to her sister, she said, "Look, Evvie. You got one, too."

But Evvie didn't seem to care. "Go see Mommy." She turned and marched across the lawn, her booted feet leaving shallow impressions in the snow.

"Hang on, sweetie." *Oh, God.* How in the world would she explain why her mom wasn't in that house waiting for her? As she started off, she heard Paisley's voice.

"Is Mommy home?" She sounded confused.

Cole dropped to a crouch. "No, sweetheart. She's not."

"Evvie's going to be sad." The girl sounded awfully sad herself.

"She is. But we're here for her. Hailey and I, we've got her." He tugged a braid. "You can be sad, too. I know I am. Your dad and I were best friends growing up."

"You were?"

"Yep. We used to ride bikes and go snowboarding... We had a lot of fun together."

"Can I go inside now?" Paisley asked.

"Yeah, of course." He stood up, laughing. "When did I become a boring old man?" He yanked the wool beanie off his head, slid his fingers through his hair, and jammed it back on. His high cheekbones, the strong jaw, and those

eyes that revealed more than he wanted anyone to know…
He was just so damn striking.

"You're not boring. You're amazing."

He watched her as though waiting for her to drop the
but in the sentence.

"I'm serious. You better watch it, or I'm going to do
something crazy like kiss you." Hiding her grin, she
hurried to catch up with the girls.

Evvie had both hands on the doorknob, her mittens
tossed to the ground. "Open."

"Hang on." Cole inserted the key and unlocked the
door.

While the girls ran straight for the kitchen, Hailey
registered the stillness, the chill. A throw pillow was
tossed onto the floor. A coffee mug sat on the dining
room table, a pink lipstick imprint on the rim. The coat
closet was ajar, one hanger jutting out as if someone had
just jerked a coat off before running out. "A life
interrupted."

Cole shut the door behind him, making it marginally
warmer. "What's that?"

"They were probably in a rush to get the kids settled
with the neighbors before they left. Or maybe they
dropped them off the night before and left first thing in
the morning. Either way, they were off on a grand
adventure, so excited to have some time alone." But she
bet they couldn't wait to come back, to get home to their
girls. The idea of time away would seem better than the
reality. They'd just want to hug their babies.

A powerful sense of loss closed over her, an
unbearable, suffocating weight. Because of course, Lindsay
and Darren would never hug them again.

Cole watched her intently, as though ready to catch

her if she fell. But she wouldn't do that. She picked up the pillow and put it back on the couch.

But I can. I can hug them and make them feel safe and loved.

"Deborah also said we should let them see our own grief." Cole spoke quietly. "We shouldn't hide it from them. And that, even if they can't express it, their primary concern is their own safety." He let out a sharp exhalation. "Actually, right before we left the house, Paisley asked if she was going to live with us."

"What did you say?"

"I deflected. I told her they'd stay with us for Christmas. But I think what she really needed to know is who's taking care of her. I told her I have a job playing hockey in Boston, but that I'd be back every chance I got."

"Do you really think we should lie?"

His gaze snapped over to her. "I didn't. I'll be back as often as I can."

"You told me you'd be back for Christmas, but that was it. You said you'd be hyper-focused on your season."

"That was before she asked me the question, and I realized I can't do it. I can't just walk away from them." He looked her right in the eyes. "From you."

Awareness exploded in her chest, sending sparks raining down through her body. The soles of her feet tingled in the aftermath.

His fingertips brushed the back of her hand. "I'm not going to let you do this by yourself. In every way that I can, I'm going to be here for you and the girls."

Her cheeks flushed hot. She wanted that. Wanted him. Too much.

Embarrassed, she turned away and busied herself with adjusting the hanger and shutting the closet door. They'd only been together a few days. What was she doing falling under his spell?

What nonsense is this? She wasn't the type to get all fluttery over a man.

Besides, once he got back with his team, she doubted he'd think much about her or the girls. "Well, we'll see."

"What does that mean?"

"It means we're feeling big things right now because we're with them. They're two helpless, sweet, adorable little girls. Of course, we're going to get emotional. But once we go back to our real lives, it'll fade." In fact, that explained the intensity between them. It was their situation.

"Jesus, Hailey. I haven't stopped thinking about you in ten years. You think I'm going to fly back to Boston and forget about you now? That I'm going to blow off Darren's *daughters*? What do you think of me?"

Good question. "I honestly don't know. If you'd asked me a week ago, I would have said you're a guy who puts himself first. You do whatever you feel like doing and don't care about the consequences to other people. But now that I've spent time with you and seen you around the girls? I think you're really insightful, sensitive, and caring. And it scares the ever-living hell out of me."

"Why?" The urgency in his voice, the appeal in his eyes, told her how much she'd upset him.

Because I'm falling for a man who's leaving the day after tomorrow. And spending too much time fantasizing about what his touch would feel like. Last night in bed, she'd yearned for his warm body beside hers. She'd wanted to feel his arm wrapped tightly around her.

"Hailey—" he began.

But right then, the girls raced out of the kitchen.

Paisley dumped a bunch of crayon drawings and magnets at their feet. "Can I bring these?"

"Yeah, of course." Cole held one up. "I like this. We'll put them on my fridge."

"Okay, we're going to our room now."

They watched the girls run off. "They really don't get it, do they?"

"Well, that's the thing. We don't know what they understand. That's why we just have to be here, ready to answer questions and look for signs that they're struggling."

"We should go with them."

He gave her a nod, and together, they headed down the hallway. Family photos lined the walls, and she stopped when she saw one of the four of them at the lake. "I remember this."

Cole crowded her, his scent invading her senses, his heat burning her right side. "I didn't fuck anything up that day."

What an odd thing to say. "We had so much fun together." They were on Cole's boat, Darren fishing, his legs dangling off the side, as both women held up a fish they'd caught. Cole had his hands on the wheel, twisting around, his eyes on... *her*.

There was no denying the look in his eyes. He wanted her.

And not like a man hoping for a hookup.

He looked at her in awe. If it wasn't her in the picture, she'd think he was looking at a girl he knew he could never have.

And didn't that just sum it all up? That was Cole's experience. What he'd been trying to tell her. It was why he'd been so awkward around her.

I wish I'd seen that back then.

They turned into the bedroom to find two single beds, a tall white dresser, and a little plastic table with two chairs, all set for a tea party. There wasn't much in the way of décor, and the only toys seemed to be contained in a big red tub, but the walls were covered with the girls' artwork.

As she took it all in, her gaze snagged on a framed poem.

You're the sun, the moon, the stars…the entire galaxy. You are my universe. I love you with everything I am.

"What's this?" she asked Paisley.

"That's what my mommy says to us every night before bed. My daddy framed it."

"I love that." She lifted it off the hook. *We're definitely taking this.*

A clatter drew their attention. Evvie came out of the bathroom lugging, a plastic step stool. "Dis mine."

"Okay, sweetie." Hailey took it from her. "I got it."

"See Mommy." On a mission, the littlest one ran out of the room.

"Mommy?" Paisley dropped a stuffed moose and ran to catch up with her sister. "Where?"

"Oh, boy." She and Cole hurried to join them, watching as they disappeared into the last room on the left.

When they hit the threshold, they came to a hard stop. It was Lindsay's bedroom. She knew immediately because her scent hung in the air, the same perfume she'd worn in high school. The pillows still held the impression of their heads, and the bed was unmade.

The girls' smiles faded. She wondered if they, too, felt

the vast emptiness of the space without their parents' spirits filling it. Paisley stayed with them, as Evvie dashed to the closet and peered inside.

Hailey's stomach rolled. *Oh, God. She's looking for her parents.*

A moment later, the three-year-old flung open the bathroom door. She stood there, staring.

Hailey held her breath, the devastation so heavy it threatened to sink her. She wanted to go to the little girl, hug her and promise everything would be all right, but she remembered what the therapist said and, instead, gave her some space.

Slowly, Evvie turned to them, eyes filled with a silent plea.

Hailey's stomach wrenched as she watched the little girl grapple with a dawning understanding. Cole was on the move. Before he even reached her, the little girl lifted her arms. When he picked her up, she cocked her head and said, "Where Mommy and Daddy?"

And here it is. Step one in grasping that her parents had died.

"They're gone, sweetheart." He blinked several times and pressed his lips together. After a moment, he sucked in a breath. "Mommy and Daddy died, and they're not coming back. But they love you more than anything. And they asked Hailey and me to take care of you."

"Want Mommy." The tremble in Evvie's voice filled Hailey's soul like a scream.

"I know." Cole didn't waver. Not a bit. "And trust me, your mommy and daddy didn't want to leave you. They would only ever want to be with you, but they had a car accident, and they're not coming back."

Evvie wrapped her arms around Cole's neck. "I want my mommy. I want Daddy."

"I know you do." Cole gently swayed with the little girl in his arms. "I know."

Silent tears turned to sobs, and she buried her face against his collarbone. "*Mommy*."

"I know, baby. I know."

When Paisley hugged his thigh, Cole lowered himself to the floor. Hailey joined, and the four of them clutched each other as Evvie unleashed her fear, confusion, and sorrow in heart-wrenching tears.

Hailey gently caressed the little girl's back. "It's okay, sweetie. It's going to be okay." Her words meant nothing, but she just felt so helpless.

"Your mommy loves you so much," Cole said. "You're—"

Lindsay's letter popped into her mind. "The sun, the moon, the stars…the entire galaxy. You are your mommy's universe."

Paisley patted her sister's arm, murmuring something only the sisters could hear. Evvie reached out, and the two girls held hands. The tears stopped falling, and her little body shuddered.

And then, it was just peaceful.

The powerful bond between the four of them charged through her. She'd always longed for a home—the kind where you could walk into your childhood bedroom and know it hadn't changed a bit even though you were an adult now, where the neighbors across the street waved, and the mail carrier made a crack about your online shopping problem.

But in this moment, she understood something.

That elusive feeling of home? It wasn't a house. It was the people.

Yes, she understood the four of them were temporary. They'd find a family for the girls, Cole would return to Boston, and she'd be back in her studio apartment.

But she got it now, what home truly meant. She hadn't missed out on some town where she could put down roots and grow old in. She'd missed out on making the kind of friends who became your chosen family.

For now, she and Cole were their family. And that's how she'd treat them.

"Hey, you know how the fairies make magic boxes?" Cole asked. "What if we made memory boxes? You guys can fill them with all the things that remind you of your parents."

"Like what?" Paisley asked.

"Well…does your dad still have that green baseball hat?" he asked.

Paisley smiled. "Mommy makes him keep it in the garage."

"It stinky," Evvie said.

"That's because it was his fishing hat." Hailey remembered how they'd take turns whacking the bill. It'd go sailing into the lake, and Darren would dive in to retrieve it every time.

"How about I get it, and you guys take a look around for all your favorite things?" Cole asked.

"Oh, I know." Paisley got up. "Come on, Evvie. Let's get our blankies."

Cole set the littlest one down, and the girls, still holding hands, headed into the closet. "When I get the hat, I'll grab the boxes from the car. Be right back."

"I was so wrong about you." She could see she'd taken

him off guard because he jerked to a stop. "There's nothing superficial about you. You've listened to me, apologized to me, and you've never once—not for a second—run from the scariness of our situation. You handle the hard questions like a champ. I see you, Cole Montgomery. And I'm so sorry I didn't before." She quickly headed after the girls.

In their parents' closet, Paisley's little bottom poked out from a row of dresses. She emerged with a storage box. "Look." Opening it, she pulled out a baby blanket.

"This is so pretty." Hailey ran her fingertips over the embroidery.

"Mommy made it for Evvie." Next, Paisley pulled out a pastel pink and blue throw. "This one's mine."

Since her friend couldn't sew, Hailey had offered to make quilts for the girls, but Lindsay had insisted on doing it herself. For Evvie, she'd bought a kit, and for Paisley, she'd taken a knitting class. Neither blanket came out perfect, but both held all the love Lindsay had for her children. "Your mommy loved you so much. These are amazing." What else would they want? "What else would you like to put in the memory box?"

"The rocks we painted?" Paisley asked.

"Sure. Go grab them."

Cole came back into the room with a stack of framed photos. "We don't want to forget these."

"For sure. They can tell us about each picture. That's how we'll keep the memories alive. Oh, you know what might be fun?" She turned to the girls. "You can tell us about all the trips you've taken and things your family did together, and Cole and I will write them down and put them in the boxes."

"That's a great idea." He smiled at her warmly.

Evvie thrust a sweatshirt at her. "Dis Mommy."

Hailey got a distinct whiff of Lindsay's perfume. "Did your mommy wear this a lot?"

"Yes." Evvie nodded with such sincerity. "Mommy weared it."

As the girls continued to collect things—their dad's walking stick, his watch, and a pair of ratty slippers—Hailey went into the bathroom and found the bottle. She'd spritz it on their stuffed animals to keep their mom present for them.

She'd also take the jewelry box just in case there was a family heirloom in it. Anything she could pass along to the girls as they got older would be cherished. At three, Evvie knew her parents the least, so Hailey would be sure to tell her stories.

As they headed back to the car, loaded with boxes, Hailey said, "That was good. Tough but good."

He popped the trunk and set the boxes inside. "I'm damn glad we're in this together."

"Me, too." Her heart clutched.

She could see it so clearly, the four of them together. *A family.*

The hope that flared threatened to burst into flames, and she had to snuff it out. She just had to.

She was getting carried away in a fantasy.

He's leaving the day after tomorrow.

There's no happy ever after here.

Chapter Nine

As Hailey hung framed photos in the hallway, she overheard the conversation between Cole and Paisley. They were talking about how Evvie had broken down earlier, and how she'd done such a good job comforting her little sister.

"I like the way you take care of her, but you know you can cry, too. I've got Evvie, but I've also got you."

What a good man.

After they'd come home from the Leesons, they'd made cocoa and built a fire, and then they'd gone through the boxes. There'd been as much laughter as tears, but it had left her hopeful the girls would come through this all right.

While Cole had bathed the girls, she'd started hanging some of the family pictures around the house. Even if they were only here a few weeks, they should always feel the presence of their parents.

She reached for the next one on the pile and saw it was from the courthouse wedding. Happiness sparked at the sight of the happy couple, laughing with unfettered joy.

Cole, the best man was laughing, too. Slightly hunched over, he was clapping and looking right at Hailey.

There wasn't a hint of anger or resentment between them. They'd put aside everything to celebrate the marriage of this couple that had loved each other madly until the very end.

These two made it so easy to believe in happy ever after.

Cole reached the top of the stairs, carrying Paisley in his arms. "The princess is ready for bed."

Quickly hanging the frame, she gave the girl a hug. "Goodnight, sweetheart."

"'Night, Hailey."

It was a shame he had to leave so soon. The girls were growing close to him.

And so am I.

A few minutes later, Cole came back. "Need a hand?"

"Oh, there's only one more."

"I got it." He picked up the last one. "Where do you want it?"

She stepped back. "Maybe here?" She made sure they were low enough so the girls could actually see them. "Are they asleep already?"

"Evvie's out like a light."

"Well, aren't you just the child whisperer?"

Tapping a nail into the wall, he chuckled. "That girl lives hard, and then she conks out." He set the hook on it. "This is a good idea."

"I hope so. I thought about checking with Deborah. Like, will it hurt them more to be reminded of their loss? Is it too soon? But it just seems worse to shut them off from the life they had less than two weeks ago."

"That makes sense to me."

"I know Lindsay wanted to save those blankets, but I put them on their beds anyway. Seems more important than preserving them."

"I agree." He seemed distracted.

"Today was tough, huh?"

"Sure was. But we make a damn good team."

"We really do." Finished, she had no reason to linger in the hallway. But some inexplicable force held her to him. If she were bolder, if she were the type of woman who could handle casual sex, she'd lift that T-shirt up and run her hands all over his abs and across his pecs. She'd press against him to feel his hardness everywhere. But she wasn't that woman. "Well, goodnight." She put the hammer in the toolbox, and he dumped in the nails.

Before she could go, he grasped her wrist. "This afternoon, you said you might do something crazy. Just so we're clear, you can kiss me anytime you like."

Her blood went hot. The only sound in her body was her heart beating like a drum. She had no words, no witty comeback. Nothing but a need so wild she got up on her toes and set her hands on his chest. "Okay, maybe just one." And she kissed him.

Soft lips. Warm. Just a hint of hot chocolate. He opened his mouth slightly—enough for her to get that hit of what it would be like to lose herself in this man.

And it was so delicious, so seductive, that she pulled away.

Wrong place. Wrong time.

Wrong man.

If touching her lips to his could send her up in flames, what would it be like to get closer? It would be all-consuming.

And she couldn't do that.

No. I'm here for the girls.

She started to walk away.

"Hold on."

At his command, her steps faltered. Desire had her in its painful grip, arousing her nipples to hard peaks and stroking a pulse between her thighs. She wanted him so much.

"Let me just say one thing. What's happening between us is not because of our situation. It's not because we're stuck in a house together."

Finally, she relented. It was time to stop lying to herself. "Yeah, I know. I'm just not sure what to do about it. Because no matter what's going on here"—she waved a finger between them—"our focus has to be on getting the girls through this awful time."

"No." His features hardened. "I don't agree." He came up to her, caging her against the wall. "That night—"

"Oh, no, you don't." She tried to dart out from under him. "We're not talking about a date from ten years ago."

But he didn't budge. "We sure as hell are." And his firm tone brooked no argument.

It was obviously important to him, so she gave him her full attention.

"I wanted to impress you." He let out a frustrated breath. "No, I wanted you to like me. When Mrs. DeMarco asked where you'd moved from, you said, 'I've lived everywhere.' And then you said, 'Well, except Washington State. I've never been there.'"

"Wait, *that's* why you took me there?"

"Yeah, and I knew you wouldn't want some snooty dinner in Seattle, so I thought Snoqualmie Falls would be good and…" Bright pink blossomed on his cheeks. "Romantic."

"It *was* good. It was amazing." They'd sat at a window overlooking a waterfall. "I can't think of anything more romantic." His body heat warmed her, and the energy between them crackled. Her gaze traced the bow of his plump upper lip, and she wanted a deeper taste of him.

"But I took it too far. I should've brought you home after dinner."

That's for sure. "Why didn't you? If it had just been dinner, everything would've turned out differently."

His gaze cut away sharply. Whatever she'd said had hit him hard. It took him a moment to recover.

"I'm sorry," she said. "What did I say?"

"Nothing. It's just… I know that, and I regret it. I regret a lot of things I've taken too far."

"I don't understand, though. Why did you bring me to that party? Why did we have to see your hockey friends?"

"We didn't. But dinner wasn't going well, and I could tell you wanted to be anywhere other than with me." He dropped his forehead to hers. "So, when you went to the bathroom, I texted my friends, asked them what I could do to salvage the date." And then, he took a step back. "I fucked up. I should've just accepted that you didn't want to be with me." He folded his arms over his muscular chest. "I should've just brought you home. I'm sorry."

She wanted him back. The heat of his body, that searching gaze that made her feel so very *important* to him, and the potential for more. More touches, more secrets shared, more intimacies.

The hell with it. Even if she never saw him again after he left, she would never regret grabbing his shirt, yanking him to her, and pressing her mouth over his. Wholly unprepared, he stumbled against her. But this man did not hesitate. No, he dove right in.

Licking the seam of her mouth, he slid inside. The moment their tongues touched, her senses sharpened, and she became aware of the silky strands of his hair, the slick heat of his mouth, and that scent that connected with something deep inside her.

Something that made her forget everything but the taste of him, the urgency of his touch, and the hot thrum of desire beating in her bloodstream.

He reached for her ass, those big hands giving it a lusty squeeze—God, that was hot. Lifting her against the wall, he stepped between her thighs. *Yes.* Lust blazed a path along her limbs, turning her inhibitions, her doubts, and her thoughts to ashes.

Angling her face, he deepened the kiss, taking over, sweeping her away with his passionate desire.

No one had ever wanted her the way he did.

And she needed it. Needed someone to want her, to chase her to the ends of the earth and never give up on her. *Cole's that man.* His body was telling her what she'd always longed to hear.

And God knows, she'd never wanted anyone the way she wanted him.

Hearing a sigh from the girls' room, she started to ease away, but he cupped the back of her head and held her in place. "This might be my only chance, and I'm going to take my fill of you." And then he kissed her so thoroughly, so desperately, she knew she was spoiled for life.

When he finally pulled back, he kissed her chastely once, twice, three times…and then he let out a shaky sigh. "Holy shit."

For a moment, she couldn't speak. Couldn't think. Her entire being was still caught up in that kiss. And then, she stuttered out a laugh, showing him her hand. "I'm shaking."

He set her down and took a step back. "I'm good, though." His knees buckled. "Totally unaffected."

She grinned. "I see that." Loving this moment with him, she clasped her hands around his neck. "They'd love this, you know. All Darren and Lindsay ever wanted was for us to be together." Every time she let her hopes run wild—maybe they could work out—*why not?*—she got a stab of fear. *He's leaving in two days.* And when he got back on the ice, all this intensity would fade.

She had to get it through her head. They would never be a couple. "Well, we've got to get up early."

Once again, he reached for her. "Hailey?" He traced her bottom lip with his thumb. "I wish I'd gotten it right. Taken you to the homecoming dance, to prom...been the jock you dated. I wish I'd had the confidence to be the guy you needed."

She sighed. "Let's not forget my part in it. Things might've been different if I hadn't been so determined to shut everyone out."

"You're not shutting me out now."

"Nope. Though I probably should." But...why? Why not enjoy the heat blazing in his eyes? *So what if it's temporary?*

All she did was work. Her life was devoid of passion, lust...all the powerful emotions. She guessed she liked it that way because it was safer. A childhood filled with anger, resentment, and fear had her seeking out stability and peace as an adult. "Kiss me again, Cole. One more time."

Those sexy lips brushed over hers, and she came alive. His touch was an awakening, a celebration. She flung her arms around his neck, desperate for more. Up on her toes, she pressed against him, her hips shifting, seeking relief from the throb between her legs, the glowing ache that only needed friction to burst into flames. His breath caught in his throat before he deepened the kiss. With his hands on the rise of her ass, he jerked up hard against him. "There are other places I want to kiss you."

Yes. God. She devoured him, her hands reaching under his shirt, meeting his smooth, hot skin. She was on fire, pure sensation, and when the ache grew too much to bear, she moaned.

And that was what snapped her out of it.

They couldn't do this with two children right down the hall.

Yes, she wanted him. Of course, she did. But… "I can't. You're still leaving the day after tomorrow."

He let out a defeated sigh. "I know."

She shifted out of his hold. "Goodnight, Cole." She'd gotten halfway down the hall, when he called her name. She didn't turn around. If she saw his mouth still wet from her kiss, the lust-lazy eyes, she'd surely go running back. "Yeah?"

"Best kiss ever."

She grinned.

Sure was.

Sleep was not going to come. Not when Cole kept reliving that kiss.

In all the time he'd known her, Hailey had given him very clear fuck-off vibes. Like their one and only date when she'd barely tolerated him.

Which, of course, was the reason he'd made the fatal mistake of taking her to that party. He'd needed to win her over, so he'd gone for something more. Something bigger than dinner on the side of a mountain.

Spectacular fail.

Lying on his back, he stared up at the ceiling. He hadn't closed the curtains, so moonlight filled his room with a silver glow. *Damn.* He couldn't stop thinking about the way she'd clung to him and kissed him like she couldn't get enough.

Sensation streamed through him, and he palmed his aching cock. He wanted her so badly. She'd starred in thousands of fantasies, but she'd been so uptight around him, so serious and responsible, that he couldn't tell what she'd be like in bed. Now, with that kiss, he knew.

She'd be fucking wild.

She just needed to be comfortable with someone.

She likes me.

And I didn't have to do a damn thing to "win her over."

Closing his eyes, he pictured her riding him, features slack with pleasure, her bouncy curls cascading down her back and pooling on his thighs. He wanted to cup her tits and rock up into her...fuck her harder and faster...get deeper...all the fucking way.

He could never get close enough to her. He was insatiable.

Sexual tension wound him up so tightly, he shoved the sheet off and got out of bed.

I'm not jerking off.

What if one of the girls walked into his room?

Instead, he picked up his phone and sorted through texts and emails from his coach and teammates.

Connor: We need you back here, man.

Illy: You're playing Thursday, right?

Coach: Let me know when you get the MRI results.

He answered as best as he could, but his mind kept fast-forwarding to the morning. He'd have to wake Paisley up earlier, give her more time. Easy enough, but what about her hair? Obviously, he knew not to brush it, but what did he do instead? He'd failed at making a basic ponytail.

Bunching pillows behind his back, he did a search.

How to wake up a kid
How to handle curly hair
How the fuck do I give one hundred percent to my team while Hailey's alone here with Darren's daughters?

He calmed his ass down because there was only one answer.

You take it one step at a time, just like you keep telling her.

Since the next step came bright and early tomorrow morning, he read articles and watched a couple of video tutorials on braiding. Something caught his attention, and he clicked on a link to a parenting forum.

Oh, here we go.

It was a treasure trove of information.

Since there hadn't been any activity in the last couple of hours, he doubted anyone was around, but he figured it couldn't hurt to lay out his situation and see if anyone had advice for him.

Not a minute after hitting Send, the replies started coming in.

This is fantastic.

After he'd gotten a world of information, he was ready to try out some of the ideas. He wondered if Hailey would let him practice on her.

Kidding.

Well, but actually…if she was awake, he could go see her—*nope. Not cool to show up in her bedroom.* He'd just shoot her a text. If she were sleeping, she'd have her phone on silent.

What the fuck's the matter with you? You're not a kid anymore. In high school, he'd followed her around like a little puppy. *You're not doing that shit anymore.*

Leave her alone.

Because as much as he wanted her, he couldn't risk the emotional fall-out with the kids. When he fucked up—and he would—they'd be on bad terms, and that wasn't fair to the girls. Hailey was smart not to take things further with him.

The best gift he could give all of them was distance. He'd provide for them, he'd be there when they needed him, but he wouldn't risk their well-being by getting too close. Inevitably, he'd take things too far like he always did.

The nanny had been right about one thing: he was a menace.

You're going to get yourself killed one day. You'd just better hope you don't take someone with you.

Truer words… He'd nearly taken Booker.

Fuck. Now, he was wide awake. He needed to get out of bed, read a book, do something to switch things up.

First, he'd check on the girls. He'd gotten a baby monitor for their room so he could hear if they had nightmares. He knew from personal experience how upsetting they could be. When he'd had the bad nanny, he'd wake up in the night sweating, sheets twisted around him, heart pounding. He didn't want that for the girls.

They kept the door ajar, a night light plugged into the wall, so he could see them clearly tucked into their double beds. Evvie was sprawled on her belly. With her chubby little cheek and cute, puckered lips, she held a fist right in front of her mouth.

His gaze slid to Paisley, and he got the shock of his life when he found her watching him. He came into the room and sat on the edge of her mattress. "You okay?"

She nodded, looking wide awake.

He had an idea. "Come with me."

As he popped into her ensuite bathroom to pick up some supplies, she sprang out of bed, slid her little feet into her moose slippers, and then the two of them padded down the hall to his bedroom. "I think you and me are night owls."

"I'm not an owl."

"You sure? Because you've got that beak." He tapped her nose, and she broke out into a grin as bright as sunshine. "It's an expression, silly. Owls are awake at night, not during the day, so that's where it comes from. It just means people who stay up late. Come here." He led her to his bathroom and turned on the faucet in the tub. "Since mornings are tough for you, I thought we could get you ready the night before school."

Paisley stood watching, oddly trusting him enough to see where he was going with this conversation.

"You take your bath, we set out your clothes—"

"But what about my hair? If I sleep on it wet, it sticks out, and I hate it."

"Well, that's the thing. I talked to some parents about your hair texture. Turns out, we can braid it the night before, so when you wake up, you step into your clothes, and you're ready to rock and roll. You want to give it a go?"

"I don't know how to braid it."

"Well, I think I might know." He pulled out his phone and tapped the screen a few times until he got to the last tutorial he'd watched. "I learned from this. So, what do you say? Should we give it a try?"

She smiled and nodded, immediately pulling up her nightgown.

Once he got the water nice and warm, he tipped her head back, readying it for the shampoo. Since he didn't have a cup, he used his hands. In the quiet of the bathroom, the only sound the splashing of water, he figured he'd take the opportunity to weigh in with her. "I'm glad I got to see your house." He'd read that to make sense of the world, kids made things up, which made it important to get them talking. What if they got it in their heads that their parents had gone on vacation and intentionally didn't come back? He'd try to get her to open up so he could clarify things.

When she didn't answer, he tried a different track. "You excited about Christmas?" If it didn't work, he'd let it go for tonight.

"Yes." That brought a smile.

"I want to be sure it's fun for you guys. Is there anything in particular your family liked to do?"

"Daddy plays music all day long, and Mommy does this." She screwed up her face and shook her fist. "'Turn it *off*.'"

He loved seeing her animated. "Are you talking about Christmas carols?"

She nodded. "He loves them."

"And your mom couldn't stand them?"

"Mostly just because he played them all day long. But then, he'd play her favorite song, and they'd start dancing."

"What was her favorite?"

She hummed a tune, but he had no idea what it was.

"Yeah, your parents loved each other very much. And you…" He tipped her chin so he could look into her eyes as he rinsed out the shampoo. "You're what all that love made. So, you're just a big ole bundle of love."

After he'd finished bathing her, he grabbed a towel and wrapped her up in it. Holding her closely, he looked right into her eyes and saw a lost, scared little girl. "I got you, little one, and Hailey's got you, too. I don't know how just yet, but I promise you, it's going to be all right. I'm going to make sure of it."

The girl let out a huff of breath and tipped her head onto his arm, and he held her like that for a long time.

Chapter Ten

THE NEXT MORNING, HAILEY SET HER ALARM, determined to make the process of getting Paisley to school way less dramatic. She'd seen the detangler on the Leesons' bathroom counter, and she'd also grabbed some elastics that she knew from experience worked well with thick hair. She also checked the most recent family portraits to see what styles the girls liked.

All set, she peered into their bedroom. The covers were flung back, the sheets a tangled mess, nightgowns on the floor, and the bathroom light was still on.

No girls. Huh.

Curious, she hurried downstairs to find all three of her roommates in the kitchen, dressed and ready for the day.

The girls were eating toaster waffles slathered in peanut butter. The little black dots on top looked suspiciously like chocolate chips. Why did that look so tasty? They chatted easily, Cole with his back to the island—closer than before but still not sitting with them—and the sisters tucked in tightly to the table, their legs swinging in and out.

Most notably, Paisley's hair was beautifully braided.

You've got to be kidding me.

Cole *did that?*

Hailey pulled out her phone to record the best center in the country eating waffles with two little girls.

Finished, she pocketed her phone and entered the room. "Well, good morning. How is everyone?"

"Look, Cole braided my hair." Paisley held them both out.

"I see that. It looks beautiful." She smiled at Cole and mouthed, *Wow.*

"He gave me shock-let chips." Evvie had peanut butter smeared around her mouth and melted chocolate on her fingers.

"Hm." She approached the table. "I want to find that revolting, but it looks really good."

"If you want me to make you one, just ask." Cole had a certain gleam in his eyes. "I like when women ask for what they want."

A sizzle went through her body.

Okay, mister. Don't be doing that sexy innuendo around the kids.

It was hard enough to mask her feelings when they were all together. "Oh, that's not a problem. I know just what I like."

His eyes flared.

And then, just to tease a little more, she said, "Mm, yes. Cole, I really need you to make me…a waffle. Right now."

"Yes, ma'am." He popped up. "It would be my pleasure." His voice lowered on that last word, giving her a look that let her know exactly how he'd treat her in bed.

Ugh. After a fitful night of erotic dreams, she did not need this.

But she did need to make Paisley's lunch, so she met him at the refrigerator where he was pulling the box of waffles out of the freezer.

"After I get Paisley on the bus, feel free to tell me more about what you want." His voice was rough, husky, and she closed her eyes to imagine hearing it in the dark of a bedroom, moonlight slanting in through partially closed blinds, his hands on her hips, her bottom tilted, as he drove her up the mattress with forceful thrusts.

Oh. Desire streaked through her, bright and hot, and her eyes popped open. "You're such a tease, getting me all worked up when we'll have Evvie with us." She focused on lunch. "Do you want a sandwich?" she called to the little girl.

"Cole made my lunch. I helped him."

She looked into the brilliant blue eyes of this man she'd underestimated in every possible way. "You did?"

"Yep. We did it together last night."

"But I saw you put her to bed. You said she was out like a light."

"Me and Cole are night owls," Paisley said.

"How late were you guys up?"

"She was asleep at eleven." And then, he lowered his voice so only Hailey could hear. "I think she was scared and just needed some companionship. As soon as I did her hair and made lunch, she fell right to sleep." His forehead creased in concern, and she wanted to soothe the worry lines. "Are you mad?"

"*Mad*? What? No. I'm impressed. How did you learn how to braid?"

"It took some trial and error, but I got tips on a parenting forum and watched some tutorials. I think it worked out all right."

141

"You joined a *parenting* forum?"

His easygoing smile faltered. "Yeah, they jumped at the chance to help out."

"I can't believe you did that."

"Why?" His tone was curt.

"No, I mean, I just didn't expect—"

"Me to be resourceful?" A dark cloud crossed over him. "To give a shit?" He brushed past her and strode across the kitchen to drop a waffle into the toaster.

Dammit. She joined him at the counter. "I'm sorry if I insulted you. I'm truly impressed with everything you did." His scowl turned even darker, and she grew flustered. "I mean, you know, with everything you're doing." She'd never once seen him angry. And it was formidable.

Turning his back on the girls, he whispered harshly, "I don't need a pat on the head for doing what any man in this situation would do. I don't know why the hell they chose me as your partner in this situation, but like it or not, they did. So, get used to it because I'm all you've got."

———

Cole was pissed. She'd talked to him like he was a kid who'd taken a leak in the toilet for the first time. Not like a man responsible for two children.

He thought he'd made progress with her, but she'd clearly never see him as anything but the asshole he was in high school.

On the way back to the house after getting Paisley on the bus, he'd checked his phone. A dart of fear had pierced the back of his neck when he'd seen the voicemail from the Renegade's doctor.

"Hey, Cole. It's Mark. Sorry to call so early, but I've got a

full day ahead of me with the team. Listen, the results of your MRI are in, and I'd like to meet with you first thing this morning to discuss them. Let me know if that works for you."

Fingers stiff from the cold, he'd texted him right then.

Be right there.

Then, he'd asked Hailey if she was okay watching Evvie while he headed into town for a quick meeting. She hadn't minded, so he'd come straight to the rink.

Now, Mark pointed to the image on his laptop. "You can see the tear right here. The good news is it's small. We can get in there and fix it before it gets worse."

"Arthroscopic surgery, right?"

"Exactly."

"Well, that sucks. But okay." He hopped off the examination table, wincing upon landing. "I'll talk to my trainer and get it scheduled for next summer."

Mark's eyebrows shot up. "I don't know what it'll look like six months from now, but I can guarantee it won't be small anymore. It's not my call, but if you were on the Renegades, I'd advise you to do it now. And like we've said, the sooner you get it done, the sooner you're back on the ice."

"I hear you. I have a game on Thursday, so I'll deal with it after that."

Mark's gaze never wavered. "The more you play on it, the bigger the tear will become. Just walking on it's a risk."

"Yeah, but it's small..." He knew he was full of shit. It sounded stupid just saying it. "Look, you know I can't miss any more games."

"I know if you play any more games, you risk a much longer rehab than six weeks."

"*Six weeks*? I can't miss six games, let alone six weeks."

"The choice is yours. But if you want a long career, you'll take care of a torn meniscus while it's fixable."

Fuck my life.

In the passenger seat of Jaime's car after surgery, Cole called his coach to give him an update.

The gruff, older man answered on the first ring. "So? How'd it go?"

"It was simple and quick. They got the job done."

"Good. All right, well, you might as well stay in Wyoming through Christmas. Give yourself a week off the knee, but then get your ass back here, and we'll get you started in physical therapy."

What he was about to say would not go over well. And maybe if he hadn't gone to the Leesons' home yesterday and seen the drawings covering the refrigerator, the little tea party set up on a kid-sized table in their shared bedroom, and the framed photographs lining the hallway, he could've walked away. But these girls had been loved wholly and completely, and now they had no one.

Only me and Hailey.

He didn't have a shred of doubt about his decision. "I can get the therapy I need here."

"Okay, but you need to train."

"I know that. I can do it here."

"No, the hell you cannot. You can't train with another team."

"I'm not talking about the Renegades. There's a world-class training center here run by the Bowie brothers. It caters to Olympic athletes, so they've got the best therapists in the world. I've also got the rink I grew up on, so I'm all set."

"We're thirty-three games into this season. You need to be here with your team. You're the captain."

"I know that, and I'm in touch with the guys every day. Look, you know I want to be with my team. I want that Cup. But I'm out for six weeks—"

"For fuck's sake, Cole, you can't be away that long. I understand about the kids. I get it. But you need to be here. You're going to have to hire a nanny."

"No, *you* don't get it. You haven't looked into their eyes and seen how scared they are. They've lost their mom and dad, their home...everything they've ever known. Those girls have nothing. Except me, Coach. Do you understand that? If I walk away, they become wards of the state."

"What about the co-guardian? Set her up with a nanny, and she'll be fine."

He blew out a breath, giving himself a moment to pull himself together. He did not want to go off on his coach. "I didn't choose this. I don't want it any more than you do. But here I am. And I'm not walking away. Not when I know I can get the right treatment here. The best use of my time is to stay here and get them situated in a home."

"You don't know how long that will take."

"No, but I'll have a much better handle on the situation in the next six weeks."

"Four." His coach spat the word out. "You're back in four weeks."

After he disconnected, Cole dropped the phone into the cupholder. "That went well."

"For what it's worth, I think you made the right decision," Jaime said.

"Yeah. It wasn't really a choice." As they drove down 191, the bison preserve was a blur of white snow. "Maybe if I hadn't spent time with the girls, but…"

"You did."

"Yeah."

"Are they messed up?" Jaime asked. "Crying all the time?"

"Not at all. The littlest one, Everly? They call her Evvie." He grinned. "She's just a ball of joy bouncing around the house. And, man, does she love her food."

"And the older one?"

"Paisley's…special. I can't explain it. She's got an old soul." He chuckled. "She's cool."

"Sounds like you're bonding with them."

"I'm not staying." He needed to be very clear. "I'm not adopting these kids." He tipped his head back against the headrest. "It's a tough situation. I want them to feel safe, but at the same time, I don't think we should let them get too close to us."

"How can you not? You can't take care of them and deliberately keep them at arm's length."

"I just worry that if we let them attach, and then we leave, we'll be fucking them up even more."

"I'm no expert, but if you're going to weigh the options, I'd think it's better to be a good, healthy, positive transition for them than an indifferent one."

He thought about the bad nanny and instantly knew his friend was right. "I've been wrestling with that one from the start, and you've just cleared it up."

Declan had followed them home in Cole's Land Cruiser, so as soon as they got home, his friend helped him out of the car and handed him his crutches. Once he had his balance, the three of them headed up the walkway.

Jaime gave a chin nod to the decorations. "That's it? That's the best you could do?"

"I figured you'd at least have live reindeer." Declan pretended to be disappointed. "It's so...basic."

The idiots looked at each other and burst out laughing.

"Do you guys remember when we were supposed to get fitted for our tuxes for prom?" Jaime asked. "We thought we were going into town to rent them, but then we get a text from this asshole"—he elbowed Cole—"telling us to come to his house. Who was that designer again?"

Declan chuckled. "Van Bryson."

"First of all, the man was staying at my dad's place." Cole was feeling good. He could have the painkillers to thank for it, or it could have something to do with being back with his friends. *Maybe a little of both.* "Secondly, he's the one who suggested it. It wasn't my idea. He wanted to try his hand at a western-style tux." It wound up being his signature look the following season. "And did we not look like badasses?" He dug into his pocket for the key and let them into the house.

All conversation ceased.

"You're shitting me," Jaime said quietly.

"All that's missing is a dog," Declan said. "To bring your pipe and slippers."

With two Christmas trees, a festive garland strung along the stone mantle, a fire crackling in the hearth, and little white lights blinking everywhere—his house looked like a scene from a holiday movie.

But what made it a home were the two little girls and the gorgeous woman sitting around the coffee table, making decorations, drinking hot cocoa with clouds of whipped cream on top, and happily chatting away. Busy bopping their heads to the Christmas carols piped in through the speakers, none of them noticed the men who'd just entered.

Declan clapped him on the back. "No wonder you're rehabbing in town."

A mix of emotions grabbed hold of him, and he stood on a precipice between wanting to see their faces light up at his approach, get wrapped up in all their warmth and happiness and sweetness…

And walking right back out the door.

Because Coach was right. He *did* belong with his team. *And Hailey's doing a great job. All she needs is a nanny and my financial support. She's got this.*

But right then, he noticed her expression. Awareness bloomed on his skin. *Something's wrong.* She sat with the kids, helping Evvie wipe a gob of glue off a popsicle stick, acting like everything was good in the world, but she kept glancing at her phone, the tension pulling on her features.

"What's wrong?" When all three of them jerked their gazes over to him, he realized he'd sounded too aggressive.

As always, Jaime broke the tension by joining them. "Hey, girls. What'cha workin' on?"

Evvie got to her feet, showing him their pipe cleaner and glitter stick decorations. She danced in place, eyes wide with excitement, and Jaime acted like it was the most incredible thing he'd ever seen.

Meanwhile, Cole held Hailey's gaze. *Talk to me.*

Without breaking the connection, she stood up and walked over to him. She only broke away to greet Declan. "Hey, I don't know if you remember me. I'm Hailey Casselton."

"Of course. Hailey." He reached out a hand. "Declan Cadell. And that's Jaime Dupree."

"It's nice to see you both again."

"What's going on?" Cole turned Hailey away from the group. "You get some bad news?"

"I don't know. It might be nothing." She waved her phone. "My company's in the news today. They're saying they could go out of business by the end of the year. But that doesn't make sense. I mean, I know they're not as popular as they once were, but it's Abbott's of London. Part of the reason I wanted to work there was that I knew they'd never shut down."

"What's Abbott's of London?" Declan asked.

"If you have sisters, I guarantee they wore the nightgowns when they were little. They've been around forever. I mean, honestly, it's not the most exciting job in the world, but it's prestigious, so it's a gold-plated, you know? With that on your résumé, you can go anywhere. I'm sorry. I'm babbling. I just never in a million years imagined they'd go out of business."

"Crappy time to find out the news," Declan said.

"I know." She pressed a hand to her forehead. "Who's hiring around the holidays? The thing is, they don't have to close. They just have to diversify. They've been making the exact same thing for a hundred years." She glanced at her phone again. "A few of us in the design group are talking about it. Everyone's freaking, talking about polishing résumés and calling on connections. But it's such an obvious fix. They need a stronger online presence. They could add a men's line or partner with a brand like Disney to produce princess gowns. There are just so many things they could do to reach a new audience while remaining conservative."

"Have you pitched your ideas?" Cole asked.

"Oh, no. No, they're a family company, and it's only in the last decade that they've let in outsiders. They make all the big decisions."

"If they're in crisis, they might be open to ideas," Declan said. "Couldn't hurt to try."

Hope flickered in her eyes. "I wouldn't even know where to begin. I'm good at designing and sewing and sketching... I know texture and textiles. What do I know about the business side of things?"

"Actually, my girlfriend's opening a store in town," Declan said. "She didn't know much either, so she joined a group called the Petticoat Rulers. It's all about women supporting other women in business. You can join them and get all the help you need."

"Oh, no. I'm only here for a few weeks. I'm not part of the community."

"Phinny moved here in the summer, so she's only got a few months on you. Don't worry about it."

"You think?" She looked so hopeful.

It made Cole want to shake the world until everything fell into place just the way she wanted. "Text me her number, and I'll make sure Hailey gets it. They can talk."

"Sounds good."

"Okay, well, we've got to get to the rink." Jaime gestured to Cole's knee. "You going to be okay?"

Hailey shook her head, her cheeks turning pink. "Look at me going on and on about some stupid news report. I'm so sorry. Come on. Let's get you off your feet." Hooking her arm through Cole's, she led him to the couch.

He glanced behind to find his friends smirking. Okay,

sure. Maybe he *could* get around just fine on his own, but he sure didn't mind Hailey fussing over him.

Once the guys reached the door, Jaime called, "You need anything, let us know."

"It's a good thing it happened over Christmas." Hailey beamed a warm smile. "We plan on staying home and making cookies and all that good stuff."

"Cole Montgomery, domesticated." Jaime nodded. "It's a good look, my man."

"I'll text Cole the link to the Petticoat Rulers, so you can check it out. Might be good for you." And then, Declan closed the door behind them.

"They're nice."

"You sound surprised."

"I guess I am. I never really thought about it, but looking back, I think I lumped you all together."

Carefully, he lifted his leg and set it on a corner of the coffee table. He winced at a shock of pain.

"Here, let me grab you an ice pack."

"I'm fine, Hailey. Really. I can get it myself."

"That's the painkillers talking. Once they wear off, you'll be blubbering and moaning." She grinned. "For my sake, let's get ahead of it."

Evvie came up to him. "Look I made."

It was a sticky jumble of red and white pom-poms, green and silver glitter pipe cleaners, and plastic snowflakes. "Prettiest ornament I've ever seen. Want to go hang it on the tree?"

"No. For Cole."

"I get to keep this? Man, I'm a lucky guy. Thank you."

"You gots a boo-boo?" She patted the bandage wrapped around his knee.

That got Paisley's attention. "Why are you wearing shorts?"

"Because I had surgery on my knee this morning."

"What happened?"

"I had a tiny tear, and they made a little cut right here." He pointed to the hidden incision. "And put in the smallest camera you've ever seen. Then, they snipped the tear right off. Simple."

"Does it hurt?" Paisley asked.

"Not a bit. I have to stay off it for two days, but I'll be rarin' to go by Christmas."

Hailey came back into the room. "Here you go." She set the ice pack on top of the thin bandage. "Thirty minutes."

"Okay, nurse Casselton."

"Excuse me for looking it up." She rolled her eyes. "What did you think I'd do when you told me you were having *surgery*? It should be a quick recovery, but—FYI—your thighs are going to look like these popsicle sticks if you don't exercise them." She grinned. "Just saying."

"Yeah, yeah. Believe me, no one knows how fast muscles atrophy better than someone who gets paid to build them." The girls went back to their art project, and he reached for Hailey's hand. "Hey, I'm sorry for the timing of this."

"It's not your fault, and I'll only have to wait on you hand and foot for a couple of days." She turned serious. "Are you bummed about your team?"

"Sure. It sucks, but..." He hunched a shoulder. "It'll enable me to help out here."

"Yeah, I was wondering about that. How does this affect your plans? Are you still leaving right after Christmas?"

"Actually, I'm staying for six weeks. I'm doing my physical therapy here."

"In Calamity? Are you serious?"

"Yep. It makes the most sense."

"You're going to stay here for six weeks?"

"I am."

"Oh, my God." She fell back against the cushion. "Is it terrible to say I'm relieved? I know you need to be with your team, and I can totally do it alone. But...God, just knowing you're here to help...I mean, I'm so stinking happy about that."

Surprisingly, he was, too. "I talked to the guys. Since you've got to work, and I have to train, Declan's going to find us a sitter. But yeah." He reached for her hand. "It's you and me. We're in this together."

She squeezed. "You and me." They were just three simple words, but when uttered in a whisper filled with yearning, their meaning changed.

He looked at their joined hands, his big, battle-scarred, and veiny, and hers so slender and elegant, and his heart flipped over. He'd been touched by a thousand people in his lifetime—trainers, doctors, friends, teammates, lovers. But only this woman's had the power to transport him out of his ordinary world and into someplace magical.

"Cole?" she asked quietly. "I'm really sorry about this morning. I just think I've been let down by so many people that when someone exceeds my expectations, I'm kind of blown away."

"Your mom?"

"Honestly, other than you and Lindsay, pretty much everyone's let me down in one way or another. I think it's the kind of people my mom hangs around. They're all flaky and self-involved."

He liked this moment with her. Holding hands on the couch, the girls working happily on their ornaments, the house smelling like pine and cinnamon.

It struck him that he'd never—not once—just hung out in his home. He either had a rowdy group of guests with him, or he was alone and anxious.

And he only knew the difference because of how content he was right then.

Content. Huh. He'd never felt that before.

"But you haven't let me down." Her voice went soft, full of affection. "I'm just really sorry for taking my personal issues out on you. You didn't deserve them."

"We're good." They were so much more than good. He was on fire for her, and given how she'd kissed him, she might feel the same way.

He'd be here for the next six weeks.

Holy shit. Could he finally get to be with her?

Chapter Eleven

SINCE SHE WANTED TO GIVE THE GIRLS ROBES FOR Christmas, Hailey asked her mom to overnight some fabric. She bought supplies and then found a room in this giant house where she could spread out and work.

It looked like a craft room of some kind. One sage green wall held two dozen wrapping paper dispensers. Every occasion was represented from baby showers to children's birthdays, major and minor holidays, weddings, and graduations.

A massive hutch took up another wall. It had nooks for scissors, bows, and tape and a rows of ribbon rods in the center.

Lost in her work, Hailey startled at the phone vibrating on the island counter. When she saw Cole's name, she opened the text.

Cole: Heard from the PI. He's found some distant cousins of Lindsay's mom. They're less than twenty miles away.

Oh, wow. That was…wow. *It's good news, though, right?* It was the outcome she'd hoped for. But Christmas was only a week away, and they had so many plans for the girls.

She set aside her scissors to respond.

Hailey: Should we go now or after—

She stopped typing. They should definitely go after. *Delete.*

Hailey: I guess we'll—

She got rid of that one, too. Something about the situation made her uncomfortable. She started again.

Hailey: Has he contacted them?

"Not yet."

Her body jerked at the sound of that deep, sexy voice, and she swung around. "You scared the crap out of me."

"Sorry."

"No, it's okay. I've just been alone for a couple of hours." She stood up, smoothing her hands down her jeans. "What do we know about the family?"

"Nothing, really. Just that they're in Driggs."

"Where's that?"

"Idaho. It's on the other side of the mountain, about forty-five minutes away."

"So, if they live so close, why didn't Lindsay know them?"

"I don't know."

"Well, it's a red flag, for sure. Before we reach out, we

should find out more about them. See if there's a reason Lindsay didn't know them."

"Maybe she did. Maybe her mom had a falling-out with someone."

"I think she would've told me. We used to talk about everything." There was no need to rush. They'd just gotten the information. The family would still be there after the holidays. "Let's put this on hold. We can talk about it after Christmas." What was that terrible tug, that unwillingness to let the girls go?

"Hailey?" The gentleness of his tone didn't match the size and musculature of this big, badass hockey player. "We have to give them a chance. You know that, right?"

Caught out, she tipped her head back and laughed. "God, Cole. I do. I'm just—"

"Reluctant to let them go. I get it. I feel the same way. But that's what we're here to do. And I'm not sure we should wait. What if they're good people? What if the girls could have a real family holiday with cousins, grandparents, aunts, and uncles... If that's what's waiting for them, don't we need to give them that?"

"Oh, fine." She sounded like a petulant child. She was joking, of course. But also, she wasn't. Because now that the possibility existed, it no longer seemed like a slam-dunk solution. Now, she could see the problems. "I just need to meet them. I'm sure I'll feel better about everything when I see that they're kind, loving people."

"I'm not sure we'll get to know them that well from one meeting."

He was so damn patient with her. So understanding. And that was what allowed her to fall apart just a little. "Then, we'll need to spend more time with them. We can't just hand them over. Not until we're sure we've found the right home."

Coming close, he held her face in his hands. "We don't have to hand them over at all." He gazed into her eyes, absorbing her fears, her worries, and her doubts. "We'll tell them we're there to let them know Lindsay passed away, and that's it. We'll only mention the girls if we like what we see."

He was so calm, so in control. So steady. "Okay, that works." While she was a hot mess. "Look at me. I don't know why I'm reacting this way. I've only known them a few days."

"It's been a pretty intense couple of days. And we've been given a big responsibility here. We have to do right by Darren and Lindsay." He reached for her hand and intertwined their fingers. "Hey, it's okay. We're just going to meet them. Nothing more."

"I know. I think I'm just as scared we'll find the right family as I am that we won't. And believe me, I know that doesn't make sense because neither of us is in a place to become parents."

"I know I'm not. But if you're good with it, then I'll tell my guy to go ahead and set up a meeting sooner than later. And I'll ask him to dig a little deeper, too, okay?"

"I guess so."

"There's no problem with waiting until after Christmas, if that's what you want." He waited patiently for her to decide.

"No, it's fine. I think I'd feel differently if Lindsay had mentioned them." *And that's the problem right there.* "It keeps coming back to that, doesn't it? If they had anyone other than us, we wouldn't be here right now." That's what she was worried about.

"It does. But we'll give them a chance?"

"Yes. Of course." Unsettled, she needed to change the subject. With a sweep of her hand, she took in the island and hutch. "Who has a room for wrapping presents?"

He broke into a grin. "Crazy, right? It's the former owner's." He looked around. "I've never been in here before."

"What?" She acted shocked. "But where do you wrap your presents?"

He laughed. "Usually, I let the company I order from wrap it."

"Well, good news. On Christmas Eve, we'll have a wrapping party in here. Just you and me, some jacked-up eggnog, a charcuterie board, and…" She made a grand gesture to the big-screen TV. "*It's a Wonderful Life*."

"Sure, and when I wake up, we'll watch *Die Hard*."

"Yeah, but is *Die Hard* really a Christmas movie?"

"One hundred percent."

This. All this goodness that flowed between them…it was exciting and fun and everything missing in her life.

He took in her sewing machine, fabric, and all the supplies. "What're you working on?"

"I'm making robes for the girls."

"Robes? That's kind of random." He touched the fabric. "I like that."

"I know, right? Yeah, it's definitely a departure from what I usually make."

"Which is?"

"Sexy lingerie." Just for a moment, she held her breath, waiting for his reaction. From the time she was a teenager, sketching bustiers, corsets, and lacy bras, people had been making remarks about how naughty she was or suggesting she model it for them. *So insulting*. And so dismissive of her art.

But Cole didn't react like that at all. He just asked, "So, you went from that to flannel nightgowns at Abbott's?"

She smiled. "Yep. It was the best offer I got out of college."

"No lingerie companies?"

"I had interest from some start-ups, but I really wanted an established, high-end company. And with this job, I can do the work in my sleep, and then have the nights and weekends for creating my own line."

"So, what got you into robes?"

"As you can imagine, the materials for lingerie are specialized, and one day, a couple years ago, I was buying supplies and I discovered this new fabric. I fell in love with it. And since then, I've been working with the textile factory to come up with my own patterns and colors. Here. Let me show you." She pulled up some images on her phone.

"I like that. Have you been selling them?"

"No, not yet. I've been building inventory… Well, I was. Unfortunately, my mom gave them all away." It still made her furious, but it was her mom, and she wasn't about to badmouth her. "She saw an opportunity for me to launch my business, and she gave them away. It won't take me long to make new ones." *Ha. Really? It took eighteen months to make them.*

"How many did she give away?"

"A couple dozen."

"I'm stuck on the way you worded it. You said your mom *gave them away*. *She* saw an opportunity… Were you looking for one?"

"No, I came home from work to find them all gone." *Ugh*. This was making her mom look bad. "She had my best interests in mind. She thinks I'm too cautious, wasting my time at a company where I can't be creative."

"What do you think?"

I think it's none of her damn business. "I have a plan. I live modestly, so I can save up two to three years of living expenses. Then, I'll go out on my own."

"Is it a conflict of interest to sell your stuff while you're working?"

"No. I mean, I wouldn't want my employer to know. They'd probably fire me, but it's not a legal thing. I'll just feel more comfortable about it if I have some money and inventory saved up." She perched her bottom on the edge of the table. "But I talked to Phinny, and she invited me to the Petticoat Rulers meeting tomorrow night, so I'll bring a robe and get their input." As promised, Declan had texted her the link, and she'd been so excited about the group's resources.

"I'm surprised they're meeting so close to Christmas."

"Yeah, it's actually more of a holiday party, but Phinny said they always talk business, so to just come. Mostly, I want their help with Abbott's, but they have a couple of designers and some boutique owners in their directory, so I'd love to hear what they think about my plan."

"Makes sense." He came closer, fingering the material. "I like the way this feels."

"Yeah, I love it. When I wear it, I feel like pure—" She shut her mouth before finishing that sentence.

The way he looked at her, his eyes all hot and hungry... Yeah, he knew exactly what she was going to say. He prowled closer. "I think you need to finish that sentence, Hailey. Pure what?"

The walls in the room seemed to close in on her. Her body tingled with awareness. She wanted to say it. But she knew what would happen if she did. He would kiss her, run those hands all over her.

God, she wanted that. She lived with an ache to be near him, to be filled by him. And now, he was going to be here for six weeks, so why not?

Why not?

She licked her dry lips, and he followed the path of her tongue. "Sex."

"If you feel like pure sex when you wear that robe, you're going to make a fortune off them."

"Wouldn't that be nice?"

His eyes were on her mouth, while she had to force herself not to look at the bulge in his jeans. She wanted to unbutton him and pull him out, feel the hot, hard length. *Hard for me.* "Is it warm in here?"

He chuckled, but nothing could hide the yearning in his eyes. "I just walked in the door from training, and Leddy needs to get home. Otherwise, I'd see how hot I could make you. We'll continue this conversation after the girls are in bed."

He started out the door, and she panicked. "Cole?" *God, let him go.* Why did she need him so much? She'd never needed anyone before.

She didn't *want* to need someone.

What did she want anyway? All he could give her was some really good sex.

But that's the thing, isn't it? It was so much more than sex. *It's about wanting someone so desperately you can't get close enough, not through kisses, not through sex, not through anything bodies could do.*

It was about souls crying out for connection.

When she didn't say anything more, he held up his phone. "Let me get back to the PI. I'll book the sitter, too, while she's still here." And then, he left.

Leaving her a hot mess.

Already in bed, Hailey heard voices in the hallway. She quickly got up and peered out the doorway to find Cole carrying Paisley to bed. She didn't like to interrupt their private evening ritual, so she got back under the covers.

For the third time, she read the letter Abbott's of London had sent to all their employees that afternoon, apologizing for the news report, but explaining that it was true, that their sales had been flagging over the last several years, and they were considering their options.

The group chat had gone nuts with speculation, but Hailey didn't have the bandwidth to give it at the moment.

She heard a knock at her door. "Come in."

Cole poked his head in. "I talked to the PI. We're set for tomorrow."

Dread raced through her. "Can we get a sitter at such late notice?" She wasn't ready for this.

"Yeah. Leddy's down to do it."

"But it might snow, and I have to wash my hair, and Evvie's been asking me to take her ice skating."

"And the dog needs a bath?"

She aimed a finger at him. "Yes. And that, too."

He gave her a warm and compassionate smile.

"But I *guess* I can reschedule."

"Good. Then, we'll plan on leaving around ten, okay?" He hesitated in the doorway. The normally confident man seemed worried.

"You want to come in?" She patted the mattress. When he sat down, she said, "I thought you were all gung-ho about this, but now I'm wondering if you're as worried as I am. Tell me what you're thinking."

"The same thing you are. No matter how great they are when we meet them, no matter what right things they say about taking care of the girls, we really don't know what'll happen after we drop them off."

"No, we don't. They might seem like the nicest people in the world, but we don't see them when they're angry or frustrated. We don't know how they're going to treat the girls. It's scary. I mean, if you met my mom, you'd love her. You'd think she was the best, but I hated how she raised me." The admission hung in the air between them. Oddly, she didn't feel guilty. She'd needed to say it, and she knew she could trust Cole. She let out an awkward laugh. "Boy, it feels good to say that out loud."

"What did you hate?"

"She didn't line up the next gig when she knew her current job was ending. She got a thrill out of not knowing where we'd land next because she trusted the universe would deliver her a job." It was like popping a cork. All the bubbles came flying out. "But no job meant we couldn't pay rent or buy food. She had no savings. None. But she didn't mind. Nope, she'd just spin the wheel and see which friend would take her in next. Nothing filled me with dread more than this particular smile she had when asking someone to feed us. 'How about filling a couple of bellies for old times' sake?' Or 'You got another steak for an old friend?'"

Interestingly, he didn't cringe. He just…stayed intent. "Must've embarrassed the hell out of you."

"It disgusted me. I became great at reading people's

expressions. If there was even a hint of exasperation or resentment, I would refuse to go. Which forced her to come up with a plan B since she wouldn't go without me. I can't tell you how many nights I spent in a sleeping bag on someone's floor. And the thing is, people don't mind letting you crash for a night or two, but after that, they want their space back. And sometimes, they were so over it they just pretended we weren't there. I think it was a passive-aggressive way to get my mom to move on already. But did she get the hint? Nope. She was oblivious." Such awful memories. "The things I heard at night…"

"What does that mean?"

"It's just like, they could be on their best behavior for a day or two because a kid was in the house. After that, they'd go back to getting high or drunk or having very adult conversations. I'd overhear breakup calls and sex behind closed doors. But honestly, you can forget all that. Hands down, the worst thing for me was the hunger. I never want to see another can of beans as long as I live. I hated that my mom let me go without food. I hated that she pretended it was some great adventure. It wasn't. It was cruel. And that's why it's so important for me to earn a living, pay my own rent, and buy my own food."

"I get it." He sifted his fingers through her hair. "I'm so damn sorry she put you through that."

She found his touch so soothing she closed her hand around his wrist so he wouldn't ever stop. But she'd talked enough about herself. Given his A-list dad, her indigent childhood was nothing he could relate to. "What about your dad?"

"My dad's the best." He gave a boyish grin that was lightyears away from the expression she'd seen during a face-off on the ice. "We're tight."

"But?" She said it in a teasing tone.

He nodded. *That's fair.* "I don't have a lot of complaints about him."

"Even though he wasn't around a lot?"

"You know, I always understood that my dad was important. And I don't mean because he's a famous actor. It's the way people look at him. Everyone lights up. They genuinely like my dad. He's never caught in a scandal because he leads a clean life. He's respectful to everyone, and this thing he does? This movie franchise? It employs a shit ton of people and makes audiences around the world happy."

"But what about you?" It made her heart hurt to think he justified his father's absence by saying he made *other* people happy. Who made Cole happy? "Didn't it suck to not have a parent around?"

"It did, but keep in mind, he was always in touch with me. He called or texted every day... He came home every chance he could, even if it was only for a weekend."

It seemed he'd just accepted that he wasn't worth more from a parent than *staying in touch.* "Do you mind if I ask about your mom? I've never heard anyone mention her."

"There's nothing to say, really. They met in a pub during the filming of the first movie. They had one night together, and he never saw her again."

"Uh, I think you're missing a few steps there. If he never saw her again, how did you wind up in his care?"

He grinned. "Oh, that little detail? She was a local girl, married. She was just having fun with the American actor..."

"Trevor Montgomery was her hall pass?"

"It's only a hall pass if your spouse is in on it. In this case, she wound up pregnant and tried to pass me off as her husband's. I was two when she died, and the guy had a paternity test done. When he found out I wasn't his, he started asking around. Wound up calling the location scout who got a hold of my dad's agent. As soon as he got the results of a paternity test, my dad flew out there to pick me up, and that's that."

"So, with your dad gone so often, you were essentially raised by nannies?"

He gave a slow nod. "Yep."

"Home must've been a lonely place."

"I mean, my nannies were paid well to hang out with me, so I always had someone to play with." And there was that cavalier guy she'd known in high school. Everything was a joke, covering his emotions with jokes and charm.

But she knew him better now. She could picture Cole as a little boy, alone in a mansion, and she ached for him.

I wish I'd been kinder to him. I wish I hadn't rejected him so meanly.

"So, you had decent nannies at least? They were good to you?"

"Mostly."

She didn't like the way his gaze ticked away from her. "What're you not telling me?"

"Nothing. One of them wasn't great, but the others were fine. I was close with the last one."

"Define 'wasn't great.'"

"She didn't hurt me. Nothing like that. She just ignored me. My dad was gone for months at a time. It's not like he came home at the end of the day, and he could see how she'd treated me."

"Cole, what are you saying? Did she not take care of you?"

"No, no. She did. She just couldn't stand to be around

me, so she was always on the phone or watching TV. She liked to hang out in the screening room and watch movies."

"You didn't tell your dad?"

"I honestly didn't know. I was a kid. And not an easy one, at that."

He was only confirming her fears about this meeting tomorrow. It made her sick to think they could drop these girls off with people who seemed good but wound up being neglectful.

"And also, she came from a respected agency in Los Angeles. She had great credentials and references. So, my dad trusted her."

"How did he finally find out?"

"Teacher conference. She mentioned my dirty clothes and hair."

"God, Cole. It literally makes me ragey to think you were neglected."

He gave her an affectionate grin. "You gonna kick her ass?"

"If I'd known you back then, I sure as hell would have. What a horrible person to treat an innocent child like that."

"In any event, after that, my dad put in a nanny cam, caught her fucking off, and hired someone new. He felt like shit about it and was pretty hard on the next couple of nannies, but then we found Miss Mary, and she stuck. She was great."

"Well, that's good. How long did you have the bad one?"

"A couple years." With a thoughtful expression, he gazed at the navy blue comforter. "The truth is, I was always a pain in the ass, always getting into trouble. So, it wasn't entirely her fault. If you knew the things I'd done…"

"Like what?"

"Too many stories. I wouldn't know where to start."

"Start with the first one that comes to mind."

"All right. My buddies and I were into dirt biking. One day, right when it was time for everyone to go home, I came up with the brilliant idea to ride our bikes out of the top floor window of the barn."

"What?"

He gave her a look that said, *See?* "Most of us landed okay in a big mound of hay, but one guy…he broke his arm. So, you can see why she couldn't stand me. I was always doing shit like that. By high school, I was stealing my dad's Piper Cub…" He winced. Looked physically ill. "Well, that's a story for another day." He got up. "I'll see you in the morning."

"Whoa, whoa, whoa. Get back here. What was that?"

But he just kept on going, closing the door behind him.

Well, did she go after him?

Or did she leave him alone?

Chapter Twelve

COLE PLUMMETED.

It was a heady experience, the weightlessness, the clusters of lights and velvet mountains capped with glittering white snow. One by one, his friends' parachutes deployed, the familiar whomp triggering the anticipation of a landing. No matter how many times they BASE jumped, they never knew what forces of nature might fuck them up.

First, Jaime landed, the chute dragging him into a jog. Then, Declan. Then, Cole. Elation soared through him. Laughing uncontrollably, he high-fived his buddies, but the look on Declan's face jerked the joy right out of him. He whipped around to see Booker coming in too fast. Way too fucking fast.

Fuck, fuck, fuck.

Cole shouted, but no sound came out of his mouth. He tried again and again, certain if only his friend could hear him, he could stop the inevitable impact. He screamed, clawing at his throat to release the warning. Instead, he watched in horror as his friend hit the ground.

His legs crumpled beneath him.

In a cold sweat, Cole tried to run, but his legs were tangled in the parachute. *Fuck. Fuck.* He frantically kicked—

Miraculously, he was freed. The relief was so intense that he jerked up—only to find Hailey kneeling on the mattress, her cool hand on his damp forehead. Instantly, he calmed.

"You all right?" Her tone was gentle, but she had panic in her eyes.

Heart thundering, he dropped his head to the pillow. The tightness in his chest made it hard to take a full breath, but damn, was he glad to see her. "Sorry." He choked on the last syllable.

She took his shaky hand firmly in hers and snuggled up against him. "It's all right." She smelled like coconut, her skin soft, her voice soothing. Gently, she ran her fingertips along his bare arm. "I got you. You're all right."

Once the worst of it passed, he let out a breath before covering his eyes with a hand. "Shit. I woke you up. You think I freaked out the girls?"

"You weren't that loud, and I was awake." With her fingertips, she scraped the hair off his forehead. "You want to talk about it?"

"No." Not when he was still brushing off the shadows. He rolled to see her. "What're you doing up so late?"

"Couldn't sleep."

"You worried about tomorrow?"

"So worried. But it's not just that. I have so much on my mind."

"Okay, let's talk about it. A sports therapist once gave me the best advice. All those worries and fears and doubts that keep rolling through your mind? Get them out of your body. Either write them down in a journal or confide in someone. Just get them out."

"You journal?"

"No."

"Who do you talk to?"

"Mostly myself."

She nudged him. "That's the same thing as letting them roll through your mind, you knucklehead."

He laughed, and it felt good. "It's different for me. I've got years of practice taking care of myself."

Cole. She rested her cheek on his shoulder. "Well, now, you have me."

Oh, he liked that. Liked how close they'd become. Only a few days ago, she'd thought the worst of him, and now, she was comfortable enough to get in bed and cozy up to him. He reached for her hand. It was a light touch, and he wanted so much more. But she didn't, so he restrained himself.

Besides, what more could he want than to have Hailey in bed with him holding his hand?

It was perfect.

"Don't you think we should talk the nightmare out of your body?" She'd shattered the mood. When he didn't respond, she reached across his chest to hug him. Her breasts pressed against his biceps, and he found that to be the sweetest, simplest gesture of intimacy and trust he'd ever experienced. "Is this the first time it's happened?"

"No."

"Is it the same one every time?" She was determined to get it out of him.

"No."

"Is it about the girls?"

"No."

"If you really want me to drop it, I will. I'll go back to bed and leave you alone. But you just told me how important it is to get things out of your body. So, I'll ask you one more time to tell me about the nightmare."

Put it this way. He wanted her to leave far less than he wanted to talk about that night. And he really, really didn't want to talk about it. Particularly with her. She'd go back to thinking the worst of him.

But if he had a chance in hell with her, he had to share even the parts of him he couldn't stand. And so, he rolled onto his back and stared at a ceiling awash in milky moonlight. "It's about the night I ruined my best friend's life."

"Wait, is this a dream? Or did this actually happen?"

"It happened."

"Okay." The word came out in a whisper as she clasped their fingers together. "I'm listening."

"So, you know I was going to play for the Renegades, and Booker was headed to LA?"

"I remember."

"Declan wanted a college education, so he was going to play for Michigan, and Jaime was going to Canada to play in the junior league for two years. Well, the night before we were all going our separate ways, Jaime found out his parents had to sell the ranch. It'd been in the family for generations, and he made the choice to give up hockey and stay home and help them out. He was pretty shaken up by it, so he asked us to come over for one last bonfire." Anxiety kicked up, and his hands went clammy. He pulled away.

But she wouldn't let him. She grabbed him and rested their joined hands over her heart. "Go on."

"That's all it was supposed to be. A bonfire at Jaime's.

Then, I show up with the keys to my dad's Piper Cub." If he had one shot to go back in time and right a wrong, it would be that night. "No one but Jaime wanted to go. The other guys were packed and ready to get up early to catch their flights. But I pushed them into it. My dad's got a cabin at the top of a cliff that overlooks all of Jackson County." He swallowed, his throat tightening the closer he got to the bad part. "We hung out, we drank—typical stuff. And then, Jaime wanted to jump."

"Jump?"

"BASE jump."

"Oh, right. Okay. I remember you guys did crazy things like that."

"I was down for it, but Declan and Booker didn't want to. And they were right, of course. Everything would've been fine if we'd just stayed at the ranch, had the bonfire—"

"Tell me the story without beating yourself up. Just get it out of your body."

"It will never be out of me. I ruined someone's life."

She squeezed his hand, a signal for him to stay on track.

He'd try, but it wasn't easy. "Declan and Booker had no choice but to jump—how else would they get down the mountain? They couldn't fly my dad's plane. Jaime landed first, then Declan, then me. All of us had perfect jumps. Couldn't have gone better. It was such a high, like the perfect way to say goodbye. Our last hurrah." Blood pounded in his ears, and his pulse beat like he'd just been chased down a dark alley.

"And then?" Her voice in the dark room was like a caress to his guilt-laden mind.

"And then we turned to watch Booker's landing, and

we could tell right away it was going to be bad. There's this thing called turbulence. It happens just above the ground. You can't see it, and you can't anticipate it."

"And it got Booker."

His eyes closed as he saw it all over again, his friend's body rushing to the ground. And the moment he hit, Cole flinched.

Hailey squeezed his hand. "It's not your fault."

"It is. If I'd let it just be a bonfire—"

"Nope. You have no control over the forces of nature. But go on. Tell me the rest."

"That's it. That's the story. He hit the ground hard. His legs…" He ran out of air.

"He broke them?"

"Worse." So much worse. "He was in physical therapy for a year. I ended his hockey career. If I'd just let it be a bonfire, if I hadn't made them fly up to the cabin—"

"Cole, honey. You have to stop doing this to yourself. You're caught in an endless loop of what-ifs, and no good will ever come of it. It won't change what happened. It won't fix it. You have to let it go. It's literally toxic to your well-being."

"Fuck my well-being. I ruined my best friend's life."

"What happened to him? After rehab?"

"He went to Yale. Got an MBA. He's a sports agent now."

"Oh, wow. I didn't realize he'd fallen so low. Yep, you're a monster all right."

He cut her a look.

"Let me ask you something. You truly believe you ruined this man's life, right?"

He kept watching her, wondering where she was going with this.

"Okay, so if that's a fact, then tell me what your self-loathing will do for him? Does it give him satisfaction to know you're drowning in guilt and regret? How does it make up for the life you supposedly stole from him?"

"I don't know. We haven't really talked since the jump."

"You've got to be kidding me. You have no idea if he even blames you?"

"Of course he blames me. But no. His parents moved back east, and we didn't talk to him until last summer."

"Are you saying you didn't visit him in the hospital?"

"We tried. Believe me, we did everything we could to see him, but his parents kept us out. And then they moved without telling anyone."

"That's awful. I can't believe they did that."

"You can forgive me but not them? He nearly died. Of course, they didn't want me around their son."

"And *this* is why I don't forgive them. Look at you. Look how you're suffering. They should've let you see that he was okay. They should've let you *apologize*. They did a terrible thing not letting you have some kind of closure." She lifted her head to look him in the eyes. "I think you need to see him. Talk to him."

"I did. Last summer, our coach passed away and left us his hockey team. We all came to the funeral, and then afterward, we met at Jaime's. The minute the subject came up, Booker left. Didn't tell us he was leaving, didn't say goodbye. He just slipped out the door and drove off. So, yeah. He blames me. And I get it. Because of me, he endured the worst pain imaginable, and he lost his shot to play hockey."

"Meanwhile, you're the Phenom."

Guilt engulfed him. Swallowed him whole. He closed his eyes to fully sink into it.

"Ah, there you go." Her tone held the lightness of a revelation. "You're living his life."

Yes. The life he would've had.

"The thing is, you don't know if he'd have been a great player. Maybe he wouldn't have cut it at the professional level. How many kids with great potential flame out? How many get injured? You have no idea how things would've worked out for him."

"The only thing I care about is that, once again, I took things too far, and Booker paid the price."

"Okay, you've got a God complex. Got it."

"What does that mean?"

"You're responsible for the velocity of wind, the timing of it? For how he landed. That's some supernatural powers you got there."

"No, I'm responsible for getting him out of bed."

"I thought Jaime got everyone out of bed? And wasn't it Jaime's idea to jump? Okay, forget it. Let's stop. I'm never going to see it the way you do, and I doubt anyone else will. But it seems you're getting something out of staying in that endless loop, so there's no point in talking about it anymore."

No, there really wasn't.

"But let me say one last thing, okay? Do with it what you will. The guilt, the shame, all the negative stuff won't give Booker back the life he could've had. There's nothing positive or constructive that'll come out of it. So, maybe instead of giving it power over you, take action."

"What does that mean?"

"Well, what can you do to make it right?"

"I have no idea."

"You took away Booker's chance to play hockey. Can you create a scholarship for kids who want to play hockey but can't? Can you support a rehab facility? I don't have the answer, but I would love to see you get out of the loop and turn all that energy into something positive."

"You're pretty smart, you know that?"

"Yeah." She nestled in against him, the coconut scent of her shampoo filling his senses. "I know."

"You going to sleep here?" His voice sounded rough. Mostly because he wanted her to stay but didn't think she would.

"Too tired to get up." She snuggled more deeply and let out a sigh. "Wrestling your demons really took it out of me."

He grinned. "What about the girls?"

"They've got their own beds."

"Okay, smart-ass. What if they walk in here and find us in bed together?"

She stilled. "You want me to leave?"

"I want you to stay." He tightened his hold. The scent of her hair, the heat of her body sent him back to their kiss. The slick heat of her mouth, the tangle of tongues, and clutch of her hands.

Oh, shit. Blood rushed to his cock.

No, no, no. That's not what she's here for.

She'd come to see if he was all right. *She wants to sleep.*

Then again, her lips parted, softened, and her eyes went sultry.

Did she *want* him to kiss her? "Hailey?"

Her hand came up, and she tenderly brushed his hair back from his face.

"Sometimes, I look at you, and I think I'm having a heart attack."

"That doesn't sound flattering. What does that even mean?

"You have to know this is different for me. I was crazy about you back then, and I never stopped thinking about you. It's been years of kicking myself for blowing it. So now, to be with you…for you to want me…."

She gave him a soft smile.

"It hurts." He caught her wrist and brought her palm flat to his heart. "Do you feel that?"

Though she couldn't miss the thundering of his heart, she didn't answer.

"That's how happy I am. How scared I'll blow it again. How much it excites me just to have you here in bed with me. Even if you never want more than this, I'm happy."

"I want more, Cole." She lifted up and whispered in his ear, her silky hair brushing across his cheek. "I ache for you."

Fuuck. Rearing up, he toppled her onto her back and claimed that sexy mouth. He breathed in the scent that drove him wild, felt her heart pounding and the press of her hands on his back.

And when he got lost in the taste of her, he was just gone. Gone in the erotic dance of their tongues and the restless shift of her hips. Desire enflamed him, fueled by her breathy moans, and the passion of her kiss. His hand slipped under her thin T-shirt, skimmed her smooth skin, and cupped her bare, plump breast.

Jesus. Sensation exploded in his chest, sending out licks of fire.

She arched into his touch, pressing harder into his palm, and he yanked up her shirt to close his mouth over her nipple. As he licked her into a frenzy, she arched her hips, rocking against his cock, her gasps feeding his need to pleasure her.

He cupped her other breast, his thumb flicking back and forth over the nipple.

"Cole. I can't…I need…"

"Tell me what you need, and it's yours."

She stopped writhing beneath him and gazed into his eyes. After a moment, she broke into a grin. "I believe you."

All at once, he understood. She'd begged her mom to get an apartment, to put food in her belly, to let her stay in one school system—to give her the basics of life—and the woman had never given it to her.

As long as she's mine, she'll never have to beg for anything. Nothing would make him happier than giving her everything she wanted.

And right now, he knew exactly what she needed. Leaving a trail of kisses down her belly, he yanked off her panties and licked into her molten core. Her knees lifted, and her fingers slid into his hair. When his tongue found her hard bud, she cried out, and he circled, moving faster in synch with her hips and in response to the fingers fisting in his hair.

Cupping her ass, he brought her up against his mouth and feasted. The heat and womanly scent of her drove him to palm his hard, aching cock.

"Oh, God. Don't stop…don't…oh, my God." And then her body convulsed while her hands kept him right where she needed him.

As if he'd stop. He loved it. Loved every second of her orgasm.

And when she sighed, when her ass crashed back to the mattress, he stretched out alongside her. She wrapped her arms around his neck and kissed him. "Got a condom?"

Hell, yeah. But something in her tone held him back, and he caught the slightest glimmer of fear in her eyes. He figured he knew what it was. Tomorrow, they might find a forever home for the girls. If so, he'd go to Boston, and she'd head to New York.

He wanted her. Always had, always would. But he couldn't bear to see the regret on her face in the morning. Have her skim past him in the kitchen, avoid looking at him.

"We have a big day tomorrow." He kissed her on the mouth. "Let's go to sleep."

He sensed her reluctance, and he knew how easy it would be to slide into her slick, hot core and pound into her welcoming body until he relieved this unrelenting ache. But he lived by intuition, and he'd listen to it now.

Because tomorrow? All of this might change.

And he'd go back to life without her.

She was holding his hand.

As soon as they'd gotten into his Land Cruiser and buckled up, she'd reached for him like it was the most normal thing in the world.

And let me tell you something. That simple gesture had gotten him all worked up, and he'd had to busy himself with loading directions into his car's navigation system so she wouldn't see how deeply she affected him.

And now, finally, after two and a half hours, they'd reached their destination.

"Well, this looks promising." Hailey watched out the window. "Every yard looks neat and well-kept." The grip of her hand countered the brightness of her tone. She glanced down at her phone. "It's 2165." And then, she looked at the curb. "This one's 2153. So, it's on the right side of the street. A few more down."

It was a classic suburban neighborhood with one-story houses, multiple cars in each driveway, and small patches of lawn covered in snow.

Once they found the correct address, he eased to the curb. He cut the engine, but neither made a move to get out of the car.

"Do you think he got the numbers wrong? Should we text him?" On the entire block, only this house had stained vinyl siding, a small porch crammed with dirty toys, and a tarp covering a quarter of the roof.

"I can ask, but I'm pretty sure it's right."

She looked at him. "Is it wrong that I want to tell you to floor it? Get me out of here?"

"It's not wrong to tell me, but we have nothing to lose by meeting them. We don't have to hand our girls over to anyone we're not comfortable with. We've only been looking a week."

"Yeah, but the investigator said he didn't have anyone else."

"He'll keep looking. Maybe he'll have luck with Darren's biological parents."

"But those records are sealed."

"He's got connections. This is what he does for a living, and he's very good at it."

"Okay." Her gaze wandered out the window again. "One step at a time."

He reached for her hand, kissed her palm, and said, "I promise you this. Unless we find Mary fucking Poppins behind that door, we're getting back in the car, and I'm flooring it."

Emotion wrenched her features. "I know it's crazy. I haven't known them that long, but..." And then, she whispered, "I love them."

She was killing him. "I care about them, too." *And I'm crazy, head over heels for you.* "Come on. Let's go meet Lindsay's mom's second cousin."

Stepping out of the car, he swung around to her side and met her on the sidewalk. "Okay, let's do this."

No one had shoveled the walkway, so their boots crunched on the snow. Midmorning, the sky was overcast, only adding to the darkness of their moods.

"They're the only house on the block that doesn't have Christmas decorations."

"That's not a mark against them." Her step faltered on the uneven terrain, and he reached for her elbow. "We don't know what holidays they celebrate."

"I know. It was just an observation."

"No, you're determined to give the girls a blow-out Christmas."

Finally, she smiled. "I am."

After ringing the bell, they huddled together against the cold. A baby cried, children shouted, and footsteps pounded. "Knock it off," someone snapped. "I gotta get the door."

It swung open. A woman with dark circles under her eyes and a messy bun stood before them, a baby on her hip. "Hey. You're Ilona's people?"

"Yes, we knew her daughter. I'm Hailey, and this is Cole."

"Are you freaking kidding me right now? You're Cole Montgomery. Holy—" The woman hitched the baby higher, a soggy diaper making a squelching sound. "Hey, I'm Tina."

"And you're Ilona's cousin, right?" Hailey asked.

"I mean, yeah, but we didn't know her at all." She looked at Cole. "Shouldn't you be in Boston right now? How did you know Ilona's kid?"

"We all went to high school together." He wasn't going to get into a conversation about hockey. "Anyhow, we didn't know their extended family, so we hired an investigator to let everyone know of Lindsay's passing."

"That's Ilona's daughter," Hailey said.

"Why? Is there an inheritance or something?" She peered behind them. "Looks like it's starting to snow. Come on in." The woman led them into the house, the floor littered with toys. "Go on and sit down." She gestured to a couch. "I'll just get this one a bottle."

Two older kids raced into the room, shooting each other with foam darts. A toddler held on to the coffee table to lift herself. Drool spilled out of her mouth as she gave them a toothless grin.

"Hi, cutie," Hailey said.

Tina came back, setting the baby in a mesh port-a-crib. He sat up, sucking on a bottle. "Okay, so you were talking about an inheritance?"

"Actually, no," Hailey said. "We weren't. We just wanted to let you know she and her husband passed away two weeks ago. I don't really know about their net worth. They were young and didn't have much."

"They had kids?"

Hailey's gaze shot to him. He'd already put the decision in her hands, so he gave her a moment. If she needed him to answer, he was ready.

But then, she said, "Yes. Two girls."

"Oh." The woman perked up. "How old?"

"Three and six."

"Okay, because the twins are nine." She pointed to the older two, still shooting darts at each other. "I've got another set of twins, but they're with their dad right now." She gestured toward the toddler. "This one's fourteen months, and that one—" She tipped her chin to the baby. "He's eleven months. I foster those two, but if there's some money coming with the girls, I can stop doing that." She trained her gaze on Cole. "It's expensive to raise kids." The toddler lost her hold and fell with a whump onto her butt. "But they're family, so I could do it with some help."

"Looks like you've got your hands full already." Hailey sounded tart, and he suspected she was thinking the same thing as him. That Tina wanted money from a hockey player.

"No, I can do it. If I get rid of these two little ones, I can put the girls in with the twins. The other set's girls, of course. I wouldn't put them with the boys. It'll be tight." She grew more animated. "If you want what's best for them, you should probably get us a bigger house. That way the girls can have their own room."

"I never said we were looking for a home for the girls." Hailey got up. "We're the guardians. We just thought you should know Lindsay passed away."

"You mind signing an autograph for me?" Tina didn't wait for an answer. She dashed into the kitchen and came back out with a pen and paper. As he signed, she said, "The good thing about me taking them is I've got lots of family in the area. My mom lives one town over, and I've got cousins everywhere."

Hailey was already heading for the door, so that left

him to end the conversation. "You have a great holiday now."

"Stay in touch. Let me know how it's going."

He waved a hand and called, "Will do." When he got into the car, he could feel the charged energy in the air. They didn't speak while he pulled away from the curb, but he knew she was holding it all in.

"Floor it."

He chuckled.

"I'm serious. Get me out of here as fast as you can."

"On it."

She shot him a look. "We're not letting her raise them."

Her determination was such a fucking turn-on. "No."

"She said, 'If I get *rid* of these two.' Can you imagine? Those babies are in her care—she's all they have in the world right now. And she's willing to 'get rid of them' for a big pay day from a Boston Brawler." With every sentence, she grew more agitated. "She didn't even look when the little one fell. Not one muscle in her body twitched to make sure that baby didn't get hurt."

"I saw."

She stared out the window, unseeing. As much as he wanted a window into her mind, he gave her space and focused on getting them to the highway

"All this time, I believed we'd find the right family for them. Tina made me realize we might not. And if we don't, then I have to adopt them. God, that's terrifying."

"Understandably. But again, we're only one week into this search. It's possible the PI will find the biological parents. They might have a big, extended family who'd take the girls in. There might even be a couple in Calamity who can't have kids of their own. We just don't know."

"Intellectually, I know you're right, but emotionally, I'm freaking out because this is the first time I've considered the fact that we might not find anyone. And that opens up a million questions. Where will I raise them? What if Abbott's goes under, and I'm unemployed? I'd want to keep them in Calamity, but what kind of job could I get there?"

"I know you don't like when I throw money at the situation, but I'll be helping you with all of it. I can buy you a house in New York or Calamity or wherever you find your next job. I can pay for a nanny so you can work and not worry about bills."

"The first time you said those things, I was so pissed at you. But now I totally get it. It eases my mind to know we can provide for them. Thank you." But the skin around her eyes still tightened in worry. "I'm just a mess right now. My mind is all over the place."

"Sounds like you need to get it out of your body." He gave her a teasing grin, but he reinforced his seriousness by putting his hand over hers and uncurling her fingers. "Go on. Give it all to me."

"God, Cole. Does anyone else get to see this side of you?"

"I don't care about anyone the way I care about you, so I'm guessing no."

She kissed his cheek, lingering a moment. "You always smell so good."

"Hailey. I have to drive for two and a half hours. More talking, less distracting." He turned on his indicator and veered into the far left lane to get on the freeway. They'd agreed to make the five-hour round-trip journey in one day instead of spending the night. Now that they had their routine down, they wanted to put the girls to bed themselves. Cole liked that private time with Paisley.

"You know what's crazy?"

"What?" He loved talking to her. Couldn't wait to hear what she had to say.

"One week ago, my life was about going to work, sewing robes, and selling trendy clothes in a SoHo boutique. Now? I can't wait to get home to those girls."

He couldn't believe it, but he felt the same way.

Now that this "family" was scratched off the list, he could focus on the next step: giving the girls the best Christmas of their lives.

Chapter Thirteen

HAILEY HAD NEVER BEEN IN LOVE. SURE, SHE'D dated, but she'd never felt that spark, that attraction…that inability to keep her hands to herself.

She felt all of it with Cole. The other morning, she'd awakened with his arm wrapped snuggly around her waist, and her leg hitched over his thigh. She'd never felt safer or more cared for. Her whole life, she'd had to look out for herself. She'd never realized how scared and alone she'd felt until she'd found a partner in Cole.

Tonight, she was alone in her bed while he took care of Paisley. She wouldn't intrude on their time together, but would he come to her later? Should she go to him? It wasn't like they were a couple. They weren't having sex, so there wasn't an expectation.

She wanted to. She just didn't want a fling with a guy she cared about so much.

But maybe with the way she craved him, she wouldn't regret anything they did together. The way he'd touched her—so lustfully—and licked her into orgasm…*God*. She couldn't stop thinking about his tongue, his hands, the way he'd driven her into a frenzy. She'd been so desperate for relief that when she'd gotten it, she'd seen stars. *That* had never happened before.

And the craziest thing? None of the issues that usually troubled her seemed to matter. Like tonight, when she'd gotten home, she'd checked her email. Her boss said they'd announce their decision about the future of Abbott's of London by January tenth.

Normally, she'd be freaking out, making to-do lists, and polishing her résumé. But every time she forced herself to think about it, her mind wandered to Cole.

His kindness, his confidence…the way he handled every situation without losing his cool. And he was just so handsome, so…muscular. Which was funny because she'd never been attracted to a man's physique before. In fact, she'd mostly dated artsy types. A graphic designer, a sculptor… She liked good conversations, shared interests. A six-pack didn't make her top ten list of what she found attractive in a man.

So, why did she want to lick Cole's? How come every time he flexed his biceps, she watched, mesmerized, as they bulged? Maybe it was the physical representation of his inner strength, because nothing turned her on more than a man in control. A man who took charge.

Restless, aching, and hot, she flung herself onto her back. What was he doing now? Brushing Paisley's wet hair? She'd love to watch his big hockey hands manage a French braid, but no. That was their special time.

In high school, she'd thought she was a conquest. Now, though, she could look back and see him through a different lens. She remembered the way he always watched her, the nervous drumming of his fingers and jackhammering of his leg.

She reached for her phone and sent a text.

Hailey: Are you up?

Cole: Yeah. Just got Paisley to bed. She's out like a light.

She wanted to keep him with her, but she didn't know what to say. *Want to make out?*

Hailey: What should we do with the girls tomorrow?

Cole: Wild Wolff Village, for sure. They can skate, get cocoa, a crepe… They'll love it.

Hailey: But your knee?

Cole: Got to keep moving it. I start skating soon, anyhow.

What else could she say?

Hailey: They didn't have many toys at their house. I'm wondering if that was their philosophy or if they just couldn't afford much.

Cole: I'm going with philosophy. Don't kids get presents from birthday parties?

Hailey: Good point.

Cole: Can't sleep?

Hailey: Just a lot on my mind.

Cole: Meet me in the hallway.

Joy flared in her chest, and she tried so hard to suppress it. But she couldn't. As she found her bra and shorts and slid her feet into flip-flops, she was as giddy as a schoolgirl. Or maybe a puppy considering how she bounded over to him when she found him in the hallway.

She threw herself into his arms and hugged him harder than the situation called for. Well, the only situation that called for this kind of embrace came with near-death incidents like car accidents or house fires.

"You should always greet me like this." His hand cupped the back of her head. "Let's make it a thing."

"I'm just so glad to see you."

"We live together. We see each other every day. And didn't I just see you forty-five minutes ago?"

She pulled back and smiled up at him. "Apparently, that's too long."

He did such a good job of hiding his shadows that she hadn't noticed them until right then, when sunshine speared through the crevices and chased them away.

Note to self: share your feelings with him more often.

He worked so hard to make others happy, but who did that for him? Other than his dad, he hadn't mentioned anyone he was close with. So maybe because he gave so much, people were in the habit of wanting something from him instead of just liking him the way she did.

Because he didn't show himself to anyone other than her.

"Come on." He grabbed her hand and led her to a panel in the wall. When he pressed it, it opened.

"What in the world?" She followed him inside to find a winding staircase. "It's so dark. Is there a light switch?"

"You won't want one."

The higher they climbed, the more starlight illuminated the darkness.

And then they reached the top.

Oh, my God. In the center of the domed, glass room was an enormous telescope. "Is this...an observatory?" Against the wall sat an oversize couch, two club chairs, and a table. The other wall had a galley kitchen.

A whirring sound had her tipping her head back to watch the curved ceiling split open, wide enough to fit the telescope.

"This is unbelievable." A billion stars sparkled like diamonds, and before she could even notice the icy cold air pouring in, a blanket settled around her shoulders. "You think of everything."

"This room is what sold me on the house."

"Really? And here I thought it was the wrapping room. Or at least the bowling alley."

He chuckled. "Nothing about it sucks, but this room sealed the deal."

"It's probably better in summer."

"Probably, but we're here now." He adjusted the telescope for her, hitting buttons and turning levers.

She watched him for a moment, his bottom tight and round in those pajama bottoms, his broad shoulders stretching the Henley T-shirt across his back. "Thank you for showing me this."

"Sure." He stepped aside. "Okay, now take a look." When she didn't move, didn't speak, just stared at him, he said, "You're not looking."

"I'm looking all right. I'm looking at you." She pressed

her palm flat to his chest, feeling the rapid beat of his heart. "Because I'm wildly, thoroughly, head over heels crazy about you. Not what you have or what you can do for me but *you*."

She'd rendered him speechless.

Good. She had more to say. "Senior year, I was the new kid yet again, so I showed up with a chip on my shoulder, and I made sure to push everyone but Lindsay away. You did something amazing for me—you took me to a restaurant on the side of a mountain overlooking a waterfall—and I barely spoke to you. That was my issue, Cole. Not yours."

"I took it too far—"

She pressed her fingers over his lips and shook his head. She wasn't done. "And even now, instead of being with you the way I want—I need—I've let fear hold me back. I've told myself I need an emotional connection when we've had one all along. In all my life, you're the one person I can count on. And I don't mean for you to be on time or to help around the house. I mean I can count on your feelings for me. They've been constant since I've known you." She reached for him, desperate to be in his arms.

But his arms straightened, holding her at a distance. "No."

What? Had she read this all wrong?

"The more I know you, the more I like you, and every damn second I spend with you makes me want you more. So, no. My feelings have not remained constant. They've grown. They continue to grow." His chest rose and fell, and his cheeks darkened. "I've only ever wanted you, and *that's* the only thing that will never change."

She believed him, and it gave her roots and wings—

neither of which she'd ever had. "Close the skylight, Cole." Her quest for safety, security, had kept her in a tiny little box.

No more of that.

"You don't want to see the stars?"

"The only stars I want to see are the ones you make with your tongue."

Without even looking, he smacked the button on the wall. And then he was on her. He grabbed her ass, lifted her, and brought her to the roomy, leather couch. Setting her down gently, he held her cheeks and kissed her reverently, sweetly, drugging her with his devotion.

She needed more of him, all of him, so she wrapped her arms around his back and pulled him down so she could feel his chest against hers. The kiss deepened, turned voracious, until she was yanking up his shirt. Reluctantly, he tore his mouth away to get up. He peeled the shirt off, shrugged off his pajama pants, and said, "Get naked. Want all of you. Every fucking inch."

She'd never wanted anything more. She'd never trusted anyone more. Her shorts, shirt, and bra went flying, and she kicked off her flip-flops. The moment she lay back down, he straddled her. He kissed her with his heart, his soul, with the same urgency and desire that made her blood burn.

He kissed her cheek, her chin, the column of her neck. His hot mouth slid to her collarbone, and then he cupped her breasts, drew them together, and jiggled them. "You're so fucking hot." His hot mouth sucked her nipple, his tongue swirling and flicking.

She writhed beneath him, drawing him closer, needing more, more, more. More of his wet mouth. He watched her, the hunger in his eyes only ramping up her need.

"So sexy."

She couldn't stand it. "Now, Cole." She was going out of her mind, the pulse between her legs nearly painful. "I need you inside me. I can't take it anymore."

With a groan, he shifted lower, parting her thighs, and licking a fiery path between her legs.

"*Cole.*" Her hips twisted, and he clamped his hands on them, holding her in place.

He licked her clit relentlessly, desire bursting into a flash fire. Her fingers fisted in his hair, her hips slammed against his mouth, and she couldn't help the sounds that came out of her—desperate, urgent—and right when she thought she would never break, she would be forever caught in this excruciating sexual tension—

Stars exploded behind her eyes, and her body went spiraling through a galaxy of brilliant white lights. She soared into a weightless space of pure euphoria.

She only came back into her body when she felt the head of his cock nudging at her opening. Planting her feet on the cool leather, she hitched up her hips, desperate to be filled by him.

But he stopped. "Fuck." His forehead dropped to her shoulder. "I don't have a condom."

No way in hell could they stop now. Not when she was this close to experiencing the kind of fullness and possession she'd longed for but never had. "I haven't been with anybody in two years. And I'm on birth control."

His head popped up, his thumbs stroking the hair out of her eyes. "You sure? Because I got tested right before the season started and haven't been with anyone."

Affection flooded her. "I wish the world could see you the way I do. They think you're some slick playboy, but really, you're just nice to everyone and out there having a good time."

"Mostly, I think I was waiting for you."

"You had no idea if you'd ever see me again."

"I was waiting for it to feel the way I felt about you. It's never happened since."

"Cole."

He claimed her mouth, kissing her with such devotion, as if he needed to reinforce his words. "And now I know, it never will. Because it's you. Only you." And then, he watched her expression as he slowly pushed inside.

He lit her up, bringing her to a level of pleasure she'd never experienced. It was more than the way he filled her. It was the heat in those blue eyes, the brush of his dark hair on her skin, the grip of those big hands, and the snap of his hips that sent a zing of erotic sensation through her entire body.

"I'm not going to last." He tucked his face into her neck and drove into her. Harder, faster, deeper.

His scent filled her, his urgency thrilled her, and when he reached between them to stroke her clit, she got swept under. Crying out, she met his thrusts, their bodies slapping together, creating a heat and friction that threatened to burn down the world.

"Oh, God. Oh…Cole." Electric heat burned through her. The tension was so exquisite, so intense, she knew it would overpower it.

And then it hit. Her climax had her catapulting out of her body. She went freefalling through a bliss so perfect, she felt free for the first time in her life.

When she opened her eyes, she found him watching her intently. "Fucking beautiful." And then tension gripped his features. "Gonna come." His voice came out a growl in her ear. "Gonna come so fucking hard." With his hands on her hips, he held her in place, as he drilled into her in short, powerful pumps.

When he was spent, he fell on top of her. He was about to roll to her side, but she held him right where he was. "Don't go." She said it in a panic. "Just hold me."

She needed his weight. Proof that he was real. That *they* were real.

That she could count on him.

She'd never had that before.

Please don't let me down.

———

Cole stopped the car in the middle of the street to watch the girls' expressions in the rearview mirror. He'd just driven through the arched stone entrance, rounded the bend in the road, and then Wild Wolff Village had appeared in all its Christmas glory.

They gawked from their car seats.

Strings of white lights glittered on limbs heavy with snow, festive garlands wound around the clock tower in the center of the square, and the charming European-style stone buildings were all lit up.

As a horse-drawn sled clopped past them in the bike lane, Paisley nearly went apoplectic with excitement. "Can we ride one of those?"

"Absolutely." Hailey twisted around. "We're going to skate and drink hot cocoa—"

"And sit on Santa's lap?" The little girl's legs kicked the back of Cole's seat.

"Yes, sweetie. That's why we're here. It's time to tell

Santa what you'd like for Christmas." A wrought iron streetlamp cast a golden glow across Hailey's features. "This place is magic."

"I guess you never came here?" Since waking up, they'd been so consumed with kids, they hadn't had a chance to talk about the next before. Had it been okay for her? Were they together now? Did she think it was a one-time thing?

It wasn't for him, and he needed her to know that.

"I came here once, but it wasn't the kind of place Lindsay's family went."

"Well, you'll get the full treatment tonight." The car behind him tapped his horn, and Cole accelerated. He found a parking spot behind the lodge, and then the four of them held hands as they waited for the trolley.

With its arrival, it clanged and clacked on its tracks, and Evvie stomped her little boots in anticipation. "I gon ride dis?" Her smile was infectious, and he and Hailey shared a grin.

"Yep. We're riding the trolley."

They found four seats together, but Evvie still climbed onto his lap. She sang along to the Christmas carol playing through the speakers, and he held back his laughter because she didn't know a single word.

"So, girls, what're we doing first?" Hailey asked. "Ice skating, Santa, or hot cocoa?"

"Skating," Paisley said.

"You got it." When the rink came into sight, she reached for the bell cord, but Paisley wanted to pull it.

Ding ding. The little girl clapped her hands in delight at the sound, making Cole wonder if he'd ever felt so much happiness from life's simple pleasures. He was sure he hadn't. Once the trolley stopped, he lifted Evvie. "All right, here we are." And then the four of them headed over to the skate rental booth.

As they sat on a bench to tie their laces, Hailey asked, "How's your knee? Is it too soon to do this?"

"Timing couldn't be better. I get on the ice tomorrow anyhow." He'd called the training center to set up a time to get in the gym. It would take a few days because his team's trainer had to work with them.

As soon as he'd tied Evvie in snugly, he held her chin in his hand. "Are you ready to skate?"

She nodded solemnly like she was being charged with state secrets.

"If only she understood the top scorer in the league was the one teaching her how." Hailey grinned.

Automatically, he glanced around to make sure no one had heard her. He was here for the girls and didn't want to draw attention to himself, but fortunately, everyone was caught up in the magic of Christmas and lost in their own little worlds. "Let's do this." Holding hands, they made their way to the ice, the girls wobbling on their blades. Both were anxious but giddy with excitement.

The rink was packed with kids and teenagers as cocky as he used to be, gliding in and out of the clusters of people, so the four of them stood watching for a minute until the girls were ready to give it a go.

With Evvie between his legs, his hands under her arms, they made it about a quarter of the way around the rink before she wanted to be picked up. She seemed off tonight, so he settled her on his hip and leaned against the railing. "What do you want to do?"

"Skate, pease." She rocked her hips like she was urging a horse to giddy up.

"You got it." He skated slowly so Evvie could take in

the costumed ice dancers threading through the crowds. They were dressed as elves, and the little girl seemed to find it mesmerizing.

She had one arm around his neck, her fingers idly playing with his hair. "I hongry."

"I'll bet you are. You barely ate lunch or dinner. What would you like?"

"I want hot dog."

Wild Wolff Village was privately-owned, and it operated like a country club that residents bought into. Home owners had personal concierges, and all the stores and restaurants were upscale. "I don't think they sell hot dogs here, but I know we can get a crepe." She gave him a blank look, and he smiled. "It's like a pancake."

Her eyes went wide. "I want pancakes."

"Then, you'll have them." He waited for the other half of their team to reach them. "Hey, guys. Evvie and I are starving. We're going to get pancakes."

"Pancakes?" Paisley said.

Before he could answer, Evvie's mittened hand cupped his chin and turned him to face her. "With shocklet chips?"

"Pretty sure you can have whatever you want on them."

It took a while to get the skates off and return them to the rental desk, but soon enough, they were at the kiosk, reading the menu to the girls. Paisley chose strawberries and whipped cream, while Evvie got her wish of chocolate chips. Once their orders were ready, they found a bench and sat down.

"This is so pretty." Hailey took in the fairy lights dripping off the quaint buildings and lining the skating rink. At the end of a red carpet, Santa Claus sat on a throne beside a forty-foot-tall Christmas tree. Its limbs were heavy with ornaments and garlands, and wrapped presents sat at its base. "Didn't we go to school with the owners' kids? I have a vague recollection about that."

"We did. Do you remember Rhys Wolff? This property's been in his family for generations. About twenty years ago, it was a dude ranch. When his parents took over, they turned it into a ski resort." He pointed to the fancy hotel. "That's the main lodge." And then he gestured up the cobblestone street. "They lease out all the stores and restaurants, and homeowners have their choice of townhouses, homes, and ranches."

"Why don't you live here?"

"None of these places have wrapping rooms."

She laughed. "You could design one."

"Too much work. I don't give a sh—" He stopped himself from swearing. "I don't care about décor and all that. I bought the house because it came fully loaded."

"Makes sense." She sighed. "This was exactly my fantasy in high school. Holding hands with my jock boyfriend as we skated around the rink, sipping a hot chocolate."

"Hang on. Let me just…" He leaned back on the bench and pretended to pull a sword out of his chest.

"What's that for?" It took her a moment to understand, and then she laughed, patting his chest. "Oh, no. I didn't mean it like that. What you planned for our date was awesome. Honestly, it was beyond anything I could've dreamed up on my own. I just meant it was the kind of thing I'd imagined in my head a million times. It was why I begged my mom to let me stay here."

Too bad he hadn't given her what she'd wanted. "I

don't understand why they didn't let you stay to the end of the year. Kicking you out was pretty harsh."

"Believe me, I know. But they said they were responsible for me, and when I didn't come home until the next day, they'd decided they'd lost their trust in me." She gave an exaggerated sigh. "And to think I got so close to prom before it was all snatched away." At least, she said it with good humor.

"Who would you have gone with?" He helped Evvie cut off a piece of crepe and fed it to her.

"You'll laugh if I tell you."

He couldn't believe it. "It was Brock Dirtbag."

"Nope. It was you."

"Okay, now I know you're lying. You hated me."

"I didn't hate you, but it wasn't about that. I just wanted the four of us to go and have a nice time. I wanted to get ready with Lindsay, come down the stairs and see you waiting for me, take pictures with her parents. I wanted to hang out of the limo's sunroof with a bottle of champagne in one hand." She shook her head. "Stupid, I know. It was every cliché I'd ever seen in a movie or read in a book."

"Okay, good. I feel better, then. You never could've acted out your fantasy."

"No?"

"Nope. Lindsay lived in a one-story house. They didn't have stairs. My conscience is clear."

She nudged him. "Okay, dude. You got me there." She went quiet, resting her head on his shoulder. "Want to know the real reason I wanted it to be you?"

"More than I want to finish this awesome spinach and mushroom crepe."

"Because no one else would've looked at me the way

you did." She went quiet as though imagining it. "When I came down those stairs, I wanted my date's eyes to go wide, I wanted to see that look...the one where the guy's blown away. It's the way you always looked at me. Like I was special. Like I was the most beautiful girl in the world." She set her fork down. "I really like the way you look at me."

I could look at you like that for the rest of my life.

Because nothing had changed. "You *are* the most beautiful woman in the world." No one else made him feel that nervous excitement whenever he laid eyes on her.

Her features softened. It looked like she wasn't sure if she could believe him. He set his plate on the bench. "Hailey—"

Evvie cried out as her cocoa spilled all over her powder blue ski pants.

"Hey, hey, it's okay." Fortunately, the padding kept her leg from scorching, but she still screamed as if Wild Jack was in hot pursuit.

While he used the napkins from the kiosk to sop up the brown liquid, Hailey picked up the cup and tossed it in the garbage.

"It's all right. We'll get you another one." He started to get up, but the three-year-old flung herself at him and just started bawling. Her cheeks were red and shiny with tears, and her sobs ruined him. "What can I do, baby? How can I make it better?"

Paisley patted her sister's back, and Hailey got in line at the kiosk to buy another one.

Evvie's tears soaked through his flannel shirt, burning his neck. Her sorrow slashed through him, and he'd never felt so helpless in his life.

People in line noticed what was going on, so the chef

handed Hailey a cocoa. She hurried back. "Here you go. Brand-new cocoa just for you." She smoothed the hair off Evvie's damp forehead. "Look, it's even got whipped cream on top."

Interest piqued, Evvie sat up for just a moment, but her little features screwed up in sorrow, and then she collapsed against him. He held her, gently rubbing circles on her back and sifting fingers through her hair. Soon, she settled down, just watching the world go by. Every few seconds, she'd shudder, but she seemed okay.

Damn, that had been scary. He hadn't known what to do for her, but somehow, she'd worked through it on her own.

Maybe just being there was enough.

And wasn't that a revelation?

Hailey stroked the little girl's hair. "Do you want your cocoa? Or are you ready to go see Santa?"

"See Sanna."

"You got it." Holding her in his arms, he stood and tossed their plates in the garbage. "Let's go."

Paisley was subdued, so Hailey held her hand. "Do you know what you're going to ask for?"

The older sister shook her head.

"You don't know what you want for Christmas?"

She just shrugged, and Cole couldn't help wondering if the only thing she wanted was for her parents to come back.

That's exactly what he wanted it.

When they reached the line, he couldn't kneel because of his knee, but he leaned over. "You want to go first?"

But Evvie twisted in his arms. "I go." She landed on the red carpet in her bright purple snow boots and jogged right past the other families.

"Wait. Evvie." He started to go after her, but a dad set a hand on his arm and said, "Let her go. We saw her crying."

"Thanks, man. Appreciate it." Still, he didn't think Evvie would be learning the best lesson if he allowed it. He moved to the head of the line and scooped her up. "Hey, we have to wait our turn."

Evvie, her features still red, her cheeks still damp from tears, squirmed in his arms. "Sanna."

"Yep. But there are lots of other kids who want to see him, too."

A woman tapped his shoulder. "It's okay. Please. We've all been there. Let her go."

"That's very nice of you. Thank you." He set her down, but even before the boy currently sitting on Santa's lap got up, Evvie raced over.

"Sanna. I gots to talk to you."

White teeth shone in the mass of white beard and mustache, as the costumed man laughed. "I'm all ears." He settled her on his knee.

Cole stepped off the platform and joined the other half of his team.

"That was rough," Hailey said. "Watching her cry like that."

"Yeah." Seeing any kid cry was tough, but this one? Evvie had a piece of his heart. "I guess it's good, though, you know. Anything that triggers a release of those emotions she can't understand." He watched Santa laughing at something the little girl said. "This is some serious shit, and I'm not equipped for any of it."

"That might be the dumbest thing you've ever said."

"What? Why? The only things I've ever done involve

jumping off cliffs, falling out of the sky, and flying around on ice with blades under my feet."

"Oh, come on. You've researched grief with children, you've joined a parenting forum, you're talking to a therapist...you're doing everything you can for these children. Cole, you're *exactly* what these girls need."

She didn't know what she was saying. "I told you what happened to Booker."

"And I told *you* it wasn't your fault." She turned fully to him. "I'm going to speak for his parents the way they should have done ten years ago. Cole, we were really scared about what happened to our son, but he's okay now, and we're sorry for shutting you out the way we did. You didn't do anything different that night than you and my son did any other time you'd gotten together, but I guess it finally caught up with our boy." She touched his shoulder. "It's okay. We're all okay."

She might not be Booker's parents, but he sure felt the power of forgiveness.

It was good to hear—damn good.

But did she think she could relieve him of his guilt, and then he'd somehow be fit for these girls?

Because it didn't work like that. At some point, he'd take things too far, and someone would get hurt.

He cared too much about them to do that to them.

Later that night, Cole squeezed toothpaste onto Evvie's brush. "You have a good day?"

She nodded.

"Sorry you spilled your cocoa." He tipped her chin and opened his mouth wide to show what he needed her to do. "How about we get another one tomorrow? There's a chocolate shop in town that makes the best you've ever had in your life." *All three years of it.* He marveled at her sweet innocence and, once again, could not *believe* Darren had entrusted him with his beautiful, perfect children. He brought the brush toward her mouth, but she angled away. "Come on. The sooner you're ready for bed, the sooner we can read books."

Her chubby cheeks looked a little more flushed than usual. And—*oh, shit*—was her bottom lip trembling? *Is she going to cry again? What happened?* "Hey, hey, hey. What's going on?"

For a long moment, she stared at her reflection in the mirror. Should he say something? Do something? He could hear Hailey in the other room, and he wanted to call for her.

But he didn't have time, because Evvie looked at him and asked, "Why Mommy not want to come home to me?"

Cole broke. His heart shattered. Tossing the toothbrush onto the counter, he pulled her into his arms and rocked her, one hand on the back of her head. "She does. She wants to be with you. Evvie, sweetie, your mommy loves you more than anything." If he did nothing else in his six weeks with these girls, he had to make them understand. Flipping the lid down on the toilet seat, he sat, holding her shoulders as he looked into her watery eyes. "Listen to me. If your mommy could be here, she would. There's nowhere else in the world she'd rather be than here with you and Paisley. But your mom and dad died in a car accident. They went to heaven, and they can't come back."

A single tear spilled down her cheek. He didn't know if she understood—well, of course she didn't. How did anyone come to grips with death? But he kissed it away, tasting salt, loss, and an all-too familiar loneliness. She fell against him, and he hugged her. Burying his face in her hair, he breathed in her baby shampoo scent and wished he could make the world right for her.

"They love you, sweetheart. Never ever doubt how much they love you. If they could be with you, they would. But they can't, and that's why they sent me and Hailey. We're here to take care of you."

Jesus, if he'd listened to his coach and gone back to Boston, he would've missed this moment. Evvie might've gone to sleep believing her mom didn't want to come home to her.

She'd have more thoughts like this, and who would be here to correct them? It happened in these quiet times and with people she could trust.

He wanted it to be him. It *should* be.

But his team needed him, and he couldn't risk the damage he'd eventually do to them.

And so, his only choice was to find the right forever home.

He just wished it wasn't so damn complicated.

With the girls in bed and Hailey at the Petticoat Rulers Christmas party, Cole went to his room to watch the replay of tonight's game. They'd lost badly, and the guys were pissed off.

He pulled up the group chat of assistant captains.

Cole: Hey fellas. Just like you've been doing all year, I'm going to need you to step up and get us to the playoffs.

I trust you and know the team has the right group to lead them. Come on. Let's fuckin' do this.

He took some time to respond to his demoralized front line, his coach, and his trainer.

And then, he did something unexpected. He texted Jaime.

Cole: You catch tonight's game?

Jaime: Yeah. Tough loss.

Cole: Yep.

And then, he decided to get real with his friend.

Cole: Not sure which is harder. Watching my team lose or these girls slowly understand their parents aren't coming back.

Jaime: Good thing they've got you.

Cole: And Hailey. She's great with them.

Jaime: I meant specifically you. You understand what they're going through.

Cole: I didn't lose my parents.

Jaime: You might not remember, but you did lose your mom, your home, the only life you knew. You moved halfway across the world to live with a stranger. On some level, you get it. Probably on a lot of levels.

The revelation knocked him on his ass. No, he didn't have any memories from back then. He'd only been two and a half. But that was close enough to three to make him understand why he was so damn tied to these girls.

Cole: You may be right about that.

Cole: Sometimes, my friend, you're more than a pretty face.

Jaime: Don't let it get out.

Chapter Fourteen

Hailey stood in front of a bar called Wild Billy's. Every time the door opened, she got hit with music from a live country band, the roar of conversation, and bursts of laughter.

This is definitely more party than meeting.

She should leave. No one wanted to talk business tonight. What was she going to do, ask for advice from some woman riding a mechanical bull?

She'd rather be with Cole anyway. The best part of her day was their time alone together after the girls were in bed. They talked about everything under the sun, all while holding hands and cuddling. It was an intimacy she'd never had before, and she loved it.

She wanted his deep, drugging kisses that rendered her mindless.

She'd spent her entire life on alert—she'd had to as a stranger in someone's apartment. Even with boyfriends, she'd been self-conscious during sex. She was thinking about dinner or a project for work or, most likely, wondering how soon he'd finish. But with Cole, she lost herself completely in his touch, his scent, his passion.

They'd both come here out of a sense of obligation, a duty to their friendships with Darren and Lindsay. But the more time they spent with the girls, the more involved with them they got, the wider their hearts cracked open.

In a weird way, it felt like the family neither of them had had. It felt good to give the girls that.

Even if it wouldn't last.

The door opened yet again, and a group walked out, everyone laughing, happy. She stepped aside, torn between the pull to go back to Cole and the strange compulsion to meet these women.

Because the way Phinny had described this group made it sound like the kind of true friendships she'd always craved. Maybe it was waiting for her on the other side of this door.

"Are you going in?" a man asked, his date's arm hooked through his.

"Good question." As she laughed at her indecision, she stepped aside to let them pass. *I'm here. I might as well give it a try.* Worst-case scenario, she didn't get anything out of the night other than a good time and a few drinks.

She opened the door and let herself in. The enormous space was divided into sections. The first and closest held a packed restaurant. A little farther in was a gleaming wooden dance floor with a stage for live music, and the third area was the bar. On the far end of it, a bunch of people gathered around a mechanical bull. Phinny's text said the Petticoat Rulers had rented a private room, so she gave the hostess the group's name.

As she made her way, she watched the line dancing. She wasn't a huge fan of country music, but this band was fun, and everyone seemed to know the steps. The closer she got to the room, the more her nerves fluttered.

After a lifetime of being the new girl, of trying to fit in, she'd given up. It just hadn't been worth the heartache. Of course, she wasn't here to make friends. She was looking for business advice. Still, she could never quite kill the longing to be included.

But she didn't want to wait around for Abbott's to decide her fate.

Energy rolled in.

I'm a businesswoman.

And I need advice. When she entered the room, she hadn't known what she'd expected to see, but it sure wasn't a bunch of women twerking. She stood and watched them for a moment and realized they were making a reel for social media. A familiar song played on the phone that recorded them doing a synchronized dance.

She also realized they had their backs to her and that she was inadvertently photobombing it. Well, she'd already ruined it. She might as well have some fun. Poking her head in between two of them, she made a face and flailed her arms.

The women startled until they realized who she was, and then they screamed with laughter, which led the others to turn around and see what was going on.

"You must be Hailey." An extremely chic and beautiful woman reached out a hand. "I'm Glori."

"Way to make an entrance." A regal blonde smiled at her. She had an accent Hailey didn't recognize.

"Wait, did she photobomb us?" someone else asked.

The whole group gathered around to view the recording, and they all doubled over with laughter.

"Oh, my God, that was the funniest thing I've ever

seen. We're totally posting that." This woman had a posh British accent and was dressed like a fashion model.

"We've been practicing that stupid routine for two months, but we couldn't stop laughing long enough to record it. And tonight, we finally get our shit together, and then you walk in and just own the room. That was hilarious." She reached out a hand. "Hi, I'm Stella Cavanaugh."

"Hailey Casselton. Thanks so much for letting me barge into your holiday party."

"The more, the merrier." The woman with the British accent gave her a hug. "Hello, darling. It's me, Phinny."

"Oh, I'm so glad to finally meet you."

The happy, joyful woman wrapped an arm around her shoulder. "I want you to meet Knox. She's a wedding gown designer, so she might be in the best position to help you."

After introductions, it didn't take long before this rowdy, fun group of women got serious. As they gathered around a table, one of them—Glori Van Patten, a retired entrepreneur who'd created the Extra bar—got the meeting started. "All right, ladies. Let's fly through the meeting portion, so we can get to the food. I don't know what you guys brought, but it all smells fantastic."

"Oh, you can thank my sister-in-law for the short ribs." Knox had an elegance about her that made her seem like she was from an upper-crust family. She turned to Hailey. "She's the chef at Wally's in Owl Hoot. She's magic with food."

"I'm so glad I didn't eat before I got here." She'd been too busy with the girls.

"Well, before we start," Phinny said. "I just want to say I'm so sorry for your situation."

"Thank you. Did you know the Leesons?" It seemed unlikely, but it was a small town.

"I didn't, but then, I just moved here last summer."

"Those poor girls," Glori said. "My heart breaks for them."

"How's it going?" a lovely brunette asked. "I'm Callie, by the way."

"She runs the Museum of Broken Hearts," Phinny said. "Just in case, you know, she wants to run an exhibition on the history of lingerie."

"I love that idea." Callie reached for her hand. "How are the girls?"

Hailey considered the question. "To be honest, they don't understand what's going on. They were staying with neighbors while their parents went away for the weekend, and now they're staying with us. I think Paisley —the six-year-old—seems to grasp that they're not coming back. But the youngest...Everly..." Tears stung, and she looked down at her clasped hands. "Tonight, she asked Cole why her mommy didn't want to come back to her."

"What?" Phinny pressed a hand over her heart. "That's just awful. How can we help?"

"Cole's hired a private investigator to find some family."

"Oh, I misunderstood," Phinny said. "I thought the two of you were adopting them."

Hope took form—so thick, sharp, and real—it surprised her. Just a few days ago, the prospect of keeping them had been unthinkable. "Ideally, we'll find a good family for them. If not...it'll have to be me. Cole won't be adopting them."

"Well, you don't have to make any decisions right

now," Glori said soothingly. "I have a feeling by the time you do, you'll be ready. That's the way these things go."

"And just know we're here." Stella gestured around the table. "All of us. We're your support army."

"She means that," another woman said. "We really are."

"Thank you." She wanted to believe them. She really did. It was just…she'd been let down so many times.

"Rosie's got kids around that age," Callie said. "And I'm…" Her features softened, and her color rose in her cheeks.

"No." Knox, the most subdued of all of them, jumped out of her chair and threw her arms around the woman. "You're pregnant?"

Callie nodded, and she looked too emotional to speak. All of them started speaking at once.

"Oh, my God, I'm so happy for you."

"That's the best news ever."

"I get to be an auntie."

"You're already an aunt."

"So, I get to be one again."

"You could get pregnant and let *me* be an auntie."

"Okay, okay," Glori said. "Let's start the meeting. We can talk about all the good stuff while we're eating. Hailey, why don't you start? Fill us in on your situation."

"Well, first, let me say thank you for letting me come tonight. I know we're only a week from Christmas, so I really appreciate it. So, anyhow, I work for Abbott's of London."

"Aw, really? I used to get a nightie every single Christmas." This came from the regal blond woman. "I'm from St. Christophe."

Stella shook her head. "Don't let the dirt under her

fingernails fool you. She's not only from there, but she's a princess."

"A princess in Calamity?" Hailey asked.

"She's only a princess in her home country," Callie said. "Here, she's a shit-kicker in pink cowboy boots like the rest of us."

The royal lifted her leg for proof, and everyone laughed.

"All right." Glori nodded to Hailey. "Go on."

"Right. So, they're in financial trouble, and it's looking like they'll either sell the company or close its doors. And I'm freaking out because it's the only job I've had since I graduated FIT." Also, she could work remotely, which was important if she was going to adopt the girls.

"How can we help?" Stella asked.

"I want to pitch a third option." She pulled her sketchbook out of her tote bag. "I'm just one on a team of fashion designers, so I have no pull or influence, but it seems pretty obvious to me that if they just diversified, they could compete in today's market." She opened the book and turned it so the others could see. "I've come up with some ideas."

"These are nice." Knox seemed genuine but not excited.

And she couldn't blame her. It was just more of the same. "As you can see, the only changes I've made are the holiday themes." She tapped the Easter bunnies and carrots and colorful eggs. "But at least it will give people a reason to buy a nightgown other than at Christmas."

"Okay, so they won't vary on the style?" Knox asked. "Can you have sleeveless? Any fabric other than flannel?"

"No. They've been making the same product for a hundred years."

"Well, you wouldn't have to do anything radical," Knox said. "It can be sexy without being revealing just by changing the fabric."

Hailey thought of her robes. She couldn't agree more. "I've also got a menswear line." She skipped ahead a few pages to show them.

"Oh, this is great. I love these pajama pants." Knox reached for the book and began flipping through the pages. "Will they go for it?"

"I have no idea."

When the wedding gown designer came upon the robes, her whole demeanor changed. "What're these?"

"Oh, that's my stuff." Hailey reached for the notebook. "That's not for Abbott's."

"Well, hang on." Knox pulled it back. "These are beautiful. What fabric are you using?"

"It's a bamboo and modal mix. I design the textiles myself."

Callie pointed to the bell sleeves. "This is gorgeous. It's sexy." She smiled at Hailey. "I love it."

"Didn't you say Abbott's would only do flannel nightgowns?" Stella asked.

"Now, this will save their bacon," Knox said.

"Can I buy one?" the princess asked. "I'd probably wear it all day long."

"Brodie wouldn't be able to keep his hands off you," one of the women said.

"What? And somehow that would be different? She could wear coveralls and jackboots, and he'd be all over her."

"Well, wait," Glori said. "Why give them to Abbott's if you can sell these on your own?"

"Okay, hold on." Hailey took the book back. "These

are two separate things. For Abbott's, I only wanted to pitch the holiday and men's lines. The robes are mine. I have a plan to go out on my own after I've saved up enough to support myself for two to three years. Eventually, I'll add sleep sets, nighties, shorts, and tank tops in the same fabric."

"So, you're going to save Abbott's but not yourself?" There was no judgment in Knox's tone.

Embarrassed, Hailey scrambled to defend herself. "I'm not ready for that yet." These women were all entrepreneurs. They were all established. "And now with the girls, my timeline will have to change. But I'm going to do it. I'm going to build up my inventory and save as much money as I can."

The once positive, energetic group became subdued. They were all biting their tongues. And this was exactly why she didn't like joining already established groups. They knew each other, could anticipate each other's responses. They accepted each other. With Hailey, they were judging her, assessing her worth.

Dammit. She slapped the notebook shut. "I'm really only here to get help with my pitch. I get one shot at it, and I can't fail. I need them to stay in business."

"I'm not sure you can single-handedly save Abbott's of London." Glori's voice had gentled. And instead of being patronizing, it felt…like she cared. "That's not to say you shouldn't try. If this is important to you, then we'll help you craft a great pitch. But it's going to take a year to go from concept to product."

"I know. I just thought I'd try."

"But can we please talk about your robes?" Knox asked. "Because they're gorgeous and with sexy, sustainable fabrics, I think you've got something here."

"I know I do," Hailey said. "But I've got bills to pay, and now with the girls, I don't know how I'll manage all my expenses. That's why holding onto the job is so important to me." Even though she knew she had Cole's support, she still had to earn her own way. It was essential to her well-being.

"We offer small business loans," Stella said.

The others jumped in, talking excitedly about websites and ads, and as great as it all sounded, she couldn't help noticing their wedding rings and designer clothes. These women had wealth and the support of a spouse. None could relate to her situation as a single woman, eking out a living…possibly adopting two little girls. They were in a whole other world.

She loved their ideas, furiously writing as much as she could in her notebook. It was all such great information. "Thank you so much. Up until now, this has been a vague dream. I've never been close enough to start brainstorming the business details of it." She stuffed her notebook back into the bag.

"Well, hold on," Glori said. "We're not done with you yet. Didn't you want help with your pitch for Abbott's?"

"I do, but I've taken up more than enough time. It's someone else's turn."

"Are you kidding?" Stella asked. "You're building a brand-new business. Come on, yours is the fun stuff."

"I don't think it'll take all that long," Glori said. "Let's get to it."

They discussed the pros and cons of her themed idea and the men's line, and then drafted an email that Hailey would never have been able to do on her own.

She knew how to design and sew, but she didn't know business. And that's what it really came down to with these women. They were sharp, savvy entrepreneurs.

They intimidated the hell out of her.

After they wrapped up with her, they went around the table, and each woman had a chance to discuss her issues. Everyone was so engaged, so helpful, it made Hailey long to be part of something like this. They all seemed to genuinely like and respect each other.

As they packed up their briefcases and tote bags, getting ready to have the Christmas party, Hailey felt a surge of gratitude. "You guys, I can't thank you enough for letting me come tonight. I love the way you all just jumped right in and supported me."

"Of course," Glori said. "That's what we're here for."

"I guess I'm not used to that."

"That's the whole reason we formed," Callie said. "We're not interested in straightening each other's crowns. We're all about getting in the trenches with each other."

"And that goes for helping with the girls, too," the princess said. "So don't be one of those women who's afraid to ask for help. Once you officially join, you'll have access to our group chat. Just jump right in. Between all of us, I guarantee someone will be able to help."

"Thank you." She could only focus on digging her keys out of her tote bag. She didn't want them to see how overwhelmed she was.

As the others moved on, Phinny approached her. "You're not staying for the party?"

"I should probably get home to Cole."

"He can't handle the girls?"

"No, actually. He's great. It's just…"

"We can be intimidating. Don't let that—"

"You are. But in the best way. You're all so confident

and smart, and here I am with my three-year plan." Her high emotions were responsible for the next words that came tumbling out of her mouth. "And I've never trusted women before, so this is all new to me."

But Phinny didn't look at her like she was pathetic. "You know, I had the same group of best friends all my life. But when my situation changed—oh, let's just be honest here—when my dad cut me off, I lost them all. Now, believe me, I understood. It's not fun to hang out with someone who can't afford to fly to Ibiza on a whim. I couldn't even afford a drink in a bar."

"But they were your best friends?"

"Oh, yes. We did everything together. Until I could no longer afford it. After that, I had a hard time trusting people. When Glori brought me here, I felt like such an imposter. I'd never done a thing my entire life other than spend money and travel, and here I am trying to open a shop without a clue how to go about it. And these women are so accomplished. Imagine someone like me asking for help from a scientist who makes the most expensive perfume in the world."

Hailey looked to see who she was talking about. "Which one is she?"

"Rosie. The princess."

The woman in pink cowboy boots, black leggings, and an oversized sweater, who looked like a supermodel? "She's a *scientist*?"

"She is. And Knox isn't just a designer. She makes couture wedding gowns. And I don't use the word couture lightly. Meanwhile, my greatest claim to fame was putting together items for auctions. I'm not saying *you* feel like an imposter, but I know what it's like to feel out of your league with these women."

"I want to be in their league." So badly. "I guess I just need more confidence."

"You look awfully confident to me. In any event, I hope you'll stay for the party and get to know us as friends." Phinny gave her a warm smile before taking off.

Unsure what to do, she decided to check in with Cole. If he needed her, she'd leave.

Hailey: How's it going? You need me to come home?

Cole: Not at all. You getting good stuff out of the PRs?

Hailey: The best. Meeting's over, and now they want to have some fun.

Cole: Call me when you're ready to come home.

Half of her was disappointed he hadn't said it was total mayhem over there. She wanted the excuse to leave. The women had broken into smaller groups, laughing and catching up with each other, and she just couldn't bear standing off by herself, putting together a little plate of food.

Ugh. Not again.

Since she'd returned her rental a while ago, she'd been driving his car, so it wasn't like he could come get her anyway.

Hailey: I drove here!

Cole: I guess you haven't been in the garage?

She laughed.

Hailey: Let me guess. Car collection?

Cole: Don't you know if you needed a ride, I'd take an ATV into town? With an extra helmet for my favorite badass?

Hailey: I should come home.

Cole: Because you're not having fun?

Hailey: Because I don't know anyone
Cole: Do you want to know them?

That old, familiar yearning to be included hit like a spasm that gripped her entire body. She'd thought she'd gotten over it ages ago.

Hailey: Yes

It surprised her how much she meant it.

Cole: Then, stay. Have a good time. If you drink and need a ride, I'll come get you.

Hailey: Okay. See you soon.

Sliding her phone into the inner pocket of her tote, she looked around the room. She could stand there and watch the women have a good time with each other, or she could take a chance and join them.

And if she got screwed over, so what? She was an adult. She could handle it.

. . .

When she walked in the door at eleven, she was surprised to find Cole on the couch reading. Yellow lamplight gilded his black hair, and when he heard her come in, he got up and smiled.

Happiness whisked through her. She could get used to this, walking in the door and seeing him smile at her with such relief and affection.

She had to stop herself from running into his arms. After she took off her boots, she hung up her jacket, and still, he stood there waiting patiently with that adorable smile that told her he was as happy to see her as she was to see him.

And that was really all she needed to get out of her head and follow her heart. She ran right for him. When he lifted her off the ground, her legs wound around his waist. He held her so tightly a sense of peace rushed through her like cool water, smoothing her jagged, scarred edges. She could feel herself softening in a way only women who weren't alone in the world could understand.

"I missed you." He said it so quietly she almost didn't hear.

"I missed you, too."

He backed her up against a wall. "But you had a good time?"

"I did. It was great."

He pressed his cheek to hers. "You're so cold."

"Well, it's minus ten out there." But the warmth of his touch chased it away. She wanted more, so much more. Possibly more than he could give. "I'm cold inside, too." And it was true. She'd lived with a sense of barrenness for so long, she'd stopped acknowledging it. "Warm me up?"

He didn't even hesitate. Kissing her, he was on the move, heading to the stairs. His mouth never left hers, his tongue stroking deliciously, sensually, as he carefully climbed, and she scraped her fingernails across his scalp until she grabbed a handful of hair at the back of his neck.

In his room, he kicked the door shut before lowering her gently to his bed. The way he looked at her, like she was both precious and edible, like he wanted to treasure every inch of her and yet violate her in the most carnal ways possible, made her go hot and restless. She didn't want him to be careful. She wanted him to let go.

As he peeled off her leggings and panties, she lifted her arms, giving him a look that said, *Take what you want.* His gaze sharpened, his features hardened, and he moved over her, yanking up her blouse and pulling it over her head.

He cupped her breasts and pushed them together, his focus so intense, she had to squeeze her thighs together. His gaze snapped up to hers. "You like me touching your tits?"

"I like it better when they're in your mouth."

Heat flared in his eyes, and he slowly peeled down one cup of her lacy bra. Never taking his eyes off her, he slowly licked her nipple and then flicked it with the tip of his tongue. It squeezed into a tight bead, and then he closed his mouth and sucked.

"Yes." Desire spread so thick and hot, she melted into a pool of sensation.

Reaching underneath her, he unclasped her bra, and her breasts sprang free. She loved how they felt in his big hands, how he played with them as though he cared more about turning her on than himself.

"You're the most beautiful woman I've ever seen. I can't believe I get to be with you."

But for how long? Because if they fell apart before he left, she couldn't let it impact her mood around the girls.

Did they have a chance for a real relationship?

"Hey, hey." He stretched out beside her, one hand on her belly, the other propping his head. "What's going on?"

One step at a time. No one had ever looked at her the way he did, and if she let herself think through all the unknowns, she'd ruin this time with him. And she wanted it. Needed it. Needed him. The way he wanted her healed her broken and bruised bits.

She reached for his hand, kissing the palm. "I can't see the future. I can't see what's going to happen with us, with the girls, with my job, with my robes..."

"And you need to know how things are going to turn out every bit as much as you need to know there's going to be a roof over your head and food in your belly."

"Yes." She whispered it, so grateful someone understood.

"I can't see the future either, but I know what I feel, and I've never felt anything like this before. And if you're worried that our feelings will fade once we have sex..." He shook his head. "It's just not like that for me. I'm crazy about you. I can't get enough, and I don't think I ever will. But I get it. I'm scared, too."

She reached for him, sifting his hair through her fingers. "What're you scared of?"

"The only woman I've ever truly wanted is here in my bed. She's letting me defile her body." He broke into a devastating grin. "She seems to like me."

"She likes you very much."

"Then, you have to understand. No one in the world has the power to hurt me the way you do. The more you care, the more it hurts when you're left alone."

She was so caught up in her own worries that she'd lost sight of him. She'd forgotten his past, his hurts and wounds. She needed to be very careful with this beautiful, sexy, vulnerable man. "Cole." She rolled on top of him, kissing that mouth that brought her such pleasure.

He caught her thighs, spreading them, and lifted her right over his hard cock.

A shock of desire gripped her, and she rubbed herself all over him. "I know you're scared, but the one thing you can count on right now? Is me. You can count on me."

"Get up on your knees." Reaching between them, he grasped his cock and guided himself into her.

A shiver wracked her body, and she sank down all the way, grinding all over him.

"Ride me." That deep, commanding voice made her shiver.

Setting her hands on his shoulders, she rocked her hips. A curtain of hair fell around them, enclosing them. Their breaths met, his minty. She moaned at how he filled her, at the clutch of his hands on her ass, and his strength in controlling her body, lifting her and then punching his hips up as he slammed her down on him.

He felt good, he smelled good, and she couldn't get enough. She moved harder and faster, and soon, it wasn't enough. Rearing up, she braced her hands on his thighs. He reached for her breasts, leaving her to take control of their rhythm.

His eyes went half-lidded with lust as he watched her ride him with total abandon. "You gonna come for me?"

"Yes." She was so lost in him she could hardly speak, the single syllable coming out on a whoosh of air. "Oh, God, Cole. You feel so good."

One hand abandoned her breast to seek her clit, and the moment he touched her, she cried out. He jackknifed up to suck on her nipple, and God, the assault of sensations was too much. All three pleasure points—her breasts, her clit, her swollen, wet channel—collided and sent her into a state of arousal she'd never experienced.

"I can't...Cole, I can't take it. I can't..." It was too much, too intense. She couldn't survive it.

But he was relentless, circling her clit, sucking her nipple, and pounding into her relentlessly.

And when she exploded, the world went white. She hovered in that space of pure elations, letting it flood her until she crash-landed. Realizing only then, that he was coming, too. Hard, wild... Cole was out of control. Sweat glistened on his skin, his teeth were bared, and he grunted and cried out.

She'd never seen him lose control, and it was the most beautiful sight in the world.

Maybe this was as real and special as he made her believe.

Maybe they *could* last.

Chapter Fifteen

On the last day of school before the holiday break, Cole took Evvie with him to the training center. Since they had a daycare center, she got to be around other kids her age.

But mostly, he'd wanted to give Hailey a chance to work. Ever since her meeting with the Petticoat Rulers, she'd been supercharged about starting her own line, so she'd stolen as many moments as she could to work on her robes. He figured she could use a bigger stretch of time.

With Christmas just two days away, she'd decided to hold off on sending her pitch, which made sense, even though he knew how badly she wanted her job situation resolved.

As much as he wanted to offer help, he kept his mouth shut because he understood that her sense of security came from her own ability to earn a living. Part of that was launching this business—an income stream she could grow while she weathered career storms. The only thing he *could* do was give her time to work.

After the training facility, he'd taken Evvie into town and gotten hot cocoa from Coco's Chocolates. They'd listened to the carolers in the town green, visited a toy store so she could buy gifts for her sister and Hailey, and then they'd gone to the library where he'd opened an account for the girls.

The more he set up now, the less anxiety he'd feel when he left. Okay, guilt. He'd feel less guilty about bailing on them. He had an agency working on getting a reliable sitter, and he'd talked to Lulu Cavanaugh, the co-owner of Harley and Lu, about a food delivery service. Whether groceries or prepared foods, he wanted something in place in case Hailey got overwhelmed with work and kids.

He'd checked in with the PI and learned the man was still pursuing Darren's biological family. And, finally, he'd brought Evvie with him to the attorney's office where he'd begun the process of starting a trust for the girls.

He should be feeling good, getting all this shit done. When it was time to leave, the girls would be set.

But oddly enough, the idea of leaving didn't sit right with him.

He wanted to be the one to braid Paisley's hair. He looked forward to their private time together every night. And he needed to be around for Evvie because he was certain she still had a vision of her parents living it up in Vegas, choosing not to come home to their little girl.

And that just twisted him up inside.

The moment they walked into the house, Evvie wrenched her hand free of his and ran into the kitchen with her library tote bag. "LaLee, Paisy, yook what I got." The books crashed onto the floor, and he smiled. There was one word for that girl: gusto.

He'd had the presents wrapped, so he went ahead and put them under the bigger tree. But only because they wouldn't fit under the scraggly one. At this point, after daily art projects, the limbs were dragging on the floor. Most recently, Hailey had printed out photos of the girls with their parents and made frames out of popsicle sticks. They'd glued glitter and pom-poms on them, so they sparkled in the tree lights.

It was fucking awesome.

"Cole." Evvie shrieked.

Alarms rang in his body, and he broke into a run, practically skidding to a stop in the kitchen where Hailey was pulling a sheet of cookies out of the oven and Paisley was standing on a step stool, licking the beaters.

"What? What's wrong?"

"Yook." Evvie danced in place, shaking her booty like an enthusiastic puppy. "*Cookies.*"

"Oh, Jesus." He laughed "You scared me."

Hailey brought the tray to the counter and set it on a trivet. With a spatula, she transferred them onto a metal cooling rack. He hadn't even known he owned utensils like that.

"I have one?" Evvie asked.

But he didn't need to answer since Hailey was already offering her one from another rack.

This moment was everything he'd ever wanted as a kid. Once, he'd asked his nanny to bake gingerbread cookies with him. He'd asked Jaime's mom for a list of everything he needed—the ingredients, the cookie cutters, everything. His nanny had done it, of course. But baking cookies with someone who was paid to hang out with him took away a lot of the fun, so he'd never done it again.

Where Paisley savored every bite, Evvie gobbled hers,

getting crumbs on her hands, mouth, and chin. They were both so damn adorable.

"Good?" he asked.

Paisley nodded.

"Yummy." Evvie ran at him so hard, she crashed into his knee. The pain wasn't too bad, though—good sign—and it all but disappeared when she offered him a "Sanna cookie."

"Thanks, sweet pea." He wolfed it down and then swiveled to face Paisley. "You made these?"

She nodded with pride. She had flecks of batter on her long-sleeved T-shirt and chocolate smears around her mouth.

"Good job." He high-fived her, then brought the mixer bowl, beaters, and scraper to the sink. "You get a lot of work done?" he asked Hailey.

"So much. Thank you for that. What did you guys do?"

"We—"

"Got books, Lalee. Lots of books." Evvie picked one up and thrust it at Hailey. "Wead."

"I can't wait to read this one," Hailey said. "We'll do it tonight, okay?"

"Evvie said you took her shopping for presents," Paisley said. "I want to get presents for Mommy and Daddy."

His heart stopped beating, his blood stopped pumping, and everything in him ground to a halt. Except her words that banged around inside him like marbles in a tin can.

Thankfully, Hailey covered for him. "We can do that." She said it easily, and he was damn grateful for that. "Absolutely. What did you have in mind?"

"Mommy always gets her perfume, and Daddy needs new slippers."

"That's very sweet of you," Hailey said. "I'll bet they would've loved that."

Okay, so, he guessed they were doing this. Unsure of how to word it, since Paisley was talking present tense, and Hailey was in the past, he kept it simple. "Tomorrow's Christmas Eve, so you don't have school. We can go right when the stores open."

But instead of being happy about it, Paisley looked worried.

"What is it, sweetheart?" Hailey brushed the hair off the little girl's shoulder.

"How will we get the presents to them?" She looked at Cole. "If they're in heaven, how will they get them?"

She was so much sharper than he expected of a six-year-old, but he was relieved they were dealing with reality. "We can't. We can't get presents to heaven. So, instead of perfume and slippers, why don't we get them stockings and fill them with memories."

"Memories?" Paisley seemed confused.

"Yeah. Tonight, we can make a fire and some popcorn and hot cocoa, and you and Evvie can tell us everything you remember about your parents. Stories from how they put you to bed or funny things they did or places they liked to take you. We'll write them all down and put them in a stocking."

"Oh, I love that." Hailey's eyes shone with admiration and affection. "That's such a great idea." She touched the top of Paisley's head. "We'll hang that stocking every year, and you guys can hold onto those memories forever."

"But I want to get them presents. Mommy always gets her perfume."

Stumped, Cole turned to Hailey, who didn't hesitate. "Okay, how about we buy them and then drop them off at the homeless shelter? I think your daddy would be happy to know that someone who needs slippers is wearing them. Do you like that idea?"

But before Paisley could answer, they heard bells jingling and a deep-throated, "Ho ho ho" from out front.

Both girls looked up at him, wide-eyed, practically vibrating in anticipation. Paisley whispered an awed, "Santa?"

"It sure sounds like it." Hailey gave him a questioning look.

He held up both hands as if to say he had nothing to do with it.

"Well, let's go see." Hailey led the way.

The girls ran straight for the bay window in the living room and peered out into the dark, snowy night. "I don't see any reindeer," Paisley said.

Cole reached for the door, but Hailey stopped him. "We don't know who it is."

"City girl." He smiled. "Only one person other than me knows the gate code."

"Uh, no. Chase gave it to me on my first day."

"That was the visitor code. I changed it right after you used it." And then he opened the door.

"Ho ho ho." In a full-on red velvet Santa suit—complete with fake beard, hat, and shiny black boots—A-list movie star Trevor Montgomery stood on the porch, hauling enormous bags stuffed with presents. "I've been searching this county from one end to the other, trying to find Paisley and Everly Leeson." He glanced down at the girls who stood pressed together between Cole and Hailey.

Santa tapped each nose. "And I think I finally found them."

"You did." Paisley spoke reverently.

"Well, come on in, Santa." Cole stepped aside to let his dad in, surprised when three elves followed with even more velvet sacks.

"Is all that for us?" Paisley asked.

"Well, now, that depends. Has Cole been a good boy?"

"Oh, yes." Paisley reached for his hand. "He's very good."

For half the year, Cole faced two-hundred-pound men who wanted to bash his head into the Plexiglass, but nothing had the power to knock him out more than the feel of that little hand in his.

"And what about Hailey Casselton?" his dad asked in his Santa voice. "Has she been good?"

The elves got busy, scattering around the house. One hooked a gigantic wreath on the door, another brought a pile of food into the kitchen, and the third emptied the sacks, placing professionally wrapped presents under the enormous tree.

"LaLee good," Evvie said so quietly, so earnestly, that emotion tightened the skin around his dad's eyes.

"Well, then, they get presents, too." Santa walked deeper into the room and sat down in a big leather club chair. "All right, who's first? Who's going to tell me what they want for Christmas?"

"Me, me, me," Paisley said.

"Come on, Sanna." Evvie took off, her little bottom wiggling from side to side. "We gots Sanna cookies. Come on."

Santa heaved himself out of the chair, shot Cole a giant smile, and took off after the girls.

Watching him go, Hailey shook her head. "I've never met a movie star, but in a million years, I never imagined meeting Trevor Montgomery this way." She broke into a huge smile. "I love your dad."

"Yeah, he's pretty cool."

"But the presents…" She shook her head. "We can't give them all that. It's too much."

"They've already seen them."

"We'll have to rearrange it so they don't notice. They'll appreciate a few presents, but this many… I think we can drop some off at the shelter tomorrow and even save some for their birthdays. I don't want to hurt your dad's feelings, but this is overwhelming."

"Yeah, we can do that."

"Cole, LaLee," Paisley called. "Come here."

"Sanna eat cookies." Evvie practically screeched it.

Cole headed for the elf who was still unloading bags. "Hey, thanks for doing this. You happen to know what my dad bought?"

"Actually, I own the toy store, so I do."

"Cool, cool. This is awesome but a bit much. We'd like to drop some off at the shelter tomorrow."

"Actually, that's just for adults. There's a place in town, though, that gives emergency housing to families. You can drop some there."

"That's perfect. Since you know what we've got, you mind putting a bag together for the families?"

"You got it."

"Thank you." He hurried to catch up with Hailey and the others in the kitchen.

His dad sat at the table with a plate of cookies and a glass of milk. As always, he had the kids in his thrall by telling stories of his sleigh ride and the funny personalities of his reindeer.

"Oh, that Blixen. He's hilarious. He only eats Reese's Pieces. We try to give him kale and quinoa, and he just does this." His dad stuck out his tongue like a cat with a mouthful of hair.

The girls shrieked with laughter.

"And Donner's the prankster. Always trying to put one over on the other reindeers. You've got to watch your back around him."

"What does he do?" Paisley asked.

"Most nights after dinner, they all hang out around the campfire. They roast marshmallows and tell stories. Well, one night, they noticed Donner was missing, and when it was time to go to bed in the barn, they found out he'd switched up everyone's pallets."

"What's a pallet?" Paisley asked, mesmerized.

"Each reindeer has his own stall, and they sleep on a bed of hay. Now, you know how you like things just-so when you snuggle in at night? Well, same with reindeer. Prancer likes a special blanket his mom made for him, Dancer likes his wooly socks, and Rudolf likes the teddy bear he got for Christmas one year. So, imagine his surprise when Rudolf went to bed and found Dancer's socks instead of his bear." His dad tipped his head back. "Ho ho ho. It caused quite a ruckus."

"Were they sad?" Paisley asked. "Did they miss sleeping in their own beds?"

His dad sobered right away, realizing what he'd done. "Oh, no. My reindeer know how to make a home for themselves no matter where they lay their heads."

"How do they do that?"

"Rudolf gave Dancer his socks back, and Prancer traded the books he found on his pallet for his blanket. No, see, it's not the room that matters. It's their favorite things that help them feel safe." His dad got up. "Now, who's hungry for dinner because I brought all kinds of food." He sorted through the containers. "I've got macaroni and cheese, chicken fingers, butter rolls, green beans..." He looked back at them. "How does that sound?"

"Nailed it." Hailey got busy with silverware, while Cole got out the melamine plates. They set out glasses of milk and napkins, while Trevor served the food.

When the girls settled down to eat, Santa joined them at the island. "I don't know what I expected when I got here, but it wasn't this."

"What do you mean?" Cole asked.

"I thought the place would be a mess, kids screaming...puddles of piddle everywhere..."

"They're not feral animals, Dad."

Trevor burst out laughing. "No, I guess not. I just didn't expect you to have it all under control so quickly." He looked at Hailey. "I'm Trevor Montgomery, Cole's dad."

Her features crumpled. "But I thought... Are you telling me you're not Santa?"

With a bark of laughter, he enveloped Hailey in his arms. "No wonder my son's got a thing for you."

"Dad." Cole's tone held a warning.

Hailey just smiled. "It's great to meet you."

A crash drew their attention to the table, and Evvie shrieked before bursting into tears. Cole dashed over to the table to find she'd spilled milk all over her chicken fingers and mac and cheese. "Hey, hey. It's all right. We'll clean this right up." He brought the glass and plate to the sink, served up a new plate of food and fresh milk, and then brought it back to her.

Her cheeks were mottled, and she hiccupped, so he pulled out the chair next to her and sat down, transferring her to his lap. He smoothed a hand through her hair. "We've had a very busy day." She seemed to be responding to his calm voice, so he kept up the one-sided conversation. "How about we go swimming when we're done with dinner?"

"I swim?" She gazed up at him with watery eyes.

"Yep. You're going to swim like a shark."

"I a shawk." Evvie swished her butt on his thigh.

"You sure are."

"Go swim now." She started to get off his lap.

He set her back in her seat and handed her a fork. "Nope. Now, we eat. Then, we swim. Sound good?"

She stabbed a cheese-covered noodle with a fork and opened her mouth wide as a plate. He nearly died with how long it took for the food to get inside, as it wavered and detoured before finally hitting her tongue. Her jaw snapped shut and she chewed dramatically. "Das good."

"Well, you can thank Santa for it."

She cut a shy glance toward the man in the red costume.

His dad was watching him like he didn't recognize him. Concerned, Cole got up. "What's wrong?"

"Nothing. You're just so good with them."

"Oh, well, I've had a few days."

"He is, though," Hailey said. "He's amazing."

"So, listen." His dad clapped his hands. "What do you

say we give the girls a Christmas to remember? We can take them to Disneyland, stay in my house in Malibu. We don't need to worry about flights. We can just take the jet. They'll have the time of their lives."

Hailey reached for Cole's arm, grinning up at him. "Well, we know where you get it from."

His dad's gaze locked on the touch, then slowly drifted up to Cole. A slow grin spread across his features.

Happiness spread through him, and he smiled back. *Yeah. It's like that.*

"Let me call Spike," his dad said. "So, he can make the arrangements. They're going to love it."

Cole didn't even have to see Hailey's expression to know what she was thinking. "Thanks, Dad, but we're going for a different kind of Christmas."

"Different how?"

"We're giving them a simpler holiday. More focused on baking cookies and making ornaments—you know, family time."

"I don't have to go with you. You can take them yourselves. I'll just set it all up. Come on, Disneyland? It'll be magical."

"No, if we went, we'd definitely want you there," Hailey explained. "We just want to give them a magical Christmas at home."

"We want them to feel safe. And right now, that means they stay here with us." He could tell his dad didn't get it. "They don't need exotic locations. They don't need Snow White. They just need us and hot chocolate and a few presents."

"Gotcha. Okay. Let me go home and change. I'll come back in a swimsuit and reintroduce myself." His dad made a big show of saying goodbye to the girls, reminding them to be good, and then took off.

"I seriously can't believe that's Trevor Montgomery."

"Yeah. My dad's pretty great." But something was off, and Cole didn't know what it was.

She rubbed his arm. "Hey, you okay?"

"I don't know. We might've hurt my dad's feelings."

"What do you mean?"

"The way he so left abruptly." Almost as if he'd been flustered. "He was surprised we didn't jump on his offer. The fact that you were unimpressed with the jet and the Malibu house—"

"Are you saying I insulted him? I didn't mean to do that at all."

"No." But suddenly, he knew. "I never cried."

"What?"

"I never had a tantrum around him. I wanted him to stay." He sank into the memories, how it felt to wait for his dad to get home. The nanny would mark it on the calendar. They'd do a countdown. He could remember the anticipation, the anxiety. "And so, I didn't complain or whine or—"

"You never broke down over spilled milk." Awareness bloomed on her features. "He came in here expecting to see chaos, and instead, he saw a real family in action." Her whole body tensed. "I don't mean we're a real family. That's not what I'm saying."

"No, I know what you mean. And we do feel like a real family. You're right. He's never seen one. He didn't grow up in one."

"So, it made him uncomfortable?"

"He's always compensated for his absence by doing big, grand gestures. This whole scene is new to him." *New to me, too.* "And I think we've given him something to think about." He tipped her chin and kissed her. "It's a good thing."

You're the best thing that ever happened to me.

A fierce determination seized him.

I want to be good for you, too.

Chapter Sixteen

HAILEY BROUGHT OUT A TRAY FILLED WITH MUGS OF hot chocolate and bowls of popcorn. As she approached, she took in the scene before her.

In their pajamas and moose slippers, their hair still wet from a bath, the girls sat on the rug in front of the fireplace. Cole had his back to the couch, his legs stretched out under the coffee table, and Trevor had his feet up on a leather ottoman, a whiskey in one hand, an unlit cigar in the other.

Was it only two weeks ago she'd lived alone in a studio apartment in Manhattan, fighting for a handhold on the subway, trudging through pedestrian traffic to get to work on time?

"Okay, here we are." She set the tray down, and the girls scrambled over. "I've already let these cool, so you're okay to drink them now." She slipped red and white striped glass straws into the mugs so the girls wouldn't spill. Both of them gawked at the mountain of whipped cream with chocolate shavings on top.

"All right, let's do this." Cole grabbed his mug. "Who wants to go first?"

"What do I say?" Paisley asked.

"Anything you want." Hailey settled in across from Cole, their legs brushing under the table. Even such innocent contact made her blood go fizzy. She wanted to crawl onto his lap and feel those strong arms close around her. "Just say the first memory that pops into your mind. Don't worry about any kind of order. You can just start talking, and we'll write everything down." She picked up her pen and said, "Whenever you're ready."

"Mommy kisseded me here." Evvie patted her cheek. "She wikes my tubby teeks."

"They are pretty adorable." Cole wrote that one down. He was in charge of the littlest one's memories, while Hailey had Paisley's.

"My daddy hates milk." Paisley grinned. "It makes him do this." She made gagging noises that cracked her sister up.

Good. This was very good. While it had seemed like a nice idea, she hadn't been sure how the girls would react.

"You want to know why?" Cole asked, smiling. "It used to be his favorite thing in the world. Any time we went out to eat, he'd order milk. When he came over, he'd pour himself a big glass. He loved ice cream and cheese— anything with dairy. And then one day, we were riding our bikes across a big field. Someone got the stupid idea to milk one of the cows, and while they were doing it, while they were squeezing milk out of the udder, your dad was grossed out. He wanted nothing to do with it. And I said, 'Dude, that's *milk.* That's what you drink.' You should've seen his face. We told him that's where ice cream and cheese came from, too. His face went green and right there in the field, in front of all of us, in front of the cows, he threw up."

Everyone was laughing, and Paisley said, "Daddy was funny."

"Your dad was the best." Cole turned somber.

"I've got a memory." Trevor's deep voice came out a low rumble.

Paisley stopped sipping. "You knew my daddy?"

"Sure did. He was Cole's best friend."

"Did you come to our house?" Paisley asked.

It was questions like this that gave Hailey a ping of worry. Children had no concept of time or space, so they made sense of the world however they could. She needed to be careful, ready to untangle concepts too big for little minds.

"No, but he came to mine. And I remember one night, I couldn't sleep, so I came downstairs to find a light on in the kitchen. It was your dad. He'd helped himself to a midnight snack… And by snack, I mean a whole feast."

Paisley giggled. "Daddy ate so much food."

"He had a whole spread on the kitchen table, and when I walked in, he said…" Trevor gave a chin nod and used a surfer voice to say, "S'up?"

Cole burst out laughing. "Are you serious?"

His dad nodded.

"How did I not know this?" Cole asked.

But Trevor seemed lost in his memory. "We must've stayed up for an hour, just eating, talking…hanging out." He broke out in a soft smile, looking like he was right back at that kitchen table all those years ago. "He showed me some snowboarding videos he'd taken. He thought the world of you. He really did." And then he seemed to snap out of it. "He was a good man, your dad."

The fire snapped and crackled, Christmas carols played quietly in the background, and Cole set his warm hand on Hailey's ankle. She knew they were both steeped in memories of their easygoing, red-haired friend.

This moment of connection...between all five of them...it was just so powerful. Before, when she'd referred to them as a family, she'd immediately regretted it, but Cole hadn't freaked out at all. Because he felt it, too. How could he not?

Every day, she tried to tamp down the hope that burbled under the surface. But like a dandelion breaking through a crack in the sidewalk, it kept breaking through. And now she knew why. Because it was real.

They *could* be a family. And wouldn't that be amazing? If they adopted the girls together, she'd get to feel this sense of deep satisfaction for the rest of her life.

But not once had he even hinted about anything long-term. Sure, he wanted to be with her. But whenever they talked about the girls, it was always temporary.

Why do you do this to yourself? It was so hard for her to just stay in the moment, enjoy this time for what it was.

She had to stop thinking ahead and focus on their one goal of giving the girls a great Christmas.

It hurt to stomp down the hope, but she had to do it for her own sanity.

This is all you get.

"Okay, keep going. More memories." Hailey lifted a red felt stocking. "We've got to fill this sucker."

The day before Christmas, it snowed all day, giving them a chance to go outside and build snowmen. When they'd finally come inside, Cole had taken their wet clothes to the laundry room while she'd gotten started on breakfast. Knowing how much Evvie loved her *faffles*, she'd made the batter, thinking that maybe tomorrow morning, it'd be nice to have cinnamon rolls.

And that's when she realized she was doing it *again*. Because she was thinking about starting traditions— waffles on Christmas Eve and cinnamon rolls on Christmas Day.

She'd wanted to smack her head against the marble countertop.

What was the matter with her? Why couldn't she get it through her thick skull?

There wouldn't be any traditions.

She had to stop this.

This wasn't her family.

Trevor had come for breakfast, and when Cole was busy getting the girls dressed for the day, they'd talked about presents. He'd still seemed flummoxed by the idea of homemade gifts, so she'd shown him the unfinished collage she'd been making for his son. Since her only source of pictures came from social media, Trevor had offered to let her sort through his boxes of photos from Cole's childhood.

So, they'd left him with the girls and headed over to Trevor's home.

And guess what? It was just as much of a showpiece as his son's. Which was no surprise for the highest-paid actor in the world. A wonder of steel, glass, and river rock, it had a different, more rustic vibe than Cole's home, but it was just as over-the-top in every way.

Seeing it in person had driven home what had been missing in Cole's life. There wasn't a single drawing or pottery project—no evidence of his life outside of hockey.

It had made her want to smother him in craft projects and meatloaf and a mudroom with hooks for parkas and bins for boots.

It made her yearn for a life with him she could never have.

As they headed back on 191, the traffic slowed as they neared town. "Would you mind stopping at the Emporium?" she asked. "They sell pre-baked cinnamon rolls, so all we have to do is pop them in the oven on Christmas morning. I want the girls to wake up to that smell, you know? I want them to come racing down the stairs because they know what it means."

"And what does it mean?"

"That it's Christmas morning, and they get to open presents. We'll each take turns, opening one gift at a time so that it won't be some big feeding frenzy. They can play with their new toys while we're getting breakfast ready. We'll have a fire going and carols playing. I just want it to be so special."

As he turned right onto Main Street, he looked a little lost in thought. "Sounds like you had a great childhood."

"Oh." She could see how he'd get that from what she'd just described. "No, that wasn't...I didn't grow up like that." She let out a strained laugh. "I got that from movies."

He cut her a look.

"My mom's kind of a bohemian. We didn't stay in one place long, and she doesn't really buy into holidays." Which was a nice way of saying it never crossed her mind to decorate or spend what little money she had on presents.

Hailey might've had a handful of holidays in a place of their own, but most of the time, they were guests in someone else's. Every year was different. Sometimes, they stayed at a friend's who'd gone home for Christmas, so they had a place to themselves and tried not to make a mess. Only once did they stay with a family.

At eleven, she'd been as eager as the other children and beside herself when she saw the bounty of presents under the tree. But when it came time to open them, there hadn't been any for her, and she'd been devastated.

She'd sat still as a statue, the family so preoccupied with opening gifts and putting in batteries and assembling things, they hadn't noticed her. She'd crept to the office where she and her mom shared an inflatable mattress and cried her little heart out.

Come to think of it, that was the year she'd decided she would earn her own money and never live off people again. That was the year she *saw* her mother, the moment she'd begun to separate from her.

Trevor parked in front of Coco's Chocolates, the charming green façade and massive bay windows reminding her of a European pastry shop. "Ooh, let's get some hot chocolate. The girls will love that."

He parked and unbuckled. "They're lucky to have you."

"You know what's funny? My immediate thought was no, I'm lucky to have *them*. Isn't that crazy? Not even two weeks ago, I was freaking out about taking time away from my job, and now? Giving the girls a special Christmas is my entire reason for living. I think it's put things into perspective." Which would explain all these fuzzy feelings she had about family. It had never been a priority before, so this experience just shifted things. "I know this is going to sound corny, but I really think it's healing the little girl in me who didn't get to have any special holidays."

Trevor had his hand on the door release but didn't open it. "Can I ask you something?"

"Of course."

The interior of the car cooled quickly without the heat. "Is taking the girls to Disneyland not special?"

She wished he'd asked Cole this question. Those two needed a real conversation. "Well, you're asking a person who didn't have any traditions growing up, so it's going to be different for me."

"My son didn't have them, either. And I saw the tree he bought standing next to the one you cut with your own two hands, and I..." He sighed. "I get it. I see the difference."

She was fascinated to discover this whole other side to his personality. He was quiet, gentle, and thoughtful, whereas on social media and in interviews, he was the brightest light in the room, a larger-than-life celebrity known universally for his generous nature and kindness.

In person, he was just so relatable.

"Okay, well, I know I craved stability as a kid." *Pretty sure Cole did, too.* "If I could've stayed home and made decorations with my mom, baked cookies, and wrapped presents, I would've taken that over Disneyland any day. I think those extravagant trips are lost on little kids who just want to be with their parents. Maybe later, when they're teenagers, they'll be excited about seeing the world."

"But not for the holidays."

She wouldn't lie when he genuinely wanted to know. "No, not for the holidays. I'm twenty-eight, and I still want those traditions. I could see taking them somewhere the week after, but the holidays are for families being together."

He nodded, staring straight ahead. "Thank you for your honesty." And then, he got out of the car.

Since he starred in a wildly popular franchise about a three-hundred-year clan war, he stayed in character year-round. She didn't know if his publicist wanted him to do it or if it was part of his contract or what, but people loved it.

So, the moment he stepped on the sidewalk in his kilt, knee socks, black boots, and fisherman's sweater, people flocked to him. In Calamity, celebrities barely got a second glance, but there was something so vital, so fun, about Trevor that he pulled everyone in like a magnet.

Hm, sounds a bit like a hockey player I know.

In a classic move, an elderly woman with a selfie stick lowered it—as if to see if he was wearing underpants—but once she got her laugh, she quickly put it away. It was a running joke that had begun with the first movie: did Trevor Montgomery go commando under that kilt? She'd probably seen that headline a thousand times over her lifetime.

Itchy to get back home—because already, she missed the girls and Cole—she got out of the Land Cruiser and bought the cinnamon rolls, another gallon of milk, and some nice, thick maple bacon she'd add to tomorrow's breakfast. When she came out of the Emporium, she saw that an even larger crowd had gathered, and Trevor was in full-form, his voice loud, his laughter booming.

He just had a way about him. He made people happy. It was a gift.

A sharp pang clutched her heart. He reminded her so much of Cole, and that made her miss him fiercely. His heart needed to know that, so she pulled out her phone and texted him.

Hailey: Thinking of you.

The moment she hit Send, she regretted it. It didn't come close to expressing her feelings.

Hailey: I miss you. Seems silly, doesn't it? I've only been gone a couple hours.

She sent it, but she knew it still wasn't right. She was being too cautious, guarding herself.

It's too late for that.
You just have to go for it.

Hailey: All right, you want to know the truth? I miss you when you're just down the hall, and I count the hours every night until I can have you to myself. I want to spend every minute with you.

Protecting yourself, being so reserved, took a toll, and she only knew because of the relief she felt after letting the truth spill out of her.

He didn't respond, though, and she didn't see the three dancing dots to let her know he was going to.

That made her retreat into her shell a little and question whether she'd said too much. But who knew what he was doing right then? *Whatever.* She couldn't just stand there waiting for him to say something back.

Dropping her phone into her tote, she strode right into Coco's Chocolates. The place smelled divine, all warm and creamy with the bitter edge of freshly roasted cacao beans. Instead of buying drinks that would be cool by the time she got home, she bought gorgeously decorated boxes of cocoa mix. While waiting for her charge to go through, she sampled a truffle. Her eyes practically rolled back in her head from the creamy texture and the rich chocolate flavor. It was the best she'd ever had.

Finished with her purchase, she headed out to the car, wondering if she should let Trevor know she was ready to go, but it turned out she didn't need to. Without so much as looking at her, he parted from the crowd, waving and throwing out one-liners. "Let's get out of here."

Only when she buckled in, and Trevor edged away from the curb, did she dare check her phone.

Cole: You are my bliss.

They entered a quiet house. The smell of cinnamon and pine filled the air, lights twinkled, and evidence of little girls was everywhere. The toy kitchen Cole bought them had pots and fake food scattered all around it and remnants of their last art project littered the coffee table. Amid the chaos, Hailey noticed some new decorations. Arms full, she tipped her chin toward the vintage Noel sign. "Another visit by your elves?"

"Hey, now. If ole Saint Nick spilled his secrets, it wouldn't be magic, now, would it? But that is a good-looking sign. And it's better than the inflatable Santa's workshop he considered buying that would've fit nicely on the front lawn."

She grinned. "And what stopped him from following through with that one?"

"Even Santa can read the room." Trevor had a twinkle in his deep blue eyes. "Less is more, or some sad adage like that."

"I'm so glad I met you. I understand your son so much better."

"How so?"

She would've continued the teasing, but she sensed he was in a more thoughtful state of mind. "You both flip a switch when you're in public. Like you, he's quiet when he's home." A dark cloud passed over him, and she quickly scrambled to chase it away. "Which makes sense, of course. You're both public celebrities." When it didn't go anywhere, she grew flustered. "Your publicists must coach you on how to behave."

He watched her for a moment, as if deciding whether he could trust her. "Anywhere I go, the paparazzi's waiting for me. If you give them a smile, a comment, even just a scrap of personality, you make it so much easier on yourself. If the world likes you, then they don't harass you. I never wanted to embarrass my son, so I've played the game as best as I could."

"I wasn't judging you. I promise. It's just something I notice about both of you. I guess that's why you raised Cole here? Because the paparazzi leave you alone?" Speaking of which, where was he? She set her bags down in the kitchen and noticed a tin of Scottish butter cookies.

"Not sure I raised him exactly, but yes, that's why I chose Calamity over Malibu. Well, that, and I didn't want him to become an entitled brat."

"You did a good job on that front. He's the best man I know."

"I've seen a whole other side of him here. With you and the girls." See, he was quieter again. Subdued. Not unhappy...just introspective.

She picked up a box of berry-flavored tea. "Cole doesn't drink this. I wonder what's going on."

Hailey: we're home. Where are you?

He didn't respond. "Maybe they're in the screening room? That seems like a good way to pass the time with kids."

"Sounds about right."

Together, they searched the house, but there wasn't a trace of them anywhere. "We had the car seats, so I don't think they went anywhere." She glanced outside, thinking maybe they were building another snowman. "Well, I'm all out of ideas. We've looked in every room in this house."

"Not every room." A slow grin lit up his extremely handsome features. "Not the room that caused him to buy this house."

"We were just in the wrapping room."

Not in on the joke, Trevor tipped his head in confusion. "I don't know about that one, but there's one room we haven't checked. I can't imagine he'd bring the girls there, but it can't hurt to try. Come on. I'll tell you about it on the way."

He led her down the stairs, but instead of going into the screening or wrapping rooms, he tapped another hidden panel. "Back in the late eighteen hundreds, when only outlaws lived in this area, there was a brothel where this house now stands."

On their way down the wooden staircase, Hailey touched the stone walls. Like a cave, they were cold and damp.

"It was popular at the time, and the owner would store the loot for the men in this hidden room beneath her saloon." Trevor tapped the wall. "The only thing left of the original establishment is this cave."

"He wouldn't bring the girls down here, would he? Is there anything in it?"

At the bottom of the stairs, Trevor came to an abrupt stop. His features went slack. "Yep."

That's when she finally heard noises. "What is it?" It sounded like breathing.

He stood on the last step, his body blocking her from the room.

"Is it gross?" She didn't want to see a rat or something. "Am I going to freak out?"

He broke into a soft smile, which was pretty devastating on a man as potently masculine as him.

Peering over his shoulder, she found a charming little room lit only by lanterns. The big bad hockey player with his bulging biceps and muscular thighs was sleeping on a giant red beanbag, Evvie sprawled across his chest and Paisley tucked against his side, his arm holding her tight to his body.

They were out cold.

Books were strewn about the cave-like room, and a thick blanket was spread out in the center. On it, she found a tea pot, little plastic teacups, and a plate of shortbread cookies.

"They had a tea party," she whispered. And it was the most beautiful thing she'd ever seen.

In that moment, she toppled. Fell head-first in love with him.

How could she not? He was an aggressive, brutal hockey player, a happy-go-lucky charmer, and the man who made tea parties for two orphaned girls.

He was the most special man she'd ever met, and her heart ached to think of him leaving.

And these girls…it was more than feeling sorry about their situation or an obligation to Lindsay. A bond was growing that would last a lifetime. Even if the PI found the perfect family for them, she knew she'd stay in their lives. She'd watch them grow into strong, independent, creative, accomplished women.

"Let's let them sleep." She started back up the stairs. "I'll get started on the cocoa."

These feelings were just too powerful.

It was too hard to watch what she couldn't keep.

Chapter Seventeen

AFTER HE AND THE GIRLS CAME UP FROM THE LOOT cave, they'd found a fire going and Hailey and his dad in bright red onesies. The girls squealed, more eager for the matching pajamas Trevor had brought than the presents they were about to open.

The five of them had spent all of Christmas Eve wearing them as they'd eaten dinner and opened the gifts in their stockings.

It had been everything he'd ever wanted as a kid. The best part of the night had been the three adults taking turns reading the memories out loud. It had prompted a few more memories, which they'd quickly written down and added to the pile.

The only hitch had been Hailey. Tonight, she hadn't been her usual warm, happy, fun self. After leaving cookies and milk for Santa and putting the girls to bed, she'd gone to her room.

They'd been together pretty much constantly for most of the day, so maybe she just needed space. Except, he thought about her text messages. The first one had been cool. *Thinking of you.* He'd liked that.

The second one had tripped a switch in his chest. *I miss you.*

Fuck, yeah.

That's what he wanted to hear.

But the third—that she wanted to be with him all the time? *Holy shit.* Joy had burst in his heart, as bright and intense as a solar flare.

So, if she wants to be with me, should I reach out? Or do I leave her alone?

He'd never been in a relationship before, so he didn't know.

After he got ready for bed, he talked to his teammates, who were down that they'd lost another game. He'd let them know it was just a period of adjustment, that they'd get their mojo back with the new lineup. He sure as hell hoped that was true. Every game mattered if they were going to make it to the play-offs.

And we sure as hell will.

He got into bed, leaving the covers at his waist.

I just want to spend every minute with you.

What was the harm in reaching out? He sent her a text.

Cole: You okay?

Three dots floated across the screen, disappeared, reappeared... And then...nothing.

Cole: I get it if you need time to yourself, but if something upset you, let me know who to slay.

He sent her a GIF of a warrior with a sword.

Still no response.

That's fine.

Look, he wasn't some puppy dog who needed to follow her around and hump her leg every damn second of the day, so he got out of bed and did a few manly things like pull-ups and his knee exercises. Maybe he'd watch some porn, blow snot out of his nose or something.

Yeah. That's what he'd do. He'd watch wrestling and scratch his balls. He wouldn't act like a kid with a crush and wonder what Hailey was doing at that moment. She obviously needed some time alone.

Totally fair.

He got back under the covers and reached for his phone, ready for some porn. *So...how do you find it?* He'd never watched it. Not even as a teenager. Not sure why. Maybe he just preferred a warm, responsive body. He loved the way a woman smelled and her soft, smooth skin. The weight of her tits in his hands. That hard, beaded nipple, and the pants and sighs that told him he was making her feel good.

Shit. Now, he had wood. He definitely needed porn. *Do you just put the word into a search engine?* And then what? How do you choose which site, which video?

Fuck it. The only skin he wanted to feel was Hailey's. The only mouth he wanted on his dick was hers. Desire surged through him, hot and dark. He'd made love to her twice, but he'd never fucked her. And he needed to. Needed to yank her hips up, ram that ass up against him, and slam into her. Needed to grab her tits, feel the slick nub between her wet folds—wet for *him*—and grind against her ass as he shot his load deep inside her.

What he felt wasn't all sweet and romantic. It was carnal and wicked and hot.

He got a flash of her lips parted, neck arched, eyes closed as he fucked her. Her big tits bouncing.

Fuuck. Squeezing his cock, he wondered if he had any lube in his nightstand.

Nope. He'd hidden all that shit in case the girls went rooting around in his drawers.

He hadn't closed his curtains, so moonlight spilled into his room, giving him enough light to see his fist gripping his painfully hard erection. He imagined Hailey straddling his thighs, her silky hair brushing his skin, and those hazel eyes all sultry as she sucked him into her mouth.

Arching off the mattress, he groaned.

"You all right?" Her hushed voice shocked the hell out of him.

He jerked upright. "Hailey?"

"Yeah. Can I come in?"

"Of course." *Shit. Fuck.* Had she seen him holding his cock? He was still hard, so he pulled up the sheet to cover himself.

As she headed over, he willed his hard-on to chill out. But it wouldn't. It was very excited to see her. Even though it sure didn't look like she was trying to seduce him in her onesie and ponytail. She probably just wanted to talk about tomorrow.

Hailey and her to-do lists. The woman liked a plan.

You'd think to-do lists would be enough to deflate my dick, but no. The closer she came, the harder his heat-seeking missile got. The tension was excruciating.

Okay, she wasn't stopping at the foot of the bed. So, maybe she'd sit on the side of his mattress—*nope. Not doing that, either. Oh, fucking hell.* She pulled back the covers and slid in beside him.

And now, he throttled his dick to get it to calm down.

Maybe she needs to talk. Maybe she's sad.

He had to stop thinking about sex and be there for her.

But her scent swirled in the air, filling his senses with her vanilla skin and coconut hair.

God, he wanted her.

"How's your knee?" Her matter-of-fact tone shoved a spike into his libido, and his whole body deflated.

Here he was, two seconds away from shooting his load, and she was thinking about his surgery. "My *knee?*" As hard as he tried to pull himself out of his lustful haze, he couldn't do it when her fingers brushed his bare thigh as she turned onto her side and moonlight glowed on her creamy, smooth skin. He thought he might die if he didn't get to touch her.

Kiss her.

Slide into her slick heat.

"You're doing too much. Your training, climbing up and down stairs. I mean, it's a holiday. Shouldn't you be resting it?"

"My knee's fine." His voice came out rough as sandpaper. "Why? Do I look like I'm in pain?"

"No, you *groaned* like you were in pain."

"Oh." Chuckling, he tipped his head back and stared at the ceiling. "It wasn't that kind of a groan."

"What do you mean?" She sucked in a breath. "Did I interrupt…Oh, my God. *Cole.*" She covered her face with her hands. "I can't believe I barged in when you…" Her eyes squeezed shut, and she looked miserable. "Were you…*pleasuring* yourself?"

"Trust me, it wasn't all that 'pleasurable,' and I didn't get beyond fisting my dick."

Her eyelids popped open, and she went silent and still. He could've punched himself in the face for being so crude around her. She wasn't one of the guys. "Sorry."

Her tongue made a slow pass along her bottom lip, her gaze pinned to the sheets. Well, to where his hand still had a grip on his cock. "Shit. Sorry." He let it go, bringing his arm up and back behind his head.

But still, she stared at the pole holding the sheet up like a tent. "Can I watch?"

Electric heat ripped through him. "You want to watch me jerk off?"

She nodded.

Adrenaline burning through his system, he kicked off the covers. "Fuck, Hailey." His dick was too sensitive to rub, but he gave it a squeeze and got a punch of lust when heat flared in her eyes.

"It's so big."

"You really don't have to flatter me to get me to put-out." He gave his cock a waggle. "It's all yours."

"You sure? Because it was excited long before I got here."

Embarrassment faded away, and he relaxed into the familiar comfort of her. "And who do you think it was thinking about?"

Her gaze flicked up to his eyes. "Me?"

"Yeah, Hailey, you. Only you."

Her legs shifted beneath the covers, and she let out a shaky breath.

He gave himself a few long strokes, the flat of his hand swiping over the sensitive head.

"Do you usually use lotion?" she asked, her voice barely a whisper.

"Yeah, but I don't have any now because I didn't want the girls to find it in my nightstand drawer and start asking questions."

"So, you need some lube." It wasn't a question.

Seeing the hunger in her eyes as she watched him tug his dick, desire streamed through him hot and thick. Because he knew where she was going with this. "That's right. I need your mouth. A few licks, and I should be good to go."

"Oh, I don't know."

The sting of anxiety burned through him. "I didn't mean… You don't have to give me a blow job."

She hitched up on an elbow. "Would you stop being so careful with me?"

"Can I? Because this is new. *We're* new, and I don't know what your boundaries are. I don't know—"

"Guess what I was going to say, Cole? That I don't think a few licks will be enough. That once I get you in my mouth, I'm going to lose my mind watching you fuck it. And you want to know what else I was going to say? That you'd better not pull out because you're worried about coming in my mouth. I want it, Cole. I want you real and raw. I want all of you."

He snagged an arm around her waist and jerked her closer. "You better be careful what you say to me. I don't think you get how much I fucking want you." He burrowed into her neck, breathing her in and gently biting the tendon. Well, maybe not so gently.

"Bullshit." She scraped the hair off his face, held it in her hand, and gave it a good, hard yank. "You think I don't see you? All that unleashed energy? You think I don't see the way you look at me like you want to eat me whole? Like you don't think you could ever get enough of me?"

He went still.

This is bad.

This is so fucking bad.

She'd stripped him bare, exposed him down to his beating heart.

"You know how I grew up. You know I begged my mom to get a steady job and stop moving me from one school to another. She didn't listen. She didn't see me. I have felt invisible my entire life. So, the way you want me? I crave it. You can only go wrong if you don't show me how much you want me."

Deep in his soul, Cole heard a crack. A roar in his ears accompanied the flood of lust, desire, and an affection so pure it glistened.

She wrapped an arm around his back, hugging him close. "Give it to me. Smother me in all that want and need." She pressed her mouth to his ear. "Make love to me like you can't get enough."

Cupping the back of her head, he kissed her, aware of her breathy moans and the ankles crossing over his ass, urging him to press against her.

And then he lost conscious thought. He was nothing more than the indescribably soft warmth of her mouth and the urgent tangle of their tongues. He was the grip of her fingers digging into his back and the sway of her hips back and forth over his hard cock.

Her sighs and frantic moans tossed fuel on his fire, and he went up in flames. His hands slid under her nightshirt and stroked up her belly, roamed the curve of her ribcage, and came around to savor the plump mound of her bare breast. When he pinched her nipple, she sucked in a breath and arched her back. His mouth found the hard bead, and he licked until she was pulling his hair and writhing beneath him.

"God, Cole."

All that friction made him so hard he fucking ached. He needed to be inside her. Needed to feel the tightness of her wet heat, needed to fuck her until he could release all the tension wracking his body.

She reached between their bodies, grasped his cock, and squeezed.

"Stop. Touch me, and I'll come." He kissed a path down her belly. "Too soon. Let me take care of you first."

"Why do you get all the fun?" Both hands on his ass, she pulled him to her at the same time she shimmied lower on the bed. "Come here."

Holy fuck. He lost his fucking mind. With a grip on the headboard, he guided his cock to those pretty pink lips, and the sight of that lush mouth opening for him, that tongue taking a long, slow lick right all around his head, had his hips rocking. She didn't even flinch, just closed those juicy lips around him and sucked him in deep. Her tongue lavished attention all over his hard length, and he couldn't stop himself from thrusting into her.

"Oh, fuck. Yeah. Suck harder." A shower of fiery sparks landed on his skin, and desire twisted hard in his belly. "Suck me. Fuck." He couldn't take his eyes off her. She was so beautiful, so lost in lust. Those pink lips worked him, her hands on his ass, drawing him deeper into her throat.

She moaned, and the vibration coaxed a ragged cry out of him.

That was it. He was done-for. "I'm coming. Fuck. Fuck."

Her grip tightened, and she gazed up at him like she wanted to watch him lose control. He was so lost, so crazed with lust, that he shot his load down her throat. Each contraction sent euphoria flooding into his bloodstream until he nearly blacked out from the extreme pleasure.

When she'd finally sucked every ounce of energy out of him, he slumped face-down on the mattress. "Five minutes and a Gatorade, and I'll be back in fighting form."

She crawled up to the pillow and sifted his hair through her fingers. "And here I thought hockey players had stamina."

Deep into the night, a hot, burning desire roused him. For a bleak moment, he wished more than anything he had Hailey in bed with him. He missed her in the same way he always had, that bottomless sense of loss, that craving for the kind of connection he'd never experienced but knew in his gut existed.

But then he became aware of the weight of her breast in his palm, the scent of her hair, and her warm, soft body mashed against his, and elation streaked through him.

She's here.

Holy shit. He had her in his bed.

When his cock notched into the crack of her ass, she pushed back, wedging him deeper, and turned her cheek, seeking. They kissed like that, her hugging the pillow, her hips rocking, their bodies growing hotter, needier.

"I want you." His tongue gave voice to his heart,

letting her know through its strokes, through its erotic dance, just how much. "Need you." Lifting her leg onto his thigh, he slid into her tight, hot channel.

Moaning into his mouth, she tilted her hips, letting him slide in even deeper. All the way, until he was fully sheathed inside her.

And then he was fucking her hard, fast, his hand gripping her hip, holding her in place. Savage need possessed him. The primal urge to mate, to join, to fuse with her body and soul.

She rolled onto her stomach, arms stretched out in front of her, ass pitched high. He mounted her like a fucking animal, slamming back inside where her body clenched around him. She grabbed fistfuls of the pillow, crying out as she met his thrusts, ramming up hard against him and grinding.

It wasn't enough. Not hard enough, not fast enough. He couldn't get close enough. He reared over her, cupping her breast, and rubbing his palm over her nipple. His other hand slid between her legs. Jesus, she dripped all over him.

Her cries turned to pants, her back arched, raising her ass even higher, and then she was writhing all over his cock. "Oh, God. Oh, God. *Cole.*"

And that was all he needed to finally let go. While she shuddered, then went boneless, he grabbed her hips and pounded into her. He fucked her so hard her palms went flat against the headboard.

The moonlight turned her skin molten silver, and her body glowed. Nothing turned him on more than her hourglass shape and jiggling ass cheeks. She was beautiful. She was sexy.

And she's mine.

Fuck. Hailey Casselton is mine.

He came in hot, explosive bursts, so violent he lost his vision to a deluge of white stars.

It was only when he'd calmed down, and she'd settled back against him, that he realized his fatal error.

She isn't *mine.*

She's only mine for now. He had to remember that.

If he didn't, he'd be destroyed.

The shush of fabric and the sweep of slippers over a hardwood floor had him stirring.

"Shh. Don't wake him."

"It Cwistmas. I gon wake him up."

"No, Evvie. *Evvie.*"

Cole fought his smile, keeping his breathing steady so they'd think he was still asleep.

The slightest depression on the mattress let him know Evvie had hoisted herself up. Then, he felt her hot breath in his ear. "Waked up, sweepy head. Waked up."

A slightly deeper impression let him know Paisley had joined on his other side. Having them right where he wanted, he flung his arms out and pretended to yawn. He turned it into a roar and caught both girls around their waists. At that moment, he was so damn glad he'd put on his training shorts when Hailey had slipped out of his room at dawn to return to hers.

"Who woke up Wild Jack?" He tickled the girls as they shrieked with laughter.

"Nobody," Paisley cried.

"Oh, somebody did. And I want to know who so I can eat them."

"I did." Eyes lit with mischief, Evvie shrieked.

Laughing so hard tears spilled down her cheeks, Paisley pulled her legs up. "Stop, Cole, stop."

He quickly removed his hand, kissing her on the forehead.

"Merry Christmas." With her pink cheeks and wet hair, Hailey entered the room looking freshly showered. "Hey, you started a cuddle session without me? Let me in there." The moment she climbed onto the bed, the three of them attached to her like barnacles.

With the four of them snuggled tightly together, he and Hailey held each other's gazes, and he knew without a doubt she felt it, too.

This is what life's about.

This is what matters.

His entire life, he'd chased the next level of success. Driven to be drafted, to earn a spot on the front line, to win games, and to take home the Cup. And he'd done it. He'd had a lot of great moments.

But nothing had been as fulfilling as this moment.

"Can we open presents now?" Paisley asked.

"Presents?" In Wild Jack's voice, he started to rear up again. "There are presents in this house?"

"Yes." Both girls squealed in delight.

"They're mine. Mine. All the presents are mine."

Hailey jumped out of bed. "Oh, no. There's only one way to get rid of Wild Jack."

"How?" Paisley asked, eyes sparkling.

"With waffles. He hates them, and if we can stink up the house, he'll leave, for sure. Whoever comes downstairs first gets to put the chocolate chips on them."

"I do it." Evvie dropped off the bed with a thunk.

He lurched up, certain she'd hurt herself. But no, the

little spitfire charged out of the room, elbows pumping, behind swaying. Paisley followed.

On her way out, Hailey cast him a look over her shoulder. "You coming?"

He realized he was just sitting there, watching them leave. Despite the uneasiness creeping up his spine, he said, "Of course. Let me get dressed and brush my teeth."

Her grin flashed bright and happy.

Once they were gone, he closed his eyes and let the fear swallow him whole.

Because it struck him that he'd earned their affection. Their trust.

They felt safe and comfortable with him.

And that's when bad things happened.

His nannie's words always ran on repeat in the background of his mind, but right then, the volume turned up.

You're going to get yourself killed one day. You'd just better hope you don't take someone with you.

It was so unsettling, it got him out of bed and into the bathroom. As he grabbed the toothbrush, he caught his reflection in the mirror.

He'd hurt people. It wasn't just Booker. It was Kevin and Danny, too. He got attached, he got swept up in a good time, and then he inevitably took things too far.

But the thought of letting Hailey and these girls go...*no. I can be better.*

I'm not a kid anymore.

He closed his eyes.

I don't want to fuck this up.

Hailey cracked the last egg and dropped it into the bowl.

At her side, Paisley started whisking. "Like this?"

"Yep. Just like that. Keep beating while I pour the buttermilk, okay?"

At the table, Evvie created a design out of chocolate chips. For every piece she set down, she stuffed another into her mouth.

"Can we open presents now?" Paisley asked quietly. "Please?"

"We have to wait for Cole and grand—" *Whoa.* She'd been about to call Trevor *grandpa.* Where had that come from? She had to be more careful. She couldn't mislead the girls and get their hopes up. What if the PI found someone?

If he did, she'd have to give all this up. "We're waiting for Cole and Trevor, sweetie."

"What's taking so long?" The little girl had a hint of petulance Hailey had never heard before.

"Well, Cole's brushing his teeth." She glanced at the clock. "And Trevor should be here any minute." It wasn't even seven in the morning.

"I don't want breakfast." Paisley dropped the whisk. "I want presents."

"I know you do, and we're not eating yet. We're just getting the batter ready. I promise, as soon as the guys get here, we're all over those presents."

Cole came into the kitchen wearing navy blue Brawlers sweatpants, a white Brawlers Henley, and leather shearling slippers. Paisley jumped off the step stool, and Evvie slid off the chair. Both girls raced over to him. "He's here, he's here." Paisley clapped her hands excitedly. "We're opening presents now."

"Is my dad here?" Cole asked.

"Not yet."

He leaned over, picked up the girls, and came to the counter. Hailey laughed when she saw the chocolate hand imprint on his white shirt. "What?" He looked down, and when he saw it, his expression grew thoughtful. She wondered if that shirt meant something to him. She was ready to suggest spraying it with stain remover when he said, "That's my next tat." He set Paisley down. "Come on, my chocolate monster." And brought Evvie to the sink.

"I not a monster."

He washed her hands. "No, you're the smartest, most interesting person I've ever met."

They continued to chat quietly, as though the world hadn't shifted beneath her feet. But it had. Warmth spilled into her, spreading everywhere. She didn't know why his simple statement had affected her so profoundly. Maybe it was the permanence of it, the fact that he would ink this little girl's handprint...

It was about the sexiest thing she'd ever heard.

And the fact that he hadn't told Evvie she was pretty or fun? He seemed to intuitively understand exactly what a young woman needed to hear to bolster her sense of herself.

How he thought he wasn't good with kids was a mystery.

He barely had a chance to dry the three-year-old's hands, when she took off into the living room, shouting, "Pesents."

With the girls out of the kitchen, she finally got him all to herself. "Good morning."

He gave her that hungry look that made her go all hot and restless. And then he kissed her. Lightly, sweetly, but with a hint of what was to come. "Morning." She loved that gravelly, deep voice and couldn't wait to hear it in the dark of his bedroom.

"Last night was amazing."

He didn't answer, just grabbed her ass and hauled her up against him. Lifting her onto the counter, he put his big, warm hands on her cheeks and kissed her.

What his mouth and tongue and hands told her spoke so much louder than words. She wasn't sure she'd believe them anyway. But his grip, his passion, his voraciousness —she heard it loud and clear—and it made her swoon.

The girls squealed, and a second later, they heard a deep voice call, "Merry Christmas."

Slowly, she pulled away, kissing him softly one, two, three more times. "Your dad's here. We should go."

"Are those for me?" she heard the older girl ask.

"Some of them are. Here. Go put these under the tree."

Hailey shook her head. "He brought *more*?"

He just grinned. "Of course, he did. It's Christmas." He stepped back, helping her drop to her feet. "The others were from Santa. Come on."

Just as they headed out of the kitchen, Evvie slammed into them. "Twevor here. Pesents now."

"I know, I know." Hailey cradled the back of her head. "We're coming."

Paisley hurried toward Trevor, a few sloppily wrapped gifts in her hand. "These are for you."

"Me?" Trevor asked.

"Yes," Paisley said. "We made them."

"You *made* me something?" Trevor asked, voice full of awe. "I'm so excited."

Both girls were jumping around, and Trevor joined them. It was hilarious. She was about to join them, when

Cole reached for her. "Before we go and get lost in all the mayhem of the holiday, I want you to know that this is the best Christmas I've ever had."

"Me, too." She had so much she wanted to ask him.

What's happening here?

Are we falling in love?

She knew this was real. She knew what they were building was powerful and wonderful and could last.

But he was going to leave. And their little bubble would burst.

And then what?

He must've read her expression because he kissed her again and said, "One step at a time." He wrapped an arm around her. "Now, let's make the magic for our girls."

Our girls.

Yes.

Chapter Eighteen

After they'd unwrapped presents and stuffed their bellies with waffles, they gathered around the hearth in the living room to relax. Firelight flickered, and the girls chattered happily. Hailey could practically hear the house sigh in contentment.

She nursed her coffee while trying to look interested in the conversation between father and son, but mostly, she was fighting back emotion. Sure, it was because she was living the holiday of her fantasies. That was awesome.

But it was painful, too, because it wasn't hers to keep. She wasn't the mother to these two beautiful, spirited, funny, smart little girls. And—her breath hitched hard in her chest—she didn't get to keep that gorgeous man who surprised her at every turn.

Especially, the gift he'd given her. She'd expected a pair of luxury slippers. Maybe a gift card to a spa. Anything but what he'd done.

This wonderful, thoughtful man had created a studio for her.

A *studio*. Complete with vintage and modern dress

forms, a caddy with all the right scissors, textile chalk, curve rulers, and a rotary roller. He'd found a brush holder and filled it with every size of rounded and flat brush on the market. Colored pencils, watercolors, and sewing machines. Not just one or two, but a computerized one, a manual one, and one for embroidery.

I mean, come on. He'd thought of everything.

She didn't even know how long she'd be staying here, but he'd told her he wanted to make sure she had everything she needed to replace the inventory her mom had taken.

And what had she given him? A collage of photographs that spanned his life including this most recent time with the girls. He'd loved it, for sure. But it didn't compare to how he'd nailed her gift. He *knew* her. He knew what mattered most.

Did she even know him that well? *I mean, come on. A collage?* That was the best she could do? Or maybe he was so used to getting so little, he didn't bother revealing what he needed.

She would pay more attention. He had seemed to like the collage, though, especially the shot she'd gotten of him on the floor playing dolls with them. He was braiding hair and buttoning dresses, chatting with the girls as though it was the most normal thing in the world. As if he didn't have a single care in the world.

Not like a team captain who was missing out on a big chunk of his hockey season to take care of his high school friend's children.

She was amazed by him.

And she didn't know what to do about it.

She'd dated plenty of guys, but she could always tell pretty quickly that it wouldn't lead anywhere. With Cole, she thought about him all the time. Her body reacted to his nearness.

No one had ever meant as much to her as he did.

She tuned back into their conversation. His dad listened intently as Cole talked through his concerns about his team. The front line wasn't gelling with the guy who'd replaced him. Part of him wanted to fly out there and offer support, but he knew it was a question of how the guys worked together, and that wasn't something he could help with.

The girls played happily with their new toys.

They'd given the girls a wonderful Christmas, and she wouldn't ruin it with negative thoughts. She'd enjoy every moment of it.

Because it was beautiful and perfect. And if Trevor and the girls weren't there, she'd crawl onto Cole's lap and show him with her hands and her mouth exactly how much she loved his gift. How much she—

Her heart squeezed so hard she got off the couch. "Anyone want anything? I'm going to get more coffee." Her voice sounded rough, and she hoped the men didn't notice.

In the kitchen, she set her mug on the counter and lowered her head. She didn't want more coffee. She wanted this day to last forever. And that was so confusing because she had a life waiting for her in New York. She had an apartment and a job—well, maybe not with Abbott's. But if she needed to get another one, New York was the place to be.

All the lines had blurred, and she was so damn confused.

Arms circled her waist, and her body recognized him instantly. She could tell by his scent—the expensive soap he used, his clothes fresh from the dryer, and the potent masculinity that sent her pulse racing.

"You okay?"

"I'm happy. So, so happy." He lowered his face into her neck—one of his favorite places to be. "Why do you always kiss my neck?"

"Because when I breathe you in, there's nothing else in the world but you."

She folded her arms over his, hugging him tightly against her. "Is this real?"

"Yes."

She loved the firmness in his tone. "But you're leaving."

"I know." He spun her around. "But that doesn't mean we have to end."

"I don't even know if I'll have a job a month from now, and you're in Boston."

"I live there for part of the year. And it doesn't matter where you work. Long distance or short, my feelings for you won't change."

With an intensity that thrilled her, he caught her waist and hoisted her onto the counter. Stepping between her legs, he brushed the hair off her shoulder, never taking his eyes off her. "I'm not into you because we're under the same roof, taking care of these kids. I've been with a lot of women, Hailey—" His gaze cut away, and he briefly shut his eyes. "Let me rephrase that. I've been around a lot of women, and I've never felt this way for anyone."

"Me neither."

"When I look at you, something clicks into place. I can't explain it other than to say it's a feeling of rightness. I know it hasn't been that long, but you're my person. I can't see into the future. I can't see past this minute right now, but I know you feel right to me. You always have. And I…" He pressed his lips together in a look of total determination. "That's just not going to change."

Affection surged through her. Scraping her fingernails across his scalp, she kissed him. She loved the silky softness of his mouth, the caress of his tongue, but mostly, she loved how he made her feel. It was his body's response to her that broke down her defenses and set her free. She might've heard the words before, but only Cole's touch told the truth.

She trusted him, and that was so hard for her. She kissed him deeply, passionately, letting herself go completely, wholly, and profoundly.

"Hailey." Paisley's voice tore them apart. "This doesn't work. Can you fix it?" She held out a light saber.

"It just needs batteries." Trevor came in after her, his gaze ping-ponging between the two adults, quickly sizing up the situation.

Cole stepped back, drawing a hand over his mouth. "Let me see what I've got."

"No, no. Don't worry about it. I brought batteries to go with everything I brought." With an impish grin, Trevor took the little girl's hand and led her out of the kitchen.

But Hailey didn't care that they'd been caught kissing. She dropped her head onto Cole's shoulder, feeling freer than she had in a very long time.

Maybe this can last.

Until now, it had been a great day.

Since the girls were too wired to nap, they'd built a

blanket and pillow fort in the living room and read books. The adults had taken turns reading. His dad had used his Scottish accent, and Paisley had gone nuts over it, begging him to repeat certain words.

It had been a lot of fun until Evvie farted and cleared everyone out. They'd laughed until their bellies ached. Next, they'd gone down to the game room to play a game Trevor had brought. They'd all put on their Velcro hats and lobbed soft balls at each other. The person with the most balls stuck to his head got to choose the music for their dance party.

It was only then, with the music turned up loud and everyone rocking out under a disco ball, that he'd noticed Evvie had gone missing.

He set off to look for her, calling her name as he made his way through the house. Maybe she'd gone back to her new toys? She'd really liked the veterinary play set his dad had gotten her. She'd put on the stethoscope and listened to everyone's hearts, including all her stuffed animals. But no, he found the presents abandoned in the living room and didn't hear a peep. He turned off the stereo system and called out, using his loud and aggressive hockey voice.

Nothing.

Fuck. Now, he was getting nervous. *Where is she?*

Think. Where would she go for comfort?

An image of the Leesons' house dropped into his mind, and his skin went cold as snow.

She wouldn't try to go home, would she?

There's no way she'd leave without an adult.

Jesus, he lived high up on the mountain, miles from town.

He'd set the alarm to signal whenever somebody opened the front and back doors, but the music had been so loud in that game room it would've been impossible to hear.

His phone vibrated, and he pulled it out to see a text.

Hailey: Any luck?

Cole: Not yet.

A sound caught his attention, and he raced into the kitchen to find the pantry door ajar, the light on. He found his little Evvie with her hand inside a bag of chocolate chips.

Jesus. This kid. He drew in a deep breath to try and calm down. "What're you doing?"

She peered up at him, not the least bit concerned she'd done something wrong, and she broke into the most adorable grin he'd ever seen. "Shocklet." She held up a hand, streaked with melted chocolate.

"I see." Gently, he took the bag out of her hands, sealed it up, and placed it on a higher shelf. "Hey, you know we've been looking for you, right? You left the dance party without telling anybody."

"I hongry."

"Sure. But we've got a big Christmas dinner planned."

"I hungry now."

"I get that, but you need to let me know if you're going to leave the room, okay? We didn't know where you were." He squatted—not a good move for his knee, but he needed to get his point across—to look her in the eyes. "We were worried about you, sweet pea. I looked all over the house and couldn't find you. Please don't do that again, okay?"

Movement behind him had him glancing over his shoulder to find Hailey watching them.

"I dance wif Mommy."

A sharp twist of sorrow had him rocking back on his heels. What did she mean? Was she referring to Hailey as her mommy? Or... "You mean you used to dance with your mommy?"

She nodded. "I dance wif Mommy."

Hailey sucked in a breath, and Cole's ass hit the floor. He crossed his legs so he could settle the little girl in his lap. "Come here, sweetheart. I'll bet you miss dancing with your mommy."

"Yes. I dance wif Mommy."

"I'll be that's a really good memory, and we can write it down and put it in the stocking." Ignoring the smears of chocolate on her hands and face, he pulled her into a hug. At first, her arms remained at her side, but he could feel her little body heating up.

She pulled away and gave him an earnest look. "I go home now?"

Ah, hell. "No, baby. You can't go home because Mommy and Daddy aren't there anymore."

Hailey sat with them, wrapping one arm around Evvie and one around Cole. "Evvie, baby. Your mommy and daddy love you so much. You have to know there's nowhere else they'd rather be than with you. But they can't come back, sweetheart."

Evvie pulled away, tears flooding her brown eyes. "I go home now. Pease, Cole? Pease, I go home?"

His heart grew too big and heavy for his chest. He'd never felt so helpless in his life. There was nothing he wouldn't give this little girl, but he didn't have the power to grant her one and only wish. With everything still up in the air, he couldn't even talk about a replacement home.

"Baby, your mommy and daddy are gone, but they sent me and Hailey to come and take care of you."

The little girl sat still for a moment. They gave her a minute to digest the information, not sure what she would make of it. And then, she looked up at him. "You mine, Cole?" That little baby voice, the sincerity in those brown eyes...

He was drowning. "I..." *Dammit.* He shouldn't have hesitated like that. There was only one answer. And it wasn't a lie. He would stay in touch with her as long as she needed him. "I am."

"You mine, Cole." She settled against him and snuggled into his chest. "Cole mine." The trust this girl gave him—

He could so easily fuck it up.

But he couldn't think like that. He had no choice but to do his damnedest to be worthy of it.

Because in some way he couldn't explain, the little girl was right.

Evvie's mine.

As he stood to leave the pantry, he found Trevor and Paisley watching them.

"Can I wear my robe now, Hailey?" Paisley asked.

"Of course, you can. It's yours."

Trevor watched the scene with an odd expression, and Cole had no idea what his dad was thinking.

"Come on, Evvie." The six-year-old motioned for her sister. "Let's put on our robes."

Evvie wiggled to lift herself out of Cole's lap. "And our fifis?"

"Yeah, let's wear those, too."

"I'll get mine." Hailey hurried after them. "We'll all wear them."

"Fifis?" Cole asked his dad.

"The highland cow slippers I bought everyone."

Cole didn't get it. "Why does she call them fifis?"

"I told them they were for her 'feetsies,' so apparently that's what she thinks they're called."

Adorable. "You better have brought a pair for yourself because this clan's about to get serious with our Christmas onesies and fifis."

"Uh, no. I didn't get myself any." His dad still watched him strangely. "But I can still pass as a distant relation in my onesie."

Cole chuckled and moved to go around him, but his dad put a hand on his arm.

"You're an exceptional man. I'm not sure I ever told you that." He sounded more intense than Cole had ever seen him.

"Thanks." *Where's this coming from?* "What's going on, Dad?"

"Nothing. I couldn't be prouder of you."

They filled the next several days with family time and holiday activities. The dog sled ride through the forest, all five of them tucked under thick wool blankets, was a favorite. The girls had laughed the whole way, and Cole hadn't been able to take his eyes off them.

There was more ice skating, cocoa, and snowmen, and they made sure to give the girls loads of quiet time to play with their toys, make cookies, and read books.

On the fourth day after Christmas, his dad didn't come over. Something had been off with him for a while, so Cole used his key to get into his childhood home. Once inside, he stood in the foyer and took in the wood beamed ceiling, the gleaming hardwood floors, and the light flooding in from all the windows.

It looked the same, of course. Nothing had changed. His dad had a staff that took care of everything.

But it didn't feel like a home.

And he could only say that because his home used to be just like this one. Before slippers and fleece blankets, light sabers and sippy cups, books and blocks, were strewn all over. Before two little girls had left their mark on him, one with her chocolate handprint, and the other with her braids.

Before Hailey.

The sharp contrast between his home and the one he'd grown up in lodged between his ribs, making it uncomfortable to breathe. Because he had so few good memories here, and at his place, he had little girl giggles, and Hailey's expression when he walked into a room—

Yes, that. That right there.

Fuck.

The way her eyes warmed, and color bloomed across her cheeks.

That's what I want to see for the rest of my life.

He could have that. If he stayed alert and watched himself. He could hold onto them.

Just because his nanny had said something when he was a kid didn't mean it held true today.

Did it? "Dad?" He wandered through the house. When he didn't see him downstairs, he headed up. "You here, Dad?" He found him in his office, sitting at his desk, the glow of the laptop screen casting a blue tint on his features. "Hey. What's up? You reading a script?"

"No." He seemed disoriented, like Cole was pulling him out of a memory. "Nothing like that. You can come in."

Cole headed for the desk, expecting to find a contract or something business related. Instead, he found a recording of a Youth Hockey League game. Why was he watching little kids? "Wait, that's Kurt." He leaned in. "That's *my* practice. I was, what, twelve?"

"Thirteen."

"How did you get this?" He supposed one of the parents might've recorded it, but they usually did that for games. Not practices. "Are you stalking social media?"

"Nope." His dad shut the laptop. "I hired someone."

"What?"

His normally jovial dad looked tired. "When you first came to me, you were…God, you were cute. Cutest little kid I'd ever seen. But I didn't know what the hell to do with you. I'd just made my first break-out film, and I had to be in a hundred places at once." He scraped a hand through his longish hair that still had more pepper than salt. "I wanted to be there for you, but I couldn't. And then I did the next movie and the one after that, and I realized I was going to miss just about everything. So, I hired someone to record it all. Your practices, your games. Even the year you joined the tennis team. And yeah, I watched that footage, too. Glad to see there was one sport you weren't good at. Guess you're human after all."

"I wasn't good because Kurt told me not to join, that if I fucked up my knees or my elbows, he'd kick my ass. He told me if I wanted to be great at something, I had to dedicate myself to it. He said there was nothing wrong with playing a lot of sports and trying a lot of things, but I could only be great at one thing."

That wiped the smile off his dad's face. "He was more of a dad to you than I was."

Cole hunched a shoulder. "He was a coach. You're my dad. Why didn't I know I was being recorded?"

"I didn't want you performing for the camera. I just wanted to see you being you."

"I don't know what to say right now." He couldn't say it made him happy. No, something about it seemed off.

"There's nothing to say. I made the wrong choice. And I only know that because I've watched you this week and realize what I missed out on. What you missed out on. And I honestly don't know how the hell you're such a natural with those girls when you had no role models. None at all. You didn't have a mother, and your father… instead of giving you traditions, *holidays*, took you to exotic places around the world." He shook his head. "How did I get it so wrong?"

He didn't like seeing his dad so upset. "You didn't get anything wrong. It's the nature of your career." Just like mine. "And, come on. I don't know what I'm doing."

"But that's what being a natural means. You don't know what you're doing, and yet your instincts are spot-on. You know what to say. You know how to handle situations—"

"You're the one who gave me Deborah's number. And I'm in parenting forums. I look things up."

Energized, his dad got up. "That's what I'm saying. You think I looked anything up? *My* instinct was to make you laugh, keep you smiling, keep your mind off your problems by taking you on some grand adventure. But I watched you with Evvie the other day. You got down on your knees and looked her in the eyes and gave her the honest truth about her mom and dad. You didn't try to distract her. You didn't offer her a Disney cruise to get her mind off of it." Hands scraping his hair back, he spun away from him. "I didn't even know that bitch was neglecting you until the school called." His dad dropped his gaze to his boots, shaking his head. "It went on for years." His voice went tight, strained. "And I didn't know."

"She came from a top agency, and she'd been a nanny for twenty years."

"A shitty one." When he turned back around, tears glittered. "My *son*." He smacked his chest with a fist. "She neglected my son." His voice cracked. "I loved you from the moment I set eyes on you. When that man traded you for cash, I was caught between wanting to punch his lights out and being so damn grateful to rescue you from someone who would've treated you like his wife's bastard kid."

"I know you loved me, Dad. I never doubted it."

"I made the wrong choice. And it took me watching you with children who aren't even yours to see that." His dad inhaled deeply, straightened his shoulders, and looked Cole in the eyes. "You're a better man than I could ever be, and I'm so damn proud of you. I can't change the past, but I can do better from this moment on."

He should probably tell his dad it was all right, that he'd had a good childhood, but in this moment, his dad was more real than he'd ever seen him, and it didn't feel right to lie. "I appreciate that, but I don't really need anything anymore. I mean, I'm twenty-eight. Whatever I wanted as a kid, I'll have to create for myself as an adult."

He had never seen so much vulnerability in his dad's eyes. "I'm sorry."

"I'm not angry with you. I've always understood you're an actor first." Actually, he hadn't understood that until this moment. He'd known his dad had a big, important career, but he'd never considered that his dad had *chosen* to be a father second. "I'm no different. I'm a hockey player first, so I get it." Since the attorney's phone call, he'd had a lot of anxiety about honoring Darren's wishes—*how* to do it—but he finally had his answer.

He wouldn't do to these girls what his dad had done to him. Which meant he couldn't be a father until he retired from hockey. Between practice, meetings, physical therapy, working out, travel, games, charities, and events, what kind of father-figure would he be?

This conversation confirmed that finding them a forever home was the right thing to do.

As soon as he left, he'd call the PI.

Christmas was over. It was time to find these girls a home.

And if the idea made him a little sick to his stomach, he'd just have to deal with it.

The day before New Year's Eve, Cole watched his team lose another game. "Fuck." He ripped off his knee brace and threw it across the room. His team needed him right now. Not in four weeks. He texted his trainer.

Cole: We have to accelerate my recovery.

Trainer: Yeah, tough loss tonight. I get it. You need to get back. But you get on the ice too soon, and you'll make things worse than before the surgery.

Trainer: All I can say is you're damn lucky it was a

partial medial meniscectomy. Be patient. We'll get you there.

Every loss took them one more step away from the play-offs. He pulled up the group chat with his teammates.

Cole: Let's go, boys. I get a few games, but a skid like this isn't okay. Our effort is lackluster, to say the least, and we don't look like ourselves. Pick it up, or we're not going to be playing for much longer.

A bunch of texts came in, one after another. But there was only one that got his attention.

Ranger: We're not ourselves, asshole. You're not here.

Yeah, man. I know. I fucking know.

Chapter Nineteen

LOST IN THE STEADY THRUM OF THE SEWING machine, Hailey startled when visitors entered her studio. "Oh." She lifted her foot off the pedal and got up to greet them. "I took too long. I'm so sorry. I know you have to go."

Glori had called that morning, offering to watch the girls so Hailey could get some sewing done. Normally, she would've said no. She and Cole had worked out a nice schedule covering each other while he skated and trained, and she worked.

But her new friend had said something that stopped her in her tracks. "Let me ask you a question. If I asked Cole if he wanted me to come by and watch the kids so he could get some training in, what do you think he'd say?"

"He'd say, 'Please and thank you.'" She'd felt so small at that moment, because she knew Cole wouldn't even hesitate to take up on an offer like that.

"You're a businesswoman," Glori had continued. "You have goals that won't get met if you don't take advantage of every opportunity to work. So, I'll ask you again. I have some free time this morning at ten. I can hang out with the girls if you want to get some work done."

"Please." She'd smiled so big it hurt. "And thank you."

But it wasn't just Glori who'd shown up. It was Knox and Rosie with their children. It had turned into a playdate.

And now, all three of them surrounded her.

"What're you talking about?" Knox asked. "We're fine. Cole came home, so we thought we'd come down and see this fabulous studio your boyfriend designed for you."

"He's not my—"

All three women gave her challenging looks.

"Fine." With a flourish, she gestured around the room. "Isn't it amazing?" He's *amazing.*

Knox took in every detail. "It really is."

"This is sensational." Glori held up a robe. "How much?"

Hailey laughed. "I'd be happy to make robes for all of you."

"That's not what I asked," the older woman said. "I asked how much you're charging."

"They're free in exchange for babysitting." Glori and Knox gave her pointed looks, making her laugh again. "Okay, fine. They're a hundred bucks. And don't ask for a break just because we're friends. I'm a businesswoman."

Their serious expressions cracked into grins, and Glori said, "Three hundred it is. A perfectly reasonable price for a hand-sewn robe of this quality."

Knox rubbed the material between two fingers. "Is it weird that I want to get naked right now?"

For a woman who worked with fabric for a living, not at all. She understood. "We could give you some alone-time," Hailey said.

Rosie shrugged out of her sweater and yanked off her jeans. When she saw everyone watching, she said, "What? I'm not naked." Yet, she stood there in nothing but sexy scraps of pale pink lace.

"That's what I started out making." Hailey pointed. "Lingerie like that. But when I found this fabric, I had the same reaction as Knox."

"You wanted to roll your naked body all over it?" Knox asked.

"Oh, my God," Rosie said. "Is your husband out of town? Do you need some Gray lovin'?"

"Asks the woman who literally stripped out of her clothing to try on a robe," Knox said.

Rosie lifted her arms and gently swung the bell sleeves. "I didn't want to ruin it with my street clothes."

"But it's okay to ruin it with your skin?" Knox had a teasing glint in her eyes.

"Oh, I didn't think about that. I did shower before I came over here."

"And slathered lotion all over your body," Knox was quick to point out.

"I did. Now it's going to smell like my perfume." Rosie cut a sheepish look over to Hailey. "Sorry."

"That one's yours." She didn't mind a bit. It fit the princess perfectly.

Rosie's eyes went wide. "Look at this. I love how it's got these dark pink, green, and yellow flowers, but then you've got this peacock with its wings spread, and it's just so feminine, bold, and romantic all at once. I love it."

"Thank you." Hailey set about turning off machines and lamps. Her work for the day was done.

"You know, the Petticoat Rulers offers business loans," Glori said.

"Oh, I don't like debt. I'm still paying off my student loans. And if the business doesn't work out...then, I'm screwed."

Knox turned serious. "I want to tell you something, and please don't take this the wrong way." The wedding gown designer had a quiet elegance about her, and when she spoke, people listened. "I grew up with nothing. I had no connections, no family money...nothing. But not for one second did I ever question whether I'd become successful. Failure never entered my mind."

"I agree with Knox on that," Rosie said. "My family's made Nocturne for generations. For years, I begged them to expand our brand, add lotions and other products, and they refused. So, I became a chemist and created my own line. It was frustrating because I didn't see how to get where I wanted, but I never stopped marching forward."

"Well, I'm marching." Hailey went on the defensive. "I sketch and design. I've made dozens of robes, and I'm serious about saving money. I just want to be smart about it. I don't have a safety net." Not like Rosie who came from the royal family of St. Christophe, or Knox who married into the billionaire Bowie family.

"Are you suggesting we're successful business owners because we married wealthy men?" For the first time, she saw the hardness underneath Knox's elegant demeanor.

"No, not at all." Well, not exactly, anyway. "I've seen your wedding gowns, and I know you're unbelievably talented." She turned to Glori. "And I've had your protein bars. They're delicious."

"But you still think we had the backing of our husbands before we launched our businesses," Knox said. "And you couldn't be more wrong. I worked at House of Bellerose Atelier for years and had my own showing at

New York City's Bridal Fashion Week. *Then,* I started dating Gray. And Rosie? Sure, she's a princess, but she came to Calamity with no support. She would've been a chemist and created her own perfume if she'd grown up in a trailer like me. Nothing would've stopped her from living her passion."

Hailey wanted to assert herself, declare that she *was* living her passion, but how could she do that when her full-time job was designing flannel nightgowns for Abbott's? She lived her passion in stolen moments.

"I can't think of a single woman in the Petticoat Rulers who used her husband's money to create her success," Knox said. "And believe me, I'm not saying there's anything wrong with that. Whatever it takes. But I think fear's holding you back, and I want you to know we've all felt it, and we're here to help you through it."

Hailey probably should've been embarrassed for making such a lame assumption about these talented, strong women—of course, they'd done it on their own—but they were all kind, and nothing they said felt judgmental. She felt comfortable enough to tell them the truth. "You're right. I *am* scared. It's the way I grew up. My mom's a costume designer, and she goes from one gig to another. We've had to live off people's generosity more times than I can count, and I'm..." *Just say it.* "I'm terrified to go without. I need food in my refrigerator and a roof over my head."

"You don't have to run your business like your mom," Glori said. "We're not suggesting you 'trust the universe' to 'manifest' what you want in life."

"Wait, do you know my mom? Because that's exactly what she says."

"Oh, she's not so unique," Glori said gently. "Look,

you can only do what you're comfortable doing but just know you *can* take calculated risks. You don't have to follow your mom's example."

"But I'll tell you one thing." Knox held up a robe. "You're going to kick major ass with these. I'm one-hundred percent sure of it."

"And we'll help you any way we can," Rosie said.

It all sounded so good. "I appreciate you guys so, so much, but the thing is, I don't know if I'm staying in town. I work in New York." Even if Abbott's went out of business, she needed to stay in the city where she'd be sure to find another job.

"And if you don't?" Rosie asked. "Will you raise the girls here?"

Anxiety rippled through her. She hadn't yet dealt with the news Cole had dropped that morning, and she wouldn't think about it now. She stayed focused on the conversation. "That depends on whether I can work remotely." She hadn't heard back from her boss about her ideas for the new lines. Given the holidays, it wasn't surprising, but it kept her up at night. She needed her income and benefits.

Part of her would love to stay in Calamity and be part of the camaraderie these women shared. Not for a second had they made her feel like an outsider. Hell, she'd met them a week ago and already, they'd babysat for her.

Had she ever had a friend outside of Lindsay who was so supportive?

And as far as raising kids…of course she'd choose Calamity over New York City. But that might not be an option anymore. She couldn't avoid it any longer. She finally had to deal with the news she'd shoved to the back of her mind so she could function and get some work done.

She took in a breath and slowly let it out. "We heard from the PI."

The women tensed.

"He's found the biological mother." Saying it out loud hit like the crack of a tree right outside the bedroom window.

"Oh, wow." Knox looked as shaken as she felt.

"I know."

"What do you think about that?" Rosie asked.

"I don't know. We don't have enough information." And if she let herself go there, she'd spiral. She'd go over every possibility under the sun. Cole had urged her not to wait until they had details.

One step at a time.

"Do you want it to work out with his mother?" Knox asked. "Or are *you* their forever home?"

Am I? Every cell in her body screamed, *Yes, yes, yes. I am.* But her emotions were too high. Her instincts were unreliable right now. "I don't know. I want them to have the best life possible, but I don't know if that's with me. And if Darren's mom is able to take care of them—I mean, maybe she went on to have more kids, and if the girls have siblings, cousins, aunts, then that's a gift I can't keep them from. What do I have to offer compared to a big, happy family like that?"

"It's all right." Rosie gave her arm a squeeze. "No need to start rolling out the what-ifs. We'll wait until we have more information."

But now that she'd started talking, she couldn't stop. She'd been holding it in all morning. "It's just that Lindsay asked me to raise them. She chose me. If they'd wanted their babies with biological family, that's what they'd have done. You know what I mean?" She gave them an imploring look. "She chose me."

All three women regarded her with such compassion, it allowed her to comb through the tangle of emotions. Lindsay and Darren had made the will after they'd fallen out of touch with her and Cole. So, they'd known what they were doing—they'd assessed all possibilities and still landed on them.

Getting that off her mind cleared some space, and now she could see the real issue. "I'm invested. Wholly and completely." The tension in her body eased. "They're so...I can't explain this connection I have with them. I mean, maybe it's nothing more than a sense of protectiveness. I only know I'm desperate to help them feel safe and secure, to make up for the giant loss of their parents."

"Or maybe it's because you've fallen in love with them," Rosie said. "They make it pretty easy."

Well, look at that. It seemed she hadn't found the real issue at all. Rosie had. "Oh, I do. I really do." *I love them. I love them so much.* Why was that so terrifying?

Because I might not get to keep them.

"How will I know if it's a good family? What if I hand them over, and they don't see how fierce and smart and loving Paisley is? What if the girls don't get the attention they deserve? I don't want them to forget their parents, and I don't want anyone to gloss over their grief. And you guys, Paisley trusts me. I can't let her down. If you could see how she takes care of her sister, you'd know just how special she is." She knew it was love because it was crashing over her right then. Huge, billowing waves of it. "And Evvie's this tiny ball of energy. She stomps through life, grabbing what she wants. That girl's got a big personality, and she's imprinted on Cole like he's her duck daddy." She looked at them helplessly. "I can't have anyone crush her spirit or try to tame her. God, I do. I love them. So much." And she didn't know what to do about that. If Darren's biological mom wanted the girls, how could Hailey deny them their blood relatives? A huge extended family?

She'd been so painfully alone growing up with her mom and a constant stream of strangers. She'd have loved a big family.

She just didn't know the right thing to do. "I'm torn right down the middle."

"Right now, you and Cole are the guardians," Glori said. "The girls are yours. You'll only place them in a new home if you feel that's what's best." She gave Hailey a swift hug. "Has the PI talked to the mother yet?"

Hailey shook her head.

"Then, we have nothing to worry about yet."

There was so much power in that one word. *We*. Rosie had used it, and now Glori did.

Other than her mom, she'd never been part of a *we* before.

And that was the moment she made her decision. If she adopted the girls, she'd raise them right here in Calamity. With this group of friends who had her back.

And hopefully, with Cole.

Because their family wasn't complete without him.

Wild Wolff Village sponsored a lot of fun events on New Year's Eve. Right at sunset, the children paraded down the cobblestone streets, from one end of the town to the ice skating rink in the center. They wore glowsticks in all the colors of the rainbow, so it was a beautiful sight.

Those who didn't want to watch the kids could sign up for night skiing. Carrying electric torches, they cut a path down the mountain. Yes, it was freezing out, but kiosks sold hot coffee, tea, cider, and cocoa, plus all kinds of warm treats like churros, s'mores, crepes, and soup.

It was such a popular event, the village managed traffic by scheduling shuttles to take people from various stops throughout town.

After the parade and night skiing, everyone gathered to wait for the renowned fireworks display. Hailey and Cole had come early enough to score their own wrought iron bench, so they snuggled up together as the girls played with their lightsabers, waiting for the show to start. He'd been thoughtful enough to bring wool blankets, and boy, did she appreciate it. It was *cold*.

He picked up her hand and kissed her palm. "You okay? You're quiet tonight."

"I just want to hold onto this moment forever." Everything would change in the New Year. The PI had contacted the woman, and she'd agreed to meet with them. In a few weeks, Cole would go back to Boston. Which terrified her because, really, they'd just begun to get to know each other.

But she had now. And now was perfect. "This is the best holiday I've ever had." The village was all lit up, the rink full of skaters, and the smell of fried dough floated in the air.

"I know." He pulled her close. "You're my person, Hailey. No matter what happens, I want to be with you."

At the exact moment her heart flipped over, the first firecracker lit up the sky, and a shower of brilliant red and green sparks rained down. The girls tipped their heads back, watching in awe as the next one exploded, opening like a bright pink blossom and fanning out across the midnight sky.

Paisley turned to them, eyes wide, smile bright. "Look. It's so beautiful."

But Cole was watching her. "The most beautiful thing I've ever seen."

The little girl grabbed Evvie's hand, ran back to the bench, and climbed under the blankets. Once settled on their laps, the four of them snuggled together, their body heat warming each other, as they took in the joyful explosion of color and light.

"Happy New Year, LaLee," Cole said in her ear.

"Happy New Year, Wild Jack."

For now, she was the happiest she'd ever been in her life.

On the first day back to school, Hailey got up, ready to make coffee and help get Paisley out the door. She breathed easily, knowing she had Cole to thank for the smooth morning routine.

Of course, she had him to thank for other things, too, like the way he'd loved up her body so well last night it was as loose as a rag doll. With a secret smile for all the wicked things they'd done, she shoved her feet into slippers and threw on her robe.

And then, she opened her bedroom door to find a trail of rose petals leading down the hallway.

Uh, what?

What was her gorgeous, badass hockey player up to now?

The world saw him as aggressive and unrelenting on the ice and charming and cavalier off it. They saw him vacationing on yachts in the south of France, and they saw him surrounded by an entourage everywhere he went.

But they'd never seen him hold a teacup with his pinky out, lounge in bed with two little girls cuddled up against him as he read stories in funny voices, or look at her as if she was the embodiment of everything he'd ever wanted.

And they'd most definitely never seen him lay out a path of petals for a woman.

Nope. This is just for me.

But why had he done it? At the top of the stairs, she came to a stop to take in the literally hundreds of pink, white, and red balloons covering the living room.

And then Paisley came out of the kitchen with a big grin and a bouquet of roses. "Come on, LaLee." The girl—wearing braids and dressed for school—waited at the bottom of the stairs.

"What on earth is going on?"

"You'll see." Paisley handed off the flowers, then slid an arm through hers and escorted her across the living room.

Evvie came barreling into her with a box of chocolate-covered strawberries. "Come on, LaLee. Come wif me."

The three of them had to kick aside the balloons to get to the kitchen, where Cole stood by the island wearing a very nice suit, tie, and shiny black leather shoes.

"Well, hello, handsome." She could not believe she got to sleep with that incredibly hot man every night. "Is anyone going to tell what's happening?"

Suddenly, they were plunged into darkness, and then one by one, light bulbs on the counter lit up. It only took a moment to realize they were going to spell out *Prom?*

And then, with a grin and mischief in his eyes, Cole

was standing in front of her. "Hailey Casselton, will you go to prom with me?"

She reached for his hands. "Cole Montgomery, I would go anywhere with you."

The girls squealed and jumped up and down. "She said yes, Cole. She said yes."

"I know. I can't believe it. I'm the luckiest guy in the world."

Evvie held up a strawberry she'd already snagged out of the box. "I have it now?"

Cole just laughed and said, "Sure. But first, hand them out to everybody."

The little girl took her task seriously, choosing just the right berry for each of them. Hailey bit into the juicy treat, the creamy chocolate soothing the tart of the fruit.

"Go on and eat breakfast," Cole said.

The girls ran off to the table where she saw an unbelievable spread that included a pitcher of fresh-squeezed orange juice, a platter of pancakes sprinkled with powdered sugar, a bowl of fruit salad, strips of crispy bacon, glistening sausages, and a mound of cheesy scrambled eggs.

"You cooked all this?"

"Ha ha. That's funny." He shook his head. "No. I paid a young woman handsomely to deliver everything from Harley and Lu's this morning."

"You're amazing." She got up on her toes and kissed his mouth. "And rich."

He chuckled.

And then she whispered, "I can't wait to peel that suit off with my teeth."

"I made it easy for you." He put his mouth right at her ear. "I'm not wearing underwear."

Standing on the other side of the island, where the kids couldn't see the lower half of their bodies, she reached between them and rubbed his cock with her palm. He went rock-hard, and it made her blood go hot. When she squeezed, his hips snapped, pressing him deeper into her hand.

"Keep that up, and you're gonna get it." His whisper was closer to a growl.

"When? You're kind of a busy guy."

"After prom."

"Gosh, I'm not sure I can go with you. I have to study for a test in Algebra, and after school, I have band rehearsal."

His body shook with laughter. "Band? We're doing band now?"

"Bet you never got sucked off by a tuba player before."

"Hm, let me think about that." He tapped his cheek. "This might take a while."

She gave him a shove. "I have my hand on your dick, and you're going to play me like that?"

"Excellent point. Now, I have to get Paisley on the bus. When I get back, we'll talk about the sucking skills of a tuba player."

"Sorry, I promised Evvie I'd take her to your dad's pool."

"Damn. Fine. Guess I'll have to wait until after prom tonight."

"You're not actually serious about this, are you?"

"Oh, but I am. I've got the corsage and everything."

"But it's January. There's no prom in January. Besides, I don't even have a dress."

"That's all taken care of." He started off, but she tugged on the back of his suit coat.

"What does that mean?"

"You'll just have to wait and see." He grabbed a napkin and wiped the chocolate off Evvie's hands, and then walked Paisley out of the kitchen. On his way out, he called over his shoulder, "The hair and make-up crew will be here at three."

"You have got to be kidding me. Hair and make-up? What is this, the Oscars?"

The first crew member turned out to be Knox, who'd walked into the house with the most gorgeous pale pink gown Hailey had ever seen. The back plunged dramatically, and the top was sheer with sparkly white hand-sewn flower cut-outs.

She'd never worn anything like it. It was something only princesses and famous people wore to galas and award shows. The first thing Hailey had said once she'd put it on was, "What if I spill something on it?"

"I guess you'll have to be careful."

"I can't give it back to you with a stain, and I could never afford something like this."

Knox had smiled warmly. "It's yours, honey. This is a gift."

"What? No. You can't give me something this fancy."

"Sure, I can. I'm the boss. I can do whatever I want. Besides, I made this for a very fussy bride. We'd gone through about a hundred different sketches and concepts, and she finally settled on something. But halfway through the project, an idea popped into my head. It had taken me a while, but I'd finally cracked that woman's style. She loved the new concept, leaving me with this half-finished dress. When Cole asked me to help him out,

I knew this was the right one. So, I finished it with you in mind."

"I can't believe it. It's the most beautiful gown I've ever seen." The fabric swished each time she turned to see it from another angle. When she stopped fawning over it, she'd asked the question that had been on her mind since she'd first seen the rose petals. "Why would he go through all this effort for a prom? We're twenty-eight."

"He told me he ruined prom for you, and he wants to make it right. That man's got it bad for you."

Next, Glori had come over with a stylist, and together, they did her hair and got her all glammed up. They'd finished exactly on time because Paisley had burst into the room. "LaLee, LaLee, Cole's waiting for you. Come on."

Now, as she took one last look at herself in the floor-length mirror, Hailey couldn't believe it. She'd never been this glamorous. She turned to Glori and the stylist. "I don't even know what to say." Inside, she was shaking. "I'm overwhelmed. Thank you so much for taking the time to make me look like this."

"You're welcome, honey." The stylist finished packing up his kit and headed out the door. "Have fun tonight."

Glori came up behind her and, with hands on her shoulders, gently steered her back around to face the mirror. "Do you know what I see?"

"An overgrown woman playing dress-up?"

"No. I see a strong, intelligent, creative, determined woman. You're nothing like your mother, so you'll never make the same choices, and that means you won't wind up like her. You're safe now, Hailey. You can trust yourself. Go ahead and take some chances."

She reached for her new friend, falling into her arms, and years-worth of fear and anxiety rushed through her—

no, *passed* through her. She'd had no idea the weight she'd been carrying until she'd released it.

In their place, a sense of empowerment took over. And what a difference.

Anxiety had her wheels spinning in the mud.

While empowerment gave her energy and determination. It made her feel indomitable.

"You're right. You're so right. I *can* take care of myself." She pulled back, swiping the moisture from under her eyes. "I couldn't see it before."

"You've been running on fear."

No more. She'd make sure of it.

Chapter Twenty

SHE CAME DOWN THE STAIRS TO COLE, KNOX AND Gray Bowie, Glori, Phinny and Declan, and Rosie, Brodie, and their two children, watching and recording her descent.

Her two sweet babies clapped, jumping up and down with glee.

"You look so pretty, LaLee," Paisley said.

Evvie broke from the group to come running to her.

"Careful, sweetie," someone called, but Hailey didn't care. She scooped the girl into her arms.

"You pitty, LaLee."

"Ah, thank you, baby." When she looked up, her gaze landed on Cole, and her heart flipped over. In his black tux and white cummerbund, he looked like a model for a fancy watch ad. He could easily be the cover model of a glossy magazine.

Oh, wait. He'd already done that. A couple of times.

And he'd planned this whole night for her.

She set off for him. With one arm clutching Evvie, she

wrapped the other around her date. "I can't believe you did all this."

"I owed you." He pulled back, his gaze roaming her features. "Are you ready to go to prom?"

"Hold on, hold on. Let's get some pictures." Rosie stepped forward and reached for Evvie. "You come with me, sweet pea, so we can get Cole and Hailey over by the fireplace." She took some poses of just the two of them and then some with the girls. "Okay, perfect. You're all set."

Cole hooked his arm through hers and led her to the door.

"Curfew's midnight," one of the guys called.

"It's okay," another one said. "I've got a tracker on her phone."

"You've got school tomorrow," someone shouted.

"Ignore them," Knox said. "Just go and have fun."

Hailey turned to look at this group of friends, her little girls, and a strange sense of rightness took hold. *This is the life I want.* "Thank you, guys, for everything. I'm incredibly grateful."

Glori shooed her out the door. "You just enjoy your date."

Finally, they were out the door. He cupped her elbow, steadying her on the snowy walkway. "You look beautiful."

"Thank you. I feel like Cinderella."

Even more so when he ushered her into a warm limo. With its sleek leather seats and pristine carpeting, it was pure class. "I've never been in one of these."

He popped the cork on a champagne bottle and poured them each a glass. He lifted his in a toast. "To getting it right this time."

Her heart clutched at the thought that they might not.

"To getting it right." She took a sip, enjoying the bubbly treat. "And that goes for both of us."

"How's that?"

"It wasn't just you who messed up in high school. I didn't give you a chance. And come on, I was a horrible date."

He broke into a grin. "The worst."

"I just...wasn't in your league." She rubbed away the lipstick smudge on her glass. "And I couldn't imagine why Cole Montgomery would choose me out of every other girl. I mean, come on. I was a total outsider. I made my own *clothes.* And the hot jock on campus was asking *me* out? It didn't make sense." She shook her head. "Your dad was a *movie sta*r. Can you imagine what that felt like for a girl who stole food out of a rich man's refrigerator?"

"I liked your clothes. I liked that you were different. You were real, and you demanded honesty from everyone. I didn't care if you were an insider or an outsider. If you wore designer clothes or leggings. I didn't care. Still don't. I just like you."

The champagne bubbles must've gotten into her bloodstream because she was fizzy and happy and... God, she was soaring. "I like you, too."

He held her gaze. "And I don't want to mess it up again."

"After what we did in the shower last night, I don't think that's possible. You keep doing things like that, and I'm not going anywhere."

He tried to smile. "Trust me, I have a way of fucking up the things that matter most."

"Hey." She couldn't stand to see him doubting himself. Crawling onto his lap, she scraped her hands through his hair. "In the ten years since Booker's accident, have you fucked up anyone else's life?"

Since she was sitting on his lap, she could feel the slight flinch that went through his body and watch the awareness spread across his features. "No." He chuckled. "But that's because I don't have close friends anymore." His hands on her thighs tightened.

"Well, all I know is I'm not the same idiot who ruined the wonderful date you took me on, and you're not the boy who stole his dad's plane." The tulle of her dress billowed between them, and she had to shift it aside to get closer to him. "I was too afraid to get to know you back then, but I know you now. I see you. You're a good man, and you have to know how much you mean to those girls. And to me."

She needed him to hear her. With her hands on his cheeks, she said, "You feed my soul, Cole Montgomery." And then, she kissed him.

That first press of soft, sexy lips and the taste of champagne on his tongue, made her heart flutter. But the way he grabbed her chin, angling her for a deeper connection, the way he licked and stroked—the way he showed her how desperately he wanted her—had her tumbling into reckless abandon.

She went hot and hungry, but the dress confined her. She needed to rub against him, relieve the ache, the insistent throb.

But when he cupped her breast and squeezed, he yanked his mouth away. Breathing heavily, resting his forehead on hers.

"What's wrong?"

"I got a handful of crystals and remembered you're all dressed up. I don't want to ruin it."

"I couldn't care less about my dress, my make-up, or anything. I'd rather have your kisses."

With a firm clasp around the back of her neck, he pulled her to his mouth. He fed her need and want and lust. He made her wild. But with all the layers of tulle and silk, she couldn't feel him the way she needed, so she hiked up the dress and straddled him, and the moment his erection notched between her legs, a disembodied voice said, "We're here, sir."

The limo came to a smooth stop, but still, they didn't move apart. His breath was hot on her cheek, and she was pressed so fully against him that if she kept rocking her hips, she'd come.

"Now, when he says *here*," she began, just to break the mood. "What exactly does he mean? Where are we?"

Setting his hands on her hips, he lifted her off his lap and settled her beside him. "At the prom." He got out of the limo, smoothed out his pants, and then reached back in to help her out.

Lord, she must be a mess. "Well, hang on. Let me do my lipstick." She reached into her crystal clutch and pulled out the tube, quickly slathering the fire engine red across her lips. She didn't have a mirror, but she patted down her hair and adjusted the skirt of her dress.

And then she took his hand and stepped onto… Main Street? It was a Friday night during ski season, so the streets were crammed with red taillights and the sidewalks full of people leaving restaurants and heading into bars. The energy was alive and full of excitement.

The air was bitter cold, but her heart was warm and full. He led her into Wild Billy's, its neon sign of a cowboy riding a bull blinking against the night sky. The door opened to live country music, a rumble of conversation, and bursts of laughter.

She'd been here for the Petticoat Ruler's holiday party, and she remembered how unsure she'd felt. How caught in fear. She didn't feel any of that tonight. "This is the prom?" She took in the dance floor lined with rows of people two-stepping.

"Calamity-style." In the entryway, he nodded to a well-dressed woman who looked to be the manager. She gave him a nod before lifting the pass-through behind the bar.

Everyone was dressed in jeans and boots, sweaters—a casual night of dancing and drinking after a day on the slopes. "Okay, now I'm Cinderella at a hoe-down." In their formal wear, they got a lot of double takes. "I think I got the wrong fairy godmother."

"Would you rather we go to the Homestead Inn?" His brow creased in concern. "I thought about renting the ballroom, but I didn't think you'd have as much fun."

She tugged him close. "You nailed it. I'd much rather be here." Though she didn't know how she could two-step in her stilettos.

The manager approached, carrying a hat and a pair of boots. "Hey, Cole. Nice to see you." She handed him the black Stetson. "And you must be Hailey. I'm Dana, and I'm your concierge for the night."

"My concierge?" She said it on a laugh. "Wow."

"Yes, ma'am." She handed her a pair of the flashiest, most expensive cowboy boots she'd ever seen. She recognized the signature look of the studs and crystals. "Dolce & Gabbana?"

Dana grinned. "You got it."

She looked at Cole. "Are you going to keep this up?"

"Keep what up?"

"Spoiling me rotten?"

"I mean…" Cole reached for the boots. "I could return them."

Laughing, Hailey grabbed them. "The hell you will. I love them."

"I didn't think you'd last long in the shoes Knox brought."

"Well, you're right about that." Her toes pinched already, but she wouldn't have said a thing. They were too gorgeous.

"Is this one of her dresses?" Dana asked.

"It is."

The manager eyed the pink confection with awe. "You're one lucky woman. It's stunning."

"Thank you. I love it."

"Well, here. Hand me the shoes, and I'll keep them safe for you." Dana gestured to a chair in the waiting area.

Carefully, she sat down and pried off each delicate sandal, replacing them with the stunning, flashy boots. "These are unreal." She gazed up at Cole. "Thank you so much." As she stood, flexing her toes in the unfamiliar shoes, Dana handed her a white cowboy hat with a crystal-encrusted band. Hailey burst out laughing. "Really?"

"Cinderella's redneck ball?" he teased.

"Exactly. Let's do this."

"Hang on," Dana said. "You can't dance in that dress." She reached into the folds and undid a clasp. The outer layer of poofy tulle came away, leaving Hailey in a comfortable silk sheath.

"I have no words for how perfect this whole night is."

And then, they headed onto the dance floor, and she

danced the night away with the most handsome, kind, generous man in the world.

Everything would be all right.

She just knew it.

Under the porchlight, Cole read the text message for the fourth time.

If he went inside, he'd have to share the news with Hailey, and the bubble they lived in would pop. The longer he stayed outside, the longer he could hold onto this fantasy life.

He had the woman of his dreams.

He had two beautiful, confused, lost little girls who, for whatever reason, had come to take comfort from him.

He had the closest thing to a family he'd ever known.

And it was damn hard to let it go.

The door cracked open, and Hailey stood there with Evvie on her hip.

"*Cole.*" The little girl shouted as though they hadn't just seen each other ten minutes before he'd taken her sister to the bus. She lunged for him.

He caught her and held her close. "Hey, sweetie." She smelled like faffles and baby shampoo.

As he entered the house, Hailey said quietly, "Looks like you got some bad news."

"Not bad, no."

"Here." Hailey got the three-year-old set up at the coffee table with cookie cutters and playdough and then led him toward the kitchen where they could watch her. "What's going on?"

"I heard from the PI. He talked to Darren's mother."

Her features tightened, and she went on alert. "Okay."

They'd been waiting to find out if the woman was interested in meeting with them. Her response would decide the outcome of their lives—all four of them. "He said she cried when he told her what happened to Darren and that she very much wanted to meet the girls."

"*Meet* the girls. She didn't say adopt them. She said *meet.*" She said it more to herself. "Okay, so, when is this going to happen?" She had her eye on Evvie as she spoke. There was a fierceness there. Like she wouldn't let anyone hurt that little girl.

He blew out a breath. "This morning."

Her attention snapped over to him. "Today? Now?"

"It's tentatively scheduled for eleven." He saw her anxiety and quickly added, "But only if you want to."

"We're not bringing the girls, right? I want us to meet her first."

"We can play this however you want." He felt himself backpedaling, wondering how to rewind the clock. Half-wishing they hadn't pushed the private investigator. "Do you need more time? I can reschedule." The idea of staying in the bubble until he had to leave in two weeks worked for him, but it left the outcome in Hailey's hands, which wasn't fair. He needed to tie everything up before he left.

She let out a defeated breath. "No. We need to do this while you're still here. I want you to meet them."

"Okay. I'll let him know we'll be there."

They both watched Evvie happily chatting to herself. Sensing their attention, she looked up and grinned. "Lookit. I make cookies." She got up and ran right past them.

"Where are you going?" Hailey asked.

They both followed the little girl into the pantry.

She strained on the tips of her toes to reach a bag of frosted animal crackers. Head tilted back to look at them, she asked, "I have cookies, LaLee?"

Hailey dropped to a crouch, pulling the little girl into her arms. "Yeah, sweetie. Today, you can have all the cookies you want."

They parked in front of a cottage right across the street from the lake.

Neither made a move to unbuckle their seat belts. They sat in the quiet of the Land Cruiser, the ticking engine the only sound. Cole's stomach twisted with dread.

He would do the right thing for the girls no matter the cost to him. But he would miss them in a way he never thought possible.

"It's cute." Hailey sounded resigned.

Every house on this street looked right out of a storybook. Each was a different color, and all of them had brightly painted doors. Flower baskets hung off windows.

He took her hand. "We don't have to go in. We don't have to do anything you don't want."

"We do, though. She's family."

"So are we."

Her gaze cut over to him, watching, assessing. He saw the moment awareness hit. "You know it's funny. I always thought I'd missed out on not having siblings or aunts and uncles and all that. I guess because I never really had a lot of friends, it never occurred to me that I could make my own family." She reached for his hand. "We did that, didn't we?"

"We did." Out of nowhere, his heart raced, and his

skin went hot despite the icy wind whistling through the windows.

He wanted her. He wanted those girls.

He wanted his damn family.

She broke out in a bittersweet grin. "And we haven't even known them a month."

"You'd think time would matter. You'd think blood would, too. But if you asked the girls who their family was, they'd include us. They wouldn't even question it."

"Wow, that's…" Tears glistened, and she smiled. "You're right." She brought their joined hands to her mouth and kissed the back of his. "You mean so much to me, Cole."

"You're everything to me." He had to swallow back the tide of emotion that threatened to crush him. "*Everything*." Because he had to stay focused on meeting Darren's mom. He cleared his throat. "You ready?" He had to keep his head on right to make the best decision for the girls.

She looked past him to the stretch of grass across the street, the bench overlooking the snow-covered sand, and the sunlight-dappled lake. "The girls would love it here."

He could see it so clearly. Both of them racing out the front door holding pails and shovels, their grandma reminding them to stop at the curb. *Don't cross the street without me*. Yeah, they'd like it a lot. "Hey, let's not undervalue my indoor lap pool."

"Or the wrapping room. One day, that'll be very important to them." She unbuckled her belt. "Okay. Let's do this." She waited for him on the grass, and then together, they walked hand in hand up the walkway. "I'm scared."

He could only take short, tight breaths. "I know." If

this family turned out to be the right one for the girls, if he had to let them go, he would feel it deep and hard. He'd never forget the first time Evvie had come charging toward him, lifting her arms and settling on his hip like she'd done it her entire life. Not once had she been hesitant around him.

She'd just taken for granted that he'd take care of her.

His muscles contracted, and he squeezed Hailey's hand too hard. "Sorry."

She gave him a weak smile. She understood.

Before they even rang the bell, the door swung open, and a red-haired woman stepped out. "Cole?" She fussed with the screen door handle before it gave. "Come on in." The interior was warm and cozy and stuffed with furniture and tchotchkes. It smelled like freshly baked apple pie. "I'm Annie, Darren's...well, you know." She looked uncomfortable. "I don't know what to say."

"That's okay. I'm Cole Montgomery. And this is Hailey Casselton."

"It's nice to meet you." Hailey shook the woman's hand. "We were best friends with Darren and his wife."

"You didn't bring the girls with you?"

"No, the older one's in school," Hailey said. "The other's at a play date."

The woman wore jeans and cowboy boots, her red hair layered and down to her shoulders. "Can I get you something to drink?"

Cole didn't like seeing her so ill at ease around them. He hoped she didn't think they judged her about a decision she'd made nearly thirty years ago. "We're okay, but thank you. Why don't we sit down and get to know each other a little?"

"Yes, that's good." She sat on the love seat, offering them the couch. "I know you're a hockey player."

"Yes."

"In Boston."

"That's right." *Please don't be looking for money.*

"And what do you do?" she asked Hailey.

He was relieved she didn't want to pursue that angle.

"I'm a fashion designer. I work for Abbott's of London."

"No kidding? I grew up wearing those nightgowns. Which I guess explains why I got pregnant at sixteen. My family was very strict and conservative." She clapped a hand over her mouth. "Oh, I'm sorry. No offense."

Hailey smiled. "None taken. It's definitely conservative. But the company is great to work for."

When it seemed they'd run out of things to say, the woman rubbed her hands on her jeans. "You sure you don't want something to drink?"

"We're fine but thank you." Hailey gave the woman a kind, warm smile.

"You probably think I'm an awful person, giving up my own baby."

"What?" Hailey asked. "No. Not at all. Please, don't think that for a second."

"I appreciate that. I don't talk about it much. Well, at all. It wasn't a good time in my life." She got up and moved behind the love seat. "Me and my boyfriend, we wanted to keep the baby, but our parents...they wouldn't hear of it. They tried to scare us into going along with their plan. And boy, did it work. They said the baby would cry all day and night, that we'd only ever get dead-end, minimum wage jobs...we'd never get ahead, never realize our dreams. Of course, we broke up. He went to college, and I…well, I didn't do so well. Not at first. I had another child. But eventually, I got my act together and went to beauty school." She wore a proud smile. "And now, I have my own salon. It's not fancy, but I do all right."

"That's great." Hailey motioned around the room. "And you have such a lovely home here."

"Oh, this isn't mine. It's too expensive here. I'm over in Victor, on the other side of the mountain. This is my daughter Tate's place." She headed to the mantel and tapped a framed photograph of a young family. "Tate's amazing. I wasn't the best mom to her in the early years. Maybe that's why she's so independent and strong. She's an amazing mom to my granddaughter."

It was only then that he noticed the baby swing hanging in the doorway, the fleece blanket on the couch, and various toys on the floor.

"She's just getting the baby up from a nap. Probably changing her diaper. You know how it goes." She came back to the love seat. "Gosh, where was I? I'm all over the place right now. I'm just nervous. I've never talked to anyone about what happened back then."

"You don't have to tell us. We're just here to let you know what happened to him."

So, that's how she wants to play it. She obviously wasn't sure about this woman.

"You have to know it was a closed adoption. Of course, no one told us that. No one explained anything. I had the baby—didn't even hear him cry. He didn't make a peep. Next thing I knew, they'd taken him out of the room. That was it." She grew concerned. "Did he find a good home? I probably shouldn't even ask that. I don't have the right."

"You can ask us anything," Cole said. "He went

through a few homes, but the last one stuck. He got to stay there all through high school."

Her fingers flexed in the cushions. "That doesn't sound good. The last one 'stuck.'"

"He had Lindsay, his wife." Hailey smiled. "They were inseparable."

"I'm glad. I never had a love like that."

"Hello." A gorgeous, well-put-together woman came into the living room holding her baby. "I'm Tate, and this little bug is Josie." She had far more confidence than her mother. "I'm very sorry to hear about Darren and his wife."

Something his own mother hadn't said yet. Not that Cole was judging.

Okay, maybe he was judging a little. Those girls deserved the best, most loving home, and he wasn't convinced Darren's mother was it.

"Yes, we're all heartbroken," Hailey said.

"I'm so sorry for their daughters. How are they doing?" Tate asked.

Yet another question the mom hadn't asked.

"So far, they're okay. I think they're just too young to understand, but we've been encouraging them to remember their parents. Trying to hold onto as many memories as we can."

"That sounds impossibly hard." Tate watched her toddler gnaw on a plastic toy.

"It's actually an honor to be there for them," Hailey said. "You know, at first, I was terrified of getting it wrong. But I think I've reached the point where I realize no one can do better." She grimaced. "That didn't come out right. I don't mean that *I'm* doing a great job—"

"You are." All eyes turned to him. "You're doing a great job."

She softened. "You're biased but thank you. No, I just meant that no one's equipped to handle a situation like this, and so I think they just need someone who cares enough to try."

The sentiment hit his solar plexus like a mallet, and the sting of awareness reverberated throughout him.

He'd come out here convinced he was a menace.

Over time, he'd lost sight of that. Consumed with taking care of them, he'd forgotten about the damage he could cause. But now, thanks to the trust the girls had in him, to getting in the trenches with them—looking for solutions and finding them—he had a degree of confidence.

Hailey was right. There was no perfect family. There were just people who cared enough to keep guiding and supporting them. It was about being there.

And it was a fucking revelation.

He didn't have to be a certain kind of person. He didn't have to do anything other than care about their welfare.

That was really all they needed. Well, that and love.

And he could do the hell out of that.

He stood up. "Well, thanks for meeting with us."

The women startled, and he realized how abrupt he'd been. But he needed to get out of here. "We won't keep you any longer. We just wanted to let you know of Darren's passing."

"Oh." Tate seemed confused. "I thought…"

But Hailey was on her feet, too, and he got the feeling her urgency matched his.

Tate walked them to the door. "I'm sorry I took so

long changing her diaper. I didn't expect to find quite as much…to clean up." She laughed but it didn't reach her eyes. "Anyhow, I'm not sure where we go from here. Is there anything we can do to help with the girls?"

"I appreciate the offer, thank you. We're still figuring things out, but we'll be in touch." Hailey looked past Tate to her mom. "It was very nice to meet you. I'm sorry it had to be under these circumstances."

The older woman nodded, still standing behind the love seat.

Tate ushered them out to the porch. "I must've misunderstood. When my mother told me you'd contacted her, I thought you were looking for someone to adopt the girls. But just so you know, if that were to happen, *I* would be the one adopting them." She searched their expressions. "I wasn't sure if meeting my mother had changed your mind. She has a lot of regrets about the choices she made, and I know she'd get some peace of mind knowing her grandchildren, but the day-to-day care would come from me. I have a degree in early childhood education and own a preschool, and I know my house looks small, but it's filled with love, and that's all children need at this age."

"That's wonderful." Hailey gave out the energy of a thousand suns. "It'd be great if we could keep in touch. We'd love the girls to know their family."

And right then, he knew she was on the same page as him.

He wanted to grab her hand and run to the car.

He'd never felt happier.

Chapter Twenty-One

THE MOMENT THEY LATCHED THEIR SEAT BELTS, Hailey put her hand on his to stop him from starting the engine. "I want your help."

"You've got it. Anything you need. What do you have in mind?"

"I'm going to do it. I'm adopting the girls. But I can't do it by myself."

Hope spiked so quickly it knocked the breath out of his lungs. "You don't have to."

She tensed, her body alert. "What are you saying?"

"When you said no one knows how to handle two children who've lost their parents, that the right guardians are the ones who care enough to try...everything snapped into place. *I* care enough to try." He turned his hand over, and they laced their fingers together.

"Are you serious?" Tears brimmed.

"Dead serious."

"What...what does this mean, exactly? You're going back to Boston in two weeks."

"I want us to be a family." Frustrated with himself, he

shook his head. His thoughts were flying too fast in his head. "We already *are* a family. Hockey's my job just like designing is yours. We can do this."

"Yes, we can. I just needed to know you wanted to."

"That was never the problem. I just didn't think I was the best man—because of my past. What I've done." He shook his head again, clearing out the negativity. "And why would they want me over a blood relative? But you put it into perspective. No one's going to care about those girls the way I do. The way we do."

Tears streamed down her cheeks. "We're doing this."

"Yeah, LaLee. We're doing this." He leaned in close, breathed in her scent, and kissed a teardrop right before it hit her upper lip.

She gripped his arm. "How will this work?"

"That's for us to decide. If you need to be in New York, then we'll get a place big enough for all four of us. If you—"

"I want to raise them here. In Calamity. We have friends, and it's the right place for the girls to grow up. But what about hockey? You're gone eighty-two days a year."

He sat back, going a little panicky at the idea his career might change her mind. "I'm not going to disappear. A lot of our time together over the season will involve texts and emails and phone calls. And then we'll do what every other family does. You and the girls will visit me, and I'll come home when I can. It won't happen as much as I'd like, but you're my priority. You know that, right? You understand how much you mean to me, right?"

She nodded, eyes bright with happiness.

"So, trust me when I say I'll make sure you won't feel alone in this."

A soft smile warmed her features. "I trust you."

"We just have to communicate. You need to tell me if you're feeling like I'm not doing my share or if I'm too focused on hockey. And we'll get you help so you can get your work done."

"Okay." She brought her other hand on top of their joined ones. "You're shaking. Are you scared?"

And that was the wildest thing of all. "Not a damn bit."

He wanted this more than he'd ever wanted anything.

And he wouldn't fuck it up.

Formal adoption papers showed up the second week in January. Hailey would've signed immediately, but Cole was training, and she wanted them to do it together, so she set them on the countertop and just stared.

She couldn't believe how dramatically her life had changed in just one month.

The night she'd gotten the attorney's call, she'd had a job she could do in her sleep, lived in a tiny studio apartment, and did nothing but work. She'd had very few friends.

Now, she had Cole, the girls, and a whole group of women who truly supported her.

She was living a life she'd never imagined and *loving* it.

At the sound of a key in the back door, a thrill spiraled through her.

Cole.

Snow dusting the broad shoulders of his black parka, he yanked off his wool beanie and tossed it on the counter. "Hey." Finding her watching him, he checked the clock on the stove. "Am I late? Are you waiting for me or something?"

"No, not at all."

"Then, why do you have that weird expression?"

"I don't have a weird expression."

"You look like you're about to tell me you just won the lottery."

"This is better." She reached for the manila envelope. "Look what came in the mail."

When he read the return address, his jaw went slack. "Are those...the adoption papers?"

"They are." She handed him a pen. "I waited for you. I want to do this together."

He reached for it but then lowered his arm. "No."

"No?" He was changing his mind? *You've got to be kidding me.* "*Cole.*"

"It's too big a moment. We have to do something special."

"Oh, thank God. I thought you had cold feet."

He hooked an arm around her back and hauled her to him. "I will never have cold feet as long as yours are in the bed with me."

"You know, that was kind of romantic." She kissed him sweetly, letting her fingers sift through his cool, silky hair. "Why do you taste so sweet?"

"I had a protein shake at the gym." He brought his mouth back over hers. "Less talking. More kissing." He licked into her mouth, his hands hitting the island on either side of her, caging her in.

Her back arched, pressing her breasts against his hard chest. She would never get enough of him. "Evvie's in the other room watching a movie." But she stayed put, looping her arms around his neck. "I agree with you. Just signing it doesn't seem like enough. What should we do?"

"We need something that marks the moment."

"Something that involves the girls."

"Yeah, exactly. They should be here with us. They need to know we're a family, and that we're forever."

Forever. A different kind of happiness made a smooth glide through her body. Not the giddy kind, not the pinch-me-I-can't-believe-this-is-my-life kind. But more like a deep sense of contentment, where everything seemed to lock into place and make sense. It had been a struggle to get here, to come to the right decision, but once made, all doubts vanished.

I'm doing this, Lindsay. I'm going to raise your babies, and I swear to God, I will love them with every fiber of my soul.

"What if we rent a cabin, just the four of us?" she said. "Something really cozy where we can make s'mores over a fire and roast hot dogs? Let's pick a place where we can make this our annual tradition."

"Our family birthday."

"Yes." She loved that idea.

There was one thing they needed to discuss that he wouldn't like. But it had to be addressed. "Cole, if, for whatever reason we don't work out, we still have to commit to being a family for these girls. I know neither of us would ever cheat, so I can't imagine we'd ever hurt each other in a way that would make us hateful to each other."

"What're you talking about? We're going to work out. Of course, we are. I don't think you get it, Hailey."

"No, I do—"

"You don't. There has never been—and there will never be—anyone else for me."

"And I feel the same way, but for my peace of mind, for the girls' sense of safety and security in the world, promise me that you and I will always be on good terms. That even if we're not together, we're still going to be a family. We'll still have an annual birthday party because we'll always be their adoptive parents. Even if we're not living in the same house or sharing the same bed. Do you agree?"

"There's no scenario where you and I are not sharing a bed. That's not happening, but I see how important this is to you, so yes, I'll make that promise. If for some reason we don't work out, I'll always be their father figure, and I'll always celebrate our family birthday. I reserve the right, however, to fuck with your new boyfriend."

She laughed. "You're not taking this seriously." But she totally got why. Now that she had Cole, she couldn't imagine being with anyone else. He was it for her.

"I am. I hear you, and I agree one hundred percent. It's just that I know something you don't." His hands slid down her back and landed on her ass. "I'm a wolf, and you and the girls are my pack."

She grinned. "I think we're more like puffins, since they spend the winter apart. But I get it. We mate for life. So, the cabin?"

"Yep. But let's not sign anything or tell them about it until we're in the cabin. I want us to do it all together."

In her studio, Hailey sat at her desk. She should be working. Instead, she was reeling from the email that had just come in.

It had taken Abbott's of London weeks to get back to her, and it wasn't the answer she'd hoped for.

They appreciated her ideas but would not be going forward with them. It would take a solid year to get a men's line up and running, and they didn't have the luxury of time. As for job security, they hadn't yet made any decisions about the future of the company.

The timing was terrible. With the help of the Petticoat Rulers, she'd planned on launching her business in the next month or so, but now, she'd have to put that on hold. No way would she run through her savings on a start-up.

Yes, she knew she'd give up her studio in New York to live in Cole's house rent-free. She knew he'd cover most of the family's expenses, but she would never rely on him. She would always earn her own way and contribute to the family. That was an absolute.

She'd told her boss she planned on staying in Calamity and asked if she could work remotely, so she'd see what they had to say about that. But she had a feeling her time with Abbott's was up.

And that was okay. Eventually, she'd figure out her next move. For now, she had a family birthday to plan. Nothing was more important than that. But before she searched home rental sites, she'd talk to Cole. He knew the area better.

When she came up the stairs, she'd expected to find Cole making dinner with the girls, but the kitchen was empty, and the house was quiet.

There was, however, a black leather carryon sitting on the floor by the back door.

Is he going somewhere?

She followed the sound of voices up the stairs where she found him in the girls' bedroom, cuddled up with them on Paisley's bed. They talked quietly, and it filled her with so much affection for him.

This is my family.

When Cole saw her, he got up and headed over. But he wasn't smiling. He didn't have that glimmer in his eyes that said, *Mm, look at you. When do I get you all to myself?*

And that scared her. When he reached her, he tipped his head toward the hallway, and they both stepped outside.

"I saw the luggage," she said. "What's going on?"

"Last night, Gavin, my second line center, got slammed into the boards. His shoulder's dislocated, so I've got to get back."

"To do what?" Give his team encouragement? "You can't play for another two weeks."

"I have no choice."

"But it's only been a month since surgery."

"I'm fine." His phone pinged, and he checked it. "Pilot's ready. I've got to go."

"Wait, did the doctor clear you to play? Because last I heard, you can do serious damage if you go back too soon.

"I'm fine. If I don't go back, we won't make the play-offs."

Fear dug its sharp claw into her chest. "Okay."

He must've heard her uneasy tone because he bent his knees to be eye-level with her. "Hey, it's all right. We knew this was coming. It's just two weeks earlier than we'd expected."

"Right. True." That should've made her feel better, but somehow, those two weeks had seemed like forever into the future. And now...

"Remember what I said about long distance? It only works if we communicate. If you keep things inside, you're only going to resent me. I know this is sooner than we'd planned, but it always *was* the plan. So, tell me what're you thinking."

"I'm honestly not thinking anything." It was true. Her mind was like a hive of activity, and she couldn't grab a single, isolated thought.

"We've been in a bubble, and it's been great. And now we're venturing into the real world where we both go back to full-time jobs."

Well, he was, anyway. She wasn't so sure about her job. "I guess I'm scared that you're going to get caught up in hockey and forget about us."

A flash of pain gripped his features, and she immediately knew she'd messed up. She grabbed his hand. "Forget I said that. It's my insecurities talking. I know you. I know us. I know we'll be okay. I'm just…scared. It's all so new, and with you leaving, it feels a little fragile. But I've got this. *We've* got this."

"I'll come home every chance I get. It won't be easy, and it won't be often, but I'll do it. And you guys can come see me. Next month, we're on the West Coast for two weeks, so I'll find time in the schedule for us to spend time together. And I'll skip All-Star week to come home and be with you guys."

"No. I don't want you to miss out on anything. It just hit me harder than I expected. I'll be okay."

"*We'll* be okay. I promise." His phone pinged again. "All right. I have to go. My dad will be here in case you need anything. If you want to hire a nanny—"

"I don't. No nanny. I'll hire babysitters and ask my friends for help when I need it." She felt better. Stronger.

I mean, come on. We've got these girls that will bind us together forever.

It's going to be just fine.

She wrapped her arms around him. "I'm going to miss you so much."

He held her so tightly he nearly lifted her off the floor. "It's going to kill me to be away from you, but we'll talk every day."

"We will."

He pressed a kiss to her mouth. "I have to go."

"You're not saying goodbye to the girls?"

"I just did."

"Oh." That's what he was doing in bed with them. "What did you say?"

"That I have to go to work, but that they can call me any time they wanted. All they have to do is tell Hailey, and she'll call me. Paisley asked if it was the kind of call where we could see each other's faces, and I said yes."

"They didn't freak out?"

"They were…quiet. But it's all right because I'm going to make sure I talk to them as often as I can. I don't want them to think I'm gone like their parents."

She hugged him one more time. She would miss him so damn much.

As he headed for the stairs, she panicked. She'd been keeping something very important from him, and now, knowing he was leaving, she knew she had to tell him. "Cole?"

He turned around. Her handsome, badass hockey player with a soft and gooey center watched her like he was torn between running back to her and taking care of his team.

"I love you." She'd never said the words before, and they didn't come out with the confidence he deserved.

And it wasn't because she didn't feel it—she'd known for a while now that she was madly, wildly in love with him.

She was just terrified to say the words out loud.

She'd never been in love before.

But he'd just told her they needed to communicate, and this was the one thing he needed to hear. So, she said it again. "I love you."

He hauled-ass back to her, lifting her off the floor and backing her against the wall. "I fucking love you. Swear to God, my heart beats for you. Only you. Please don't give up on me."

"I won't."

Slippered feet shushed on the hardwood floor, and the girls came down the hallway, armed with books. Evvie shoved them at Cole's legs. "Wead."

He set Hailey down. "I can't read right now, sweetie."

"I can." Hailey grabbed some of the books. "Let's go into Cole's room."

Evvie gazed up at him. "Cole come wif us?"

"No, sweetheart. Remember I said I have to go to work? But I'll call you from the airport like I promised."

Paisley stood back, clutching the books in her arms. Where Evvie took what she wanted, her sister was more watchful and kept things inside. Just as Hailey reached for her, ready to assure her everything would be all right, Cole dropped to a knee.

"Hey, little one. Do you want to watch my game on TV tomorrow night?"

She nodded.

"Cool. At the beginning, right before I skate onto the ice, I'm going to look right into the camera and do this." He kissed two fingers and held them up. "And then, at the end of the game, I'll do it again."

She didn't answer, just held onto those books.

"Do you know what this means?" He did it again, only this time after he kissed his fingers, he pressed them to her cheek. "It means I love you. And I'm thinking about you when I'm not with you. Always. Okay?"

That worried expression broke, replaced by a grin.

He opened his arms, and both girls stepped in for a hug. "I'll see you soon, okay?"

"Okay," Paisley whispered.

Evvie pulled away to ask, "Cole wuv Evvie?"

"I love you very much." His voice sounded rougher, thicker. He glanced up at Hailey. "I should probably just go."

She put her hands on the girls' shoulders and drew them close until they made a tight triangle. "Safe travels. Call us when you get to the airport." Then, she led them to his bed, and all three crawled in. With a girl tucked on either side of her, she picked up a book and began to read.

What else could she do but keep things as normal for the girls as possible?

She had a choice to make. She could worry about him drifting away or she could trust that what they had was special and beautiful and worth holding onto.

Yeah, that.

That's the choice she'd make.

———

Cole left his book on the nightstand, so he ran upstairs to get it.

When he got to his room, he found all three of his favorite people were cuddled up in his bed. They were so engrossed in Hailey's storytelling that none of them noticed him.

His heart squeezed at the beautiful sight.

He wasn't going to lie. It hurt a little that he'd only been gone a minute, and they'd already sealed the gap. What would happen a week from now? A month? *Evvie's only three.* By the time he came home in June, would she even remember him?

He'd be sure to call them when he woke up and then reach out during the day. Maybe he'd buy some books in Boston and read to them every night. *Yeah, that's a good idea.* It wasn't like he wanted to go to bars or clubs. He wanted to be with his girls.

The longer he stood there, the more uncomfortable he grew. It wasn't that they were snuggling together. Seeing them happy made him feel good.

It was what lay ahead.

Now that he knew what a family felt like, how the fuck was he supposed to go back to his old life?

He'd managed the loneliness by surrounding himself with people. But now, he had Hailey. There'd be no disguising it. It would eat him alive.

He stepped into the room. "Hey."

His voice startled them.

"Everything all right?" Hailey asked.

"Yeah. Forgot my book."

"I'll get it." Paisley popped up. She knew right where he kept it because sometimes, after he did her hair, they'd lie in bed, reading together until she got sleepy. "Here."

He hated to lose his nightly routine with her. "Thanks, sweetie."

"Can we come with you?" she asked.

"I wish you could." Actually, they'd planned on

spending the upcoming three-day weekend in a cabin. "Why don't you?"

"Go to Boston?" Hailey asked.

"Can we?" Paisley looked at her. "I want to go."

"Go wif Cole." Evvie rolled onto her belly and dropped to her feet. She padded over to him and reached for his hand. "Go wif you."

Their reaction—fuck, it was everything. They wanted to be with him. The gap hadn't sealed. He still had his place in this little foursome.

"But Paisley has school." Hailey got up, too.

"It's kindergarten." He shrugged. "But it's no different from our plans to stay in a cabin. We'll just have the celebration in Boston. We'll rent a suite at the Four Seasons." No, she wouldn't like that. She wanted someplace cozy. He'd figure it out.

"I want to go." Paisley bounced in place. "Please, LaLee?"

This was the perfect plan. They'd get to sign the adoption papers as a family. They'd get to have their birthday party. "You guys can come to my hockey game."

"Yay." The girls jumped up and down, even though they'd never been to an arena in their lives.

He could see Hailey was still on the fence. "You have to move out of your apartment anyhow. So, after the game, we'll fly to New York. Dad's screening is Friday night." He hadn't planned on going, but excitement flared in his chest. The girls would love that. The red carpet, the glitter, the attention. He'd buy them special dresses and shoes. "What do you think? I want to sign those papers sooner than later."

"I know. I do, too."

"What if we did it over afternoon tea?"

"Ooh, a fancy tea." She smiled. "They'd love that."

"So, you'll come? I've got a game Friday night, so I can get you home by Sunday."

"Yes, we'll come. It sounds fun."

Relief swept through him.

This would be perfect.

Chapter Twenty-Two

As he did before every puck drop, Cole scanned the crowd. This was his arena, and the fans were on their feet. Tonight, they'd played the toughest opponent in their conference, and now, in overtime, only one would get the win.

It's gonna be me. It's gotta be.

That's what I'm here for.

His gaze landed on his girls. Evvie waved wildly in Hailey's arms, and Paisley had her hand pressed against the glass. Before the game started, right when he'd skated out onto the ice, he'd kissed two fingers and pressed them to the Plexiglass. Paisley had mimicked him. It had become their thing. His lucky charm.

My girls. The love he felt for those three felt too big for his heart to hold.

Enough. Worry about that after the game.

Time to focus.

Adrenaline coursing through him, he spread his feet and got low. And when the puck dropped, he smacked the other center's stick away and sent it back to his defenseman. With tons of speed, he swung up the left side of the wall and got the puck. Now, it was him and his teammate on the other side of the ice against the Viper's two defenders. Once they crossed the blue line, Cole and his guy skated in a criss-cross and switched sides of the ice. He dropped the puck to his teammate.

The other team's defender tried to jump the pass, but it was too late. He was out of position, and now, they had two against one.

Fuck, yeah. I'm open.

I'm on my one-timer side.

I need this pass.

This is the game.

Stick in the air, ready to rip the puck into the empty net, he shouted for his teammate. "*Benson.*"

His buddy dropped his shoulder to fake the goalie into thinking he'd take his shot but then quickly slid into Cole's wheelhouse.

The goalie never had a chance.

Game over.

We won.

Waving his stick in the air, grinning wide at the crowd, his only thought was the girls. He skated across the ice, tugged off his glove, and kissed two fingers. Pressing them against the Plexiglass, he waited while all three of them reached up to meet him. And the connection—even though not physical—was electric.

He couldn't stop grinning at them.

Never had a win meant so much now that he had family here to witness it.

· · ·

After a shower and a quick team meeting, Cole met up with his girls right outside the locker rooms.

"You were amazing." Hailey hugged him with one arm since Evvie was slumped against her chest. "I've never been to a hockey game. That was so much fun."

"Other than my dad, I've never had family here before." He grinned. "It didn't suck." Tugging Paisley's braid, he said, "We won because of you."

"Me?" She sounded incredulous.

"Yep. You're my good luck charm."

She beamed a smile at him.

He picked her up and said, "So, what do you think? Grab some dinner?"

"Yes. Can I get my frappe now?"

"Oh, no, honey," Hailey said. "We're not having milkshakes this late."

"But Cole promised. He said I could have a world-famous Boston frappe."

"I did, but we can get them tomorrow morning before we leave for New York. We've got a fun weekend planned."

Since New York was only a three-and-a-half-hour drive from Boston, he'd arranged a driver for the long weekend. It would streamline travel with two little girls.

He hit the release bar, and they stepped out into the freezing cold parking lot. Fortunately, the car was waiting, so they all climbed in. He got Evvie settled in her car seat, and across the way, Hailey got Paisley in hers. Once the driver took off, the girls immediately fell asleep.

Hailey shifted over, slipping an arm through his. "You were so hot out there." She rose to whisper in his ear. "I got all tingly inside."

"And when we get home, I'll take that tingle to the next level."

Hailey squirmed. "Just how big is your penthouse?"

"Oh, it's big, all right. And the walls are very well insulated."

"I can't wait to be alone with you. Watching you shout at your teammates, that mean face you gave the guy on the other team, and all those goals…" She shivered. "So hot."

"I'm glad you guys are with me."

"It's fun. I'm glad you suggested it."

"Even if Pais had to miss two days of school?"

"It won't be easy for this goody two-shoes, but I guess I'm going to have to get used to living with a rule-breaker."

"Hey, so where do you want to tell the girls? I know you wanted to rent a cabin, but is there some other place where we could start the tradition?"

"I don't think it has to be a specific place. I just like the idea of an annual birthday party. Afternoon tea would be fun, but I have to meet that guy in my apartment at noon, so it won't work in Boston."

A guy in her building owned a thrift shop, and he'd agreed to take her furniture off her hands. All she had to do was hire the trailer to get everything to his shop.

"We can make a day of it in the city. Horse and buggy ride in Central Park, the carousel, and then tea."

"That would be fun, but it's going to take me most of the day to box up my stuff. And then I have to get it all to the post office. Remember, I'm shipping everything to Calamity."

"What if we do it at my dad's screening? Never mind. That's too hectic. We want to do something private, just the four of us."

"First of all, the girls aren't going to a screening. They're too young, and they won't appreciate it. But secondly, I'm having dinner with my mom. It's my only chance to be with her before I move. Let's hold off until Sunday."

"I've got a game Sunday night." He was looking for some amazing venue when the actual event itself was what mattered. "Fuck it, let's do it when they wake up in the morning. I want to see their faces when we tell them we're their forever home." Had he ever wanted anything this badly?

"I do, too. I'm happy, Cole. Really, really happy."

He reached for her hand, pressing it to her heart. "I love that you're moving in. I love that we're a family." He was skirting around the truth. It was the molten core of a mountain, and he was circling the rim.

"Me, too."

How ironic that the guy who slammed two-hundred-pound men into the boards was too afraid to say three simple words. "The other day at my house..." He drew in a slow breath. "When you said you loved me—"

"Oh, God, no. Stop. You don't have to say it back. That was—"

"I do, though. But besides my dad, I've only ever said those words to one other person." He didn't have a lot of clear memories of his time with the bad nanny. What he had were remnants of uncomfortable feelings that clung to him like spider webs. "I said it to the bad nanny once, and she got angry."

"Angry? For saying I love you?"

"She said, 'Oh, no. It's not like that.' She was so disgusted... That's what stuck with me. It was my first true rejection, and I remember thinking I'd never say it again. I'd had this pure, strong emotion, and I'd assumed it was mutual, but it wasn't. I'd gotten it so wrong. And that made me see love in a whole new light. I stopped trusting the feeling." He gazed down at those creamy cheeks, the warm hazel eyes, and the lips that brought him such pleasure...*I get to see that face every day for the rest of my life.* "I've always known I loved you, but I didn't want to say it and have you say, 'Oh, no, Cole. It's not like that with us.'"

She unbuckled her seatbelt and hitched a leg across his lap. "Say it."

And suddenly, with her looking at him like that, all fired up with passion, it wasn't hard to say at all. "I love you, Hailey Casselton. I love you like a house on fire."

"And I love you, Cole Montgomery. You're the sun, the moon, the stars. You and the girls are my entire universe."

As much as he'd wanted to hire movers for her, Hailey had insisted on doing it herself. She wasn't going to take much with her, but she needed to go through her belongings and decide what to take with her and what to leave behind. She'd encouraged him to treat the girls to a whole day in New York City.

They'd sign the papers when they weren't so busy.

So, he'd invited his dad, bundled the girls up in parkas and boots, and taken them to Central Park where they'd bought hot pretzels from a kiosk and taken a horse and carriage ride. The girls had flipped out over the carousel, insisting on going around three times in a row. After that, they'd gotten frozen hot chocolates and chicken fingers at a favorite restaurant on the Upper East Side.

By mid-afternoon, his dad had to get ready for the premiere. The girls were dragging, so they all went home with him. Cole put on a movie in his dad's penthouse, and the girls curled up against him. He must've dozed off because the next thing he knew, boots thudded on the hardwood floor, waking him up.

All three of them looked to see Trevor enter the sitting room in a sleek black tuxedo jacket and a forest green and red kilt.

Paisley got up on her knees, her hands resting on the couch cushion. "Where are you going?"

"To a movie," his dad said.

"I want to go to a movie."

"This one's not for kids," Cole said. "Also, it's a screening, so it's not the kind of movie you're expecting. It's got fancy food, not popcorn and chocolate-covered raisins."

"I want shocklet," Evvie said.

"Hey." He tugged her ponytail. "You just had some, remember?"

"What's a screening?" Paisley asked.

"It's the first time they show a movie to the public," Cole said. "The actors walk down a red carpet in their fancy suits and dresses, and the photographers take pictures, and the press shouts your name. Camera lights flash in your face. It's pretty wild."

"Can I go?" Paisley asked Trevor. "I want to go with you."

"Unfortunately, I'm going to be working. Trust me when I tell you, you'd be bored silly."

"I won't be bored." She turned to Cole. "Please, Cole? I want to go." Bits of hair had come out of her braids, and her skin looked pale.

What she needed was a bath, some dinner, and a good

night's sleep. "No, sweetie. We're going to stay home and have fun here."

"I've got to go. I'll see you guys in the morning." His dad kissed their foreheads and headed for the door.

Paisley watched him, anxiety growing with each step he took away from her. "I don't want to stay here. I want to go with Trevor."

"Yeah, I heard you, and we'll have breakfast with him in the morning." *When we sign the adoption papers.*

The door shut, and his sweet little girl flung herself down on the couch. "Why did you let him go? I want to go with Trevor. I want to go to the screening."

"Well, like he told you, he's working, so we can't go with him. Come here, sweetie." He tried to wrap his arm around her.

But she jerked away from him. Her features pinched into a scowl, and she folded her arms across her chest. "I hate you."

He couldn't have been more shaken if she'd clocked him with a hockey stick. "What? No, you don't. Why would you say that?"

Color spilled into her cheeks, and she shouted, "I want to go with Trevor."

He'd never seen a hint of attitude before. She'd always been so quiet and watchful, so sweet. They'd always had a special bond. "Let's take a bath. I can braid your hair and read books."

"I don't want to read books. I want to go with Trevor." Her voice edged toward hysteria.

What the fuck? "Sweetie, come on." They hadn't eaten since lunch—that was five hours ago. "I'll see what I can stir up for dinner."

"I don't want dinner. You're mean, and I want to go

home."

It hurt much more than it should.

She's six. She doesn't mean it.

But it was such a familiar twist in his gut. "You're going home tomorrow."

"I want to go now. Call Hailey. I want to talk to Hailey. I want her to take me home." Now, she was crying, tears streaking down her cheeks. "I want to go home."

What do I do? He'd never seen her like this. Tomorrow, she'd leave. He wouldn't see them again for months.

I don't want their last memory of me to be negative.

I don't want her to hate me.

"I have a great idea. There's a fun restaurant where the waiters dress up and sing and dance. You'll love it. Come on. Get your shoes on."

They were in New York City.

Why not dazzle them?

Give them an experience they'll never forget.

As the limo slowed, Cole took in the flashing lights and cluster of glamorous people. Dinner had gone so great, he'd figured he'd surprise them with the screening.

He'd already texted his dad to let him know they were stopping by. They'd take a quick walk down the red carpet, a picture with Trevor, and then they'd head home.

It'd be a night to remember.

Paisley gazed out the window, eyes wide. "Is this it?"

"Yep. It's Trevor's screening."

"Yay." She clapped her hands.

Cole: We're here. Can you get away for a minute to take a pic with the girls?

Aging Movie Star: Sure thing. Meet you at the other end of the carpet.

Cole: Cool. Thanks.

He pocketed his phone. "Here's the deal. You're both holding my hand, and you're not letting go. Not even for a second. Is that clear?"

Paisley nodded while Evvie's legs kicked out in her car seat.

"Okay, good. And like I said, we're only staying for five minutes. Right?"

"Right."

"You like your new clothes?" After the diner, they'd started the walk back to Trevor's, but they'd found a children's clothing store. Paisley had spotted a pink tulle dress in the window. That's when he'd come up with the idea to give her the night of her life.

"I love my dress so much. I love it, love it, love it." She tapped the pink patent leather Mary Jane shoes they'd bought to match the dress.

Evvie couldn't have cared less about dresses, so she'd gotten black boots that looked like Trevor's, a pleated skirt, and a bright pink and blue gumball machine purse with a shiny red strap. She was fucking adorable.

The limo stopped. "Here we go." He unbuckled them.

An attendant opened the door, but before they got out, Paisley tugged on the sleeve of his tuxedo jacket. "I'm sorry for saying you're mean, Cole." She flung herself into his arms. "I love you."

With a hand on the back of her head, he held the little girl close, breathing her in and just reveling in the fact that he'd earned her affection. "I love you, too, Paisley. So much." He wanted to tell her he was her forever home—so badly—but he had to wait for Hailey.

The moment they stepped out of the car, Evvie clutched his leg. He picked her up, and she buried her face in his neck. Lights flashed, and reporters called his name. He held on to Paisley's hand tightly as he made his way along the red carpet.

Five minutes. His dad would be waiting for them. And he'd already arranged with the driver where they'd meet.

But with each step he took, the more agitated Evvie grew. Finally, she cupped his cheek and said into his ear, "Go home, Cole. Pease go home."

"We're going, sweetheart."

It was mayhem. Not only had he come back from the injured list to win a game, but he'd showed up with two little girls. It was a feeding frenzy to see who could get a story out of him.

"Cole, Cole... Where'd you get the girls?"

"Who's the baby mama, Cole?"

He was used to the bullshit. He knew how to play the game.

But then, they came for his girls.

"Hey, girly, girly. Look here. Look here, sweet thing."

"Hey, pretty little girl. Let me see your smile."

Evvie lifted her head, and flash bulbs went off in a frenzy. She screamed and writhed in his arms. He dropped Paisley's hand to make sure the littlest one didn't fall.

"Paisley." He made sure to have eye contact with the six-year-old. "Hold on to my jacket." When she hesitated, he shouted, "Now. Hold on." And then, he ditched the red carpet.

The moment he got clear, he let out a sigh of relief. "It's okay, Evvie. It's all over. We're good. It's all good." He reached for Paisley's hand, only to discover it wasn't good at all.

Because Paisley was gone.

In the first five minutes of her disappearance, he shouted her name a dozen times, scanned the crowd, and grabbed the arms of passersby to ask if they'd seen her. Then, Cole hollered, "Everyone stop. I'm looking for a six-year-old girl with curly blond hair in a pink ballet dress."

A few people looked over at him, but mostly, they went back to their conversations or continued into the theater. Panic threatened to yank him under, but he had to keep his head.

He spotted his dad hurrying toward him. *Thank God.*

"What's going on?"

"I lost Paisley." In Manhattan. On the streets.

Jesus fucking Christ.

Trevor whistled sharply. Heads snapped in his direction. His publicist came right over. "Shut everything down. We need to find Paisley Leeson, a six-year-old girl." He made a gimme motion with his hand to Cole. "Picture."

Cole had taken loads of photos of the girls to show Hailey, so he quickly pulled them up.

"On it." The woman took off.

Trevor pointed to him. "Stay right where you saw her last and don't move."

"I have to move. I have to find her. I *lost* her."

"Listen to me. She's going to look for you. She's going back to where she last saw you. Wait there. Patti's going to get security on it. We'll find her."

But it was the city. People were ruthless. If they saw a

pretty little girl...if she wandered off, looking for him... the farther she got, the less the chance he had of ever finding her.

A sickening chill slid down his spine. *Stop*. He had to stay focused. He moved closer to the red carpet, scanning every nook and cranny in the crowd, looking for that pink dress.

Evvie fisted the collar of his suit coat. "Where Paisy?"

"She's here. I'll find her." *I have to.*

"Paisy gone?"

"No, no. She's here."

What have I done?

Cole: I lost Paisley

Hailey stared at the text message. Her stomach wrenched, and she went cold.

She hadn't heard from him in a while, so when her mom had gone to the bathroom, she'd given him a quick call.

He'd said, *Can't talk right now*. And then, he'd promptly disconnected.

The hum of conversation and the clattering of plates dimmed, and the restaurant walls closed in.

Her mom sat back down. "What's wrong?"

"Hang on." She called Cole again, but it went straight to voicemail.

Hailey: What do you mean you lost her?

Hailey: Call me.

Hailey: Call me right now.

I have to get out of here. She pushed back her chair.

"Honey, talk to me." Her mom got up, too.

"Cole texted. He said he lost Paisley."

"Lost her? Where?"

"At the screening, I assume. But I don't know." They could be anywhere. She found her waitress near the hostess podium. "I have to go. Can you please get my bill?"

The woman must've understood the urgency because she gave a curt nod and took off.

When he'd said he was taking them there, she'd told him it wasn't a good idea. They'd had a long, full day. They had to be exhausted. But he'd been so upset. He'd always had such a close relationship with Paisley, so to have her say she hated him, to tell him she wanted to go home… Hailey knew that had to have hurt.

"Should we go there?" her mom asked.

Hailey tipped her head back. "I told him not to take them." She thought of the crowds, the chaos, how easy it would be to snatch a little girl off the street, stuff her in a trunk, and drive off. There would be no chance of ever finding her again.

Why does he do that?

Why isn't it enough to just be with the girls?

He always has to take things to the next level.

She called Cole again. This time, he answered.

"Hey, it's okay. I found her. She's here." Noises in the background. Honking. A distant siren. Voices.

"What happened?"

"I'm sorry. I'm so fucking sorry." He sounded choked up, and she didn't know if he was talking to her or Paisley.

He'd *lost* her. *Paisley*. She went oddly numb, even while tears spilled down her cheeks. The bill was a blur of black and white. She handed over the credit card and signed without even checking it. "Talk to me, Cole. What happened? Is she okay?"

"She's fine. Someone found her and brought her to a police officer. She was only missing for five minutes. She's okay."

"Put her on the phone."

After a moment of static, her precious little girl's voice came on the line. "Hi, Hailey."

"Oh, baby. Are you okay? What happened?"

"Evvie got scared. Everyone was yelling at us, and she got scared. Cole got us away. He told me to hold on to his jacket, but my shoe came off, and I let go."

"I'm sorry, sweetie. That must've been scary. I'm so glad you're safe. Evvie's okay?"

"Yes. We're going home now."

She could hear Cole's voice. *Hand me the phone.* And then, he came back on the line. "The car's here, so give me a second to get them in their car seats, and I'll call you back." She'd never heard that tone before. He was always so in control, so confident, but he sounded shaken.

The restaurant was humid, hot. She pushed out the door and stepped into the frigid evening air. "Okay. I'm getting a cab right now. I'll meet you at the apartment."

Hailey entered to total silence. Other than a few recessed lights, the penthouse was dark, with no staff in sight.

Thanks to traffic, it had taken her an hour to get from Brooklyn to the Upper East Side. Still, she'd expected the ruckus of getting the girls to bed. Little feet padding down a hallway, Cole shouting, *Wait, let me dry you off.*

Not this…emptiness. Where was everyone? Where were the girls? She dropped her purse on a table in the marble foyer and crossed the massive living room that overlooked the bottom half of Manhattan all the way down to the Statue of Liberty.

At the end of the hallway, she came to the guest room where the girls were staying. Peering in, she saw them sleeping together in the same bed. Still unnerved, she sat on the edge of the mattress, brushing the hair off Paisley's cheek. She pressed a kiss on each temple. "I love you, babies. I love you so much."

Then, she left the door ajar, so they'd have the light from the hallway, and headed to the room she and Cole were staying in.

She walked in to find him sitting on the bed, head in his hands. "Hey."

He jerked upright. "I'm so damn sorry, Hailey. I fucked up."

"It's okay." She sat beside him, stroking his back. "It was scary, but she's all right."

He got up and paced across the room. "I was only going to stay five minutes. I thought I had it all under control. I had her hand in mine, but the fuckers started shouting at the girls—trying to get a picture. Evvie was losing her shit, and I had to let go of Paisley's hand." It seemed less about recounting to her and more about reliving it step-by-step. "I told her to hang onto my jacket—"

"But her shoe came off, and she let go. I know." It was excruciating to witness his pain.

His gaze snapped over to her. "She said that?"

She could only nod. He was frantic, distraught... She'd never seen him like this.

"That's why she let go? Because of her *shoe*?" He scrubbed his face with both hands. "They didn't have her size, and that was the only pair she wanted, so I got her a half a size too big."

One more thing to blame himself for. "Cole, that's not your fault. I would've bought that size, too. I've done it myself for a pair of boots I loved but didn't fit." She wanted to comfort him, but when she moved closer, he held up his hand to ward her off.

Ouch. She knew he was processing. She knew it wasn't personal. But she didn't like this wall he was putting up. How did she get through to him? "Come with me. I want you to see her. She's asleep. She's safe. She's fine."

"You don't get it. I *lost* her. I had no business taking them to the screening."

She'd thought the same thing, but he didn't need to hear it. "Why did you? You said they had fun at dinner. You could've just gone home..." He didn't need her piling on the blame.

"I know that. Believe me, I know. I wanted to make it a night she'd remember. I wanted—"

"You wanted her to love you. I know. It would've hurt me, too, if she'd said she hated me. But you know that she loves you, right? She was just overtired."

"Yeah, that's the point. I knew that. And still, I took her out. I took her to a fucking screening." Closing his eyes, he swiped his hand down his face. He took a deep breath, and the next time he looked at her, he was deadly calm. "I love you, Hailey. I love those girls. But I can't be what you need me to be. I *knew* that." He looked down at his bare feet. "I just got carried away."

"Don't say that. We're brand-new to parenting. We're going to make mistakes—lots of them—and we're going to learn from them. You're blowing this way out of proportion."

"Bullshit. I never leave well enough alone. It's just what I do. Those girls deserve a hell of a lot better than what I'll do to them. I'm a fucking menace."

The last time Hailey had looked at the clock, it had been four in the morning. She must've finally dropped into a deep sleep because when she checked her phone, she saw it was nearly nine.

Shit. "The girls." She sat up to find Cole gone. *Oh, thank God.*

He's taking care of them.

Last night had been tough. He'd been so damn hard on himself. Mostly, what had kept her awake was wondering what she could say to make him see he'd overreacted. Sure, she'd have been scared, too, but he truly believed he wasn't good for those girls. She couldn't let him think like that. She'd only fallen asleep when she'd realized what she needed to say.

She'd say it now. At home, she'd throw on her robe and slippers, but this was Trevor's house, so she grabbed her jeans and a sweater and headed downstairs.

An unfamiliar show played on the TV, and each girl had a bowl of dry cereal in her lap. *That's weird.* Cole usually did something special for them. Hadn't he said he'd bought chocolate croissants yesterday from his favorite bakery?

"Morning, girls. Where's Cole?"

"I don't know." Paisley didn't take her attention off the screen.

She ran a hand over the little girl's back. "How are you feeling today?"

"Fine," Paisley said.

"When I came home, you were sleeping. But I know that must've been scary last night."

The little girl stopped chewing and turned to look at her. "I knew Cole would find me."

Hailey took in a sharp breath. She really hoped he was close enough to hear her say that. "Well, I'm sorry it happened to you. We'll be much more careful from now on."

She headed for the kitchen, expecting the scent of warm croissants. When she didn't see him there, she realized he had to be working out.

Of course, dummy. He's back on the ice.

He's got a game tonight. He can't miss training.

On her way to the gym, she found Trevor drinking coffee in his office and reading a script. "Morning."

"Morning." He had a guarded look in his eyes.

"Everything okay?" She leaned against the doorway.

Slowly, he stood.

A cold fluid entered her bloodstream. Her body knew before her mind did. "I was just going to see if Cole was in the gym."

Trevor set his mug down.

"But he's not there, is he?" She didn't even wait for an answer. "He left."

"He has a team meeting this morning."

"Please don't bullshit me. Where is he? What time did he leave?" It wasn't too late to talk to him, to convince him everything would be all right.

"He left before I got up."

"Did you try to stop him?" She understood her question was stupid. Trevor had been sleeping when his son left, but she literally couldn't stop herself. "Did you talk to him?"

It was just that Cole was slipping through her fingers. Her family, this gift she'd been given, was slowly dribbling out of her clenched hand. "He's got it all wrong. I need to talk to him." But she didn't have her phone on her. She'd left it on the nightstand. "He was stuck on the fact that Paisley said she hated him, but what he needs to understand is that she's been on her best behavior. That's why things have gone so smoothly. This whole time, she's been afraid if she pitches a fit or yells at us, we'll walk away from her. She can't risk us leaving, too. So, the fact that she could yell at him like that…it means she's comfortable with him. She trusts him. She can be herself and not worry he'll leave her."

"That sounds about right." Trevor came around the giant desk and pulled her into his arms.

"But he did it, didn't he? He left her. He left us." She took a step back. "Can I talk to him? Is it too late?"

He made a half-turn, his fingertips landing on a white envelope. She recognized Cole's handwriting. *Hailey.* Trevor slid it toward her.

With shaky hands, she opened it to find a check for fifty thousand dollars.

Of course. He'd given her the only thing he had to offer.

Money.

Chapter Twenty-Three

"Are you all right, sweetheart?" her mom asked.

Hailey and the girls met her mom at a diner near Times Square. The place was loud, bright, and had a jukebox. The girls loved it. "I'm just so mad at him."

With no idea Cole had bailed on them, Evvie devoured her chocolate chip pancakes and Paisley munched on toast. Both kicked their legs in and out under the table.

"How could he do this?" She kept her voice low. "How does somebody change their mind so quickly? One minute we're planning to sign the papers and the next..." She snapped her fingers. "He's gone. I thought I could count on him. I thought..." Emotion jammed up in her throat, making it hard to talk.

Her mom reached for her hand. "You thought you'd found The One."

She nodded, grabbing her napkin and wiping the tears before the girls could see them.

"Can I have a quarter, please?" Paisley asked.

Glad for the distraction, Hailey rummaged through her wallet and pulled out a few coins. "Here you go."

The six-year-old got up on her knees to scroll through titles that meant nothing to her, looking for another button to push. Her heart squeezed. She loved them so much, and she would be everything they needed. "Let's change the subject. I don't want to talk about it in front of them. They pick up on everything."

Her mom nodded. "Where do you want to raise them?"

"Not here, that's for sure."

"So, Calamity?"

"Yeah, I think so. I have my savings, and I know there's some money from insurance and the sale of the house. I'll buy a cottage on the lake or something like that." She was just so damn sad.

"Well, hold on. Isn't your savings for your business?"

"Mom." She let out a huff of exasperation. "My priorities have obviously changed."

"No, your *circumstances* have changed. Your passion hasn't. And running your own business is perfect for the kind of hands-on mom you want to be." She reached into her bag and pulled out a sheet of paper. "Do you see this?" She tapped the title. *Robe Wait List.* "Remember that gift shop I told you about? Well, I did it. I set it up, and I hung up one of your robes. Since we opened a week ago, we've gotten a hundred forty-three preorders. Honey, you've got something here."

That *was* encouraging. "It's something I'll look at later. Right now, I have to get a roof over our heads, food in our bellies, and a car. Life is expensive, and I have to find a new job."

"I thought Cole was going to cover those major expenses? You can live in his house and eat his food."

Irritation bristled on her skin like a rash. "I'm not like you, Mom. I will never be comfortable living off other people's kindness." *And by that, I mean charity.* Because most of the time, they didn't want to let Naomi and her kid crash at their place. They got sick of having to feed them.

"It's not kindness. It's the role he's chosen to take. Why would you say no to a house for the girls? Let him do what he's comfortable doing."

"No. He's welcome to set up trust funds or pay for their education or whatever helps him sleep at night. But I won't live off him."

"Why?"

"Because he could change his mind at any point. He could pull the plug. What if he gets married and has kids of his own, and his wife doesn't like our arrangement? What if he retires and decides he needs to be more careful with his money? I won't depend on anyone for my well-being."

"But you'll rely on a company for it? Because from where I'm sitting, Abbott's didn't turn out to be all that reliable. You want to know what is? You. Your talent. Your passion. That's something you can rely on to provide for you and the girls." She leaned forward. "Sweetheart, do it. Take the risk. You won't believe how happy it'll make you."

"I've just become a single mother." She checked the girls, but they were tapping the buttons on the jukebox, totally in their own world. "I'll be working full-time and caring for them. If there's time after they've gone to bed, I'll continue to build my inventory."

"Let me ask you something." Her mom sat back in her seat. "What are you going to say when Paisley tells you she wants to be an astronaut?"

"I'll tell her to go for it and then research what she needs to do to get there."

"And if Evvie wants to be an actor? Are you going to point out all the obstacles in her path, remind her how few people ever make it big?"

"Of course not. I'll pay for headshots and help her find an agent. I'll drive her to auditions."

"And while you're telling them they can be anything they want but working a job you hate and piling up robes in a closet, which message do you think they'll listen to, your words or your actions?"

Hailey didn't want to upset the girls' lives more than necessary, so until she found a home for the three of them, she'd live in Cole's house. She did, however, get her own car the day after she got home.

Because fuck him and his Land Cruiser. She hated that he thought he could fill her heart with promises of love and hope for a beautiful life together, and then leave her with nothing but cold, hard cash.

Money?

Really?

That check had been a slap in the face. She'd immediately put it through Trevor's shredder.

To be honest, it was the blazing anger that kept her from sinking into despair. He'd skated in and out of her life so fast he'd blown a hole right through her. If she'd never met him, she'd have been fine. She was used to being alone. It was what she knew best.

But what she'd never had before was the intimacy, the laughter, the connection, she'd shared with Cole. And now, without it...her body ached as if she'd been in a head-on collision.

The worst part was that, in those moments when she could be anything other than deeply hurt, she knew he loved her. He loved the girls.

He just truly believed he was a menace.

But it wasn't in her power to convince him otherwise, so...onward.

Tonight, she'd hired a sitter for the Petticoat Ruler meeting and had put out the word on the group chat that she was looking for someone to work part-time for five days a week. It sucked that she had to be a single parent— but not because of the workload.

It was an honor to raise these girls. And she would not let them or Lindsay down.

It was just sad because the girls would've had the best daddy in Cole.

She entered the Town Hall meeting room to find it packed. *Good.* Because she needed help.

Her friends came rushing over to greet her. Callie, Knox, Glori, Stella, Rosie...all of them gave her warm hugs.

"How was the family birthday celebration?" Callie asked. "Did you find a cabin?"

"We didn't have it." She wasn't sure how much to say. She would never badmouth Cole, and now wasn't the time to talk about it. "Cole's back on the ice, so everything's postponed."

Glori stood in front of the room. "All right. Let's get started. Everyone, please take your seats."

The group was large enough that they sat in

auditorium-style seating, instead of around a conference table like last time.

"I hope you all had a great holiday and are ready to get back into it," the president said. "We're going to skip reading the minutes since the December meeting was more of a party and get right into it. Okay, who'd like to go first?"

Hailey's hand shot up, and Glori nodded for her to go ahead. "Not me being overeager."

Everyone laughed.

"Okay, well." She pressed her hands to her stomach. "Deep breath." She looked at her friends. "I'm going to launch my lingerie business."

"I volunteer." Stella shot out of her seat. While everyone burst out laughing, she hugged Hailey. "I'm so happy to hear this."

"Woo hoo," someone else shouted.

"You got this," Callie said.

Breaking free of the bindings she'd put around herself felt exhilarating. Her mom had sure hit the target. She was a role model for her girls, and if she taught them to repress themselves and play it safe, she'd never forgive herself. "So, I'm going to need help. I'm looking for a website designer, some seamstresses, and I'm looking for boutique owners who'd like to sign contracts with me. I'd like to sell my line in stores, but I'll need a one-year contract in order to give my lingerie a chance to catch on with the different seasonal crowds that come through." She paused because this one was harder. "And I'm going to apply for a small business loan."

"Yes." Stella's fist shot into the air, Phinny clapped, and from the podium, Glori said, "We're here for you every step of the way. Count on it."

"I'm a website designer," someone called. "Here. Pass her my card."

"I own a boutique in the Owl Hoot Resort's shopping plaza, and I will absolutely sign a contract with you," another woman said.

Knox reached for her hand. "My bridal shop's in the same place, and I'm positive my clients will go nuts for your robes."

Hailey stood there, awash in gratitude for the support of these amazing women. She was still scared. She was taking the biggest risk of her life, but she believed in herself and her talent, and she wanted to teach the girls how to live their dreams.

I can do this.

I'm going *to do this.*

Cole stood on his deck, grilling meat, the thump of bass and buzz of conversation from his apartment surrounding him.

He was trying, man. He was really fucking trying to keep his focus on the game and on the season. But it got harder every day. He kept up his pep talks, encouraged his teammates, put in his training, but his joints ached, his muscles hurt, and most days, he could barely get out of bed.

Missing Hailey hollowed him out. It was a grief that kept digging, scraping, and chipping away at his sanity.

But he'd done what was best for them, and now, he had to live with it. Stabbing the steaks, he set them on a platter and brought them into the kitchen. "Grub's ready."

A bunch of guys came in, all of them talking at once.

"I'm starving."

"That looks great."

One of his players clapped him on the shoulder. "Great fuckin' game, man."

Another pulled utensils out of a drawer and said, "You're on fire."

Then, they took their loaded plates and headed back into the living room.

His team's streak of wins had dug them out of the hole and put them in the running for the play-offs, so he'd thrown a get-together the night before All-Star week.

He wasn't playing since he'd opted out when he thought he was going to sign those adoption papers.

The loss sliced so deep, he went as light-headed as if he'd actually lost blood.

Every day, he tortured himself by scrolling through Hailey's social media. Even if it killed him, he'd spend the rest of his life watching those two sweet, feisty, happy little girls grow up.

Without me.

Hailey was the best adoptive mom those kids could ever hope to have.

"Cole, man?" someone called. "Your dad's here."

Coming out of the kitchen, he found his dad wearing a kilt, boots, and a tuxedo jacket. The guys surrounded him as he told a story that made everyone laugh. It had always been like that, and he'd been proud of his dad.

All his life, he'd seen his dad as the most popular actor in the world. Revered in the press and swarmed by fans, Trevor had always been the center of attention. Even at home, he was surrounded by staff, and he was on good terms with all of them.

Only now did Cole understand how totally and

completely alone his father was. Over the years, he'd had girlfriends, but nothing had lasted. He had friends, of course, but they were all busy leading fast-paced lives.

Just like me.

Everyone liked Cole. The press had only good things to say, but he was essentially alone.

When his dad saw him, his expression lightened. He parted from the crowd and came at him, arms open wide. "Great game." He drew his son into a hug, slapping him on the back.

"Thanks."

"You've got some extra fire, huh?"

"Guess so."

When his dad pulled back, he noticed the tension around his eyes. "Hey, can we talk somewhere privately?"

"Of course. Let's go into my office."

As they crossed the living room, one of the guys pretended to trip, dropping to the floor and holding out his camera to get a shot just as Trevor walked by in his kilt. It drew a lot of laughter.

Cole just shook his head. Once in the office, he leaned against his desk. "Does it ever get old?"

"Does what get old?"

"The joke about what you're wearing under that kilt."

He waved a hand. "Nah." But then, his features tightened, and he had a thoughtful expression. "Actually, yeah. It does. That's kind of what I wanted to talk to you about. You know how I just finished reading the script for the fourteenth film?"

"Yeah."

"Well, I don't think I'm going to do it. I've pitched them another idea. Told them I'm stepping back—"

"You're *what?*"

"—and think it might be time to start a next-generation franchise. We've had the same characters for all thirteen films. Might be time to shake things up. Only so many bloody battles a man can act out."

"What will you do?"

His dad hunched a shoulder. "Retire."

Out of nowhere, a rush of anger had him pushing off the desk. "Oh, now you're going to retire? When I'm twenty-eight and don't need you anymore?"

Pain flashed across his dad's features.

"Sorry. I'm sorry. I don't know where that came from."

"Sure, you do. Everything that's happened with the girls has dredged up all the feelings we never talked about when you were a kid." He placed his hand on Cole's desk. "I can't change the past, but I'd like to make a different future for myself. For us."

"No, I shouldn't have blown up like that. I never resented you for your job. I saw how important it was."

"The first film was important. The second and third were, too." His dad watched him carefully. "You know how I grew up."

"Of course."

His dad was an only child of farmers who worked their fingers to the bone to put food on the table. They were good people, but they never caught a break and died with nothing but debt.

"I was a kid when I found out I had a son. Twenty-two. I'd had a lot of walk-on roles, and I'd done a few commercials, but that movie was my big break. And you know the film industry. You know, with one flop, I'd have been yesterday's news. You know because it's the same for you. One injury, and everything you've worked for is over. You slow down, and you're replaced and forgotten."

He did know that. "If you're ready to retire, then I think it's great. Just…don't do it for me. I love you, Dad. We're good. You know that, right?"

"No, I don't know that. I wasn't there for you, and if I go off and do this next film, I still won't be there for you. You might be twenty-eight, but you still need your dad."

"Where is this coming from?"

"Cole, you got the family you always wanted, and you walked away. I saw you with them. I saw you and Hailey together."

"What does this have to do with you?"

"Because I wasn't there. I've never been there. Not once. And now… now, I can be. Cole, you're hurting. Anyone can see it. And if I go off and make another film, it'll be more of the same thing. Me missing out on being there for you." Gazing down at his boots, he shook his head. "I saw how you were with those girls, and I should have been that way with you."

"I had knee surgery. I had nowhere else to go."

"Bullshit. Mentally, emotionally, you were one hundred percent theirs. I'd never seen that side of you, and you damn well didn't get it from me. All I did was show you a good time. My son's sad? Take him to Bali. My boy's lonely? Fill the house with strangers. Jesus, I watched you figure out what those girls needed and give it to them."

"So, what're you going to do? Buy a condo in Boston and go to all my games? Come to my parties?"

"I don't know. Maybe I'll babysit my grandkids."

Cole hung his head. "They're not—"

"Yeah, they are. You know it as well as I do."

"Dad, you've got to know I'm not good for them."

"Because you lost Paisley for five minutes?" His dad came closer. "If you polled a hundred parents, ninety-eight would admit they've lost a kid, too. At the mall, the fair, in a hotel... Come on, you have to know that."

"That's what Hailey said." He paced across the room and back to the desk. "You guys don't get it. Remember Kevin? I broke his fucking arm. And Booker?" *Jesus.* There it was again, that image of him landing, his legs crumpling. *Fuck. I'm a menace.*

"You didn't break Kevin's arm. He broke it by riding his bike out of the second floor of a barn. That was his choice to make. But so what? When I was twelve, I took my dad's tractor on a joy ride. I lost control and took out a quarter of one of his fields and then landed in a pond. That's what boys do. They work hard to kill themselves. It's amazing any of us gets to adulthood."

"No, it was never my friends' fault. They all knew when to quit. It was me. Every single damn time, right when they had to go home, I'd push it. With Kevin, we'd been dirt biking after school. Everyone had to get home for dinner. He would've been fine. Everything would've been all right if I'd just let them go, but what did I do? I suggested we ride our bikes out the window of the second story of the barn. Do you remember that speed skating idea I had on the Snake River?"

His dad nodded.

"We were on our way home from training... Booker had his sister's birthday party to get to, Declan's grandfather needed help with something. They all had to get home, and there I go suggesting we try skating on a river."

He ran his hands through his hair, pulling at the roots. "All Jaime wanted was to have a bonfire. I was the one who stole your plane and took us to the cabin. There's something wrong with me, Dad. I had the girls safe in your apartment. Everything was good. I didn't need to take them to a damn screening. When I think of what might've happened to her…Jesus." He dropped to a crouch, lowering his head into his hands. Grief roared through him, a pain so intense, so beyond his ability to stave it off, he thought he would lose his mind.

But then, he felt strong arms wrap around him. His dad didn't say a word, just held him as the pain ran through him, dripping into every crevice, polluting every cell until it had nowhere else to go. Just fucking infused his body.

And when he stood up, he was so exhausted he collapsed into his chair. "I can't hurt the girls the way I hurt Booker."

"All this time, I thought it was guilt holding you back. But your problems don't have anything to do with Booker. What happened that night's a symptom. Tonight, I finally heard the cause."

Cole waited, desperate to hear the words that might release him from this hell.

His dad put a hand on his shoulder. "Out of all the things you just said, the one thing that stands out is that every time you pushed for more, it was because you were about to go home and be by yourself."

"Not with Booker."

"It was the same thing. That was the night before the four of you were going in separate directions. Those boys were your family, and you were about to lose them. You were about to go out into the world on your own. What I hear is a boy who wanted to keep his friends with him, and to do so, he had to come up with a reason for them to stay. And over the course of a thousand wild adventures where everyone had the time of their lives, three people got hurt. Kevin broke his arm, Danny had hypothermia from skating on a river, and Booker shattered his tibia." He tipped his head back. "I really hate myself right now. Knowing how lonely, how fucking isolated my son was...I can't stand it."

"It's not your fault."

His dad banged his fist on the desk. "It is completely my fault. You want to know why I'm retiring? Because I'm lonely, too. I'm surrounded by actors, camera operators, electricians, grips...but at the end of the day, I'm alone. But you—Cole, you have a family waiting for you, needing you." He pointed to the door. Bass pounded under the roar of conversation. "You surround yourself with people just like I do, but none of them matters. The way I see it, we both have a choice. We can choose the same emptiness we've lived with all our lives—I can keep going with this franchise, and you can shut out Hailey and the girls—or we can both make the harder choice of taking a risk. You're going to make mistakes. Things are going to go wrong—that's just life. But that family loves you. They need you. What are you going to do?"

He hadn't known it before because it had been the only life he'd ever known. But now that he knew a different life—a vastly more fulfilling one—he understood the stark loneliness he'd lived with for twenty-eight years.

The fear when he'd wake up as a little boy to a quiet house, to a nanny who'd ignored him, who'd tossed food at him like he was a stray dog.

The painful ache when the other parents would bring orange slices to practice, gather in little groups, and take pictures of their sons. No one had done that for him.

The *anxiety*—yes, that was it—of sitting on the plane for a road trip. Trying to be funny, interesting…someone they'd want to hang out with.

A new energy rolled through him, and he looked at his dad. "I'm going to get them back."

Chapter Twenty-Four

EVVIE SHRIEKED, HER CHEEKS AN ANGRY RED, AND Paisley dashed out of the bathroom naked and dripping wet, giggling as she skimmed away from the towel Hailey was trying to wrap her in.

So, really, it was the worst possible time to see that name appear on the screen of her phone.

She considered blowing him off the way he'd done to her, but then she remembered the promise they'd made to each other to remain a family. "Hello?"

"Hey." Oh, that voice. Deep, sexy, and thick with remorse.

She missed him so badly. It wasn't being a single parent that bothered her. No, she loved every minute with the girls. Even the difficult times like these, because she got the reward of after, when they calmed down and snuggled with her.

It was the nights she didn't have him in her bed, his warm, strong body wrapped around her so tightly she didn't know where she began and he ended.

It was after the girls fell asleep, when she didn't have him there to talk about their days or even just to read beside each other on the couch. It was when she walked in the door, and he wasn't there to look at her like she was the sun, the moon, the stars…the entire galaxy.

She would never have that again, and it left her with a giant, brutal hole.

"What's going on?" he asked over the crying.

"Evvie's got shampoo in her eyes."

"But it's for babies. It doesn't sting."

"Yeah, I know. I think she's overtired. She had a playdate with about five other kids today. It was like a preschool up in here. Anyway, it's not a good time for you to talk to them. How about I get them settled, and then we'll call you back?"

"No. I'll wait. I want to listen."

"That sounds like a good deal. Conducting family life over the phone. It's a lot easier, and you never have to get your hands dirty." She closed her eyes, regretting the words the moment they left her mouth. "Let me calm Evvie down." She set the phone on the counter and gently dabbed the little girl's eyes with a towel. "All right now, sweetie?"

"Dat hurt." Her tone held accusation, as if Hailey had done it deliberately.

"I'm sorry, baby girl. Come on. Let's get you out of the tub." She wrapped her up in a fluffy towel, still warm from the dryer. "Now, go on and get your jammies on. I'll be right in to read to you." She stared at the phone a moment. The wound was too fresh, and she wasn't ready to talk to him. But the girls were more important than her hurt feelings, so she picked it up. "You there?"

"Yeah, of course."

"I'm sorry for saying that. It was incredibly immature."

"Don't apologize for telling the truth. You have every right to be angry with me. But I didn't call to talk to the girls. I called for you. I know this isn't the best time, but I couldn't wait another second to tell you the news."

A cry came from the girls' bedroom, and Hailey took off down the hallway to find Evvie on the floor, one leg in her twisted onesie.

"Hey, punkin. Hang on. I got it." She sorted it out, guiding her foot and arms into the other holes. After buttoning it, she put the phone back to her ear. "We should probably talk another time."

"Can you give me a second? Please? This can't wait."

The nerve of this guy. "Sure. Let me ask my cranky kids to snap out of it so you can tell me your good news." She went into the girls' bathroom and shut the door. "Look, Cole. I know I said I wanted us to remain a family for the sake of the kids, but I've changed my mind. The girls love you, and they talk about you all the time, so you're welcome to be in their lives in whatever way makes you comfortable, but I don't think co-parenting is a good idea."

"The hell it isn't. I love you, and I love my girls."

Whoa. His tone had flipped from quiet and remorseful to confident and commanding.

And it was hot.

"I fucked up big time, but I've got my shit together now. That's why I'm calling. Look, you know about my childhood, but what you don't know is that my nanny once told me I was going to kill myself one day. She just hoped I didn't take anybody with me."

God, that woman was horrible. All kids got into trouble. They tested the limits. That was how they learned about the world and their place in it. Her girls were only just starting to feel comfortable enough to act out around her.

"I've never gotten that out of my head, and after what happened to my friends, it just reinforced what she said. I was sure I was bad for the girls. That, at some point, I'd take things too far and hurt them. And when I did... fuck." He blew out a breath into the receiver. "I never should've taken them to that damn screening. Everything was good. We'd had a great day, but I hated the idea of Paisley going back to Calamity hating me, of her shutting me out. So, I did it. I took them, and Paisley got lost. I proved to myself that I was a menace."

She was impressed that he could see the truth. It was a huge step for him. "Everyone makes mistakes."

"Yeah, but until I figured out *why* I kept making the same one, I'd keep doing it. But I did. I figured it out. When I was a kid, my friends were my family, but *I* wasn't theirs. They had parents, siblings, grandparents—even foster parents—and I had someone my dad paid to take care of me. The reason I always took things too far is because I didn't want to go home to that empty house. But you and the girls, *you're* my family. I'm not alone anymore. And, yeah, I'll make mistakes just like any parent would, but I'm not a menace. I'm good for those girls, and God knows, you and the girls are good for me. I need you. I want—"

"Cole." She had to stop him. She couldn't bear the rumble of hope that threatened to mow her down. She wanted to believe him so badly. "I hate how awful your childhood was, and I'm glad you got your nanny's voice out of your head, but you bailed on us after losing Paisley for *five minutes*. What happens when Evvie breaks a leg or one of them needs stitches? Bad things are going to happen, and I'm not going to put any of us through the pain of having you bail on us again. I love you, Cole. The girls and I miss you terribly, but I just don't believe you're here to stay."

Cole sat at his desk. He was so shocked, so disappointed, he couldn't get out of his chair.

"'Night." His dad walked past his office. Noticing him, he jerked to a stop. "You okay?"

No, he wasn't. "She doesn't want me."

His dad came into the room. "She said that?"

"She said she loves me but doesn't trust me to stay." He glanced up. "She thinks I'll do it again."

"Do what? I'm not following."

"She thinks something will happen to one of the girls, and I'll flip out and run again."

"But you won't do that."

"No, I won't."

"Did you tell her what we talked about?"

He nodded, the pain lodged like a knife in his chest, making it hard to take a breath.

"Then, show her."

"How do I show her when I live in Boston? When I won't be back until June?" He got up so quickly his chair hit the bookcase. "She said she doesn't want to co-parent, Dad. She's put me back in the role of godparent."

"But that's not your role. Legally, you've adopted them."

"I'm not going to make life harder for her by forcing myself on her. She has a hard enough time trusting people and look what I did. I was every bit as unreliable as her mother." He paced across the room, gazing unseeing out the window.

"What do you want, Son?"

He spun around. "I want *them*. I want to braid Paisley's hair and read them books before bed. I want to get the soap out of Evvie's eyes. I want to take them to soccer practice and wait for the first dates to knock on the door. I want to take pictures of them at prom. I want to walk them down the aisle because I'm their dad. I'll never be Darren, but I'll do my damnedest to be as good for them as I can possibly be." The gap between what he wanted and what he could have seemed impossible to bridge. "But she doesn't want me."

"I'll say it again. Show her."

"I heard you, but I don't know how to do that." His gaze snapped over to his dad. "Are you suggesting I quit hockey?" He glanced down at the papers on his desk.

"What is that?" His dad picked them up.

A bullet train of hope roared through him. "It's an extension contract."

His dad scanned it, his eyebrows hitching up. "That's a lot of money. They must really like you."

Cole cracked a grin. "Yeah, I do all right."

"Are you going to sign it?"

"You know, for so long I've felt like I owed this team for giving me a shot."

"And now?"

"And now, I owe it to myself to find the happiness I've

always wanted. I owe it to the woman I love to be the man she needs me to be. And I owe it to the girls to be the kind of father they can count on." He snatched the contract and tore it in half.

And then, he picked up his phone and scrolled until he found the group chat with Jaime and Declan.

Cole: Know of anyone who needs a center forward?

Jaime: What the fuck?

Declan: You serious?

Cole: I'm coming home.

As the garage door lowered, Hailey unbuckled the girls. "Okay, go on and get in your jammies."

Friday night was movie and pajama night, so the girls raced up the stairs and into the house. She found the girls loved themed nights. It gave their lives a structure. Monday was Game Night, Tuesday was Bathtub Party where she let them play with Silly String and all kinds of fun toys, and Saturday was Hailey's Night Out.

Tomorrow would be her first one. She didn't have any particular plans, but her sitter would come at three, and she'd go to the fabric store, check out some boutiques, grab a bite to eat, and, if she felt like it, maybe catch a movie.

Grabbing her tote and the mail, she followed the girls inside. They were already tramping up the stairs, which gave her a moment to check out the return address on the padded envelope. It was from Boston, so she figured it was from Cole.

Throwing more money at us? If it were another check, she wouldn't shred it this time. He wasn't a bad man. He wasn't choosing to be a bachelor over a family man. He was just caught in childhood trauma and couldn't find his way out.

Well, of course, he *had* found his way out. She'd just shut him down.

Which hadn't been very nice of her.

Maybe I should check myself when it comes to childhood trauma.

She pulled out…season tickets.

Oh, come on. Like she'd fly to Boston with two little girls to see him play hockey.

She shoved them back into the envelope and tossed it on the counter. It made a thunk. *Huh.* Must be something else in there.

Reaching inside, she pulled out a key and a note.

Dear Hailey,

I love you. And I love our girls. Ever since our phone call, I've been wracking my brains, trying to figure out how I can prove to you that I'm your forever family.

I finally got it.

I love you with all my heart. And I can't live without you. Not even for a hockey season.

If you can find it in your heart to forgive me, please bring the girls to this address, and let's have our family birthday celebration.

Just us. No flashing lights or spinning wheels.

I get it. I'm enough.

ERIKA KELLY

And if you'll let me, I'll prove it every day for the rest of our lives.

Happiness flooded her. And even as her mind formulated the question—*can I forgive him?* She already had her answer. These two weeks had been the longest of her life. Of course, she'd forgive him. It was already done.

Only after wiping her tears away did she think about those season tickets he'd sent.

He couldn't live without them—even for a season. Did that mean he wanted them to move to Boston? She'd wanted to give the girls roots in Calamity. And she didn't want to leave the Petticoat Rulers—not after finally finding her people. But she supposed it would only be for a few years until he retired. And keeping the family together did seem the higher priority.

"Ready, LaLee," Paisley called from upstairs.

She'd have to figure it out later. But just as she put the note and key back in the envelope, she noticed two things. One, the map had a note on it that told her to arrive at ten tomorrow morning.

And the tickets weren't for the Brawlers.

They were for the Renegades.

It hit like a lightning strike. What did that mean? Was he in town for a game?

No, dummy. He didn't send a ticket for one game. He sent them for next season.

Does this mean…

Is Cole moving home?

Wood snapped and popped in the fireplace, and the basket of pinecones he'd placed on the hearth did its job, filling the cabin with its cinnamon scent. In the kitchen, Cole stirred the hot chocolate, his body a live wire as he waited.

For All-Star week, he had several days off, but he'd wasted no time. The moment he'd sent the letter and tickets, he'd packed his bag and headed for the airport. Of course, his team—and the press—didn't know his decision to not renew his contract yet. They wouldn't know until after he held the Cup in his hands.

Only his dad, Jaime, Declan, and now Hailey knew.

Would she forgive him?

Would she show up?

He had no idea. If she did, he'd spend the rest of his life making up for what he'd put her through.

To commit to her, to say I love you and promise forever, and then bail?

What an asshole.

He'd lost her trust, and it would take time to earn it back. But he'd never stop trying.

He'd fucked up a lot in his life, but to put the three of them through that kind of emotional whiplash was the worst thing he'd ever done.

You don't toy with their fragile hearts.

He'd forever regret stealing his dad's plane that night and the life-altering damage he'd caused Booker, but it wasn't a life sentence. And most importantly, he couldn't lock himself away so that he'd never hurt anyone else again. Life didn't work like that.

He'd keep trying to be a better man. He'd keep working on himself.

And he'd be the best damn dad to those girls he could be.

And Hailey? She'd never have to doubt him again. He fucking loved her with every fiber of his being.

If she didn't come, if she wasn't ready to forgive him, he would understand. He'd be as involved with the girls as possible and, hopefully, over time, his actions would prove his promises.

Tires crunched over hardpacked snow. His heart flipped over, and he dropped the spoon. Hot chocolate spattered on the stove. When he reached for a dishtowel, he knocked over the can of whipped cream. Adrenaline rushed through him so hard his hands shook.

They're here.

She came.

Car doors shut, and the voices he adored fill the air. He hurried across the living room and placed his hand on the doorknob at the exact moment Hailey grabbed it on her side. They looked at each other through the glass, and he held his breath.

He'd be able to read everything in her eyes.

I don't forgive you.

You're an asshole.

How could you do that to us? To these precious little girls?

Instead, she broke into a grin so happy, so sweet, so filled with affection, all he could do was fling the door open to remove the barrier. The moment he did, she was in his arms. The girls barreled into him, shouting his name.

Each hugged a thigh, Hailey's arms around his waist, and he was fully enveloped in love. A sense of peace washed over him.

I'm home.

It's going to be all right.

He got down on his knees and hugged the girls. "I

missed you. I missed you so much." He breathed in their baby shampoo scent and felt their little hands fist in his shirt.

"Let's get this celebration started," Hailey said. "Go put your backpacks in your room."

The cabin was tiny. Two bedrooms, one bathroom, a living room, and a kitchen. It was meant for them to be all over each other like puppies in a basket. The girls ran off to find their room.

Cole stood. "I'm sorry—"

But she pressed a hand to his mouth. "None of that. I know you, Cole. I know you didn't question your love for me or your desire to be in the girls' lives. I know you backed away because you love us and actually believed you could hurt us." She lowered her arm and reached for his hands. "I also know it didn't take long before you realized the only way you could actually hurt us is by leaving."

"Yes." The word came out in a rush of air. And the strangest thing happened. Out of nowhere, tears burned the backs of his eyes.

"I see you. And I love you very, very much."

"I love you, Hailey. So much I can't see straight. Knowing I might've lost you about killed me."

"Well, that won't happen again." Grinning, she pulled papers out of her tote bag. "Because I'm going to lock you down. Once you sign these, you're ours forever."

He pulled her to him and slanted his mouth over hers. He kissed his love into her, let it flow right through him and into her mouth. It had been two weeks since he'd held her and touched her, and he needed to show her how much he'd missed her.

"LaLee," Evvie shrieked.

"Cole made hot chocolate," Paisley called from the kitchen.

They pulled away, foreheads touching. "If you get the girls settled," he said. "I'll bring in the cocoa."

With one more kiss, she set off to gather the girls around the coffee table.

With a sure hand, he poured the creamy liquid into four mugs and then squirted whipped cream on top. As he brought the tray out, he took in the scene. Hailey and his girls sitting before a crackling fire. While they chatted happily, she handed them a box of crayons and white printer paper and set out the contract.

His heart was so full it ached.

This is my family.

He was so damn grateful Hailey had forgiven him and wanted to have a life with him.

When Evvie saw what he was carrying, her eyes went wide. She got up and raced over to him, slamming into his legs.

"Hang on. Let me set this down." As he set the tray down, Hailey handed each girl a straw and a spoon, and they all bellied up to the table.

This was the moment. The one they'd been waiting for. The right moment.

Hailey reached for his hand and squeezed it. "Girls, we have something to tell you."

Paisley looked up. Evvie already had a whipped cream mustache.

"Cole and I would like to be your forever family."

Paisley's features went slack. "What's that mean?"

"We know we can't replace your mommy and daddy," Cole said. "But we'd like to adopt you and make the four of us a family."

"I love you both with all my heart," Hailey said. "And there's nothing I want more in the world than for us to be a family."

They hadn't expected the girls to understand, and they'd figured over time, the girls would figure out what they wanted to call them, but for now, this symbolic signing was enough.

Hailey laid out the paperwork and pens. "Right now, we're going to sign adoption papers. Once we do, we're a family, and that's forever. We want you girls to sign, too."

Cole had his gaze locked with Hailey's, their smiles big and wide, and they signed the legal documents at the same time. Then, he handed the pen and a different piece of paper to Paisley. "Go on and write your name right here." This one, Hailey had drawn up for the four of them to sign.

A family is an unbreakable bond.

A family loves each other, supports each other, and takes care of each other.

A family's love is unconditional, stronger than mountains, and deeper than the ocean.

From this moment on, the signed parties below are a forever family.

The six-year-old took it seriously. On her knees, tongue sticking out, she painstakingly wrote each letter of her name.

When she finished, they gave Evvie a pen, and she made a fast and furious scribble.

Hailey held up the piece of paper "It's done." She reached for his hand. "We're a family."

He grabbed Evvie and hauled her onto his lap. Paisley

piled on, and then Hailey knocked the three of them down. Cole lay on his back, laughing, basking in the joy of having the people who mattered most in the world on top of him.

Nothing had ever felt so good, so right.

Nothing had ever felt like home.

Until them. This moment.

My family.

Epilogue

ONE YEAR LATER

SNOWBOUND IN A COZY CABIN, COLE LIT THE candles on their homemade chocolate fudge cake. He blew out the match and dropped it in the sink, listening to his family laugh and marveling that an entire year had passed since they'd signed the adoption papers.

Even as they kept Darren and Lindsay's memories alive for the girls, they grew closer and tighter every day. He hoped his friend was resting easy knowing they were doing everything they could to give his daughters the best life possible.

Slender arms wrapped around his waist, and Hailey hugged him. "This is perfect."

He turned in her arms. "You're perfect." Her wavy hair flowed freely, and her luscious lips curved in a smile. Even though they lived together, slept together, and talked every single day, she still made his pulse race. He would never get enough of her, never stop wanting her.

Grabbing her ass, he lifted her onto the counter. With a single kiss, his body went hot. The indescribable softness of her mouth, the sensual dance of her tongue, the way her fingers sifted through his hair...everything about her touch excited him.

Sometimes, he couldn't believe how a simple gesture like putting a hand on his thigh could make him hard. She could shoot him a private look across a crowded room, and he'd want to drag her into the bathroom.

Of course, he'd done that. Many times.

He deepened the kiss, losing himself in her scent and the taste of hot chocolate in her mouth. "You kiss perfectly." He slid her closer and whispered in her ear. "You fuck perfectly." And then, he looked her right in the eyes. "And you love me perfectly."

"It's because I care. So, so much."

She was right about that. The reason they worked so well, that they were in sync, was because they both tried so hard to hear and understand—to learn—each other.

He kissed her again, deeper this time, letting her feel his whole heart.

After a moment, she gently pulled away. "The candles are melting." She nipped his bottom lip. "More of that after the girls go to bed."

Fuck, yeah. He couldn't wait to get his hands all over her.

As they slowly made their way to the table, they started singing, "Happy birthday to us, happy birthday to us, happy birthday to our family, happy birthday to us."

The girls joined in, and when he set the cake down, Evvie crawled from her chair onto his lap. He hooked his arm around Hailey who had Paisley sitting with her, and the connection between the four of them warmed him to his bones.

My family.

He would never get over the way his life had changed.

The way these girls had brought him a happiness he never could have imagined.

Before them, he'd lived for hockey and surrounded himself with people who wanted to party on a yacht or hang out at his penthouse. People he could impress.

Now, he got to spend his life with two little girls and a woman who wanted nothing but him. He didn't have to take them on exotic vacations or push for more. He just had to show up.

And he did. Switching to the Renegades had given him more time at home, but mostly, it gave his family the peace of mind that he was there for them. Always nearby.

Raising these girls wasn't easy. He'd spent plenty of time talking to the therapist and getting advice on parenting forums, but through it all, they'd grown closer.

"Ready?" Hailey asked.

The girls nodded, and then they all leaned in to blow out the candles. Smoke drifted lazily in the air, and they clapped.

"Yay." Paisley pumped both fists in the air. "Happy Family Day."

"Happy Family Day." Hailey kissed all three of their cheeks before cutting thick slices.

Just as they picked up their forks, ready to dig in, Cole said, "Whoa. Not so fast. This is our second birthday as a family, so we're starting a tradition. Let's go around the table and say our favorite memories of the past year. Who wants to start?"

"I do." But it didn't look like Paisley had anything to say. Her lips pressed together, and her cheeks went bright red.

"Overachiever," Hailey said.

The seven-year-old covered her mouth with a hand to hide her grin.

"How about we let—" Hailey began.

"No, I'm ready. I liked when Papa won the trophy and looked right into the camera and said, This is for you Paisley." She lowered her voice to sound like him, and they all smiled.

"Hey, I mentioned Evvie, too."

"Oh, I didn't hear that." Paisley giggled.

And that made him crack up. Yes, she'd pushed their boundaries, but she'd also come to trust them enough to let her true personality show. And this girl was funny. Clever, too. They'd wanted to honor Lindsay and Darren by never taking away their titles, so Paisley had come up with Papa and Momma for her adoptive parents. And he loved it.

Loved being her papa.

Evvie was quiet, so he wrapped an arm around her tummy and said, "You know I said your name, too, right?"

She gazed up at him with a loving expression. "Can I eat now?"

He chuckled. Guess she hadn't been hurt that her sister excluded her. "Not yet, baby. Do you want to tell us your favorite memory this past year?"

"I'm not done yet," Paisley said. "I liked when we went horseback riding, and I liked when grandpa took me on the lake last summer. He made the boat go so fast."

His dad was loving retirement. At first, he'd spent a lot of time helping Hailey with the girls, but once Cole had come home in June, he'd built a pretty good life of his own. Even if people continued to check under his kilt.

"And what do you love about being a family?" Hailey asked Evvie.

"We made cookies for Cwismas. And I skated."

Back when he was a wild kid building dirt bike courses on people's properties with his buddies, his former coach had shown them how to channel their energy into a competitive sport. He and his four best friends had taken those hockey lessons and turned them into careers.

He didn't know what these girls would wind up doing, but he saw how much Evvie loved watching the figure skaters train at the Bowie brothers' complex, so he'd started her in ice skating lessons.

"Yes, I like watching you because it looks like you're having so much fun," Hailey said. "What else?"

"I don't know."

Hailey brushed the hair out of the little girl's eyes. "Can you think of anything else this year that made you happy?"

"I like when we get in bed and wead stories." She gazed up at Cole. "I like when you sing to me."

Since he had his special time at night with Paisley braiding her hair, he'd started singing lullabies to Evvie, and she loved it.

Her head fell against his chest. "I don't know." She sighed. "I just like when you love me."

Sometimes, his heart couldn't handle this much emotion. It didn't seem designed for so much love. And yet, it always surprised him by stretching to accommodate just a little bit more. "I will always love you." Hugging her, he rested his chin on her shoulder. "You're papa's little girl. You both are." When Paisley climbed onto his lap, the three of them held each other tightly. "My girls. I love you so much."

"Let me in there." Hailey wrapped her arms around

them, her forehead touching his. "*This* is my favorite memory. Right here. Right now."

He let it sink in, this love, this connection, this beautiful bond, and that's when he knew it was time. He'd been waiting for just the right moment.

This is it.

"I'd like to make a new one."

Hailey pulled away. "A new memory?"

He stood, shifting the girls onto the chair he'd just vacated, and got down on one knee. When he pulled a blue ring box out of his pocket, Hailey looked like she'd stopped breathing.

"Hailey Casselton, I've loved you from the moment I laid eyes on you at Darren's locker in twelfth grade. I blew it the first time around, and I almost blew it the second time, but now, I'm ready to be the man you need. I want to walk through life at your side. I want to bring you coffee in your studio every morning and spoon with you every night in our bed. There's nothing I want more than to wake up with you every day for the rest of my life." He was an athlete, not a poet. He would never have the right words to express how he felt about her. So, he'd keep it simple. "I just want you. You and only you. Will you marry me?"

She lunged out of her chair and into his arms, knocking him onto his ass. They kissed like nobody was watching, and he lost himself in what had to be the greatest moment of his life. "I love you," he whispered. This family had filled all the empty spaces inside him. He had everything he could ever want and more.

She pressed kisses all over his face. "I love you so much."

"So, you'll marry me?" He opened the ring box and

pulled out the diamond bracketed by two rubies, one representing each of their girls.

"Yes, yes, yes."

"Thank God." He hugged her with such force she squealed. The girls piled on top, and they all laughed and rolled around.

But he wasn't done. He gently extracted himself. Then, he lifted the girls back onto the chair and knelt before them. Taking their hands, he said, "I didn't know what happiness felt like until you girls came into my life. I didn't know what family meant until you made us one. I love you both with all my heart. Will you be my daughters from now until forever? I want to braid your hair and put Band-aids on your boo-boos. I want to watch your ice skating lessons and root at your soccer games. I want to help with your science projects and teach you how to change a tire. And I want to greet your boyfriends at the door before every first date." He pointed two fingers at their eyes and then at his own. The girls giggled, even though they had no idea what he meant. They were just happy. All of them were ridiculously happy.

He pulled two tiny rings out of his pocket.

Their eyes went wide as he slipped them onto their fingers.

"We're going to keep these in a jewelry box and only wear them for special occasions, but they're meant as a pledge of my love and devotion to you both. Will you let me be your papa forever?"

Paisley nodded and hugged him. "I love you so much."

"You my favrotist," Evvie said. "I love you."

He didn't know how he'd gotten so lucky, but he knew he'd never take them for granted.

Every day of his life, he'd wake up and earn the gift of their love.

Thank you for reading LOVE ME LIKE YOU DO! Do you want more of Cole and Hailey? I've got some fun surprises for you in this glimpse into their future! Go here for more: https://bit.ly/LMLYDhea

Can you guess what's up next in the Calamity Falls Small Town Romance series? It's Jaime and the runaway bride! Look for TRULY, MADLY, DEEPLY in March 2023!

And if you love a grumpy, tatted hockey player and want to see him fall head over heels in love with the spoiled princess he's forced to live with for a month, you're going to love THE DEEPER I FALL! This one's Declan's book!

Do you subscribe to my newsletter? Get on that right now because I've got an EXCLUSIVE novella for my readers in 2022! You'll get 2 chapters a month of this super sexy, fun romance! #rockstarromance #whenyourcelebritycrushbe-comesyourboyfriend #teenidol

Need more Calamity Falls, where the people are wild at heart?

KEEP ON LOVING YOU
WE BELONG TOGETHER
THE VERY THOUGHT OF YOU
JUST THE WAY YOU ARE
IT WAS ALWAYS YOU
CAN'T HELP FALLING IN LOVE
COME AWAY WITH ME
WHOLE LOTTA LOVE
YOU'RE STILL THE ONE
THE DEEPER I FALL
LOVE ME LIKE YOU DO

Have you read the Rock Star Romance series? Come meet the sexy rockers of Blue Fire:

YOU REALLY GOT ME
I WANT YOU TO WANT ME
TAKE ME HOME TONIGHT
MORE THAN A FEELING

Look for Jaime's book, TRULY, MADLY, DEEPLY coming March 2023! Grab a FREE copy of PLANES, TRAINS, AND HEAD OVER HEELS. And come hang out with me on Facebook, TikTok, Twitter, Instagram, Goodreads, and Pinterest or in my private reader group.

Read an excerpt from THE DEEPER I FALL

Excerpt of The Deeper I Fall

TEN MONTHS AGO

Tonight, Seraphina Maud Crutchley was a superstar.

She didn't feel like one very often. Rarely, in fact. But at this moment, with the spotlight trained on her as she stood in the middle of the ballroom surrounded by every single luminary in London's elite, she felt a wild mix of emotion: pride, certainly, but also the teensiest sense of imposter syndrome.

Honestly, she didn't know what to do with all the attention, so she smiled and kept her focus on the stage.

"The Lumley Foundation has hosted this ball for over a century." The CEO, in his black tailcoat and white bow tie, addressed the crowd of glittering donors. "Thanks to the addition of Phinny to our team, we've seen our donations quadruple. With her sparkling personality and boundless compassion, she is most certainly a bright star among us. Thank you, Phinny, for putting together such a spectacular array of auction items." He gave her a nod, and the audience broke into applause.

Her stepfather squeezed her shoulder, and her mum whispered in her ear, "I'm so proud of you, darling."

It was the most glorious moment of her life. Thanks to the blinding light in her eyes, she couldn't see the audience, so she just waved her appreciation. When the applause didn't die down, she began to wonder what was going on. The acknowledgment was lovely, but surely, she hadn't done anything *that* exceptional.

She supposed scoring a reclusive billionaire's superyacht for a week was quite a coup, but still…

This response is a bit much.

It was only when the spotlight turned away from her that she discovered the reason for the crowd's enthusiasm. Cameron Lumley had taken the stage. Shaking the CEO's hand, he grabbed the microphone. Then, her elegant, handsome boyfriend flashed his movie star smile. "Good evening."

Even though his family ran the foundation, he had no reason to be on stage right then. He might not run events, but he sure was an impressive sight. His custom-made suit hugged his broad shoulders and muscular thighs while his commanding presence captured the attention of everyone in the room. "On behalf of my family, I'd like to thank you all for your support this evening. As you know, the charity is my life's work, so it's only fitting that the woman who owns my heart now plays such a central role in it."

Surprise jolted her.

I own his heart?

They'd been together a while, but they hardly had some grand love affair. Not even close.

What's he going on about?

Her parents moved to stand on either side of her, enormous smiles stretching across their faces.

Cameron extended a hand. "Darling, please come up here."

She almost shouted *Why?* She didn't need to get up on stage. The band should start playing, and the patrons should go back to dancing. That was the order of events.

Her mum took the champagne flute out of her hand. "Don't just stand there."

With all eyes on her, what choice did Phinny have? But while her brain sent the signal to her legs, they refused to cooperate. A wave of nausea hit, and she went hot all over.

Her stepfather set his hand on the small of her back and gave her a nudge. "Go on now. Don't embarrass us."

That got her moving. As the crowd parted, she made her way to the steps. On some level, she knew what was happening, but her mind was racing, and she couldn't think clearly.

Please don't do this.

We're nowhere near ready for this. They'd grown up together but had only begun dating during their last year at university.

Casually dating.

Cameron stood center stage, while the CEO reached for her hand and helped her up the stairs. It was hard enough to move in her ball gown and shapewear bodysuit, but with her legs shaking, she moved like a newborn foal.

Which was fitting since her heart was positively *galloping.*

"Darling…" Cameron reached for her hand, kissing her palm.

And then, he dropped to a knee.

In the middle of the grandest charity event of the year, her boyfriend—emphasis on *friend*—was about to propose. "I have loved you my entire life, but it was only when I saw you coming out of Trinity Hall that I knew it was time to start our future together. Every day has gotten better, and I can't wait to spend my life with you. Seraphina, will you do me the honor of becoming my wife?"

With the audience's collective gasp, the air was sucked out of the room.

She couldn't breathe. Blood roared in her ears, and her vision blurred around the edges.

In the silence, she had the strangest sensation of floating. She could picture herself grabbing a handful of helium balloons and drifting off the stage, out the window, and sailing over the rooftops of London.

Cameron's smile faltered, and it jerked her back to the moment. She couldn't embarrass him. "Yes. Of course, yes."

Relief washed over his handsome features, and he stood to his full height. He wrapped an arm around her and faced the ballroom, raising their clasped hands as though she were a trophy.

In the middle of the audience, Phinny found her parents. She'd never seen them so happy.

But why? The moment felt surreal. She'd never gushed about him to her parents. Never once talked about marriage or babies or any kind of future with him. They were two people from similar backgrounds who had fun together. *We're just dating.*

Marriage?

Standing on that stage, she felt like a paper doll cut out.

With a tug, she was led back down the stairs.

Immediately, well-wishers swarmed them. His family, their friends...everyone was gleeful.

And it was all a lie.

Because she couldn't marry him.

Flee. It wasn't a thought so much as an alarm that rang through her body. She wrenched her hand out of his grip and made her way out of the ballroom. When she saw a sign for a powder room, she ducked inside and locked the door.

Oh, God. What is happening?

As she ran cold water over her hands, she looked up at her wild-eyed reflection. Her pulse pounded violently. Why had he proposed publicly? Now, calling it off would create a scandal.

It didn't have to be like this.

A hard rap jerked her attention from the mirror.

"Phinny?" *Cameron.* "Open up."

Angry that he'd put her in a terrible position, she opened the door, grabbed his wrist, and pulled him inside the lavender-scented bathroom. "What was that?"

His eyes flickered with hurt. "What do you mean, what was that? It was a marriage proposal."

"But why? Cameron, we're not ready for that."

"We've been dating for three years. When did you think we'd be ready?"

"I don't know." *Never.* "We haven't talked about it."

"What on earth do you think we've been doing all this time?"

"We've been *dating.*"

"Yes, on a course toward marriage. Why else would I be exclusive with someone if not with the intention to marry her? Why are you acting like this came out of nowhere? You can't pretend you didn't know it was the path we've been on."

She couldn't argue his point, and it flustered her. Because, really, it uncovered a truth that would only hurt his feelings. *I don't love you.* "I can't possibly get married now. I haven't done anything with my life."

His jaw snapped shut like he was trying to contain his anger. "Whatever you want to do, what better way to do it than as Cameron Lumley's wife?"

Obviously, that made perfect sense. Marrying into one of the wealthiest families in the United Kingdom would afford her any opportunity her heart desired. And it wasn't like Cameron cared what she did. That wouldn't change once they got married. He'd still go off with his mates on trips, and she'd go clubbing with hers. Sometimes, they'd do the holidays together, while other times, they'd be with their own families.

She knew exactly what her life with him would look like because that was the kind of marriage his parents had. And she didn't want to wind up like his mum, spending more time with her wine than her husband.

She pulled off the engagement ring. "I'm sorry, but I'm not ready to get married."

He just stared at her as though waiting for her to laugh and say *Gotcha. Of course, I'll marry you, silly!* "Are you serious?"

"Quite." His presumption that she'd just fall in line with some plan he'd never voiced irked her. "Cameron, come on. Do you even love me?"

"Of course I do." He seemed calmer as if they could now settle things. "I like you better than anyone else we know."

Well, there's a ringing endorsement for marriage. "And I like you. But I need more time."

"How much time?"

"I don't know."

"Are we talking about a few weeks?"

Weeks? "I'm twenty-four. What's the rush?"

His expression shuttered. "Waiting these three years has cost me nearly two million pounds."

She flinched as if he'd flicked cold water at her face. As soon as he married, he'd tap into his trust fund. With each child he added to his family, the monthly allowance would go up.

Quite the incentive to keep the Lumley line going.

She'd known that. So, why did it sound so ugly to hear him say it out loud?

He must not have liked her crestfallen expression because he reached for her elbows and bent his knees to look her in the eyes. "Darling, there's no one I'd rather spend my life with than you. You make me laugh…you make me happy."

"Well, yes, because I don't require anything of you."

He chuckled. "Most definitely, that's one for the plus column. But it works both ways. We give each other room to live our lives. Trust me, that's a good thing. We'll never grow restless or resentful."

I want more.

And what a bombshell revelation that was. She'd just been going along, having fun, not questioning anything, and she'd given no thought to where she was heading. Now that he'd forced her to think about it, she had to accept she hadn't done a damn thing with her life.

She couldn't say what she wanted to do exactly, but for

the first time, she felt something missing. Something between the phases of parties, clubs, and shopping and getting married and popping out babies. "I need more time."

The smile vanished. He straightened. "No."

Fear sliced through her. She might not be ready to marry him, but she'd never contemplated a life without him. Like her parents, he was a major cog in the machine of her world, and she didn't know how to operate without all of them. "No, you won't wait?"

"I have waited. Three years is more than enough." He softened. "Look, you'd make a smashing stylist. Or you and your mum could open a boutique. Once we're married, you can use a portion of the extra fifty thousand pounds a month to do whatever you want. It doesn't matter to me, but we either get married now or it's done."

"It's done? Or we're done?"

"We're done. If you're not ready to marry me after three years, then I've got no reason to believe you'll be ready by four years or even five."

"I can't imagine my life without you, but I can't marry you because you've run out of patience with me. I'm sorry, Cameron." She took in the proud jut of his chin and the look in his eyes that screamed *Are you seriously going to walk away from me?* She liked him very much. They'd had a lot of fun together. But she didn't love him.

And so, she walked out the door.

Cut from her mooring, she felt adrift...uneasy. She hustled toward the exit as though the manor were on fire. The tight silk liner of her dress and the five-inch stilettos hampered her progress, though, as people rushed toward her, eager to share the happy occasion.

She couldn't talk to anyone right then, so she hurried on. Pulling out her phone, she tried to text her parents' driver, but her trembling fingers kept tapping the wrong pads, making her delete and start over.

"Seraphina?" Her mum glided along the hallway.

"Where are you going?" her stepfather asked. "We've just opened the bubbly to toast your wonderful news. Let's find Cameron. Come along."

The moment her mum reached her, the smile faded. "What's going on?"

Phinny handed over her phone. "Can you please ask Fergus to come 'round?"

Her stepfather snatched it. "We'll do no such thing. All of our friends are here to celebrate with you."

"There's nothing to celebrate." Phinny let out a tight breath. "We're not getting married."

"Of course, you are." Andrew's eyebrows shot up. "Don't be ridiculous."

When she'd met him as a little girl, she'd called him by his first name, but since she couldn't pronounce Andrew, she'd wound up saying Dewzy. For the first time since he'd come into her life, that term of endearment didn't fit. At this moment, when he cared more about his reputation than her feelings, he was purely her stepfather. "I gave the ring back. I'm not marrying him."

"Seraphina." Her mother sounded appalled.

"I told him I needed more time, and he said he wouldn't give me any."

Clasping her wrist, Andrew led them to an alcove. "You've known each other your entire lives. How much more time could you possibly need?"

"There are things I still want to do."

"Like what?" her mum whispered harshly. "You want to shop more? Travel more? Have more spa days? What exactly are you so eager to do?"

Like a can on the road flattened by a tire, Phinny's spirit compressed under the weight of her mum's words. She'd never considered herself frivolous. She'd been living the only life she'd ever known. "I don't know. But I would rather find out than get married to a man I don't love."

Her stepfather had always indulged her, and in return, she'd tried very hard to please him. So, to see the tick in his jaw, the color flood his cheeks, truly upset her. "What on earth do you think we've been doing, Seraphina?"

"What do you mean?" A sickening feeling rolled through her.

"You don't have a proper job, you live in an apartment we own, and you use a credit card we've given you...why do you think we've been supporting you all this time?"

The great beast of fear loomed over her like a dark, menacing shadow. "I—" Her mind went blank.

"We've supported you because you were going to marry Cameron," her mum said. "And Lumleys do philanthropy, just as I've done. Just as you've been doing. *That* has been our expectation. If we thought for a moment you had no intention of marrying him, you'd have been polishing your CV and applying for jobs your last year at university. You'd have been paying your own bills upon graduation."

"Now, go and find your fiancé," her stepfather said. "And get things back on track. Or the locks to your Knightsbridge apartment will be changed by morning."

"What?" She could barely process his words. He couldn't possibly mean to throw her out onto the streets?

"Darling, please." Her mum patted his arm.

Oh, thank God. Her mum would always take care of her. They were a team. Her parents were upset. She understood that. But they'd never make her marry a man she didn't love.

But then her mum's features hardened. "Let her make some calls, see which of her friends will allow her to sleep on their couch until she gets a job."

About the Author

Award-winning author Erika Kelly writes sexy and emotional small town romance. Married to the love of her life and raising four children, she lives in the southwest, drinks a lot of tea, and is always waiting for her cats to get off her keyboard.

https://www.erikakellybooks.com/

facebook.com/erikakellybooks

twitter.com/ErikaKellyBooks

instagram.com/erikakellyauthor

goodreads.com/Erika_Kelly

pinterest.com/erikakellybooks

amazon.com/Erika-Kelly/e/B00L0MLWUY

bookbub.com/authors/erika-kelly

Made in the USA
Middletown, DE
02 February 2023